B*Witch

PAIGE MCKENZIE
AND NANCY OHLIN

LITTLE, BROWN AND COMPANY

New York Boston

Copyright © 2020 by Paige McKenzie and Nancy Ohlin

Cover art copyright © 2020 by Sweeney Boo. Cover design by Marci Senders and Angelie Yap. Cover copyright © 2020 by Hachette Book Group, Inc.

Little, Brown and Company
Hachette Book Group
1290 Avenue of the Americas, New York, NY 10104
Visit us at LBYR.com

First Edition: July 2020

Little, Brown and Company is a division of Hachette Book Group, Inc. The Little, Brown name and logo are trademarks of Hachette Book Group, Inc.

The publisher is not responsible for websites (or their content) that are not owned by the publisher.

ISBNs: 978-1-368-02876-9 (hardcover), 978-1-368-04593-3 (ebook)

Printed in the United States of America

LSC-C

10 9 8 7 6 5 4 3 2 1

To everyone who has ever had to hide their light.

Every flight begins with a fall.

—GEORGE R. R. MARTIN

To whom it may concern:

Please read this message quickly, and in private. I have posted it to a few select sites in the hopes that it will reach like-minded souls, and I will be deleting it shortly.

I am a descendant of Callixta Crowe. For those of you who don't recognize the name, she was one of *the* most powerful witches in history. Perhaps the most powerful. She lived and died in the late 1800s; she perished as part of the Great Witch Purge of 1877.

Other than that terrible event, which has been written about in history books, the subject of witchcraft is shrouded in much mystery. Witches make up a very small percent of the population. They practice in deep secrecy (if at all) because of societal prejudice—many non-witches consider them to be abnormal, freakish—and because of the anti-witchcraft law of 1877, also known as Title 6 of the US Comprehensive Code, Section 129:

> *Whoever engages in or promotes the practice of Witchcraft may be punished by Death or term of imprisonment or any other penalty the Court may deem appropriate.*

I wish to begin to unshroud the mystery now, for reasons I will explain in a moment.

Here are some things you may or may not know about witches.

The majority of witches—at least, *known* witches—seem to be female, although there are male witches as well. Magical powers are hereditary, often skipping generations. These powers manifest at puberty, although in rare instances, they manifest earlier or later. Some people may live out their entire lives without ever realizing that they have powers. Even those who *do* discover their abilities may never learn how to use them, especially given the near-total absence of spellbooks and other resources. Or they may choose *not* to use their abilities—because of 6-129, because of anti-witch prejudice, because they're afraid to reveal their true selves to their friends and families. Because they want to fit in.

Fortunately, the years since the Great Purge have been relatively "kind" to practicing witches. Some (*some*) non-witches have become more tolerant and accepting, at least in private. Enforcement of 6-129 has grown more relaxed, and the penalties, too. No witches have been executed since the Great Purge. Sentences have decreased over the decades, from "life in prison" in the early 1900s to "six to twelve months" more recently.

Younger violators of 6-129 were once reported to the juvenile police, but this convention gradually ceased after the 1960s.

Now a teen or tween witch caught practicing at school might receive a suspension or expulsion or similar, depending on the school's policies. At home, that witch might be grounded, have privileges taken away, or similar, depending on the family.

However, the tide seems to be turning back toward the Great Purge times. I believe that a new and dangerous intolerance is brewing in this country. Anti-magic voices are emerging, and because of them, witches may face renewed prejudice, punishment, and peril. Some of this intolerance may be connected to the patriarchy feeling threatened by powerful women, as with the Great Purge. Although this is likely not the whole picture. I am still investigating.

I could be wrong about this disturbing regression; I sincerely hope I am. But in case I'm not, I wanted to make sure that my ancestor Callixta's legacy doesn't die, that *magic* doesn't die. I wanted, too, to prepare all witches out there for what may be coming.

To this end, I am including a link here to a manuscript Callixta left behind. It is an opus consisting of spells, potion recipes, and many, many words of wisdom (including her theories regarding witch genetics, gender, etc.), and as far as I know, it is the only such compilation available. (Despite its uneven enforcement, 6-129 continues to have a chilling effect on books, websites, and other means of disseminating magical information.) All copies of Callixta's manuscript were presumed destroyed in the Great Purge, but parts of it survived and have surfaced. I have made it my life's work to find these disparate pieces, put them together, and create a legible, comprehensible, and usable document. The work is not complete yet, but I believe I can no longer wait to share it with the world.

For the past 139 years, witches have been forced to teach themselves magic skills, invent their own spells, and in general try to be their true best selves in a vacuum of knowledge and community. I hope Callixta's manuscript will help them reach the next level (and beyond) in their personal journeys. I hope, too, that it will help them defend against what appears to be a rising groundswell of hate.

Please use it well.

I will be removing this message and link within twenty-four hours and taking extreme measures to cover my digital tracks, for safety reasons.

Love and Light

☆

PROLOGUE

She hadn't expected the end to come so soon.

After all, her scrying mirror had told her that she would live to be a hundred: a silver-haired old lady with a dozen pampered rescue dogs and a closetful of Chanel.

She wasn't even sixteen yet. Her birthday was next month; she knew that her parents had planned a party for her at the country club. A live band, a photo booth, goody bags full of Lush Bath Bombs and Tiffany's trinkets, her cousin Nell flying in from London . . . the works.

Why had she been brought here? Was this a random act of evil? It wasn't related to what she'd found in his car, was it? Whatever the case, her instincts told her that she should get the hex out, that it was her only hope. Unless help was on the way? But that was a long shot; she couldn't count on that.

Straining against the ropes—the knots were like cement—she wriggled in the red chair and searched her brain for an escape spell, one of the ones from Callixta Crowe's secret witch manual. (She'd been online during the brief, miraculous window when the link to it had appeared and disappeared eighteen months ago.) *Pertroll?* Nope, that was for when you'd misplaced your "communication apparatus," aka phone. *Oblitus?* Nope, that was for when you'd forgotten to finish your "studies," aka homework. (She'd already deployed that spell twice, and it was only the first week of the new school year.)

Honestly, she hadn't really advanced beyond the day-to-day essentials; she hadn't even known for sure about her witch-ness until Callixta's manual. In fact, maybe her scrying skills weren't as far along as she'd thought—maybe designer clothes and rescue dogs were *not* in her future. Plus, she'd bought that mirror at Target.

What about that shape-altering spell, *amitto*, that could make you "dispense with the discomfort and indignity of a corset" (i.e., drop a dress size)? She had almost mastered it (not to lose weight or look skinnier, since she believed in body positivity, but for disguise purposes should the need arise). She could try to tweak it for her current predicament and wriggle out of her bonds.

Suddenly, the woman appeared at her side, quiet as a mouse. She was carrying a silver tray with a tea set on it; she placed it on an antique table next to the red chair. The cup, saucer, and pot were antique—bone-white, with an intricate floral design.

"These flowers are called angel's trumpets. Are you familiar with them?" the woman asked pleasantly.

She shook her head, confused. Wary. What was her captor up to now?

"They're a marvelous addition to any garden—as long as they receive the proper amount of afternoon sun, of course. And see these? These are doll's eyes." The woman pointed to clusters of tiny black dots that flecked the rim of the cup.

Doll's eyes . . . what the hex? The girl squinted. *Ew*, the dots *did* look like little eyeballs.

"Shall I be Mother?"

"W-what?"

The woman tipped the pot over the cup, releasing a thin ribbon of steaming tea. She added a generous dollop of honey and stirred. The silver spoon made a soothing tinkling noise against the porcelain.

The tinkling stopped, and the woman lifted the cup and touched it to the girl's lips. The girl froze. *It's happening.* She had seen the poisoned tea move in horror movies.

"No!" She squeezed her mouth shut and turned away.

She *thought* she'd turned away. But the geometry of the room had shifted like a kaleidoscope, because now the woman was behind her— in front of her?—and the girl was drinking the tea, almost willingly. It was pooling inside her mouth and trickling down her throat. It had a warm, green, slightly bittersweet taste that was masked only slightly by the honey—lavender honey, her favorite.

No! She jerked back from the cup, spat out the tea, and twisted the other way in the red chair.

But the kaleidoscope shifted again, and the woman was right there, feeding her more tea.

"Good girl," she purred.

No, no, no.

"I brewed the petals and stems along with the leaves. Delicious, isn't it?"

No. Yes.

She closed her eyes. The tea *was* delicious. A lovely fuzziness was starting to settle in, as though she'd been sunbathing all afternoon by the pool—listening to music and the distant hum of a lawn mower, a glossy magazine splayed across her stomach. Her familiar nearby, protecting her even in his sleep.

Adele was singing to her through her earbuds.

'Cause there's a side to you that I never knew, never knew . . .

She smiled, feeling the sun on her face.

'Cause I heard it screaming out your name, your name.

A shadow moved in the window. Another person. The woman had been talking to him earlier. His name was Mark or Matt or . . .

The kaleidoscope shifted one last time.

A cat brushed up against her, purring.

Then there was no more.

PART I

CALLING THE QUARTERS

To protect the circle, four elements must always be summoned at the beginning of the rite. I usually go with Spearow in the East, Charmander in the South, Squirtle in the West, and Diglett in the North. But only on weekdays. Weekends, I have a whole other system.

(FROM THE GRIMOIRE OF BINX AKARI KATO)

✫ TWO DAYS EARLIER . . . ✫

CATEGORY FIVE FREAK-OUT

Magic is personal and should be
kept away from prying eyes.

(FROM *THE GOOD BOOK OF MAGIC AND MENTALISM*
BY CALLIXTA CROWE)

Iris pressed her face against the cool metal locker—number 1693, was that even the right one?—and fought the urge to vomit all over the black-and-white checkerboard floor. "Stop it, stop it, stop it. You're being such a *baby*," she whispered to herself. A panic attack on the first day of school; seriously, what a cliché.

She heard footsteps passing behind her, voices rising and falling. Were people talking about her? No, they were talking about stuff that was actually interesting, like *"Who got Mr. Ferguson for English?"* and *"Why did they paint the cafeteria Day-Glo green over summer vacation?"* and *"Did Shaquille really break up with Taryn because of what Hannah said?"*

Iris *did* have a good excuse for her Category Five freak-out. Kind of. Sort of. This wasn't just the first day of school; it was her first day at

Sorrow Point High, where she knew absolutely no one and which was three thousand miles—more like three thousand light-years—from her old school. Not that she hadn't had her occasional anxiety spirals there. But still.

It had started this morning. Iris had left the house, made a U-turn, gone back to her house, and changed her outfit . . . four times. The neighbor lady, Mrs. Wendlebaum, had been puttering around in her herb garden and called out, "First day of school, huh? Butterflies in your stomach, dear?"

Iris stifled another wave of nausea. This was not butterflies. This was the creature from *Alien* wanting to explode its way out of her chest. This was her heart pounding a bloodred Dothraki battle cry in her ears. This was the Mage-Rage Potion from her favorite video game, *Witchworld*, shock-waving its way through her system.

Behind her, the hallway chatter seemed to have shifted away from teachers and cafeteria decor and breakups.

"They're holding a meeting at the community center this weekend."

"No way! The mayor's a total pacifist. She'd never let that happen."

"Well, it's happening. Axel's going, and so's Brandon."

"Speaking of . . . did you guys hear about the gravestones at the cemetery?"

"You mean the . . ."

The voices faded away.

Gravestones? A mystery meeting? But Iris didn't have time to dwell on these distractions because she was *this close* to throwing up; she could taste acid and her breakfast (extra-pulp OJ, hot chocolate, blueberry oatmeal) in her throat. She made herself inhale deeply for six counts, hold for six counts, and exhale for six counts. Her skin buzzed and prickled. The pounding in her ears subsided by a micro-decibel. Crisis temporarily averted?

Her therapist—not her occupational therapist or her social skills therapist but her therapy therapist—had taught her the deep-breathing trick and other techniques. *Distract your brain! Touch something soft, like a silk scarf. Smell a bottle of perfume. Listen to classical music. Name ten European capitals. Calculate the square root of 14,400.*

The tricks worked, sometimes. The daily one hundred of Zoloft helped, too. But what she *really* needed to make this panic-attack-from-hex go away was a nice little calming spell.

There was just one problem with that. Magic was forbidden. Illegal. So far, Iris had managed to stay out of trouble. In New York City, where she used to live, and around the rest of the country as far as she could tell, the federal anti-witchcraft law, called 6-129, seemed to be only loosely enforced. Also, Iris, no doubt like most witches, had always been careful to keep her identity secret and do her craft on the q.t. (most of the time, anyway).

Plus, the consequences for the witches who *did* get caught breaking 6-129 hadn't seemed *too* end-of-the-world and horrible. Some girls at her old school had gotten suspended for making potions in chem class. Another girl had been expelled for trying to morph Principal Ellison into a hamster. The hygienist at Dr. Singh's office had gotten fired for using spells to clean teeth. Stuff like that.

But . . . things were changing. A new president, David Ingraham, had taken office in January, and he was really, really anti-magic. (According to rumor, his youngest daughter had been a witch and died in some mysterious magic-related incident.) He said bad, untrue things about witches and witchcraft all the time, either in the regular media or on his social media. He'd announced recently that he was working with Congress on a bill to seriously beef up enforcement and punishment for 6-129 violators.

And his message had found an audience. After he became president, a national hate movement called Antima—"Anti-Magic"—started to surface. And what was up with that name? Had they deliberately riffed on "Antifa," the antifascist movement, when they were the polar opposite of that? Evil jerks!

Iris had learned from the news and online that the Antima were made up of small local factions with one goal in common: eliminating witchcraft for good. What would that even look like? Did they want to go around hunting down everyone with the teeniest amount of magical powers, and . . . what? Iris was worried (okay, maybe more like terrified) that this was their goal, because lately, they'd begun to amp things up. A couple of their rallies in Washington, DC, had turned violent. Last week, Iris had seen on TV that a Texas witch was beaten up by an Antima gang called the Sons of Maximus and left for dead.

Iris hadn't personally encountered any Antima members in New York City (that she was aware of, anyway). She hadn't heard about any Antima incidents there, either. As for Sorrow Point, she and her family had just moved here, and she'd only visited a few times before, so she didn't know it well. But it seemed like such a cute town (despite its name—seriously, *it* could use some Zoloft). She couldn't imagine the Antima wreaking havoc here, holding rallies and harming witches. Still, she would be very discerning and super, super careful regarding if and when she used magic.

Like maybe now? The acidy oatmeal-OJ-hot-chocolate combo was rising in her throat again. She had to get her anxiety level down, fast. She wouldn't do anything dramatic—just an itsy, bitsy, under-the-radar spell from Callixta Crowe's confidential witchcraft manual (a printout of which she'd accidentally stumbled upon in her old public library, hidden under a boring book jacket with the title *The History of the Finnish War 1808–1809*).

She peered around to make sure no one was looking. A sea of pastel-clad girls swept by. *Argh*. Why had she settled on all-black after the multiple outfit changes? She looked like a lump of coal in a basketful of Easter eggs. Black had been the go-to in New York, but obviously not here.

The pastelly girls disappeared around the corner. The coast was clear. Iris reached into her backpack, pulled out her phone, and pretended to check it. With her free hand, she touched her smiley-face moonstone pendant.

"*Cessabit,*" she whispered. "I am peaceful. I am confident."

The moonstone warmed. It sparked against her skin—tiny electric sparks like the fizzy emanations from a firecracker.

Nothing.

"Oh, come *on. Cessabit!* I am peaceful! I am confident!" she hissed through clenched teeth.

Seconds later, the nausea began to diminish. The pounding in her ears stopped. Her heartbeat slowed to normal. Her whole body calmed.

Yes!

Buoyed by her success, she impulsively added another incantation.

Underneath her lump-of-coal sweater, her faded black *1984* tee—WHO CONTROLS THE PAST CONTROLS THE FUTURE—morphed imperceptibly into a cute, stylish pink top.

"With ruffles," Iris whispered.

The neckline blossomed into a semicircle of rose-colored ruffles. *Nice!* She wriggled out of her sweater and stuffed it into her backpack.

Someone bumped into her from behind, *hard*. Her backpack tumbled to the floor, spilling its contents.

Startled, Iris spun around. A guy stood there, glaring at her. He wore black jeans, black boots, and a black shirt with a shoulder patch. (So some people here *did* dress in all-black.) His dark hair was super-short and streaked with blue.

"Oh! I'm sorry!" Iris blurted out, although why was she apologizing? *He'd* bumped into *her*.

The guy didn't reply, just continued glaring at her. His shoulder patch had a stark, almost geometric design of what looked like a birdcage suspended over a bonfire. It seemed familiar—and it was definitely creepy. Flustered, Iris dropped to her knees and grabbed at her belongings: her sweater, pens, notebooks, phone, and a tube of Pretty in Pomegranate! lip gloss. (Fortunately, she'd left her wand at home.) Her panic and nausea were seeping back. Had the guy seen her perform the calming spell?

As she reached for the lip gloss tube, the guy stepped on it. The sole of his boot just missed her fingers as he kicked it and stalked off. It skidded across the checkerboard floor and pinged against a locker.

Iris rose to her feet unsteadily. She realized that her hands were shaking, and that she had stopped breathing.

She remembered where she'd seen that shoulder patch before.

On TV. The story about the Texas witch. The Antima members the reporters had interviewed were wearing that same patch.

"Hey, are you okay?"

A tall, cute guy picked up her lip gloss and handed it to her.

"Um . . ." Iris's throat felt dry.

He bent down and scooped up the rest of her stuff. "Are you new here? I don't remember you from last year."

"I . . ."

Iris took her backpack from him and made herself do more therapy-breathing—six in, six hold, six out. She was safe. The scary guy was gone. *This* guy seemed nice. And he wasn't wearing an Antima shoulder patch—just a plain white polo shirt and khakis.

"Yup, I'm definitely a big ol' newb. And thanks. Um, so, I think I'm supposed to go to my homeroom now. Can you tell me where—" She pulled her schedule out of the side pocket of her backpack, scanned it quickly, and flipped it around. "Sorry, upside down! Can you tell me where Room 125 is?"

"I can show you. By the way, I'm Colter. Colter Jessup."

"Bond. James Bond," Iris joked in a British accent. Yeah, could she *be* more awkward? "JK, I'm Gooding. Iris Gooding."

"What year are you, Iris?"

"I'm a sophomore."

"Me too. Hey, did you get Cram for algebra?"

"Cram? Hmm, let me see. . . ."

Iris adjusted her glasses and looked over her schedule as Colter gave her the lowdown on teachers—who was easy, who was difficult, who had perpetual bad coffee breath. As they rounded the corner and passed what appeared to be the library, Iris closed her eyes briefly, touched her moonstone pendant, and mouthed the word *cessabit*. Everything was fine. The Antima guy probably hadn't seen her perform the spell; and if he had, she could always track him down and do a memory-erase.

Still, the fact that he'd been wearing that shoulder patch upended her rosy assumptions about Sorrow Point being a witch-friendly (or at least not a witch-hostile) town. There *were* Antima members here.

"Sanchez talks way too much about his cats in class," Colter was saying.

Something grazed the back of Iris's neck.

She slapped a hand against the spot. What the hex? She turned—but there was no one, nothing there. Except for a couple of students up ahead, this section of the hallway seemed to be deserted.

Or not? Iris turned the other way and spotted three girls in the doorway of the library. A girl in a Juilliard hoodie, a girl with pink hair and a Hello Kitty backpack, and a girl in a green boho dress with soft auburn curls down to her waist.

They were staring at her.

"You'll totally get A's, though, if you do the extra-credit labs," Colter was saying. He paused and reached into his pocket. "Sorry, someone's texting me."

Iris inched closer to him as he checked his phone. She pulled out her own phone and typed a gibberish text while side-eyeing the three girls. Why were they looking at her?

Wait . . . could *they* be Antima, too? There *were* female Antima members apparently, which was messed up, since Iris had heard that witch hatred might be related to men being scared of O.P. women.

Then she noticed the auburn-haired girl holding something at her side, pressed into the velvety folds of her dress. Iris's pulse began to go bonkers again. Not with panic this time, but with excitement.

No. Way.

The girl pivoted slightly to whisper something to the two others. Now Iris could see the object more clearly.

It was just a fountain pen.

"Sorry 'bout that." Colter tucked his phone away and smiled at Iris. "I can take you to Room 125 now."

"Thanks!"

They continued walking. *I am peaceful*, Iris thought. *I am confident.*

She touched the back of her neck, wondering.

FLUFFY BUNNY

A lone witch has powers.
A coven has a multitude more.

(FROM *THE GOOD BOOK OF MAGIC AND MENTALISM*
BY CALLIXTA CROWE)

"So is she one of us?" Ridley asked Greta in a low voice as they emerged from the library doorway.

"I'm not sure. I couldn't get any information from the . . . you know." *Divining spell,* Greta finished silently.

She tucked Flora into her vegan leather backpack. To the world, Flora looked like an antique fountain pen; Greta had enchanted it to appear that way. She undid the enchantment only if she happened to be using the wand alone or with her two coven-mates somewhere safe.

"She's probably just a *Witchworld* newb. You can tell from the twitchy fingers and the dark purple eye shadow. All the Level One gamers wear it," Binx declared. "Or she might be a fluffy bunny."

Ridley frowned. "A fluffy *what*?"

"Fluffy bunnies are kind of like faux-witches," Greta explained.

"So they want to be members—excuse me, *faux* members—of an oppressed minority? Like, that's their goal in life?" Ridley said skeptically.

"Well . . ."

Ridley had a point. Besides, Greta could swear the girl had mouthed the word *cessabit*—one of Callixta's simple calming spells—while touching the moonstone pendant around her neck. *That* was a super-witchy move. Ridley and Binx had witnessed it, too.

Footsteps. The librarian, Mr. Kasich, suddenly appeared from around the corner, swinging a faded brown messenger bag.

"Good morning, girls! I trust your summer vacations were enjoyable? Can I help you find some books?" he called out.

"No, thanks, Mr. Kasich! Maybe later," Greta replied with a wave.

She hooked arms with Ridley and Binx and speed-walked them down the hall.

The three of them ducked into the alcove with the trophy displays, and Greta cast a *calumnia* spell. (She'd perfected it to the point where she could just *think* the word, and it would manifest 99 percent of the time.) *Calumnia* could scramble their private conversation so that anyone listening would think they were discussing makeup or the weather or froyo flavors or something equally banal and boring. It reversed automatically if a non-witch entered the conversation. (Not for the first time, Greta felt huge gratitude for Callixta's book; before its existence, her skills had been so limited.)

"Okay, we're in *calumnia* mode. So there hasn't been a new witch at our school since forever—that we know of, anyway. It's just our coven and Div's coven," Greta mused out loud. "If this girl is a witch, maybe we could invite her to join us? She might be looking for a community. And it would be nice for us to have a new member."

"Really? I think we're fine with just the three of us." Binx studied her nails, which had been painted to look like red, white, and black Pokéballs. "Well, maybe *fine* is an overstatement. But you know what I mean."

"I don't know. When *I* moved here, it was really wonderful for me to meet you guys and have this coven. I never knew any other witches besides my aunt Viola," Ridley admitted. "And besides, the more witches the better, right? According to Callixta, any group spell gets more powerful with each added witch."

Binx's face lit up. "Ooooh, excellent point! If we could snag a fourth member, we'd have more power than the Triad. I'll do some research on the new girl ASAP!"

"This isn't a power grab," Greta told Binx. "I was just thinking that the new girl might like being part of our coven. *If* she's a witch." She sniffed and added, "Plus, our kind of craft is *so* much better than *theirs*. Their way is toxic and negative. Curses and poisons and—"

"Ummm . . . I think that makes what you're doing a power grab, then," Binx interrupted. "Good Witches, four, Bad Witches, three. The Good Witches win!" She pumped her fist in the air.

"Ha ha," Greta said with an eye roll, even though Binx was kind of right. But kind of *not* right, because wasn't it the job of a coven leader to welcome new members? And keep the flame of Callixta's legacy alive? Callixta's magic was about love and light, not darkness and control (which were Div's and Mira's and Aysha's things). "I'm serious. The world doesn't need another Div clone. So, yes, okay, *could* you do some research on the new girl? Find out who she is, where she's from, if she might be one of us? We should figure all this out before Div gets wind of her existence."

Ridley glanced at her watch. "Guys, can we continue this conversation later? We need to get to homeroom. I've heard that Ms. Nasser loves to give detentions for tardies."

"Fun fact—the detention room has excellent Wi-Fi," Binx said. "You can poach it from Sparklebutt's office." Principal Sparkleman had become Principal Sparklebutt last year after accidentally sitting in some art class glitter.

"I prefer my Wi-Fi without the detention. Ridley's right; let's talk about this later," Greta suggested.

She adjusted her backpack on her shoulders and started toward the stairwell. Ridley followed at her heels. Binx followed, too, speaking into her phone, which had some sort of bright yellow Pokémon case today. Actually, she was speaking *at* her phone. Greta could just make out the words *light* and *sesame*.

A few seconds later, half a sesame bagel materialized in Binx's other hand. Lightly toasted, with butter.

"Breakfast," Binx explained, taking a bite. "Overslept," she added with a mouthful of bagel.

Alarmed, Greta glanced around. There were students up ahead, but none of them seemed to be paying attention to Binx. "Can you please not do that stuff in public?"

"What's the big deal? We're in *calumnia* mode, right?" Binx finished off the bagel and licked her fingers one by one. "Mmm, butter should be its own food group. Besides, why *shouldn't* I use magic to make myself breakfast? Why should I starve because of a law that was created by a bunch of sexist old dudes in the Middle Ages?"

Not this again, Greta thought. "The 1870s wasn't the Middle Ages. And *calumnia* doesn't scramble things *visually*. We need to be more careful than ever about hiding our identities."

"Why? We've never gotten caught. And even if we *did* get caught, so what? We can just hang out in detention together. Or, if we get suspended, that'll give us more time to stay home and practice spells," Binx pointed out.

Ridley bit her lip and said nothing.

"Yeah, well . . . I didn't want to freak you guys out, but just before we met up, I passed a couple of students near the cafeteria, and I think they were wearing Antima shoulder patches," Greta explained.

Ridley grabbed her arm. "Excuse me, *what*? Where did they come from? There weren't any Antima students here *last* year!"

"Who were they?" Binx asked Greta.

"One of them was Axel Ngata. I think the other one is Orion something."

"Orion Kong. I know him, and I know Axel, too. They're total posers. They're probably just wearing the patch because they think it looks B.A.," Binx scoffed.

"Still. The Antima are horrible. That poor witch down in Texas . . . and did you hear about the latest? The police . . ." Ridley's eyes shimmered with tears. "The police are letting her attackers go. They claim there's no 'evidence,'" she added, making air quotes.

"*Seriously?*" Binx burst out. "That really is Middle Ages. What's next, torture chambers? Someone needs to do something about this!"

Greta was about to reply when a rustling in her dress pocket caught her attention. She reached in and extracted a folded-up piece of paper.

She unfolded it and gasped. A cry escaped her lips.

"What's wrong?" Ridley asked her.

"It's a shadow message!"

Trembling, Greta held out the piece of paper for Ridley and Binx to see. The handwritten letters were glossy and black, like crow feathers:

Ridley stepped back, swiping at her eyes with the back of her hand. She looked terrified. "W-where did you find this?"

"In my pocket. Just now. I don't think it was there before, but I'm not sure. Do you . . . I mean, could it be from the Antima?"

"Lemme see." Binx grabbed the shadow message and squinted at it. "Yeah, no, it's not from the Antima. It's from those tea-brewing trolls!"

"You mean Div's coven?" Greta asked.

"Yeah, it's totally them. I recognize Mira's handwriting. This is so annoying." Binx crumpled the shadow message into a ball and pitched it at a nearby trash can, missing.

Greta rushed forward to retrieve it and placed it inside her backpack in a small recyclable bag containing a rosemary sprig. (She always carried rosemary with her, for such occasions; it had protective properties.) "We should keep it. Just in case it's *not* them, and we need to try to use spells to identify the writer."

But Binx was already texting Mira on her Pokémon phone. *"W . . . T . . . F . . . you . . . think . . . you . . . can . . . scare . . . us . . . with . . . a . . . stu . . . pid . . . NOTE?"* she read out loud as she typed.

Greta sighed. Binx had some sort of third-grade inter-coven feud going with Mira and Aysha; they were always pranking each other (which Greta wasn't entirely happy about because it increased the chance of exposure— but Binx wasn't one to be told what to do).

Although to be honest, Greta *hoped* the shadow message was from Div's girls.

Because if not . . .

The image of that witch in Texas flashed through her mind. The stretcher carrying her out to the ambulance, the blood gushing from her forehead, news cameras everywhere. An elderly neighbor saying in a disapproving tone, *"I didn't know she was one of them."*

Greta had heard about Antima factions popping up in the South . . . in the Midwest . . . in Florida . . . in California and Arizona.

Had the movement finally reached Sorrow Point, Washington?

✳ 3 ✳

TECHNOMANCER

Do not dismiss the old ways in search of
disposable magic. Trust your power.

(FROM *THE GOOD BOOK OF MAGIC AND MENTALISM*
BY CALLIXTA CROWE)

Even though it was only Day One, Binx already approved of her
first-period English class. The room had even better Wi-Fi than the
detention room, and she had no problem piggybacking. Also, the teacher,
Mr. Dalrymple, seemed super out of it during his lecture on Romantic
poetry. He alternated between long, moody pauses and lots of wild ges-
turing out the window (at the trees? at the delivery trucks? at the blue-gray
Puget Sound in the distance?) while talking about unrequited love and
the ephemeral nature of life. But all this was just fine because it made
him pretty much oblivious to Binx's nonstop under-the-desk typing and
texting.

Of course, she could fool the best of them, oblivious or not; she had
mastered the art. She was a technomancer (aka cyber-witch), which meant

that she could use magic to enhance and accelerate all computer tech. For example, her phone and laptop automatically interfaced code with spells (like when she'd ordered her virtual genie/assistant Uxie to make her a bagel earlier). She'd developed this specialized form of magic by combining the information in C-Squared's—aka Callixta Crowe's—witchcraft book with her own considerable cyber skills.

Binx was good at the little details, too. For this class, she'd chosen a seat in the back row, far corner. Her yellow pleated miniskirt perfectly camouflaged the Pikachu case. She worked the tiny phone keyboard on her lap, her gaze fixed on Mr. Dalrymple; but whenever the teacher had one of his drama moments (*"Love is my religion!" "His soul shalt taste the sadness of her might!"*), she allowed herself a quick peek at the screen to take in data.

Which she did now, since Mr. D. was busy emoting about immortality or Grecian urns or whatever.

Still no response from the Triad of Evil. *Grrrr.*

Binx had texted Mira (and Aysha, too) about a dozen times—before homeroom, during homeroom, en route to English, during English. But they hadn't responded. Nothing. Nada. Had they blocked her again? She'd thought about texting Div, but . . . well, Div was scary. Especially with that familiar of hers, an albino Brazilian rainbow boa that sometimes traveled with her thanks to an advanced invisibility spell. (Binx did not like the way the snake looked at her.)

They *had* to have written the shadow message and then used a spell to make it magically appear in Greta's pocket. Maybe it was in retaliation after the little incident at Starbucks last week? It had been so fun watching the expressions on Mira's and Aysha's faces when they realized their iced mocha fraps had been switched out for a powerful burping potion she'd whipped up. But maybe it wasn't worth it, after all, if the consequence was the pretend-shadow note and Greta (and Ridley) getting all freaked out and paranoid.

"She dwells with Beauty—Beauty that must die!" Mr. Dalrymple exclaimed, shaking a fist at the outside world (or maybe at the scruffy pigeon on the windowsill?). Another drama moment . . . Binx took the opportunity to check on the status of her other project, i.e., her password-capture algorithm, which she'd supercharged with a special spell. She needed the password to the Sorrow Point School District server to gather intel on the girl with the dorky purple eye shadow and see if she might be one of them.

And if she *was* a witch, then what? On the one hand, yeah, it would be awesome to outnumber Div's coven and dominate in the group spell department. (Binx knew Greta felt the same way, although not because she wanted power for its own sake, but because she disapproved of Div's kind of magic.) On the other hand, a new member would alter the balance. Would Purple Eye Shadow Girl be a positive or a negative?

"Turning to poison while the bee-mouth sips!" Mr. D. cried out.

Binx had the password. *Sweet.* A few more keystrokes, and ten seconds later, she was in the school district server. More keystrokes led her to the list of new students along with their ID photos.

Gotcha! The girl was a third of the way down the list. In the grainy photo, her eyes were averted, and her smile seemed strained:

IRIS EVANGELINE GOODING

SOPHOMORE

112 SYCAMORE STREET, SORROW POINT, WA

And here were Iris's transcripts from her previous school in New York

City. There were tons of medical records and other records, too. There was also something called an Individualized Education Program; apparently, she received accommodations like extra time on tests because of her generalized anxiety disorder and other special needs.

None of this told Binx whether or not Iris Evangeline Gooding was a witch, though.

No matter. At least they knew who the girl was now. Binx opened an app quickly that would magically download the files to an untraceable off-site server. She also sent a group text to Greta and Ridley with Iris's name, grade, and home address along with the message:

Our Fluffy Bunnelby with the eye shadow. You're welcome.
(And yes, Greta, that's a Pokémon reference.)

They didn't text back. *Of course.* Ridley was too obsessed with rules to text in class, and Greta's phone was probably buried in her vegetarian backpack under bags of herbs. They also refused to engage in hexting (hexing via text), which Binx did with Mira and Aysha regularly. (Last weekend, Binx had hexted them by making their outfits smell. They had hexted back by causing her to start doing jumping jacks where she happened to be standing, which was the movie theater downtown.) The Iris girl wasn't a priority, anyway. The real priority was making the Triad confess to their latest crime.

Because it was one thing for the two covens to argue, disagree, throw shade, spell-block, hext, or perform more serious pranks. (Although Binx *had* maybe crossed a line when she'd pretended to kidnap Aysha's familiar, Nicodemus, an Alaskan noble companion dog, for like five minutes; even though she didn't have a familiar of her own, she was aware that witches and their animals had crazy-strong bonds.) It was another thing altogether to impersonate the Antima and issue threats. That was unacceptable, and they knew it.

Binx's phone vibrated—not with an incoming text but an enchanted security alert she'd recently installed to warn her about hackers, intruders, and other potential dangers. Had the school district bureaucrats detected her unauthorized access? But that seemed unlikely, since their system was older than dirt. Still, she logged out of their server, just to be safe. She also went off-line in case her piggybacking had tripped any alarms—again, not possible, but it was always smart to be ultra-cautious.

Was the danger of a non-virtual nature, then? She casually put the phone facedown on her lap and glanced around.

Her desk neighbor seemed to be watching her; she didn't know his name. He wasn't spying on her, was he? He was probably just admiring her pink hair (it had been cyan last spring, and ice blue before that, and rainbow before *that*) and her super-*kawaii* good looks, right?

Binx knew how to handle boys. She went back online, pulled up an Instagram photo, and slanted the screen in his direction. It was a Crabby Cat meme that said: R U BOREDS 2?

Her desk neighbor blushed and smiled. Too easy.

Binx made a Crabby Cat face at him, which caused more blushing and smiling, then she picked up a pen and pretended to pay attention—now Mr. Dalrymple was pontificating about the concept of the sublime, which was the power to provoke ecstasy through art.

Her phone vibrated again—*another* warning? It wasn't re: the desk neighbor, though; he was listening intently to Mr. D. jibber-jabbering about the sublime.

Binx scanned the rest of the classroom. No one was looking in her direction; everything seemed normal and calm and boringly business-as-usual. She waited a minute, then two, then three. The warning didn't repeat.

Probably a glitch, Binx thought with a shrug. The security-alert enchantment was brand-new; she'd recently started using it on the recommendation of her online friend ShadowKnight, who was a technomancer, too, the only boy witch Binx knew personally. She quickly disabled the enchantment (so it wouldn't keep false-alarming). She would ask him for advice re: debugging the next time they communicated.

Although . . . she hadn't heard from him in days, despite her leaving him a bunch of (encrypted) messages. Last week, he'd said something about his parents almost learning about his witch identity (which he'd kept from them since discovering it himself at age twelve . . . apparently, they were super anti-magic). Was he okay? Had he gone even deeper underground to avoid their scrutiny? It was bad enough having annoying parents (Binx could so relate); but it would be terrible to have parents who were not down with the witch thing and might kick their kid out of the house or whatever. (Binx's mom and dad didn't know about her being a witch, and she planned to keep it that way. Not that they'd disown her, but she didn't like confiding in them about anything because of their general obtuseness.)

Or maybe ShadowKnight's parents had found out about his activism group? He'd mentioned to Binx that he was part of a new, top secret political movement. He hadn't said much about it, just that they called themselves Libertas and that they were working to try to get the anti-witchcraft law, 6-129, overturned and replaced by an anti-witch-*discrimination* law. Which would be *amaaaazing*.

Lately Binx had been wondering if she should maybe join Libertas;

6-129 was vile. She could use her technomancing talents to help bring an end to it and protect the rights of witches. Also, maybe the Libertas people had ideas about how to make the Antima go away?

But . . . *nah* . . . Binx wasn't big on groups. It was hard enough being part of a coven and having to follow Greta's "rules," like *"Stop hexting Mira and Aysha in public!"* and *"No magical bagels at school!"*

Still, she reminded herself to try to reach ShadowKnight again.

A ROSE BY ANY OTHER NAME

Magic in others is not always obvious.

(FROM *THE GOOD BOOK OF MAGIC AND MENTALISM*
BY CALLIXTA CROWE)

By the time the second-period bell rang, Ridley was in her seat and all ready for class. A mint-green notebook labeled US HISTORY was open to the first page with the spine carefully pressed flat. She loved new notebooks—the clean fields of white, the faint blue horizontal lines. She always opted for the narrow college ruling versus the wide ruling; it looked cooler and, of course, more *collegiate.*

She picked up her mechanical pencil (because she didn't like making mistakes in indelible ink) and wrote the date at the top of the page. The first day of her second year at Sorrow Point High. Her first day freshman year had been way less . . . *distressing.* Sure, it had been emotionally challenging in its own way—a new city, a new school, a new life—but there was a different (and less anti-witch) US president back then, and the Antima movement didn't exist yet, at least not openly, and Ridley had felt relatively safe practicing the craft in secret on her own. And soon after, she'd met Greta and Binx, and they'd been able to practice the craft together . . . still in secret, but *together*.

But *this* first day of school was different. Greta's account of the two guys wearing Antima shoulder patches had been jarring. Ridley had *never* seen Antima members in Sorrow Point.

And despite Binx's occasional rebellious flouting of the law (as in this morning's bagel incident), their coven had (*knock on wood*) never gotten caught. Neither had Div's. They had all managed to pass as regular old non-magical humans.

Until now. That disturbing shadow message. Was it just another Triad prank, as Binx had suggested? Or were the Antima onto Greta? To their whole coven? And if so, what were the Antima going to do with the information? Report them? Torment the girls with more threats? Show up at their houses in the middle of the night and spray-paint hateful words on their doors? *Attack* them (and then would the police look the other way, like they had in Texas)?

Callixta's descendant had suggested that the Antima hated witches because they hated powerful women. But did they hate girls like Ridley even more because she was Black and also trans? Or did the Antima hate all witches equally? (In the last presidential election, the other candidate—a Black lesbian—had almost defeated David Ingraham, creating a ripple effect of increased racism and prejudice against the LGBTQIA community.)

Not for the first time, Ridley wondered if she should just give up witchcraft. It wasn't worth it if it might bring more pain and hardship to her family; they'd already been through so much. *Too* much. Plus, there was her future to think about, especially college. (She'd been dreaming about the Columbia-Juilliard double-degree program since forever, and it probably didn't accept applicants who were known witches.)

But if she gave up witchcraft, it would really, really complicate her life. Not that her life wasn't already complicated, but still.

Quandary, Ridley wrote in her notebook. *Dilemma. Conundrum. Predicament. Catch-22.*

"Good morning, everyone!"

Ridley erased her word salad and turned her attention to the front of the room. But wait . . . where was Ms. Hua? The person standing at the blackboard had a buzz cut and retro rhinestone glasses and was not Ms. Hua.

"I'm Ms. O'Shea," she announced to the class. She picked up a piece of chalk and wrote on the blackboard: *O'SHEA.* "I'm filling in for Ms. Hua while she's on maternity leave for the next few months. In the meantime, I'll be taking you on the awesome journey that is the birth and evolution of our country. I'll also be assigning weekly quizzes and short papers, so you'll have that to look forward to!" She grinned and gave a thumbs-up.

Ridley sat up. *A sub who isn't going to just show movies? Fantastic!*

The door opened and closed, and a girl rushed in. "I'm sorry, I got lost!" she apologized breathlessly to Ms. O'Shea. "I didn't know that 232 and 232R were in different parts of the building."

"No worries. Welcome, have a seat."

The girl pushed a strand of honey-blond hair out of her eyes and glanced around the room. Her gaze landed on the empty seat across from Ridley's. She hurried down the aisle, shrugged off her pink suede backpack, and sat down.

"Did I miss anything?" she whispered to Ridley.

Ridley shook her head.

"Oh, whew!"

The girl smiled at Ridley. Ridley smiled back. Was she new? Ridley didn't recognize her.

Ms. O'Shea began taking attendance, calling out names from a clipboard. Halfway down the list, she said, "Penelope Hart?"

The girl raised her hand in the air. "Here! Present!"

Penelope. The name made Ridley think about the brave and clever heroine in *The Odyssey* by Homer. She'd read the ancient Greek epic at her old school back in Cleveland.

Penelope, Ridley scribbled in her notebook, then erased it. She brushed away all the rubber crumbs.

"Ridley? Ridley Stone? Are you here?"

Several kids had turned around in their seats and were staring and pointing at her. *Oops.*

"Yes, hi! I'm here!" Ridley said, rainbow-waving. Her mind had been on *The Odyssey.* Or maybe on Penelope.

After attendance came the distribution of the syllabus (was the plural *syllabuses* or *syllabi*?). As Ms. O'Shea handed them out, Ridley became aware that Penelope was trying to get her attention.

"Psst!"

Penelope slanted her notebook toward Ridley. On a blank page, she'd written:

I love your name! were you named after Ridley Scott the director?

So Penelope liked movies; they had that in common.

I wish! I loved Alien and Alien Covenant.

Yeah, and don't forget Blade Runner!

How can anyone forget Blade Runner? Wait, did you mean the original or the new one?

The original. The new one had a different director, right?

Right! I think his name was

Footsteps. Red Dr. Martens with purple shoelaces . . . Ms. O'Shea was walking down the aisle toward them. "Here you go," she said, handing a syllabus to Ridley.

"Thank you, Ms. O'Shea!"

Ridley quickly slid the syllabus over her notebook. She realized that her heart was racing. Was it because she'd almost gotten caught writing back and forth with Penelope? Or was it because of Penelope, who was cute and nice and also a cinephile? Ridley made a mental note to ask her if she'd seen *The Matrix*, which was pretty much the best movie in the history of movies, in her humble opinion (plus it had been made by two of her heroes, Lilly and Lana Wachowski, both trans women).

Ridley forced herself to focus on the syllabus. Her lips moved silently as she read over the list of topics:

The European Colonization of the Americas
The Colonies
The War for Independence
A New Nation
Federalism and Slavery
The Civil War

Reconstruction and Jim Crow
The Birth of the 20th Century

She read over the syllabus again, then picked up her pencil and circled *pre-Civil War history* (which she'd always wanted to learn more about) and also circled *federalism* and scribbled in the margin: *What other countries in the world have a government based on federalism?*

She noticed Penelope noticing her marking up the syllabus, and smiling. Ridley smiled back and shrugged.

The rest of the period seemed to fly by as Ms. O'Shea read from a dog-eared paperback called *The People's History of the United States.* Once in a while, Ridley paused in her diligent note-taking to glance over at Penelope. Penelope was *not* taking notes; instead, she was doodling . . . eyes? Yeah, definitely eyes. Eyes with curly lashes, eyes with dark, dramatic wings, eyes encircled with tiny moons and stars. What was her obsession with eyes? Whatever the case, she was a really good artist.

When the bell rang, Ridley hastily finished her sentence (*"C. Columbus and his crew were responsible for enslavement and genocide . . ."*), closed her notebook, and put it in her backpack along with her syllabus and mechanical pencil. Her phone, which was tucked away in an inner pocket on silent, glowed faintly and indicated that she had three new texts from Binx. Were they updates about the "fluffy bunny" from this morning and/or the shadow message?

Regarding the latter, Binx seemed to be convinced that Div, Mira, and Aysha were behind it and that *their* coven should call them out on it, respond with fire and fury. Sure . . . maybe? Ridley prayed that Binx was right about their authorship of the shadow message. Still, she wished that the two covens could just get along and stop with the back-and-forth pettiness. It was exhausting; plus Ridley had better things to do, like work on that new transformation spell (transformation was Ridley's thing) and that other new spell, too.

"So, what class do you have next?"

Penelope was hovering beside Ridley's desk. Up close, she smelled like roses. Was that her perfume?

"Um . . . uh . . . I have French. Room 291R. What about you?"

"Spanish. Room 284R. I didn't realize before that *R* stands for *rear wing*. Do you want to walk together?"

"Sure!"

Ridley stood up, slinging her backpack over her shoulder. As she followed Penelope to the doorway, she thought: *It's been ages since I made a new friend.* Mostly, her social life consisted of hanging out with Binx and Greta—mainly Binx, who had become her best friend despite the fact that they were both private people. Or maybe *because* of it? Being a witch necessarily meant that you had to keep a distance from others because you never knew who might figure out your identity and turn you in to the principal or the police. (Even worse, you never knew who might be Antima, which used to not be a problem here but now it apparently was.)

"See you tomorrow, Ridley. You, too, Penelope," Ms. O'Shea said as the two girls passed her. "Oh, and, Ridley—there are tons of other countries whose governments are based on federalism. I'll be sure to include that in our federalism discussion!"

"Um . . . okay?"

That was bizarre. How did Ms. O'Shea know that Ridley had written down that federalism question on her copy of the syllabus?

Just outside Room 232R, the hallway swirled with students heading to their third-period classes. Penelope stopped and started to turn right; then she pivoted left, bumping into Ridley. Ridley blushed as she stepped away.

"Sorry! I am such a klutz. Which way do we go?" Penelope asked.

"*That* way," Ridley said, pointing right. Why was her face so hot? "So, do you have Señora Quintana for Spanish? Everyone says she's—"

"Pen! Penelope!"

A guy strolled up to them. He wore a white polo shirt and khakis, and he looked like an Instagram model.

Oh, right. He had been talking to the new girl this morning. Colter something.

"How's it going? How are your classes?" He draped his arm around Penelope's shoulder and kissed her hair.

Penelope leaned into the curve of his arm. "Good! Do you guys know each other? Colter, this is Ridley. Ridley, this is my boyfriend, Colter."

Colter thrust out a hand and beamed at Ridley. "Awesome to meet you, Ridley."

Ridley took his hand and shook it. His grip was warm and strong, but she barely registered it. Her brain was still stuck on the words *my boyfriend*.

"Awesome to meet you, too. Oh my gosh, I forgot my French textbook in my locker," Ridley lied. Suddenly she had to get out of there ASAP. "See you later, Penelope."

"Okay, see you later!"

"Nice meeting you," Ridley added to Colter, even though she'd already told him that, then turned on her heel and headed in the opposite direction.

It's been ages since I had a crush, she thought. The last time had been in eighth grade, back in Cleveland; she and Natashya had dated for a few months before everything fell apart.

But that was back then. And now here she was, having her first crush in ages, and the girl already had a boyfriend.

Ridley stopped and U-turned in the middle of the hallway. The third-period bell was about to ring, and she had to get all the way to Room 291R.

As she doubled back past the history classroom, she saw Ms. O'Shea standing in the doorway.

Watching her.

What the hex?

And then an odd, random thought occurred to Ridley. She'd run into Ms. Hua over the summer at the grocery store—in July?—and she hadn't *looked* pregnant. Was she really on maternity leave? Or had something happened to her?

Stop being so paranoid, Ridley chided herself.

Still.

She glanced over her shoulder. Ms. O'Shea was gone.

✳ 5 ✳

HOT AND COLD

Our minds are more powerful than you may think.

👁

(FROM *THE GOOD BOOK OF MAGIC AND MENTALISM*
BY CALLIXTA CROWE)

\\ 'm so glad that you were able to meet with me this morning. Thanks for giving up part of your study hall!"

Mrs. Feathers leaned forward on her bright blue yoga ball and smiled kindly at Iris. She reached across her desk for a small brown ceramic bowl.

"Can I offer you some M&M's? They're kind of my weakness."

Iris hesitated; sugar could sometimes make her even more anxious and agitated than usual. "Maybe just one. Thanks, I mean, thank you!"

She started to pick up a yellow one, then gravitated to a green one instead. But what about the red, or the orange? *Argh*, it was impossible to decide.

"I have a hard time with choices," she admitted as her hand hovered over the bowl. "My therapist, Francesca—well, actually, she's not my therapist anymore, but she was my therapist back in New York City—she says it's because I'm worried about making the wrong choice and then being locked into that choice, and then what? What if I pick the yellow M&M, but I was really supposed to pick the red one, but it's too late and I can't go back and un-eat the yellow M&M . . . well, I *could*, technically, but that would be gross and really rude, right? Like, what am I going to do, spit it out and go for the red one instead?"

Mrs. Feathers nodded sympathetically. "You can take all the time you need to pick out your M&M. Or take one of each color. Or take the whole bowl. Or I can put the bowl away for now and you can decide later, when you feel ready. This is an M&M-safe space." She smiled again.

Iris had no idea what an "M&M-safe space" was, but that was okay. Mrs. Feathers, who exuded a sort of hippie-grandma aura, seemed nice. Nicer than Mr. Zabel, the social worker at her old school, who used to make a sour-pickle face whenever Iris showed up at his office (which was often).

Iris made herself do some therapy-breathing and settle back in her chair. She felt less crazy and chaotic than she had this morning before homeroom. She hadn't run into the mean guy with the Antima shoulder patch again, and she hadn't seen any of the three girls she'd felt watching her, either.

Although she hadn't gotten an Antima vibe off of them.

Was it possible . . . could they be witches, too? Iris had never had a witch friend; it would be so cool to have witch friends to hang with.

"So I just wanted to say hi and introduce myself and all that," Mrs. Feathers said. "If you'd like, I can also go over your IEP with you and make sure you know what accommodations you're entitled to. I plan to touch base with all of your teachers, as well."

"Does the IEP have the thing about loud noises? Because of my sensory processing disorder? I think my mom had that added last year."

Mrs. Feathers typed something on her computer keyboard. The computer was beige and boxy and ancient-looking. "Yes, it's definitely on your IEP. We have noise-reducing headphones in every classroom for use during tests and quiet work time and whenever else you might need them. We can also give you your own pair to carry around in your backpack."

"Really? Cool."

Iris picked up an orange M&M, thought about eating it, then changed her mind and set it carefully on her lap. She was glad that Mrs. Feathers was familiar with SPD. The fact that Iris's neurodivergent brain scrambled sensory input, at times interpreting soft sounds as loud and loud sounds as unbearable . . . or making her averse to the slightest physical contact one day, then wanting to slam into furniture (or into other kids in the playground, when she was younger) the next . . . or being unable to tolerate the feeling of mashed foods in her mouth . . . was usually confusing and off-putting to those around her.

As Mrs. Feathers typed something else, her gaze drifted to Iris's pendant.

"Is that a moonstone? It's very pretty. You rarely see moonstones that color."

Iris reached up and curled a fist around the smiley face, not to calm herself but to hide it from Mrs. Feathers, although it was a little too late for that, like un-eating an M&M. She was usually fine wearing her pendant openly, since people didn't recognize the yellow gem (moonstones were usually more moon-colored). The fact that Mrs. Feathers had identified it was kind of unsettling, since moonstone could be associated with magic. (And, in Iris's case, the association was correct.)

"Gosh, is *that* what it is?" Iris exclaimed, trying to sound surprised. "I always thought it was just some random stone. Mostly I just like the smiley-face part; it cheers *me* up."

"Well, we all need that, don't we? Whenever I'm having a sad or bad or mad day, this is what I look at to cheer me up."

Mrs. Feathers picked up a framed photo and turned it around. A gray cat with a couple of bald patches was meatloafing on a couch. It had one milky blue eye and another that appeared to be scarred shut. In the background, a little golden kitten was curled up in a sleepy, furry puddle.

"These are two of my kitties. I found *her*"—Mrs. Feathers pointed to the gray one—"under a highway, badly injured. The vet wasn't able to save the one eye, and she can barely see out the other."

"Aww, poor kitty-cat."

"She's a strong girl, though. A survivor. I named her Loviatar."

"Loviatar?" It sounded like one of Iris's medications.

"Loviatar is the blind daughter of the Finnish god of death," Mrs. Feathers explained.

"The god of . . . *death*?" Iris repeated, frowning. Why would someone want to name their cat after a death god's daughter?

"Loviatar isn't like her father. In the myth, she becomes a powerful shapeshifter and warrior. She also tries to steal the sun, moon, and stars. Of course, the only thing *my* Lovi tries to steal is my breakfast, lunch, and dinner, right off my plate. Same with my other pets." Mrs. Feathers chuckled.

"LOL! I mean, that's funny!"

"Does your family have pets, Iris?"

"Yup. My little sister has a pet mouse, Lolli McScuffle Pants, and my little brother has a hamster named Hulk. They're new, we just got them from the Sorrow Point SPCA, I bet you didn't know you could get non-cat and non-dog pets from there? We've also had Oliver P. and Maxina for a while; my parents adopted them from a cat rescue place on the Upper West Side. That's in New York City. Let me tell you, they were *not* happy about the cross-country relocation thing."

"Why did your family decide to move here?"

"After my dad died—that was in May, so basically four months ago—there wasn't a lot of money. Not that we ever *had* a lot of money but there was even less, like my mom wasn't sure how we were going to pay the rent or buy groceries. New York's crazy-expensive. So my grandma Roseline, she's my mom's mom, said we should move out here and live with her in her house, and Mom could work at her restaurant—Café Papillon. Do you know it? It's part diner and part art gallery and part bead shop. On Orchard Street next to the tattoo place? Anyhoo, so Mom and Nyala and Ephrem and I, and Oliver P. and Maxina, we packed up and moved here. Yay."

Iris twirled her finger in the air, then stopped abruptly.

"Gah! Sorry, no offense! I am such an idiot! I'm sure Sorrow Point is super, super cool. I'm just not used to it. It feels, well, *foreign*. Which is a dumb thing to say because it's not foreign, it's still the same country."

"That's tough about your dad," Mrs. Feathers said softly. "My father died at a young age, too, so I know what it's like to suffer that kind of loss." She blinked and pinched the bridge of her nose.

Was Mrs. Feathers about to cry? Iris had never seen a teacher cry. Although technically Mrs. Feathers wasn't a teacher but a social worker. Same difference, though.

"I'm sorry about your dad," Iris murmured.

"Thank you."

"Death really sucks."

"Yes, it most definitely does."

Now *Iris* wanted to cry. She pinched the bridge of her nose, hard, wondering if this was a stopping-tears trick. *Hmm.* It worked, sort of. Although now her nose hurt.

The bell rang, signaling the end of second period. Iris tried to remember what came after study hall. *Oh yeah, French.*

"Okay, well, *merci beaucoup!*" She picked up her backpack and jumped to her feet. As she did, the orange M&M that had been sitting on her lap fell to the floor and rolled under a bookshelf. "*Argh!* My M&M!"

Mrs. Feathers pushed the brown ceramic bowl toward her. "No problem. Here, have another one."

"No, I'll get it, I don't want to mess up your office."

"Really, it's—"

Iris didn't hear the rest of Mrs. Feathers's sentence as she dropped to her knees (*ouch*) and crawled over to the bookshelf. She tried to peer under it, but all she could see was dust. And a piece of paper . . . maybe a newspaper clipping?

Iris reached in to retrieve it. As her fingers grazed it, a white-hot heat seared through her.

"*Ow!*"

"Are you all right?" Mrs. Feathers called out sharply.

Iris's brain buzzed and prickled. An image came to her . . . signs held high in the air by angry-looking people. The signs had numbers on them.

What the hex?

"Iris?"

Mrs. Feathers was next to her, bending down with a worried expression. Iris scooted back from the bookshelf and stood up, wobbly and dazed. She inspected her fingers; there was no burn mark, and no pain, either. In fact, they felt perfectly cool.

Had she had an SPD moment? This was happening to her more and more lately. She'd touch some object, and weird mental images would come rushing at her.

"Sorry! I was looking for the . . . and I accidentally touched a hot . . . except I think it was probably cold or regular temperature, and my brain went into . . . Never mind, I have to get to my French class."

Mrs. Feathers glanced at Iris's hand, her brow wrinkled in concern. "Are you sure you're not hurt? I think there might be an old baseboard under there. Do you need to see the nurse?"

"No, I'm good. Bye, *au revoir*!"

Iris saluted (why?) and headed into the crowded hallway. She pulled her schedule out of her backpack side pocket; what room was her French class in? Room 291R. Her brain was still a little bit buzzy and prickly. She wished there were a permanent magical cure for her SPD, and for her anxiety disorder, too (which also had initials—GAD, for Generalized Anxiety Disorder). But she didn't remember seeing anything like that in Callixta's witchcraft manual.

Of course, Callixta said that magic was mainly about intention. If a witch could powerfully and deliberately *think* a thing, she or he or they could make it so. Spells, potions, mirrors, wands, and such were mostly just ways to enhance and channel the magical energy of the intentions. So maybe Iris just needed to, well, *intend* more strongly?

Make my SPD and GAD go away . . . NOW! N-O-W! I MEAN it! she thought, squeezing her fists.

Nope. Still the same. Big surprise. (She'd tried this before, many times.)

Sighing, she headed down the hall toward what she hoped was Room 291R, where a familiar-looking girl rushed past her in a navy-and-white Juilliard hoodie. It was one of the three girls who'd been checking her out that morning.

Iris watched as the girl went into Room 291R. So they were going to be in the same French class.

Iris decided to sit *far* away from her, just in case.

6

SMACKDOWN

Covens should be united against
their common enemies.

(FROM *THE GOOD BOOK OF MAGIC AND MENTALISM*
BY CALLIXTA CROWE)

B
y lunchtime, Binx still hadn't heard back from Mira or Aysha. *Jerks.*
But no matter. She had the next forty-five minutes to track them
down and force a confession out of them. She'd magically hacked into
their class schedules and confirmed that they had A-lunch, too, so locat-
ing them shouldn't be too difficult.

She also hadn't heard back from Greta and Ridley re: her brilliant
detective work about Iris Gooding. Whatever . . . They could discuss
what to do about Iris over lunch after they'd dealt with the Triad.

Binx made her way down the main hall toward the cafeteria. Posters
about homecoming, clubs, and athletics plastered the elegant cream
walls. (She noticed that fencing tryouts were in November . . . *Excellent.*
She'd always wanted to take up the sport.) A maroon WELCOME BACK,

STUDENTS! banner hung cheerily from the high, molded plaster ceiling. The building, she'd heard, used to be a fancy resort in the late nineteenth century. Then it was closed and boarded up for decades. Then it was eventually reincarnated as Sorrow Point High. (The mood *was* very *The Breakfast Club* meets *The Shining.*)

I wonder if there are ghosts here, Binx thought, then chuckled to herself. She didn't believe in ghosts. Witches, yeah, but not ghosts.

As she neared the cafeteria, she spotted Jennifer Liu and Joel Katz semi-hidden behind a fake potted palm tree, kissing. *Ew.* JennJo had been dating since kindergarten, practically, but get a room! Then she saw that approaching them from the other direction were . . . *yessss!* Mira and Aysha. Perfect timing.

Binx was about to call out to them, but before she could, they sauntered over to JennJo like a pair of hungry panthers that had just found their prey. Aysha murmured some words under her breath. Then she flipped one of her boxer braids over her shoulder and touched Joel's arm.

"Hey, sweetie. Love your shirt. Really shows off your pecs."

Aysha's hand snaked up to Joel's collar, and she pulled him toward her. His body peeled away from Jennifer's, propelled toward Aysha's as though magnetized. Jennifer's jaw dropped. Mira watched, smirking.

"Hey, Aysh. How's it going?" Joel said dreamily.

"Better now that you're here, baby," Aysha cooed.

"Ex-*cuse* me!" Jennifer put her hands on her hips. "Aysha, what do you think you're doing? Joel, get away from her!"

"But she's way hotter than you," Joel pointed out matter-of-factly.

Jennifer's chin quivered. She looked as though she were about to burst into tears. "H-how can you say that? W-why are you being so m-mean?"

"I'm not being mean, I'm just being honest."

Jennifer gasped and folded her arms across her chest. She started to say something, then ran off, her shoulders shaking with sobs.

Aysha and Mira cracked up as they watched Jennifer flee. "Come here, princess," Joel murmured to Aysha, leaning in for a kiss.

Aysha put her hand on his chest and pushed him lightly. "Yeah, no, that's not happening. You're kind of a loser."

"Uh . . ."

Joel wandered off with a dazed expression. Binx rolled her eyes; this was classic Triad nonsense. Where had they learned how to do that, anyway? She didn't remember any unshipping spells in C-Squared's book.

For a second, Binx toyed with the idea of trying a counterspell on JennJo (they might be the poster couple for obnoxious PDA, but they didn't deserve *this*), then changed her mind; she had important business to attend to, and besides, she didn't want to take any unnecessary risks (unlike the bagel, which had been *very* necessary).

Binx caught Mira's and Aysha's attention and motioned them into a nearby alcove. The alcove contained a single vending machine with a handwritten out of order sign on it (unoccupied, good). She cast a quick calumnia spell.

"*Calumnia* mode," Binx announced. "Wow. That was super-mature of you."

Aysha smirked at Binx, taking in her yellow outfit. "Says the girl who's dressed like a Minion. Or is it SpongeBob SquarePants? You're really pushing the fashion envelope today, Beatrix Kato."

Binx fake-smiled so hard that her teeth hurt. Aysha knew better than to call her by her full name, which she loathed (seriously, why should she suffer because of her father's obsession with an olden-day bunny-ologist?). But Binx herself knew better than to act like she cared, especially around the Triad, especially around Aysha, who took no prisoners.

"Yeah, I was going for Bart Simpson, actually. We need to discuss that shadow message you guys wrote."

Mira wrinkled her nose. "What shadow message?"

"You know exactly what I'm talking about."

"Seriously, I don't!"

"Is this a joke? Are you messing with us?" Aysha asked Binx suspiciously.

Binx hesitated. Mira and Aysha both seemed legit confused. Or were they just legit lying? Knowing them, likely the latter.

Her phone buzzed with a text. She glanced at it quickly. It was a message from Ridley:

Where are you?

Binx wrote back:

Vending machine room near the cafeteria. With the Triad minus D.

Ridley and Greta appeared seconds later.

"Calumnia?" Greta whispered to Binx, who nodded in response.

"Yeah, so, they're claiming they didn't write the shadow message," Binx explained to her coven-mates.

"We *didn't*!" Mira insisted. "What *is* this shadow message, anyway?"

Greta reached into her backpack and pulled out the clear bag that contained the note plus a sprig of rosemary. Ridley cast an anxious glance into the hallway, then positioned herself next to and slightly behind Greta, to block the view of the shadow message from any passersby.

Aysha and Mira checked it out.

"That's not from us," Aysha said immediately. Mira nodded in agreement.

"Liars. That's your handwriting, Mira!" Binx exclaimed.

"That is *not* my handwriting. I always do my Ys with those cute little loops," Mira said, tracing the shape in the air.

"Look, we know you wrote this, so you'd better just—"

Binx stopped. Something was climbing onto her shoulders. No, not climbing . . . *slithering.*

It was a snake. A big, long, white snake. It wrapped itself around Binx's neck until its silver eyes were just inches from her brown ones. It flicked its tongue and made a hissing noise.

Binx knotted her fists to keep from screaming. Her skin grew icy cold—with fear? Or had the creature already injected her with poison, and she was about to die? Or . . .

"Guys? A little help?" she whimpered to Greta and Ridley.

"Help with what?" Ridley asked, confused.

"Um, the giant deadly reptile?"

"They can't see it, Beatrix. At the moment, only you and I have that pleasure."

Div sauntered up to their group, leaned against the vending machine, and smiled. Or sneered. Or a little of both. With her all-white outfit, long platinum hair, and ghostly pale complexion, she matched her familiar's albino palette. Binx barely registered Div's use of her full name; at the moment, she was too terrified about her impending demise.

"Why are you bothering my girls?" Div asked Binx. Her voice, as always, was deceptively soft and silky.

"I'm not! They're the ones who started it! With the stupid shadow thing!" Binx protested.

"Div, what are you doing to Binx? You're not using Prada against her, are you?" Greta demanded.

Sighing, Div reached out, patted the snake, and whispered to it in some foreign language . . . or maybe it was a spell? The terrible creature loosened its grip on Binx and slithered onto Div's arm, then settled contentedly around her shoulders before becoming invisible again, or invisible to Binx, anyway, since no one else had been privy to its appearance, apparently.

"*Seriously?*" Binx gasped as she rubbed her neck.

"Div, that's not cool," Greta said angrily.

Div turned to Greta and cocked her head. "Greta. You haven't been sleeping well, have you? I can see it in your face. The puffiness, the black circles. I'll text you a recipe for my new relaxation tea. It's quite . . . powerful."

"Your last 'recipe'"—Greta made air quotes—"turned my skin blue and it took three days to wear off. So, no thank you! Binx, are you okay?"

"No, I am *not* okay. I was just trying to get to the bottom of the note drama, and—"

Div plucked the bag from Greta. Her snakelike green eyes fixed on the shadow message inside.

Then she pulled something out of her white leather backpack and held it up for the other girls to see.

It was the exact same shadow message. Even the handwriting was identical.

"Wait, *what*?" Binx exclaimed.

"I found this in my locker just now," Div explained. "It looks like you and I have a common enemy, Greta."

"Can you guys put those away?" Ridley said nervously. "*Calumnia* only works on what we're *saying*, remember?"

"Yes, thanks for the reminder," Greta said, complying.

Div rolled her eyes but complied as well.

"*Now* do you believe me?" Mira said to Binx.

"Not particularly," Binx shot back. "You still could have written the shadow message. Shadow *messages*, plural. You know, as some sort of super-prank 2.0?"

"*You* could have done that, too, Kato," Aysha accused.

"Can we please consider for a second that it wasn't *any* of us?" Greta pointed out.

"Maybe we should try some scrying spells," Div suggested.

"Maybe we should just burn them," Ridley said.

"What about—"

"You girls are blocking the vending machine," a voice interrupted.

The six witches spun around. A guy stood nearby. A junior . . . Brandon something. He gestured impatiently at the vending machine.

Then Binx's gaze landed on his black T-shirt.

An Antima shoulder patch.

Whoa.

Had the *calumnia* spell held, or had it automatically cut out when Brandon showed up? Had he seen the shadow messages before Greta and Div hid them out of sight?

Before anyone could say anything, Div coughed into the crook of her arm and at the same time whispered: *"Praetereo."*

A memory-erase spell.

Brandon blinked and frowned. His brown eyes looked muddled. "Did I . . . Are you all in line for the vending machine?" he asked, confused.

"We were, except that it's out of order. Isn't it so annoying when that happens?" Div sidled up to him and slipped her arm through his. "I think they put in a new vending machine by the salad bar, though. Here, let me show you."

Smiling, she steered him out of the alcove, chatting lightly about sports drinks versus sodas.

Binx's gaze moved from Ridley (who looked totally freaked out) to Greta (ditto) to Mira (ditto) to Aysha (ditto, although she was trying her best to hide it).

Binx was right there with them.

So there really *were* Antima at the school now.

Which meant that the shadow messages might not be a Triad super-prank, after all.

Which was not good.

7

CHOICE OF EVILS

Magic is a choice between the Light and the Dark.
The choice is ultimately yours.

(FROM *THE GOOD BOOK OF MAGIC AND MENTALISM*
BY CALLIXTA CROWE)

Div sat at the pearl-colored vanity table in her room and scrutinized the three jars in front of her. Each one contained a different lock of hair.

She'd come home early from school, skipping the last two periods, to study her copy of the shadow message and determine its true origin. (She'd faked a fever, which was perfectly easy to do with a *calor* spell—also, Nurse Jacinta was beyond gullible). She had the big house to herself— Uncle Paul was at his law office, and Aunt Marta was doing a three-hour Pamper Yourself package at the spa, as she did every Wednesday—which meant that Div could practice magic openly and also let Prada roam freely. No doubt her familiar was slithering around the kitchen, searching for something small and wriggly to squeeze to death; she was overdue for a meal.

Aunt Marta had been talking about getting a little purse dog, which would *not* be a good idea . . . at least not for the dog.

The jars. Div considered them for a moment, then rearranged the order from left to right, based on priority. Now the jar containing Binx's hair (from her cyan phase last spring) was on the left; the one containing Greta's curly auburn hair was in the middle; and the one containing Ridley's coily black hair was on the right. Div had been collecting these samples secretly for the past year or so, with a tiny pair of cuticle-trimming scissors and some distraction spells. (She had hair samples from other people, too, stowed away in the back of her closet in neatly labeled jars. Who knew when they might come in handy?)

She set the shadow message on top of Binx's jar. She needed to rule out the possibility that someone in Greta's coven had authored it. If that *were* the case, Binx would be the most likely culprit, given her personality and her predilection for childish stunts.

Also, to be honest, Binx had skills. Even though Greta was the self-appointed leader of their coven, Div sometimes wondered if Binx might not be the superior witch—or at least the more *creative* witch, willing (like Div herself) to experiment with and expand on the limited teachings in Crowe's book. (In fact, Div had tried to poach Binx from Greta over the summer, but to no avail. The girl had actually laughed in her face—*so* obnoxious.)

Div hadn't let on to the others at lunchtime, but she'd been greatly unnerved by the double shadow messages and the vending machine interloper with the shoulder patch (she'd learned that his name was Brandon Fiske, and that he was a junior). She was aware, of course, of the Antima's activities around the country, the escalating violence and virulence of their methods. For months, she'd been following a number of different Antima subgroups on social media (they all had stupid, self-important names like the Truth Bearers and the Guardians of Light and the Sons of Maximus), for strategy purposes. She wanted to understand the enemy. Their beliefs . . . their goals . . . what they meant when they called witches like her "abominations of nature" and "threats to society" . . . why they considered themselves "heroes" and "patriots." (Some Antima, though, apparently didn't have an online presence, and organized and communicated in some other way—Div wasn't sure how.) She wondered if Brandon was the only Antima at their school, or if there were others.

She wondered, too, if the Antima were driven by sexism and misogyny (which was one theory). Although from what she could tell, there *were* female Antima members. But why would they join a cause that was anti-women? Of course, they could be doing this for protection, to make sure the Antima didn't turn against *them*.

And did the Antima have an extra layer of animus against queer women? She and Aysha were both bi; so was Greta.

She touched Binx's jar. Hopefully Mira and Aysha were right. Better to deal with childish stunts than with the Antima.

"Aequo," she murmured.

No reaction. The shadow message didn't shimmer or change color, and neither did the lock of hair.

She envisioned shimmers and colors in her mind. *"Aequo!"*

Still nothing.

Frowning, she repeated the enchantment with Greta's jar, then Ridley's. No shimmering, no color changes.

So it *wasn't* them.

Which meant that the Antima might have her in their sights, after all.

Which was a problem. A *serious* problem.

Div grabbed her phone and scrolled through her contacts to find Greta's number. They would deal with this threat together; they would *end* this threat together. Back in eighth grade, when they'd had their little coven of two, they'd been an incredible team. They'd both been skilled at harvesting the natural world for magical use. Herbs, plants, minerals . . . whatever could be found in nature, they could utilize as ingredients for their craft. And they'd been so *good* at it. They'd inspired each other, challenged each other (and this was way before Crowe's book).

Then Div had started to explore the darker aspects of the natural world. While Greta continued to focus on healing and fixing and growing, Div began to focus on manipulating and breaking and destroying. She tried to get Greta interested in this new direction, too, but to no avail. Greta was just too . . . *pure.* So stubbornly dogmatic with her *magic-can-only-be-used-for-good* nonsense.

Then, around the time when Div started teaching herself about necromancy, Greta had left their coven and formed her own.

Div looked down at her phone. There was Greta's name in the middle of the *N*s. *Greta Navarro.*

No. She didn't need Greta anymore. They were the past. She had her girls now.

Mira Jahani. Aysha Rodriguez.

She fired off a text to them; the last period should be wrapping up.

My house, ASAP.

K, Aysha wrote back immediately. Mira responded with a car emoji.

Good. They were, as usual, respectful of her status as coven leader and never disobeyed her.

Div had met Mira and Aysha at the beginning of ninth grade. The pair had been BFFs since elementary school, and even as their interests began to diverge (while Aysha grew into martial arts and wolves, Mira grew into fashion design and celebrity blogs), they'd stuck together because of their history. *And* because it turned out that they were both witches—the only ones they knew of in Sorrow Point or anywhere else. (Their discovery moments had happened during a game of two-person flashlight freeze tag that had resulted in Mira actually freezing Aysha's shirt, and vice versa.)

Div had never really noticed them before last September, when they'd all ended up in the same freshman history class. One day, she overheard the two friends planning to use a spell to alter their report cards to give themselves all A's. Later, Div had confronted them privately and pretended that she was going to report them to the principal. They'd immediately tried to cast a double memory-erase spell on her, to which she'd responded with a powerful counterspell along with the words *Nice to meet you, too.* She'd then suggested that the three of them form a coven with her as leader. (Mira and Aysha were the first witches Div had ever come across aside from her mother and Greta, and she liked the idea of bossing lesser witches around, just as her mother had done to her before she moved to Barcelona with her boyfriend.)

Setting her phone down on the dressing table, Div gazed at the shadow message that lay, unchanged and unshimmering, on top of Ridley's hair jar. She swallowed nervously. She needed to distract herself while she waited for the girls to show up.

Holding up her hands, she regarded her French-tipped nails. *"Blancus,"* she commanded, and the French tips morphed into a dark purple, the color of bruises. "Yeah, I don't think so."

She reiterated the spell and at the same time pictured a silvery-white shade in her mind, changing her nail color again. "Better."

Leaning back in her chair, Div blinked at her reflection in the mirror. She was pale. So pale. She looked like those women in Victorian England who ate arsenic wafers to make their complexions ashy-white. (Another poison called belladonna, which was Italian for *beautiful woman*, was used for this purpose, too, and also to enlarge the pupils—big pupils had been, for some reason, desirable back then.)

Div could appreciate the application of poisons for beautifying purposes, although she herself had little need for them. She preferred to use her toxic concoctions to hinder and harm her enemies, her detractors. She got her recipes not just from Crowe (who, like Greta, had been too virtuous and earth-motherish to go there) but from her own research and experiments. Of course, she couldn't imagine actually *killing* someone with one of her potions, unless it was in self-defense or in defense of one of her witches.

Still, she wondered . . . could she kill, say, an Antima member? Not in self-defense or defense of others, but because the Antima were scum? She tried to picture herself doing this. Maybe? Probably not. Although it was an interesting idea and reminded her of something her uncle mentioned once. A legal concept. Choice of evils. Sure, it was evil to kill someone, but what if that someone himself was evil?

Outside, car doors slammed. Mira must have driven herself and Aysha over in her Miata. Mira wasn't supposed to drive anyone under twenty who wasn't a relative, not until she'd satisfied a few more Washington State DMV requirements, but the one time she'd been pulled over, the police officer had let her go (without magic intervention) because she was the daughter of a local political VIP. (Mr. Jahani, a councilman, was running for mayor of Sorrow Point in November.)

The police. Div frowned into the mirror. With the new anti-witch US president and now Antima in their community, would the Sorrow Point Police Department start cracking down on witches and witchcraft? And what did this mean for her coven? Extra measures might have to be taken to hide their magical identities and activities. (Mira had some pull with the police, but not *that* much pull.)

She texted the girls and told them to come up. A minute later, they bustled into her room.

"There was an accident on Pine, otherwise we would have been here even sooner," said Mira breathlessly. She plopped down on Div's bed and adjusted her gray snakeskin boots. "These are killing me, they're way smaller than when I bought them. I wonder if Binx cast a shrinking hext on them?"

Aysha crossed her arms and leaned against the wall. "So what's up?" she asked Div. Aysha wasn't big on small talk.

"We need to figure out who wrote the shadow messages, of course," Div replied.

"I still think Binx fake-wrote both of them," Mira said.

Div was about to tell her the results of the *aequo* spell she'd just cast. But she decided to hear Mira out, in case she had new information.

"Do you have any proof?"

"Um, her personality? *That's* your proof. She loves to pick fights with us."

Okay, so no new information.

"That girl seriously needs to get a life," Aysha piped up.

"Actually, I find her quite interesting," Div said.

Mira and Aysha exchanged a glance. "Of course, if you say so!" Mira said quickly.

"Interesting how?" Aysha asked.

"She's a cyber-witch," Div pointed out. "I don't know any other cyber-witches, do you?"

"*Yoooooou're* not thinking about trying to recruit her again, are you?" Mira asked Div suspiciously. "'Cuz the last time, she said she'd rather eat all her devices than be in our coven."

Div shrugged.

Aysha strolled over to the bed and sat down. "We don't need that laptop witch. If you want to expand our coven, I have a better idea. *Two* ideas, actually."

"Oh?"

"What two ideas? You didn't tell me, Aysh!" Mira complained.

"I wasn't sure. I'm still not sure. But there might . . . *might* . . . be two new witches at the school."

"What?" Div was surprised to hear this. Besides themselves and Greta's coven, she knew of no other witches at Sorrow Point High. The arrival of two new witches could be huge. Fantastic, actually. "Once again, is there any proof?" she asked Aysha.

"Not exactly. Well, sort of. So, there's these two girls in my English class. Iris something and Penelope something. Iris was sitting across from me. She was wearing this moonstone pendant, and I saw her holding it and whispering to herself like a couple of times during class. And the other girl, Penelope, she was sitting in front of me, and her backpack was hanging from the back of her chair, kind of open, and I thought I saw a deck of tarot cards inside. I used a quick *mobilus* spell to move them into the light a bit"—Aysha was talented at telekinesis—"and yup, they were definitely tarot cards. Handmade. Really good art, actually."

Div considered this. If these new girls, Iris and Penelope, were indeed witches, and Div could convince them to join the coven, that would increase their ranks to five. Group spells with five witches would be so much more effective than with just the three of them. Five witches, combining their powers, might give Brandon Fiske and any other Antima at their school—even in all of Sorrow Point—a run for their money.

And if she could convince Binx to join them, too, then maybe Ridley would follow. That would make it seven.

And then finally, Greta would have no choice but to come back to her.

The bedroom door creaked on its hinges, and Prada slithered in. Her stomach area protruded with whatever she'd caught and killed downstairs. She raised her head and flicked her tongue at Mira and Aysha.

Mira fluttered her fingers at Prada. "Um, hey, hi, gorgeous snake!" she squealed nervously. Even though Mira and Aysha had been coven-mates with Div for a while, Mira in particular was still skittish in the presence of Prada, who'd tried to bite her once for raising her voice at Div. (Mira had never made that mistake again.)

Prada slithered slowly toward the bed. She paused next to Mira's snakeskin boots.

The color drained from Mira's face. "Ohhhh! Yeah, these are fake. Pinkie-swear! Div, can you please tell her these are fake, *please*?"

Div sighed again. She knew Mira wasn't lying; she often shopped for knockoffs and discount labels and used an enhancement spell to make them look designer.

"Come," Div whispered to Prada. Prada obeyed immediately, slithering over to the vanity table and coiling herself at Div's feet. Mira let out a loud, dramatic exhale.

Aysha turned to Div. "So what do you think? About Iris and Penelope, I mean."

"Let's come up with a plan to get to know them better," Div suggested. "We can't take any risks, in case they might be Antima in disguise, or whatever. But if they *are* witches, we should recruit them."

"That's a super-smart idea!" Mira exclaimed.

"So glad you approve," Div said sweetly. "Now, back to business. We need to resolve this shadow message matter. First, let's do a group *aequo* spell with these hair samples. I did *aequo* on my own, before you got here, but I want to repeat it with the three of us."

Aysha stared at the jars. "Does that hair belong to—"

"Yes," Div interrupted. "I don't think that the shadow messages were written by their coven, but we should be certain. And if it's definitely *not* them, it's likely the Antima, and we need to try a different scrying spell that doesn't require hair samples." Or maybe get the hair samples somehow, she thought.

"Got it." Aysha nodded and slipped down to the white shag rug and assumed a cross-legged position. Mira did the same.

Div went to her closet to retrieve some candles and gems that she kept hidden in a tampon box, then joined them on the rug. As she arranged the items in the middle of their circle, she felt a renewed sense of resolve and confidence. Everything was going to be okay. Her witches were here. More witches might be joining them soon. Not to mention that she herself had more power and practice than anyone she'd ever known.

The Antima didn't stand a chance.

She had this.

8

OBFUSCATORS

A person of the magical sort may use her abilities
to serve Justice as she sees fit.
But take heed of the consequences.

(FROM *THE GOOD BOOK OF MAGIC AND MENTALISM*
BY CALLIXTA CROWE)

Ridley decided to take a shortcut through the new development on her
way to Binx's house. Greta had called an impromptu coven meeting
to solve the mystery of the shadow messages, while Binx was still holding
on to the slim possibility that Div and her coven had faked them and were
lying about it. They were undeniably skilled at deceit and . . . what was
that word? Oh yeah. *Obfuscation.*

Greta had also instructed Ridley and Binx to cast *pleukiokus* spells
(Callixta's book, Chapter 14) for extra protection. Ridley had done so in
the girls' bathroom right after lunch. Now, walking, she could still feel
the spell's effects; it was like the sensation of wearing an invisible cloak.
Still, she made herself continue to *think* about the concept of protection

in case the spell wore off; better safe than sorry. Especially now that the Antima had infiltrated her school—but Ridley didn't want to think about them. Out of sight, out of mind (and vice versa).

Also, what was up with the new history sub, Ms. O'Shea? There was something *odd* about her. Unless Ridley was imagining it?

Turning left onto Lilac Street, she decided to distract herself by tapping a complicated bariolage rhythm against her leg. Bariolage was a violin technique that involved layers of sound—one line a steadily held note, another line a melody, and so on. This particular bariolage was from Bach's Partita in E Major. Ridley hated Bach. She didn't hate listening to his pieces, which were almost diabolically elegant, but she hated performing them, because there was no wiggle room for mistakes. Nowhere to hide. But her teacher, Mr. Jong, was making her learn the partita for next year's competitions. In fact, she would have to play it for him at their lesson next week. All six movements, from memory.

Grrrr.

Ridley sighed and glanced around. The new development, called Seabreeze, was actually not on the sea (more obfuscation); she couldn't even see Puget Sound from where she was. Only half of the houses were finished; the other half were still under construction. The finished ones were all the same—beige McMansions with faux-Greek columns, six-car garages, and pool cabanas that were nicer than a lot of people's actual homes. The unfinished houses were in various stages of metamorphosis—everything from wood-beam skeletons on dusty, barren lots to almost completed structures with cheerful orange FOR SALE signs. There were short, truncated sidewalks-to-nowhere in front of the finished houses and no sidewalks at all in front of the unfinished ones.

Her phone buzzed as she turned onto Coyote Way. She paused the bariolage and blinked at the screen, which morphed from black to neon pink. Then rainbow. Then a demented Hello Kitty with bloody fangs. Then back to black.

What the . . . ?

Ridley held the phone at arm's length, wondering what Aysha and Mira were up to, and which counterspell she should use to negate whatever evil they had sent her way. Also, why were they pranking *her*? They usually went after Binx.

Hello Kitty popped up again, this time with a cartoon bubble over its head:

You're on your way right?

Ridley exhaled. Binx. She should have guessed.

She typed a reply:

Nice special FX. Yup I'm on my way, there soon.

Great, I shall have the snax ready.

Ridley tucked her phone back into her pocket and continued down Coyote Way. She always looked forward to going to Binx's house; it was big and beautiful and had an *actual* view of the sea, as well as a hiking trail down to the beach. Resuming her bariolage, she began leaping nimbly from one sidewalk-to-nowhere to another, which for some reason made her think about *The Matrix* (although honestly, what didn't make her think about *The Matrix*?). The leaping added another layer of complexity to the already complex bariolage rhythm.

Just then, a silver SUV came speeding from the opposite direction, blasting EDM at full, earsplitting volume and killing Ridley's musical groove. An empty soda can flew out of the driver-side window and landed in a sagebrush bush.

Ridley's eyes widened. *Really?* Did *everyone* have to be so disrespectful?

Stepping behind a palm tree (Greta had taught her the name of this particular kind, a Chinese Windmill, which could thrive even in the Pacific Northwest), she shrugged off her backpack and rifled quickly through its contents. Random notebooks, a copy of *Cloud Atlas*, sheet music, her grimoire (which she'd disguised as a creative writing journal) . . . ah, there it was. Her wand, Paganini. (She'd made it herself, just as Greta and Binx had done with their wands, and enchanted it to look like a violin bow, in case any non-witches ever caught sight of it.)

Ridley generally limited her use of magic in public, but the SUV driver needed to be taught a lesson. Besides, there was nobody else around. She pointed Paganini straight at the soda can. Actually, not a soda can, but a beer can, she saw now. *Figures.*

She closed her eyes and mentally transformed the beer can into a flying object.

"Alata," she then murmured under her breath. She pictured its aerial path back to the SUV.

She opened her eyes. The dented beer can rose obediently and rocketed toward the SUV. When it was parallel with the car, it curved right and shot into the driver-side window.

Yes!

The SUV braked with a furious screech of tires. The EDM cut out. Ridley thought she could hear a string of swears, and her mouth twitched up in a smile. *Mission accomplished.*

As she waited for the driver to leave, she ran her hand idly across the rough tree bark and wondered if she should add palm oil to her new healing potion recipe. She admired the new shade of red on her neatly trimmed nails: Crimson Secret.

Another string of swears, and the driver shifted into gear. Good riddance.

Except . . . the SUV wasn't going away. It was going in *reverse*. Toward her.

No no no no no.

The SUV stopped near the palm tree. The driver jumped out of the car, slammed the door behind him, and headed straight for her hiding spot. "I can see you back there, you little witch," he growled.

Little witch? Was that just an expression, or . . .

Ridley's heart was pounding so hard in her chest that she could feel it drumming against her rib cage. She had to do something. Distract him, make an escape. She jammed Paganini into her backpack and stepped out from behind the tree.

"You must be confusing me with someone else," she began.

Then froze.

It was *him*. Brandon Fiske. The guy who'd interrupted the two covens by the vending machine.

"You threw that can at my car, didn't you?" Brandon demanded.

Ridley forced herself to smile. "What? *No!*"

"You did! And you're not getting away with it!"

Brandon moved closer to her, so close that she could smell the sweat and grass and dirt on his lacrosse clothes. He raised his fist as if to hit her.

Ridley stumbled backward. *"Muto!"* she cried out.

A second later, Brandon vanished, and a stinkbug materialized on the pavement where he had been standing.

Ridley exhaled. Her entire body was shaking. Then she began running as fast as she could. As she turned onto a dead-end street, she glanced over her shoulder and murmured: *"Muto! Praetereo!"*

Brandon rematerialized next to the palm tree. He looked around with a confused expression (the same expression he'd worn after Div cast *praetereo* on him at lunchtime) and got back into his SUV.

The memory-erase spell seemed to have worked. *Whew.* Ridley slowed to a jog and cut across an empty construction lot to Briarwood Street.

"Ridley! Hi!"

Now what? Alarmed, Ridley stopped and pivoted in the direction of the voice. A girl was walking toward her on Briarwood. Short, blond, pretty—

Penelope Hart.

"Hi!" Ridley said. She was pleasantly surprised to run into Penelope, but also worried—had she seen Ridley's interaction with Brandon? Was *another* memory-erase spell in order? She quickly checked out the line of sight between them and Coyote Way. She couldn't see the palm tree or Brandon or the silver SUV.

"Hey! Hi! Do you live around here?" Penelope called out.

The girl seemed cheerfully unaware. Maybe the memory-erase spell wasn't necessary.

"Yeah, sort of." Ridley gestured vaguely toward the east. Her house was on the other side of Seabreeze, in an older neighborhood full of raised ranches and bungalows. "How about you?"

"We just moved here from Ojala Heights. Well, not 'just.' Back in June. Our house is at the end of Blackberry Lane." Penelope pointed. "It's that one on the corner that looks like an ugly French castle. Sort of a dog-puke color."

"Dog-puke, that's one of my favorite colors," Ridley joked, folding her arms over her chest.

Penelope laughed. "Right? Couldn't they have picked a *nice* shade of brown, like Sienna or Twig or Aphrodite Blush?"

"Aphrodite Blush?"

"Sorry. It's a lipstick color. I'm a little obsessed with makeup, can you tell?"

Penelope cupped her hands around her chin, framing her face. She wore two—no, three—shades of beigey eye shadow, so artfully applied that it was impossible to tell where one ended and another began. Her lashes were long and curled ever so slightly, and her brows were perfectly shaped. She wore a rose-pink lipstick and matching blush.

Staring at Penelope's face, standing so close to her (there was that really nice perfume again), Ridley felt a little wobbly inside. She swallowed once, twice.

"And I'm also a beautuber," Penelope was saying.

"Beautuber?"

"I have a beauty channel on YouTube. It's called *Just Face It with Penelope!* You should check it out. Not that you need it; you're already gorgeous!"

Ridley's cheeks grew hot. "Um, thanks."

"You're welcome!"

"So where are you—"

Ridley's words were drowned out by the sound of an approaching car. She turned and saw the silver SUV speeding down Brentwood.

Oh no!

She instinctively grabbed Penelope's arm and pulled her back from the curb, then frantically ran through various defense spells in her mind. . . .

The SUV neared, EDM on full volume, then kept going. Brandon hadn't even glanced at them.

The *praetereo* spell had held.

"Thank you! Wow, that person was going way too fast!" Penelope exclaimed.

"They should get a ticket," Ridley agreed.

Penelope closed her eyes and took a deep breath. "Whew, okay, that's better." She opened her eyes. "What are you doing now? I was on my way to Starbucks for my pumpkin spice latte fix because, you know, September. Do you want to come along?"

"Definitely!" Ridley said eagerly. And then she remembered the coven meeting. Could she skip it? No. Not with the whole shadow message issue looming. "Oh, wait. I can't. Sorry. I have to go to my friend Binx's, for this, um, thing."

"No worries. Another time. Oops, I have to get this, I'll see you at school!"

Penelope turned and spoke softly into her phone. "Hey, Colter. No, I'm not home, I'm on my way downtown."

Colter. Right. Boyfriend. Instagram model.

Ridley waved to Penelope and walked away. She felt exhausted suddenly; the Brandon encounters had wiped her out physically and emotionally, and then to pile on a chance encounter with Penelope? It felt like the universe was messing with her. Was this what everyday life was going to be like now? Having to be even *more* secretive and careful about her witch identity? Enduring ugly confrontations with Antima members? Casting memory-erase spells constantly?

And why did Penelope have to have a boyfriend?

Her phone buzzed with another text. She pulled it out and glanced at the screen.

Now Hello Kitty was sinking her fangs into the neck of someone who looked a lot like Ridley.

"Ha ha," she said, cracking a smile.

On the other hand, being a witch definitely had its benefits. Like having witch friends (especially ones who made her smile). Like being able to live as her true self. (She knew there were other paths to achieve that, but this was *her* path.)

She hurried her steps toward Binx's house, making a mental note to look up Penelope's YouTube channel later.

9

BROWNIES, MILK, AND MAGIKARP

The consequences of Magical work can
sometimes be unpredictable;
even the strongest intention can result
in the unintended.

(FROM *THE GOOD BOOK OF MAGIC AND MENTALISM*
BY CALLIXTA CROWE)

"Come on, ShadowKnight, where *are* you?" Binx snapped at her phone.

"I do not understand what you are saying," her virtual genie/assistant Uxie replied in a robotic voice.

"I need to find ShadowKnight. Where is ShadowKnight?"

"I do not understand 'Shallow Night.'"

"Never mind, Uxie."

Sighing, Binx sat down on her bed and scrolled through her DMagic app again. She'd developed it to send and receive encrypted messages. Not just encrypted, but super, super, magically encrypted. She'd sent her technomancer friend four messages in the past four days, and he hadn't answered any of them—or even read them, as far as she could tell. (Read messages were indicated by a nerd-glasses icon.)

Binx took a beat to fire off another enchanted Hello Kitty meme to Ridley, then checked the *Witchworld* Sub9 discussion board, which was deeply buried in the cyber-recesses of the game. It was where she'd stumbled upon the temporary link to C-Squared's witchcraft book back in March 2016. It was also where she'd first met ShadowKnight, this summer. After a few weeks of group posting, the two of them had started sending private messages to each other. That's when he'd revealed to her that he was a witch, and she'd revealed to him that *she* was a witch, too. (She didn't know his real name or address or any other personal info about him, and vice versa.)

There was no sign of him on Sub9, either. Although there *was* a semi-interesting debate brewing about the use of *Witchworld* hexing hacks. And also a link to an article about increased police crackdowns re: witchcraft across the country. *Not. Good.*

Binx wasn't a worrier; nevertheless, she was beginning to worry. Had ShadowKnight's parents discovered that he was a witch . . . and not just a witch but the member of a secret resistance movement? Had the police?

Or had the Antima? Binx really didn't appreciate the fact that they suddenly seemed to be real and present and close by, not just bad news happening in faraway cities (although of course, Binx had no idea what city ShadowKnight lived in). The image of that Brandon guy's hideous shoulder patch throbbed in her brain. The symbol of the cage over a bonfire. That was how they used to burn witches during the Great Purge, according to the history books.

A sudden loud noise startled her, and she leaped to her feet. *Oh, that.* It was just the doorbell—some dumb classical music sound bite that her mom had downloaded to replace her *previous* dumb sound bite, from an old-person rock song. (Yoko Yamada, when she wasn't teaching at the university or writing one of her boring academic treatises on gender equality, was way into the midlife-crisis home improvement.)

Binx's phone lit up with the security-video feed. Ridley was standing at the front door, biting her nails (was that a new bad habit?). Behind her, Greta was hurrying up the driveway, clutching an Organic Bliss canvas shopping bag to her chest.

Binx would have to try to contact ShadowKnight again tonight. Pocketing her phone, she headed downstairs, crossed the vast wood-and-glass living room, and opened the door.

"Hey, guys!"

"Sorry I'm late. I had to stop by my house first," Greta said breathlessly. She held up the Organic Bliss canvas bag. "I come bearing fresh herbs from my garden for our ritual. Also a contribution to the coven meeting snacks . . . brownies!"

"Thanks. Are the brownies from Organic Bliss? I bet they're made from hemp dust and pinecones and recycled dairy-free cardboard," Binx joked. She stuck a finger into her mouth and pretended to gag.

"Ha ha. They're actually yummy. Wait till you try them."

"If you say so. Come on in, you guys. It's just us; the parental unit is at work."

Binx waved them inside and closed the door, then cast a quick *obex* spell to make sure that no one could enter while they were having their coven meeting. She noticed that Ridley was still biting her nails.

"You seem stressed. Are you okay?"

"Yes. Well, not really."

Ridley told them about a run-in she had with an SUV driver who turned out to be Brandon . . . *again*. "He called me a 'little witch.' I don't know if he meant an actual witch or if it was just a random insult. I had to cast *praetereo* on him."

"Oh, Ridley!" Greta leaned over and hugged her. Greta was a big hugger. "I'm so sorry. You must have been scared."

"I shouldn't have used *alata* on his beer can. I should have just let it go," Ridley murmured.

Binx was *not* a big hugger, but she joined in anyway. Her best friend and witch sister was upset. "I probably would have done the same thing. And not reversed the *muto*. That way, he'd stay a stinkbug for all of eternity."

Ridley snort-laughed into Binx's shoulder. "Yeah. Maybe that's our solution. Maybe we should just morph *all* the Antima members into stinkbugs."

After a moment, the hugathon broke up, and Binx led the others into the kitchen. "Let's grab some beverages to go with the non-animal-cruelty brownies. I think we just got a big Fresh Delivery order, so we should be set. I have popcorn and pretzels upstairs."

Inside the kitchen, Binx opened the enormous La Cambusa refrigerator and peered inside. "We've got like six different kinds of fruit juice, ginger ale, root beer, regular seltzer water, flavored seltzer water, caf and decaf iced tea, caf and decaf iced coffee, lemonade, limeade, sports drinks. And milk. Milk goes with brownies, right? We've got regular milk, chocolate milk, and almond milk."

Greta chose almond milk, and Ridley and Binx both chose chocolate milk. They carried their beverages and the brownies with them upstairs.

Ridley paused in front of a painting on the second-floor landing.

"Is that a Robert Rauschenberg?"

Who? "Sure. Yup," Binx replied.

"Is it new? I never noticed it before."

"I guess?"

"Wow, I've only seen Rauschenbergs in museums."

Ridley always seemed to be in awe of Binx's house and the fancy possessions that her parents had accumulated over the years. Binx didn't really care about stuff like that, as long as she could decorate her own room however she wanted and have her privacy. Strangely, Binx had never been to Ridley's—Mr. Stone apparently needed a lot of peace and quiet at home because he worked different shifts for his paramedic job and slept at odd hours—so she had no idea what it was like. She *had* been to Greta's house; they used to hold their coven meetings there because her parents were aware of Greta being a witch (and Binx and Ridley, too) and wanted to be supportive. But Teo, Greta's twelve-year-old brother, had walked in on them once while they were setting up a spell, and Mr. and Mrs. Navarro didn't want him to learn about the girls' witch identities in case he might accidentally spill the secret, so they'd decided to move the default location to Binx's. Binx's mom was clueless about her being a witch and was hardly ever home (her dad, ditto, plus he lived in Palo Alto now), so that was a plus.

Once inside Binx's room, they assumed their usual places on the pink shag rug. Binx had arranged cushions in a circle: a Japanese wave one for Ridley, psychedelic flowers for Greta, and a purple crocheted one for herself. (She'd made it over the summer while watching wild animal documentaries on TV . . . because, bored.) She had also arranged the candles—tall beeswax tapers in mismatched silver candlestick holders as well as small votives in little glass cups. As she closed the curtains and proceeded to light the candles, her pink room glowed gold, and the girls' shadows danced silently on the walls.

Greta reached into her Organic Bliss bag and set out the brownies; they were in a hatbox covered with old-fashioned-looking bird stickers.

Binx picked up a brownie and bit into it. *Huh.* It was actually pretty good. Maybe she could get the recipe? She scarfed down the rest and chased it with chocolate milk and a handful of popcorn.

"You both did the *pleukiokus* spell on yourselves, right?" Greta asked.

"Yup," Binx replied. Ridley nodded.

"Good. Keep repeating it every day, for protection."

Greta next pulled out the clear bag with the shadow message. She extracted the note carefully—the sharp smell of rosemary filled the air—and laid it down in the center of the circle. The glossy black words—*YOU AND YOUR KIND NEED TO DISAPPEAR*—looked even more ominous by candlelight.

"Let's start our group scrying ritual. The Goddess may be able to help us figure out the shadow message's true origin."

"Yeah, her, or maybe Victini," Binx said, picking up her Pokémon deck. "I usually use Charmander for fire, but today, I'm going with Victini because it's a psychic type *plus* a fire type." Quickly scarfing down a second brownie, she crisscrossed her legs and fanned four cards in her palm. "I have another substitution, too. For water, I'm going to use Magikarp instead of Squirtle. People always say Magikarp is useless, but I think it has potential. Like, it's kind of an underdog. Or underfish, I guess."

"Underfish, that's hilarious!" Ridley said, cracking up. But Greta just looked confused. She was not up on Pokémon characters and lore. (Also, being a coven leader and a perpetual worrier, she was kind of like a stressed-out mom with no sense of humor.)

When calling the quarters (their coven always commenced their magical gatherings with this ritual, which they'd adapted from C-Squared's book), Binx usually liked to begin in the South. The South was fire, an element she could relate to; it was a powerful tool if you knew how to tame it, but it could burn you if you weren't careful.

Binx knew that a Pokémon deck wasn't a standard witchcraft item. But there was no "standard" in magic, with the exception of C-Squared's book, which hadn't really been available until that descendant of hers put it online for like a minute. And still, most likely, not all witches had a copy or had even seen a copy. (Binx, of course, had managed to download it onto an untraceable off-site server.)

Also, she'd known about her witch identity since she was thirteen. So between then and the appearance of C-Squared's book, she had (like many witches?) developed her own magical methods and magical tools (in her case, her phone, her computer, and her Pokémon cards).

Binx turned to face southward, which meant orienting her body toward the pink NOT UR BABE poster above her bed; Ridley and Greta followed suit. "Go, Victini!" Binx said, laying the card on the floor.

"Be with us, Michael," Ridley murmured under her breath. She believed in angels, and the archangel Michael corresponded with the South and with the fire element.

"We honor you, Pele," Greta added quietly, invoking the Hawaiian volcano goddess. Greta, who was way into goddesses, rotated through different ones that represented the elements; sometimes, she even made up ones of her own, like when she went through her "Ignisia the Flame Goddess" phase based on a short story she'd written in elementary school. She placed a sprig of peppermint next to Victini. (Greta used both fresh and dried herbs, but she preferred fresh because she felt they were more powerful, more closely connected to nature.)

Next was the water element in the West. Binx pivoted toward the window; the curtains had parted slightly, revealing a dark gray sliver of the Puget Sound in the distance. "Go, Magikarp!" she said, placing the card. She briefly touched its long, whisker-like barbels to give it extra strength. These barbels were white, which meant this Magikarp was a girl; the boy Magikarps had tan barbels. *Girl power!* she added silently.

"Be with us, Gabriel," Ridley chimed in.

"We honor you, Aphrodite," said Greta. The Greek goddess had been created out of sea foam. She placed some lemon balm leaves next to Magikarp.

North was the earth element. "Go, Diglett!"

"Be with us, Uriel."

"We honor you, Gaia the Earth Mother." A sprig of vervain.

And finally, the East, the air element. "Go, Spearow!"

"Be with us, Raphael."

"We honor you, Feng Po Po." Parsley.

The three witches sat very still, eyes closed, taking in the magical energy that was being generated by the ritual.

The first few times Binx had participated in the calling of the quarters with Ridley and Greta, she hadn't felt a thing except maybe sore and cranky from sitting cross-legged for so long or bored by the repetitive incantations. She'd even had (brief) second thoughts about having joined a coven. Then one day, at the fourth or fifth or sixth coven meeting, it had happened—the electric thrumming in her chest, the adrenaline jolt, the sense of power and purpose . . . and at the same time a sensation of being surrounded by a palpable white light of protection. It had been . . . *amazing*. Epic. Better than reaching Level 20 in *Witchworld* and acquiring the Staff of Immortality.

Not to mention it was nice to have other witches to hang with. (*Real* witches, not virtual ones.)

After a while, Greta broke the silence.

"Goddesses, angels, and Pokémons—"

"For the hundredth time, Poké-*mon*, no S," Binx corrected her.

"—Pokémon, please help us solve the mystery of this shadow message.

Who sent it, and why? And please help protect us from whatever malicious intent is behind it. Love and light."

Binx cracked open one eye. Greta had steepled her hands in prayer and was murmuring something under her breath. "Sorry. I'm adding a prayer for Gofflesby. He's been sick," she explained without looking up. Ridley reached over and squeezed her arm. Binx did the same. She knew how Greta felt about her familiar—a cat with the weirdest name ever.

After a moment, a breeze materialized from nowhere. The curtains fluttered. The candles flickered and danced.

A tiny spark flew through the air and landed on the shadow message. A glowing orange fault line began to sizzle across the paper, sprouting baby flames.

"Uh . . . people? Hello? We have a little problem," Binx announced.

Greta and Ridley opened their eyes, too.

"Holy machines!" Ridley cried out.

Without a word, Greta pulled her wand, Flora, out of her sleeve and aimed it at the quickly escalating flames. *"Restinguere!"* she commanded, her face tight with concentration.

But instead of extinguishing, the fire cascaded up, up, up like a slo-mo volcano eruption. All three girls jumped to their feet and backed away. Ridley grabbed Paganini from her backpack. Binx found her wand Kricketune (which looked like a gaming console, for disguise purposes) among the strawberry-shaped twinkle lights and anime indexes on top of her dresser. *"Restinguere!"* they shouted in unison, brandishing their wands at the fire.

In response, the mini-inferno hissed and shrieked . . . but continued to rise.

Binx turned and directed her wand toward Magikarp. *Help us!*

In response, the Magikarp card shimmered—or maybe it was just the flames reflected in her UV coating?—and in the next instant, the three glasses of milk (almond, chocolate, chocolate) began to levitate. When the glasses were a foot or so above the fire's apex, they tipped over.

Milk gushed out. The flames sizzled and faded and died with a gasp of gray smoke.

Binx exhaled and nodded gratefully at Magikarp. "Thanks for putting out the fire, buddy."

Magikarp stared up at Binx with her large, vacant eyes.

Next to Magikarp, the shadow message was perfectly unscathed, the paper a pristine white.

"Why didn't it burn?" Ridley asked nervously.

"I don't know." Greta bent down to study the shadow message. "Wait . . . what's happening?"

Binx and Ridley bent down, too. *Whoa.* New letters were materializing at the bottom of the paper—faintly at first, then clearer and clearer.

No, not letters. Numbers.

1415.

"What the—" Binx began.

Just then, the classical-music doorbell chimed through the house.

Greta yelped in surprise. Ridley spun around on her heels and aimed Paganini at the window, then the door. Binx grabbed for her phone and checked the security camera feed.

Div, Mira, and Aysha stood at the front door.

Div seemed to be shouting up at the security camera. Binx activated the audio.

". . . need to talk. We have a serious problem!" Div yelled.

"Um, we're kind of busy at the moment?" Binx replied curtly.

Greta shook her head. "If Div is coming to *us* for help, there's something really wrong," she whispered to Binx and Ridley.

On Binx's phone, Div was holding up a piece of paper to the security camera.

It was her copy of the shadow message.

It, too, had numbers on it.

1415.

10

THE DREAMLESS ONE

The Natural world is full of Magic.
Harvest it with care and love.

(FROM *THE GOOD BOOK OF MAGIC AND MENTALISM*
BY CALLIXTA CROWE)

"We need a plan," Div told Greta as she slid behind the wheel of her white Audi.

Greta didn't respond as she carefully buckled her seat belt. After Div and Mira and Aysha had shown up unexpectedly at Binx's house, the six witches had gone around and around trying to figure out who'd written the shadow messages and also who'd enchanted them (to catch on fire, then not catch on fire, then mysteriously sprout the numbers *1415*). Was one force at work, or several forces? Were they witches or witch-haters or some of both?

The two covens had gotten nowhere, and so Div had offered to drive Greta home in order to speak privately, coven leader to coven leader. Greta had balked at first. She didn't feel comfortable being alone with Div. First of all, she didn't trust her. Even now, she wasn't 100 percent certain that Div and her girls *weren't* behind the shadow message business. (Ninety-nine percent, maybe, but not a hundred.)

And there was their personal history, too. Back in eighth grade (before they even knew Binx and Ridley and Mira and Aysha), Greta and Div had formed their own little coven, and the two girls had been so close. Then one day, Div had tested Greta's "strength" (she'd called it that, but really, it was more like "unquestioning, unconditional loyalty") by making Greta watch as she fed a small, helpless little creature to her familiar, Prada. Div had known how much Greta loved animals and she'd wanted to see what Greta would do. What Greta had done was leave their little coven—leave their friendship—and she'd never come back. The breakup had been a long time coming as far as Greta was concerned. The two of them had been developing divergent magical paths—Greta's positive and nurturing, Div's negative and toxic, and that incident had been the last straw.

Greta now knew that underneath Div's cool, confident exterior was a cruel soul. Greta couldn't stand cruelty. It was anathema to her. Like Callixta, Greta believed that love and light should be the abiding principles in magic.

". . . clearly the work of the Antima," Div was saying. She turned on the engine, backed smoothly out of Binx's driveway, and headed left onto Cliffside Drive. "We have to stop them before they follow through on their threat."

Greta folded her hands in her lap. "Stop them how? Maybe the best thing to do is to lie low. Maybe even take a break from using magic. We need to keep our witches, and ourselves, safe."

"You don't seem to be grasping the situation," Div said coldly. "The Antima appear to be onto us—or at least onto you and me. They're capable of *anything*. Their shadow messages said that we should 'disappear.'

Plus, as far as I know, aside from you and Aysha, the rest of us have kept our witch identities a secret from our families. If our families find out . . . if the school finds out . . . well, I'm not sure that all the memory-erase spells at our disposal can contain the fallout. Also, and this is a terrifying thought, but what if the Antima convinces the police and the government to start arresting child witches, teen witches?"

"Oh!"

"Not to mention the fact that we need to think *offense* as well as *defense*. The Antima are evil, and they need to *go*."

Greta winced at the angry edge in Div's voice. She touched the raw amethyst pendant at her throat, to center herself. *Love and light.*

"Okay, well . . . say that the Antima *did* write those shadow messages," she said after a moment. "But they don't use magic. They're *anti*-magic. So who enchanted the messages, and why? And what does 1415 mean?"

"Aysha googled 1415 on our way here. A lot of random things came up. Like, the year 1415 was the beginning of the Hundred Years' War in France; some king invaded someone else's kingdom. Nothing relevant." Div swept her white-blond hair over her shoulders. "We should perform some scrying spells to see if '1415' is part of someone's personal information. Maybe it belongs to the author of the shadow messages?"

"Good idea." Greta shifted in her seat. "So, I've been wondering . . . Who at the school might know that we're witches?"

"Speaking for myself and my girls, *no* one. We're very careful."

"So are we."

"Right, uh-huh."

Div's tone was skeptical, arrogant. As usual. But Greta wasn't going to bite.

"And who do we know at our school who are Antima, or who *might* be Antima?"

"There's Brandon Fiske, of course," Div pointed out.

"And this morning before homeroom, I saw these two guys wearing the shoulder patches. One of them was Axel Ngata. The other one was named Orion; Binx said his last name is Kong. She thought they were just posers, but . . ."

"Kong. He's in my algebra class. Okay, so that's *three* possible Antima members that we know of. Let's go back to the 1415 spell. Do you know of any witches at the school besides us?"

Greta hesitated. She thought about the girl from this morning. Iris Gooding. Could *she* have enchanted the shadow messages?

Greta wanted to meet her, learn more about her, and, if she *was* a witch, invite her to join their coven. Unless, of course, she was connected to the shadow messages and the numbers. But likely, Div would want to ask Iris to join *her* coven, as well. If she knew about Iris's existence. Which, hopefully, she didn't.

"Not really, no," Greta lied. "Do you?"

"No."

Greta wondered if Div was lying, too. She closed her eyes and tried to read Div's emotional state. This was a magical skill she'd been cultivating for a while, and sometimes, it provided her with useful information.

But not today. Not with Div. As usual, she was inscrutable, a wall of deep shadows.

Greta opened her eyes and blinked against the sunlight. "So what do we do now? What's our plan?" she said out loud.

"Why don't we split it up?" Div suggested. "Why don't my girls and I look into Orion Wong and Brandon Fiske and Axel Ngata, see if we can trace the shadow messages to any of them? You and your girls can try to figure out if there are any new witches at our school who may have enchanted the shadow messages . . . or witches who *aren't* new who've managed to keep their identities a secret." She added, "And we should *all* keep an eye out for additional Antima members. There may be more of them beyond the three."

"Okay. Sure." Greta pointed. "My street is the next left. Junipero Serra Drive."

"Yes, I remember."

Greta remembered, too. Back in eighth grade, they used to spend a lot of time at each other's houses: making teas out of herbs in Greta's garden, writing spells in code in their diaries, concocting potions out of random ingredients and storing them in empty lotion bottles . . . basically freelancing it, since Callixta's book had not made its way into the world yet. They'd also done a lot of non-magic stuff together. Like watching old black-and-white movies, drawing portraits of each other, and playing board games (neither girl liked losing).

Was it during *Casablanca* that Div had kissed her? Or *Sunset Boulevard*? Somehow, Greta had suppressed the details of that day.

"You can just drop me off here. I'll walk," she said abruptly.

"No problem, Gretabelle."

It was Div's old nickname for her.

Flushing, Greta grabbed her backpack and exited the Audi without saying goodbye.

Greta opened the gate that led to the backyard of her house and headed over to her garden. She needed to text Binx and Ridley to fill them in on her conversation with Div, explain about the assignments. But first, she wanted a moment to chill, to get her equilibrium back after the long, unsettling day.

Her garden always calmed her. She set aside her bag and knelt down on the grass. The lawn was damp from a mayfly-brief shower that had passed through about an hour ago; the air smelled like rain and moss and lovely, unidentifiable green things. The wetness seeped through the knees of her thin wool tights, but she didn't mind. She never minded getting messy when she was in nature . . . even if "nature" in this case was her family's small backyard, boxed in by Mrs. Mianowski's house to the right and the new neighbors' house to the left.

The garden was called Bloomsbury. Greta had named it that because she wanted to inspire her charges to bloom, plus she'd learned about something called the Bloomsbury Group in a dusty old art book at her father, Tomas's, used-book store, the Curious Cat. Bloomsbury was a neighborhood in London filled with elegant gardens. In the early 1900s, the writer Virginia Woolf, her sister Vanessa Bell, and other Bloomsbury artists and intellectuals had met regularly to have interesting discussions, create, and support each other's work. Kind of like a coven.

Bloomsbury—*her* Bloomsbury—was not elegant, exactly. It was wild and overgrown, a mad jungle of herbs, flowers, foliage (and even weeds, because as far as she was concerned, they were plants, too). She had tried this year to be more orderly than in previous years, dividing everyone by height, color, growing season, sun and soil preferences, and of course, magical properties. But the plants seemed to have minds of their own, no surprise, and had extended themselves into one another's territories. Some, like the black-eyed Susans and foxgloves, had reseeded like crazy. Some, like the partridgeberry and creeping fig, had tentacled their way over and across and made friendly—or not so friendly?—curlicues around their neighbors.

Still, they all managed to grow and thrive. Perhaps it was Greta's magical green thumb. Or perhaps it was the Goddess's way, spinning beauty out of chaos.

The marigolds caught Greta's eye. They badly needed to be dead-headed. She leaned forward, plucked the dried-up blossoms, and slipped them into her pocket. She could brew them for a tea, or maybe steep them in milk to make a lotion—Teo was constantly falling or bumping into things, and marigold lotion was good for bruises and sprains.

Marigolds had other magical properties. For example, according to Callixta's book, sleeping with a marigold under one's pillow could bring on prophetic dreams. The thing was, Greta never *had* dreams, prophetic or otherwise—or if she did, she never remembered them. She'd tried the marigold-under-the-pillow trick several times, just to see if they could cause her to have a dream, *any* dream, but nothing had happened. She'd tried other remedies from the book, too, like wild asparagus root and peppermint. Still nothing. Obviously, she was destined to be one of those dreamless people. Which was kind of depressing—it was like there was an entire part of her that she would never know, like roots growing too deep under the loamy earth.

A whisper-light sensation tickled her brain. . . . Something was mentally nudging Greta for her attention. She glanced up; her familiar, Gofflesby, sat in the kitchen window in sphinx position, his large emerald eyes fixed on her. His mouth was slightly open, and his chest rose and fell in an irregular rhythm. He let out a long, wrenching cough.

Greta's heart clenched like a fist. "I know, little one. I meant to tell you before, I've been working on some new potions for you. I'm going to take you back to Dr. Slotnick, too. The last time we saw her, she told me about these new medicines that are good for kitties with chronic respiratory infections."

Gofflesby continued staring and panting and coughing. The thing was, he was just barely out of kittenhood. Two or three years old, max. Greta had found him this summer hanging out in Bloomsbury and eating the valerian and silver vine, and after making sure he didn't have another owner, she'd adopted him as her familiar. Cats this young shouldn't be sick all the time. It wasn't normal, and it most definitely wasn't fair.

Greta was a witch; surely she could cure him? What good was magic otherwise? What good was *she*? Sometimes, she seriously questioned whether she had any business being a witch. Much less a coven leader. Half the time, she felt as though she was making it up, improvising, pretending.

And now, on top of Gofflesby's illness, she had to deal with the Antima. . . .

Oh, right. Greta pulled out her phone and fired off a quick text to Binx and Ridley, detailing her conversation with Div.

"Hello, my love!"

Greta's mother, Ysabel, emerged from the back porch lugging two canvas bags, a pile of library books, and a basket of cookies. She walked over to Greta and planted a kiss on the top of her head. The air filled with her jasmine-and-lemongrass perfume.

"Hey, Mama."

Gofflesby had vanished from his window perch. In her mind, Greta imagined him padding up to her room to take a nap in his favorite spot: on top of her mandala-print comforter in a pool of sunlight, snuggled below the large dream catcher that he sometimes pawed at.

"I need to deliver more bath soaps and soy candles to Organic Bliss," Ysabel was saying. "Sparrow said the last batch is almost sold out, can you believe it? After that, I need to return these books to the library and drop these gluten-free goodies off at Angelina and Jack's—they just had their baby, did I tell you? Babies, *plural*, twin girls, Zadie and Zoe—and pick up Teo from coding club. I hope he didn't get into a fight with that Sasha girl again. How was your first day of school?"

Her words tumbled out in a rush of breathless, happy energy. She was always like that, even when things around her were not so happy.

Greta rose to her feet and pocketed the rest of the dead marigold blossoms. "School was fine. Can we make another appointment with Dr. Slotnick? Soon? Gofflesby's still coughing." She hated asking this; she knew money was tight. The vet bills for Gofflesby had been piling up along with the other bills; she'd noticed the unopened envelopes on the kitchen counter.

"Poor kitty. I thought he seemed less coughy lately, but you would know better. My friend Lamar told me about a homeopathic remedy he uses for his pug's asthma. I can find out the name of it for you."

Pug asthma? "Um, okay. Thanks, Mama."

"Of course, honey. Your dad is doing inventory at the store, so he'll be a little late. Do you mind making dinner? The avocados are probably ripe by now, so I'm thinking guacamole. There's leftover lentil soup from my Climate Coalition meeting. It's that recipe you like from *Veganomicon*, except we were all out of tarragon so I had to use marjoram instead. Oh, and maybe a nice salad, we still have a few of those heirloom tomatoes from the farmer's market."

Before Greta could reply, Ysabel leaned in and hugged her, the canvas bags and library books and cookie basket crushed between them. "Love you! Don't forget about the— Sorry, I lost my train of thought. Maybe it'll . . ."

Her words trailed off as she turned and hurried toward the driveway, leaving a jasmine-and-lemongrass cloud behind her. A moment later, the family's ancient Volvo station wagon sputtered to life and disappeared down Junipero Serra Drive.

Greta blinked.

Someone was standing in front of her house. It wasn't Mrs. Mianowski or one of the other neighbors; it was a stranger.

Alarmed, Greta took a step back until she was half-hidden behind Teo's Cozy Cocoon tree swing. She remembered Div's comment about the police; could it be an undercover detective looking for witches? Or could it be an Antima member? Orion or Brandon or Axel or someone else? She searched her mind for a spell she could use to defend herself if necessary. Maybe *repellare*? The person was hanging out next to the family's other car, a VW bug that was parked in its usual spot at the curb. His or her back was to Greta, but then he . . . she? . . . pivoted slightly to look around.

It was a she. A familiar she. Straight black hair, glasses, really pretty, a Zooey Deschanel–Audrey Hepburn vibe . . . wait, was that Iris Gooding?

Yes, it definitely was.

What was *she* doing here?

Greta retreated farther behind the tree swing. She watched curiously as Iris pulled a phone out of her pants pocket and swiped at the screen, shaking her head and muttering to herself. Was Iris looking for her?

Also, how did Iris know where she lived . . . or even who she was?

Now Iris was touching something at her throat—the moonstone pendant she'd been wearing this morning? Then she began walking down Junipero Serra, her stride suddenly quick and confident. So she *wasn't* here to see Greta. After a block, Iris turned onto Sycamore.

Greta decided to follow her. Casting a quick *pleukiokus* spell on herself (the second of the day, for extra protection), she headed out into the street.

11

DEAD WITCHES

Your enemies will not always appear in
human form.

(FROM *THE GOOD BOOK OF MAGIC AND MENTALISM*
BY CALLIXTA CROWE)

After the coven meeting, Ridley and Binx decided to take a walk to
the mall, which was near Binx's house. It was one of their favorite
unwinding activities.

As they strolled down Cliffside Drive (there were no sidewalks, just
the quiet road bordered by deep woods), Ridley found herself looking
over her shoulder constantly. The events of the day had left her feeling
totally rattled. And confused. Were they dealing with other witches or
witch haters . . . or both?

The sudden buzzing of her phone startled her. Binx's phone trilled at
the same time.

"It's a message from our fearless leader," Binx announced.

Greta had texted:

Div and I talked (I know, I know), and we have assignments
for all of us. Our coven is going to try to find the witch/
witches who may have cast a spell on the shadow messages.
Their coven is going to investigate Orion, Brandon, and
Axel to see if they wrote them. And in general, we should
all be on the lookout for other possible Antima members
at our school. But don't confront them (obviously). We need
to stay safe.

"Women and girls can be Antima, right?" Ridley asked, glancing up from her phone.

"It's backward, but yeah. Why?"

Ridley told Binx about the new history sub, Ms. O'Shea. "I don't know if she's Antima or what. But I felt like she was watching me—observing me."

"Let's add her to the list of people to check out, then," Binx suggested. "We can't be too careful. We've never dealt with any Antima around here. They could be super clever and super organized."

Ridley shuddered.

"Okay, well . . . I have history again tomorrow, second period. Friday, too. I'll watch her like a hawk."

"I can try to find some info on her online. O'Shea, like *O-S-H-E-A*?"

"Exactly."

Ridley read over Greta's text again. "So . . . are Greta and Div theorizing that their shadow messages were enchanted by a witch at school? Who? It's only us and the Triad. And maybe that Iris girl. If there are any other witches, they've been keeping it a secret. And they're going to be even *more* secretive now because of the Antima." She paused and added, "Is the idea that this witch, whoever it is, is trying to *warn* us? Or give us a clue? I mean, why cast that bizarre spell that made those numbers show up? Sorry to ramble. I'm just thinking out loud."

"Who knows? I guess that's part of our homework assignment, to figure it out." Binx wrinkled her nose. "I'm not super down with the idea of working with the Triad on this. They're so annoying. But if it means we can catch whoever's threatening Greta and make the Antima go away, then I guess it's worth it."

They fell silent as they turned onto a gravel driveway at the entrance of the Sorrow Point Cemetery, off Cliffside Drive. This was their usual shortcut; the other end of the cemetery led to a hillside overlooking the back of the mall parking lot.

It was weird, but Ridley found the cemetery calming. She liked the winding paths that crisscrossed the grounds, dense with sycamores and pine trees. She liked the silvery-green clumps of old-man's beard that dripped from the overhead branches. Sometimes she harvested the mossy lichen and made a healing potion out of it; whenever her little sister Harmony had one of her maybe-it's-real, maybe-it's-not-real colds, Ridley gave her the potion in a spill-proof kids' cup full of chocolate milk.

Strolling through the cemetery also made her feel closer to Daniel, even though his actual gravesite was back in Cleveland. Ridley had picked a tree in this cemetery that she called "Daniel's tree." It was a maple like the one in their old backyard, with two thick, gnarled branches like arms going in for a hug, except a different variety—an Oregon maple. Which was perfect, because the Oregon Ducks had been Daniel's favorite college football team. Sometimes she visited it the same way she would have visited his gravestone, if it were here.

You jerk, she thought angrily. Tears stung her eyes, and she brushed them away quickly.

"Hey, are you okay?" Binx said, looking concerned.

Ridley was touched; Binx didn't usually do concern. "Not really. But I'll get over it."

Binx hooked her arm through Ridley's. "Don't stress. We have our *pleukiokus* spells to protect us, right? And we won't let the Antima hurt Greta. Or any of us. We'll Moonblast their sorry butts!"

Ridley made herself smile. Binx didn't know that her tears were about her big brother, not about the Antima. Ridley had never told Binx about Daniel, or about all the other stuff having to do with her old life back in Cleveland. She hadn't told her about being a trans girl, either. Someday she would, though. Hopefully soon.

She was just glad Binx was her best friend. It had been this way since last September, when she'd first met her two coven-mates. Of course, Greta was awesome—nurturing and protective and kind, like a big sister. But Ridley and Binx had just *connected*. They laughed at the same stupid stuff. They liked to binge the same TV shows. They had long conversations (at the mall, at the beach, during sleepovers) about magic, especially in terms of discovering their own unique paths as witches—Binx as a cyber-witch and Ridley as a . . . whatever she was meant to be. (She wasn't sure yet, she was still figuring that out.)

And speaking of figuring things out . . .

"Hey, Binx? Do you know a girl named Penelope at our school? She moved here, like, over the summer," Ridley said casually.

"Penelope. Hmm. What's her last name?"

"Hart. She told me she has a YouTube channel. It's called *Just Faces* or something."

Binx lit up. She always got excited about anything and everything online-related. She began scrolling and tapping and typing on her phone.

"They really need to put a cell tower in this place," she murmured under her breath. After a moment, she held up her phone for Ridley to see. "Her?"

A YouTube video began to play. Penelope's smiling face filled the screen. She wore a pink V-neck blouse, and a small heart-shaped tattoo (or birthmark?) peeked out from under the neckline.

Ridley felt that wobbly-on-the-inside feeling again.

"Hey, guys! It's Penelope! Soooo . . . many of you have been asking me about how to rock a dark lipstick without looking like the undead. Today's tutorial is all about dark *matte* lipsticks, and tomorrow's tutorial will be part two, dark *glossy* lipsticks."

Binx hit pause.

"Yeah, that's her," said Ridley.

"She has over sixty-five thousand subscribers. Impressive. So, what about her?"

"Nothing. I met her today, that's all. She's nice. She's dating this guy, Colter—"

"Colter Jessup?"

"He was the guy talking to Iris Gooding this morning."

"Yup, Colter Jessup. Mira used to go out with him. It was, like, ages ago."

Ridley blinked, surprised. "Mira and Colter? Really?"

"I'm pretty sure. Wait, let me check her social."

Binx resumed her scrolling and tapping and typing. Ridley tried to imagine Colter and Mira dating. Mira seemed kind of shallow, like she was into surface more than substance. If that was the kind of girl Colter liked, then what did that say about Penelope? Or maybe there was more to both Mira and Colter than met the eye? Ridley didn't know the guy. Maybe he was just as great on the inside as on the outside.

Ridley and Binx were getting close to the hillside that sloped down to the mall. In her peripheral vision, Ridley saw Daniel's tree to the right, by a cluster of laurel bushes. There it was, not the tallest tree in the cemetery, but not the smallest, either. A teenager. Its large, verdant leaves fluttered in the breeze. A crow hovered on a low branch, preening its shiny black feathers. For a moment, Ridley wondered if Daniel might send her a sign . . . but how? By making the crow speak to her? By rearranging the leaves into symbols?

Dumb, she chided herself.

Still, she wished she could talk to him. About what happened. About Momma and Daddy. About everything.

"Got it!" Binx announced. "Sorry it took forever." She held up a photo of Mira and Colter in front of Dahlia's Ice Cream, which was downtown. Mira's arm was outstretched in selfie mode as she and Colter exchanged a kiss. Mira's hair was different . . . shorter.

"Huh," Ridley said.

"I would totally date him, too," Binx murmured. "He's a snack."

Ridley shrugged. "I guess so. If you like that type." Which Penelope obviously did.

"What's not to—" Binx stopped in her tracks. *"Pleukiokus,"* she murmured under her breath.

Ridley stopped, too. "Binx?"

"Say it—*now!*"

"P-pleukiokus," Ridley blurted out. "You're scaring me. What's going on?"

Binx put her hands on Ridley's shoulders and spun her around. She jutted her chin at a row of gravestones just beyond a grassy berm.

In a garish red hue, someone had spray-painted the word DEAD on one and WITCH on another. Ridley stifled a cry as Binx snapped a quick photo of the atrocity with a shaking hand. She grabbed Ridley's arm and tugged.

"Let's get the hex out of here."

The two girls ran, putting the horrible message behind them, but every time Ridley closed her eyes it was as if the words had been burned across her retinas.

DEAD WITCH.

✳ 12 ✳

RESCUE ME

Psychometry and prophecy are powerful sisters
in the practice of Magic and Mentalism.

(FROM *THE GOOD BOOK OF MAGIC AND MENTALISM*
BY CALLIXTA CROWE)

ris speed-walked down Sycamore Street, wondering how she'd managed to get so lost on her way home. She'd had to stay after school to
meet with her bio and algebra teachers, and figure out if there might be
overlap with what she'd studied at her old school. Now she was late, and
her mother was counting on her to watch Nyala and Ephrem while she
helped Grandma Roseline at the restaurant.

Iris was thankful for the GPS app on her phone, which was named
Ravenscroll. (Phones were *kind* of like scrolls carried by ravens, right?
As in, methods of communication? Or maybe she was just a big, giant
dork.) She'd hardly ever needed the app to navigate her old neighborhood in Harlem, which had numbered east-west streets that went in
nice, neat chronological order and north-south streets with manageable

names like Riverside, Broadway, Amsterdam, Convent, and St. Nicholas.

But Sorrow Point was a different story. Nothing was chronological or manageable. Lots of streets had almost identical names, like Loma Linda Avenue, Loma Linda Drive, and Loma Linda Boulevard. Others dead-ended unexpectedly. Others looped in on themselves so that Iris kept returning to the same spot like a rat trapped in a maze.

Her street, too, had many variations on its name: Sycamore Street, Sycamore Lane, Sycamore Crescent, and also North Sycamore Road, South Sycamore Road, and South Sycamore Road Extension. Iris had been fine up until she'd accidentally turned onto Sycamore Crescent, which had dead-ended in a cul-de-sac (which was not a thing in New York City). So she'd had to retrace her steps, get back on Alameda (*Road*, not Street or Drive), and keep going. Along the way she'd found herself on a street called Junipero Serra, stopped in front of a peach-colored bungalow with a cute little VW bug (the place made her feel inexplicably safe), and consulted Ravenscroll.

Finally, she was on Sycamore *Street*. She could see her grandmother's house down the hill, just past the little bodega with the mean lady who'd yelled at Nyala for touching a candy bar without buying it. Iris had been *this close* to casting a hex on the nasty storeowner, Mrs. Poe.

Ravenscroll made a tiny *ping!* sound, and a message lit up the screen. A reminder about an upcoming appointment with her new therapist. *Oh, joy.* Iris didn't know why she couldn't just keep seeing her old therapist, Francesca, by Skype or FaceTime or whatever. (Maybe a virtual reality videochat spell? Was there such a thing? Obviously not in Callixta's time, but maybe some modern-day witch had invented one?) Iris had been with Francesca since she was seven. Nine whole years. She seriously didn't want to start with some stranger who didn't know anything about her or her life. Iris's mom was also in the process of finding her a new occupational therapist and maybe a new social skills therapist, too. Moving across the country seriously sucked.

Of course, lots of other things seriously sucked, too. Like having anxiety and sensory processing disorder to begin with. Like needing magic to find her way home . . . to not throw up on the first day of school . . . and other basics.

Like not having her dad around. That super, royally, infinity sucked the most of all.

Iris was almost at Poe's Market. She wanted to pop in to buy some gum—it helped with her SPD-related need to bite and chew—but she wasn't in the mood to deal with mean Mrs. Poe right now.

In front of the store, a skinny, scruffy black cat sat on a wooden bench licking its paws. Its fur was matted, and its right ear was just a stub.

"Hey, kitty," Iris called out. "Do you live here? Can I pet you?" She extended her hand and approached it slowly.

Just then, three guys burst out of the bodega, slamming the squeaky screen door behind them. One of them was ripping open a bag of Doritos. The other two were swigging from cans covered with brown paper bags.

The Doritos guy was from school. The nasty one who'd bumped into her and kicked her lip gloss. The one with the Antima shoulder patch.

Iris ducked behind the bench.

"—yeah, and she was playing all hard to get at first, but a few drinks loosened her up," he was saying.

The other two fist-bumped him and nodded in agreement. "Way to go, Orion," one of them said.

"Thanks, Brandon."

Orion stopped in front of the wooden bench and hurled a couple of chips at the black cat. It hissed and leaped off the bench and skittered away. The three of them laughed uproariously.

Iris waited until they were looking the other way. Then she stood up and attempted to proceed unnoticed toward the store entrance. She'd rather face mean Mrs. Poe than these cretins.

But Orion saw her and cut her off. He stepped in front of her. He was standing too close.

"*You* again! Where're you going in such a big hurry?"

He seemed to grow even taller and broader—or maybe it was Iris shrinking into herself. His breath reeked of Doritos and beer, like hot garbage. Her brain buzzed and crackled in confusion. "Um . . . excuse me . . . I have to . . ." Dizzy and frightened, she backed away.

But Brandon and the other guy were right there; they'd flanked her while her back was turned. *Oh no.* They were both wearing Antima shoulder patches. Iris's gut clenched. They were *all* Antima. They must know she was a witch. There was no easy way to slip away from them.

The third guy waved his drink through the air lazily and eased forward even closer to her. "What's your name, babe? I'm Axel, but you may call me the Ax. Wanna party with us?" He quirked an eyebrow and smirked at his friends when Iris remained paralyzed.

Brandon had crept even closer and was lightly running the knuckles of his free hand along her upper arm. "Yeah, what's the matter? We're not scaring you, are we?"

Iris's skin screamed. She wanted to punch and kick, but her overloaded brain wouldn't cooperate. Everything had become too confusing. Too much was happening, more than she could process. She tried frantically to think of a spell to make it stop. What would Jadora from *Witchworld* do in this situation? But Jadora's magic couldn't help here in the real world. . . .

An ammonia odor filled the air.

"*What the . . .*"

Orion and Brandon and Axel fanned out and stared down at their shorts.

They had all peed themselves.

Suddenly they were swearing and blustering and covering their crotches with their backpacks. Mumbling various excuses, they rushed away—Orion and Axel on foot, sprinting in opposite directions, and Brandon to a silver SUV parked nearby.

Safe. She was safe. Apparently, they'd been too drunk to exercise bladder control. Iris sank down on the bench, trying to corral her spinning thoughts and ease the itchy-crawly screaming of her skin. She shuttered her eyes and did some therapy breaths—six in, six hold, six out. The black cat had returned and was circling her ankles, purring.

When Iris opened her eyes again, her field of vision shimmered. Sun. Sky. Wildflowers.

Breathe, she told herself.

"Are you okay?"

Iris's head shot up. A girl emerged from behind a gnarled pine tree and was walking toward her.

"I . . . um . . ."

"Those guys are disgusting."

"Um . . . yeah."

The girl sat down on the bench and smoothed the skirt of her green velvet dress. She reached down and petted the black cat and murmured to it, occasionally glancing up to make sure the three guys were truly gone. They were.

Iris finally recognized her. It was the girl from this morning, at school, in the hallway. The one with the wand . . . *correction*, fountain pen.

"I'm Greta."

"Hi . . . hey . . . I'm Iris."

Greta continued petting the cat and speaking softly to it. Her skin smelled like lavender. Sunlight glinted on her long auburn hair and separated the individual strands into red and gold and copper.

Iris's buzzing, crackling brain began to still itself. The lavender was nice. Calming. She tried to piece together what had just happened. Had those Antima guys really peed themselves at exactly the same moment? Slowly, things clicked into place and Iris looked over at Greta. Maybe the fountain pen hadn't been a fountain pen, after all.

"Did *you* do that?"

Greta stopped petting the cat. "Do what?"

"Make those guys pee?"

"Ha ha, that's funny. How would I even do that?"

Iris stared at her. Greta stared back, her eyes cool and guarded.

But there was something else in Greta's expression. She seemed amused, pleased with herself.

She *had* made the Antima guys pee. With magic.

"You're a witch, too!" Iris burst out before she could stop herself. "I didn't know there even *was* a making-people-pee spell! Oh, and this morning at school? Your fountain pen wasn't a fountain pen. It was a wand, wasn't it? Am I right? Did you cast a spell on me? What kind of spell was it?"

Silence. Greta resumed petting the cat.

"Well?" Iris prompted her.

"You said 'too.'"

"Excuse me?"

"You said, 'You're a witch, *too*.' Are you telling me that *you're* a witch, Iris?"

"Um . . ."

Iris fiddled with her smiley-face moonstone pendant, stalling. She'd said "too" accidentally, and now she couldn't un-say it. *Dumb*. Should she do a memory-erase spell?

She'd never told a single living soul about her powers. She'd barely even known (or known of) any witches—just those girls who'd gotten into trouble at her old school, plus Veronica in Dr. Singh's office, and they hadn't known that she, too, was one of them. The only witches in Iris's life were Jadora and the others in *Witchworld*, and they didn't really count.

Now here was a *real* witch, sitting right next to her.

Someone just like her.

Someone who had rescued her from the Antima.

"Yes," Iris whispered.

She waited for the sky to break open and unleash dark clouds and lightning and thunder. She waited for the police to show up and arrest her. She waited for Orion and Brandon and the Ax to reappear.

Nothing happened.

Greta smiled. "Well, that's awesome."

"It is?"

"Yes. It's *really* awesome."

Iris frowned, suddenly wary. This conversation seemed too easy. "You . . . you're not tricking me, are you? You're not an Antima member pretending to be a witch, are you?"

"Oh my gosh, no. Those guys were Antima, though—but you probably knew that."

"How do you know *I'm* not?"

"I could be wrong, but I'm pretty good at reading people's feelings. I've been trying to teach myself. I don't sense any hatred in you."

"Yeah, no, that's not me. The only thing I hate is when my breakfast cereal gets soggy . . . oh, and when my clothes itch. Actually, JK, there's a lot of stuff I hate. But not witches. Because *I'm* a witch, and . . . never mind, sorry, I'm talking too much. I do that when I'm nervous."

"Why are you nervous?"

"I'm *always* nervous. Your mood-ring magic can probably sense that, right? 'Nervous' is my middle name. JK again, it's Evangeline."

"That's pretty."

"Thanks. Anyhoo, of course I'm nervous now, because it's the first time I ever . . . I've never told anyone that I'm . . . and it's terrifying. But also cool. But also terrifying."

"I know what you mean."

The black cat jumped up and curled itself onto Greta's lap, purring.

"Hey, little one. You're going to make Gofflesby jealous," Greta murmured to the cat.

"Who's Gofflesby?" Iris asked.

"My familiar. Do you have a familiar?"

"No. I mean, my family has pets. But I don't know how you can tell who's your familiar and who's *not* your familiar, so maybe they're *all* my familiars, or maybe none of them are."

"Oh, you'll just know," Greta said, sounding unbelievably wise. "Have you read the book?"

"You mean Callixta Crowe's book? Am I pronouncing her name right?"

"Yes and yes."

"Only like half of it. I picked it up by accident in the library one day—but I didn't check it out because I was worried that . . . well, the *law* and all that. I read like a bunch of chapters and took some notes, but that was it. The next time I went back to the library, it was gone."

"So you didn't read the chapter on familiars?"

"No. I'm only kind of familiar with familiars—get it, 'familiar with familiars'?—from *Witchworld*. That's a video game, FYI. But maybe you already know that, so sorry if I'm being redundant. Anyhoo, it's not like I'll find a dust dragon or a screaming unicorn or an ice-breathing devil squirrel in the *real* world, right?" Iris laughed awkwardly.

"Right. Well, according to Callixta, your familiar can simply be an animal you feel a special connection with. They don't have to be magical or whatever. And you can have more than one familiar at a time. Or no familiar at all."

"Oh! I didn't know."

Greta stroked the black cat between its ears; it lifted its head, purring with pleasure. "You said you'd never told anyone about your being a witch. That probably means you've never been part of a coven, right?"

"A coven? You mean like the Raven's Rage Coven in *Witchworld*? Or the Healing Hearts Coven? I don't like that one, though; the witches act like they're nice but they're totally not. But you're talking about a *real* coven, right? So, no." Iris blinked at Greta. "Why, have you?"

"Uh-huh. Two of them. The first one turned out to be . . . it was a bad fit. But the one I'm in now . . . well, it's really great. I kind of started it. If you're interested, maybe you could think about joining."

Iris pushed her glasses up the bridge of her nose and sat up very straight. "Really?"

"Really. Let me talk to the other girls. Maybe you could come to one of our coven meetings, check it out?"

"Really?"

Iris couldn't believe her luck. She'd made a new friend—her first one since moving to Sorrow Point—who also happened to be a witch. A *nice* witch. *And* she'd just been invited (or sort of invited) to her very first coven meeting (not to mention her first social gathering of *any* kind since Abigail Roth's disco-themed holiday party last year, which had been kind of a disaster—okay, a *huge* disaster, because Iris had hidden out in the bathroom the entire time because the loud music had hurt her ears).

"I have like a million questions to ask you. Like, how many witches are there at your . . . I mean, *our* . . . school? How do they . . . and *you* . . . keep it a secret? Are those three Antima guys dangerous? They are, aren't they? How long have you known you're a witch? What about the other witches in your coven? Those girls I saw you with this morning . . . are *they* in your coven? The Juilliard fan from my French class and the pink-haired one?"

"Ridley and Binx, yup." Greta picked up the purring black cat, set it down on the bench next to Iris, and stood. "I so want to answer all your questions, but I really need to go. I promised my mom I'd make dinner. Can you put your number in my phone, so I can call you or text you later? Oh, but before I go—speaking of the Antima . . . and by the way, I cast a memory-erase spell, *praetereo*, on those three guys, so they won't remember what happened here . . ." She paused and seemed to consider something. Then she nodded to herself. "I want to show you something."

Greta reached into her backpack and pulled out a small, clear bag. Inside was a bunch of rosemary sprigs and a piece of paper with words and numbers on it.

Iris felt a sensation of icy cold spreading through her body.

"W-what is that?" she asked nervously.

Greta slid the paper out of the bag and held it out for Iris to see. "Callixta calls these shadow messages. Did you get one, by any chance? Or did you happen to cast a spell on this one?"

"*What?*" Iris peered at the writing:

YOU AND YOUR KIND NEED TO DISAPPEAR
1415

The sensation of cold intensified. Iris crossed her arms over her chest, shivering.

"Wow, that's creepy. And rude. No, I didn't get one of these, and no, I didn't cast a spell on it. Where did you get this? And what's 1415?"

"I don't know. I found it in my pocket before homeroom this morning. Another witch at our school—she belongs to the other coven—found the exact same shadow message in her locker. So you didn't get one?"

"Nope."

"We think it might be from the Antima. Maybe even one of *those* guys." She gestured vaguely in the direction the SUV had driven off. "Plus, someone—a witch—seems to have enchanted it . . . enchanted *both* of them. We don't know who, or why."

"That's so weird!"

Trying to ignore the cold, Iris leaned in and read the shadow message a second time. Her head and Greta's head were almost touching.

The shadow message seemed to be calling out to her, trying to get her attention.

"Could I?" Iris reached for it.

"Are you sure you want to handle it?"

"I'll be careful, I promise."

Iris took the shadow message from Greta and laid her hand on it. The cold immediately dissipated and was replaced by heat. She took a deep breath and let her eyes close.

The images came to her, fast and furious. *Flames. A crow skeleton. People shouting. A girl in a red chair, tied up with ropes.*

1415.

14.

15.

A, B, C, D . . .

"Iris? Are you okay?"

Iris's eyes snapped open.

"It's . . . they're . . . I think fourteen and fifteen might represent the fourteenth and fifteenth letters of the alphabet? So, what is that?" She quickly counted off on her fingers. "*N* and *O*, right?"

"How did you—" Greta gaped at her. "You figured that out just from touching the shadow message?"

"Yeah. It's been happening to me more and more. I touch stuff, and these images appear. I'm not sure how, or why. But sometimes they're clearer than other times, and this time it was really clear. So *N* . . . *O*, 'no'? No to what? And why was it in code?"

"I . . . I don't know. I'll have to think about it."

"And hey, Greta?"

"Yes?"

Iris wasn't sure if she should tell her new friend about the other images that had come to her. The flames, the crow skeleton, people shouting . . .

. . . and Greta tied up in a red chair, a prisoner.

Of course, these visions might be nothing. She probably shouldn't scare Greta unnecessarily.

"Be careful," Iris said simply.

13

RETAIL THERAPY

Be wary of witch-hunters who may be
disguised as witches.

(FROM *THE GOOD BOOK OF MAGIC AND MENTALISM*
BY CALLIXTA CROWE)

By the time Binx and Ridley reached the mall, they were out of breath
and completely freaked out. Who had spray-painted DEAD WITCH on
those gravestones?

Antima, obviously.

Binx leaned against the outside of a photo booth, panting. She quickly
texted the photo of the defaced gravestones to Greta with the message:

R and I just saw this in the cemetery. Antima???

Greta texted back:

That's terrible!!! Whose graves?

Binx wrote:

> Not sure. I'll blow up the pix when I get home and try to read the names. R and I are at the mall now.

Greta wrote:

> Be safe. I'm in the middle of something, but I'll text you again in a few min. I have news.

Binx slid her phone into the pocket of her yellow jean jacket. She told Ridley about her plan to digitally enhance the photograph later.

"Good idea. Ugh. That was so creepy."

"I think we need some retail therapy," Binx suggested. "How about Auntie Anne's for pretzels, and then Michaels for supplies?"

Ridley gave a thumbs-up. "Agreed."

They linked arms and headed toward the center of the mall. Binx could hear Ridley quietly repeating "*Pleukiokus*" with each step, as though she were keeping time or sounding out a rhythm. Binx herself was on heightened alert, side-eyeing each person they passed to see if they were wearing an Antima shoulder patch. (Did Antima wear other symbols, too? She would have to research that.)

At Auntie Anne's, the two girls ordered their standbys: a cinnamon sugar pretzel for herself and a pepperoni pretzel for Ridley. Then they made their way to Michaels. Michaels was one of their favorite stores because it was the perfect place to buy witchcraft supplies without appearing to buy witchcraft supplies. Cute little glass bottles with cork stoppers were ideal for storing potions. Cool pens were good for writing in grimoires—for Ridley at least, since Binx kept hers entirely on her phone. And of course there were other items that were useful, like candles, beeswax, and bags of gemstone chips.

Binx and Ridley grabbed a couple of shopping carts. Peering around, Binx noted that the store seemed relatively empty, which was a plus . . . just a couple of moms with their kids and a few Michaels clerks in their cheerful smocks. At the cash register, a woman in a black leather jacket and red Dr. Martens was talking to the cashier. (Binx made a mental note to order boots like that for herself; they would go really well with her new skater dress.)

"Do you want to wander or do you have a shopping list on your phone?" Ridley asked Binx.

"Both. I definitely need some seashells and feathers. I've been"—Binx glanced around and lowered her voice—"experimenting with potions that have a bio-cyber interface."

"*Calumnia,*" Ridley cut in. "Okay, now we can talk. Explain."

"So we use herbs, flowers, and other plants for potions, right? And other natural, biological ingredients like beetle wings and . . . oh, *snap*, remember when we used Kyle Morrison's grody-toady toenail clippings to try to create a new type of polymorph potion? *That* was epic."

"*Ew.* Of course I remember. It was a complete fail. Go on."

"The bio-cyber interface will happen if I'm able to link up my cyber capabilities"—Binx held up her phone—"with real-life stuff like seashells, feathers, toenails, plants, cat whiskers, whatever. Like with nanotechnology, when scientists can literally *change* the molecules in your body by inserting you with point-one-micrometer nanite bots and then remote-controlling those bots with external computers?"

"I *still* don't know what that means. You're talking sci-fi gibberish."

"No, I'm not. I'll send you some links about nanotech, you should read up, and *then* you'll understand. Your problem is, your magical mind-set is outdated. You're so stuck in the olden days with your palm-reading and numerology and all that Gen-Grandma craft. You're insanely smart—what's your GPA these days, like six-point-five?—and you like science, right? You need to get with the program."

"Maybe. I'm more of a traditional girl, though. I *like* the grandma stuff from Callixta's book. Did ever I tell you that I have an antique Ouija board? It was a present from my aunt Viola, and I keep it hidden in my desk at home."

"Hmm. Well, I invented a magical Ouija board app that'll blow your Ouija board out of the water."

"You're on!"

"I shall hold you to it!"

They meandered through the aisles, past the picture frames and the unfinished-wood birdhouses and the early display of Halloween decorations. (Ridley picked up a couple of plastic skulls.) Binx eyed two skeins of yarn—one violet-purple and one charcoal-gray—and reminded herself to come back for them sometime soon. (She planned to crochet beanies and fingerless gloves for her witch sisters, for Christmas.) When they reached the aisle with the feathers, Binx tossed several bags into her cart: duck, turkey, ostrich, and pheasant, dyed and undyed. She also grabbed half a dozen peacock feathers and two long red boas.

She tucked a peacock feather behind Ridley's ear and draped one of the boas around her neck. "Very glam!"

Ridley struck a supermodel pose. "Why, thank you!"

Binx draped the second boa around her own neck as they went off in search of seashells. They looped back to the front of the store and finally found the seashells near the bins of rainbow-colored fake flowers.

Binx added several bags of assorted small seashells to her growing pile and a couple of large white-and-pink conch shells. She considered a bag of dried brown starfish. "Starfish aren't shells, are they?"

"Nope. They're echinoderms."

"Do you know if they have special properties? Never mind, let me look it up in my grimoire." Binx swiped at her phone. "Okay, got it! So according to these notes, starfish are associated with the heavens and with instinct and intuition and a ton of other stuff. They make good amulets or charms if you're sick or hurt or need renewal. Plus, there's the pentagram shape, which has all sorts of mystical meanings."

Her phone trilled and she glanced at it as Ridley pulled her own out of her pocket.

"It's Greta again," Binx announced. "'I just met Iris, and she's definitely one of us,'" she read out loud. "'She was getting harassed by Orion and Axel and Brandon.' Oh no! 'I invited her to come to one of our meetings.' Um, hello? Maybe you could have, like, asked us first? 'BTW, Iris thinks that 1415 is a code for the word "no."' No what? And how does she know this, exactly?"

Ridley didn't answer.

"Earth to Ridley!" Binx elbowed her.

"A-*hem*." Ridley elbowed her back. "I want to check out cupcake pans, do you want to check out cupcake pans?"

"What? Are you mental? Why would I want to check out—"

"Hi, Ms. O'Shea! How are you?" Ridley called out loudly.

The new history sub? Binx coughed and slid her phone into the pocket of her jean jacket.

A woman was pushing her shopping cart toward them. She wore a black leather jacket and red Doc Martens. It was the person from the cash register.

So *this* was Ms. O'Shea? Binx's gaze moved to her jacket. No Antima symbol of any kind. But maybe she was wearing a shoulder patch *under* her jacket? Or maybe she just didn't advertise her loyalties?

Ms. O'Shea moved closer. Binx's muscles tensed.

"Hi, Ridley! Hi, Binx! What're you up to?"

"J-just getting a bunch of stuff for my mom and little sister," Ridley said nervously.

"How did you know my name?" Binx asked Ms. O'Shea suspiciously.

Ms. O'Shea raked a hand through her short black hair and smiled. "I know quite a bit about you, Binx. And about you, Ridley. And about Greta, too."

Ridley exhaled sharply. Binx felt the blood drain from her face.

Stay calm. Don't panic. Figure this out, Binx told herself, trying to still the sudden pounding of her heart. She searched her brain for a spell. Should she do a memory-erase? Or something more . . . combative? In her peripheral vision, she saw Ridley reaching into her backpack, probably to retrieve her wand.

Binx reached into her backpack, too, and pulled out Kricketune (disguised, as usual, to look like a gaming console). She pointed it at Ms. O'Shea. "Are there more of you here? Is the mall the cool new meeting place for the Antima?" she snapped sarcastically.

Ms. O'Shea fluttered her hands. "Absolutely not! Please, it's not what you think."

Binx eyed the exit, which was just past the candy display. Should they just run for it? Then she noticed the contents of Ms. O'Shea's shopping cart.

Inside the cart were small glass bottles with cork stoppers, beeswax bars, and two bags of amethyst chips.

What the hex?

Ms. O'Shea slipped off her retro rhinestone glasses and pointed them at her cart. *"Donare,"* she said softly. The bags of amethyst chips rose slowly and traveled through the air. One landed in Binx's cart, and the other in Ridley's. "I love amethyst, don't you?" she added merrily.

Binx and Ridley gaped at her.

"You're . . . you're . . ." Ridley stammered.

"Exactly," Ms. O'Shea said, then held up her glasses. "And this is my wand, Theia, named after the Greek goddess of vision. Can I buy you guys another pretzel at Auntie Anne's? We have a lot to talk about."

"I first noticed the three of you about a month ago. At Misthaven Beach," Ms. O'Shea explained as she took a bite of her jalapeño pretzel. The three witches were sitting around a table in the food court, protected by a *calumnia* spell. "It was around sunset, and you guys were toasting marshmallows over a bonfire."

Binx thought back to that day. "But the beach was totally deserted."

"It was, except for me. I was taking a walk on the far north end. You wouldn't have seen me. But I saw *you.*" Grinning, Ms. O'Shea pointed to her glasses. "Theia magically enhances my vision so that I can see across great distances. From where I was standing, I could tell that Greta was enchanting each of your marshmallows to make them perfectly golden-brown. You, Binx, were using a spell to stoke the fire. And you, Ridley, must have gotten concerned about privacy, because you morphed the air into a heavy fog and surrounded yourselves with it."

"Holy machines! You *saw* all that?" Ridley sounded alarmed.

I so need to score a pair of those Theia glasses, Binx thought.

"I did. And needless to say, you girls need to be more careful. Especially now that the Antima movement has spread to Sorrow Point."

"Is that why you came to our school?" Binx asked curiously.

"Yes, in part. My coven and I—"

"Oh my gosh, there's another coven in Sorrow Point?" Ridley exclaimed.

"Not here. Way north of here, in the mountains. I'm there every weekend. My coven's mission is to keep a lookout for young witches and mentor them, help them. After I saw you guys on Misthaven Beach . . . well, the school needed a history sub, so I jumped at the chance."

"So Ms. Hua is really expecting a baby? She didn't . . . she isn't . . ." Ridley stopped and shook her head. "I thought that maybe something *bad* happened to her. Sorry, I guess I was just being paranoid."

"No worries. And yes, she really *is* expecting a baby. She was having a rough second trimester, though, so she asked to take her leave early. She's fine, and the baby's due around New Year's."

"Oh, whew," said Ridley.

"I also know about Div and Mira and Aysha. Well, as of today, anyway," Ms. O'Shea continued. "At lunch, I happened to pass by that little alcove with the vending machine, and I saw the two of you and Greta having an intense-looking conversation with them . . . except that from what I could hear, you all seemed to be talking about what to wear to the Homecoming Dance. I had a hunch, so I did a quick scrying spell and realized that *calumnia* was in effect."

"Huh!" Binx took a bite of her cinnamon sugar pretzel.

"See, I *told* you! *Calumnia* isn't perfect because it doesn't scramble stuff visually," Ridley reminded Binx. "In fact, we should all be smiling right now because all these food court people could be watching us!" She fake-smiled.

Binx fake-smiled, too, wondering if Ms. O'Shea knew about Iris Gooding being a witch (according to Greta, anyway). She made a mental note to tell Ms. O'Shea about Iris after she'd had a chance to talk to Greta first and confirm that Iris was indeed one of them.

As they snacked on their pretzels, Binx and Ridley filled Ms. O'Shea in on the shadow messages, the 1415 hexes, and the defaced gravestones, as well as their belief that Orion, Brandon, and Axel were Antima members.

When they'd finished, Ms. O'Shea said, "Wow, those shadow messages must have been scary for you. The graffiti on the gravestones, too. And no, I didn't hex the shadow messages, and neither did any of the other witches in my coven. Maybe I could take a look at Greta's? And Div's? And yes, those three boys are on my radar, too. Although . . ." She hesitated.

"What?" Ridley prompted her.

"It's entirely possible that they're just wearing the shoulder patch and acting like bigoted jerks, but not engaging in any of the more extreme and violent Antima activities. Not yet, anyway. We think, though, that there's a more serious Antima presence in Sorrow Point. Some bigwig who is organizing and financing a powerful new Antima faction."

Binx would have said something smug to Ridley about how she'd been right—Orion and Axel *were* posers. Except she wasn't happy to hear about this other news.

"Who's this bigwig?" she asked Ms. O'Shea.

"We don't know. We're trying to find out who he—or she—is."

Ridley was tearing her pepperoni pretzel into tiny pieces. Binx noticed that her friend sometimes did that with food (or a piece of paper or whatever she happened to be holding) when she was anxious. "Can't you and your coven just do a superpowerful scrying spell and uncover this person? You guys must be really advanced witches, right?"

"I *wish* we could do that," Ms. O'Shea said with a sigh. "But as you probably know from Callixta Crowe's book, and from your own experiences, too, I'm sure, the practice of magic is imperfect. And unpredictable. Otherwise, we witches could just scry and memory-erase away the Antima. Disable them, even. Them, and all other evil in the world."

Binx began tearing her own pretzel into tiny pieces, too. It *was* kind of therapeutic. But it also made her feel more agitated. And angry. It wasn't fair that she and other witches had to meet like this, in secret, strategizing ways to keep from being terrorized by a bunch of random witch-haters who had no reason for their prejudiced attitudes. Just before the Great Purge, there'd been a plague that had killed tens of thousands of people, and the government had decided (wrongly) to blame witches for it and order their arrests and executions.

But that was then. This was now. Witches weren't a threat to anyone, and they deserved to have equal rights.

The Antima had to go. The 6-129 law had to go, too.

Binx gathered all the torn-up pretzel bits and popped them into her mouth. She remembered to fake-smile. (Someone really needed to create a *calumnia* 2.0, to cover visuals.)

And then she smiled for real. An idea had come to her.

There *was* a way to fight back. ShadowKnight had told her all about it. She had to get in touch with him ASAP. If only she could figure out why the hex he'd disappeared.

14

THE SEARCH FOR LOLLI MCSCUFFLE PANTS

The act of finding your Familiar
is an individual endeavor.
No spells are needed; just an open mind.

(FROM *THE GOOD BOOK OF MAGIC AND MENTALISM*
BY CALLIXTA CROWE)

"*You must hand over the Sapphire of Truth immediately or face the full wrath of the High Council!*"

"*You mendacious maenad! You wouldn't know Truth if it hit you over the head like Hedren's Hammer of Halcyon Magic!*"

"*How DARE you!*"

Iris pushed her glasses up the bridge of her nose and hunched over her laptop as Ilyara and Draska, the two most powerful witches on the Valkyrie Valley High Council, squared off. Should her own character, Skotadi of Sirren, intervene or stay hidden behind the Crystal Cauldron?

The wrong decision could mean instant death, or worse, being demoted to her previous level. Death was the lesser of two evils here because she could just respawn at her prior position outside the Fortunale Fortress. Losing a level was a *huge* problem because it had taken her forty hours of play to achieve the jump.

Her room was a crazy mess—clothes spilling out of dresser drawers, pools of hardened candlewax, and empty Pasta-in-a-Cup containers everywhere. Her gems, potions, and tarot cards (homemade by her . . . art wasn't her strong suit, but oh, well) were all hidden away in her closet in an old cardboard box marked WINTER CLOTHES/DO NOT THROW AWAY. She really should do a major cleanup; she still wasn't completely unpacked from the big move last month, and what she *had* unpacked was a chaos salad. But today was Wednesday, and Wednesdays from six to nine p.m. Pacific time meant triple XPs (Experience Points) for battle wins and double value for newly acquired Firx, which were the currency in the *Witchworld* world. Her character had already accumulated 1,200 XPs in the battle against the Enochian Elves and banked an additional 500 Firx—enough to buy a new scrying mirror at Beeble's Bazaar or maybe even a Shadow Shield, if the merchant Mungledoc was open to bargaining.

The IRL cleanup could wait. So could her English, history, and French homework. She—or rather, Skotadi—needed to come out of hiding, put on her big-girl pants (an expression her therapist Francesca used to use), and join the fight; the question was, on whose side?

If Francesca were here, she would probably point out that Iris was in extra-intense gaming mode because she'd had an extra-intense day. It had been Day 1 at her new school. She'd been harassed and assaulted by three jerks (*Antima* jerks). She'd revealed to another human being that she was a witch. She'd received scary images (and the word *no* in secret code) from a shadow message.

Experiences like this tended to fire up Iris's anxiety, and gaming was a good way to throw a blanket on the flames.

Of course, Francesca didn't know that she was a witch. Iris had always been super-extra-cautious about keeping that part of her life a secret, even from her therapist, who was a cool person, and even from her family members, who were (besides her little sister Nyala) mostly cool, too. She didn't want to take any chances that someone outside her family-therapist circle, someone *not* cool, might find out.

Iris cranked up the volume on her Tegan and Sara album just as the song "I'm Not Your Hero" came on. *Argh.* Not exactly the right sentiment for dealing with this stuff. Or for going into a nasty cyber-battle.

Although it occurred to Iris, not for the first time, that *Witchworld* was the one truly "safe" place to be a witch. The world seemed to be fine with witches as long as they were fictional.

"*Lolllllli! Lolli McScuffle Pants!*"

"*Shut up, Nee-Nee. I can't hear my movie!*"

Nyala and Ephrem were yelling and fighting downstairs. Sighing, Iris typed an AFK (away from keyboard) status, paused the music, and rose from her desk chair. Mom was working at the diner with Grandma Roseline, which meant that Iris was officially in charge, i.e., she had no choice but to intervene in *this* battle. Stepping over a pile of yesterday's (or last week's?) clothes, she trotted down the carpeted stairs.

"*But that doesn't mean I wasn't brave,*" she sang under her breath. "*Oh yeah, ooo-ooo, la la la la la la . . . I'm glaaad no one can hear me siiinging . . . oh yeah . . .*"

Her siblings were in the living room. Ephrem was sitting about six inches from the TV set—which was playing *Jake and the Neverland Pirates*, one of his favorite shows—and slurping from a grape juice box.

Nyala was on her hands and knees, peering under the ancient brown corduroy couch.

"Hey, guys, what's up? Ephrem, that's *way* too close to the TV."

"She's *bothering* me!" Ephrem exclaimed, pointing a stubby finger at Nyala. His lips were ringed with purple juice.

Nyala glared at Iris over her shoulder. "Lolli's missing. Did you take her?"

"Um, no? Why would I take your pet mouse?"

"'Cuz you *would*, jerkface."

"Do not call me that. Seriously, what happened? When did you see her last?"

"I was cleaning out her cage, so I put her in a little shoe box with the rest of my banana from lunch, but now she's not there anymore and what if she's dead? What if Oliver P. and Maxina *ate* her?"

"Cool!" Ephrem said excitedly.

"Shut *up*, you stupid brat!" Nyala shouted.

"*Guys!* Okay. Plan. Nyala, check and make sure Lolli's not in the bathroom, then put Oliver P. and Maxina in there and close the door. You can lure them in with the cat treats—there's some in the kitchen drawer with the Tupperware lids. Ephrem, stay here and watch another episode of *Jake* and, um, keep an eye open for Lolli." With the tiny creature loose, Iris didn't trust her clumsy little brother not to accidentally step on her if he moved from his spot. "I'll search the rest of the house. Everybody watch where you walk."

"What if Lolli's *already* squashed?" Nyala wailed.

"She's not. Calm down, okay? I'm going now; you guys have your orders."

Retracing her steps out of the living room, Iris looked right and left and down (and even up—what if Lolli was a climber?). She tried to remember the spell Jadora used whenever her familiar, a Bothnian bird-cat, went missing (which was often because the superwitch's many enemies were often snatching Baxxtern as a way of weakening and distracting her); maybe she could use it for inspiration? (There *was* a finding-lost-familiars spell in Callixta's book, but she couldn't recall that one, either.) Iris had no idea what it felt like to be so bonded to an animal. She had yet to meet a familiar of her own. Maybe it was okay, though; not all the witches in *Witchworld* had a familiar, and Greta had mentioned that Callixta said it was okay to be familiarless (was that a word?).

She remembered Greta mentioning *her* familiar. Goffle-something. Did the other witches in her coven have familiars, too? Did most witches IRL?

Iris proceeded to search the rest of the house—kitchen, dining room, the den with the futon couch (Kedren's new "bedroom" for whenever she was home from college), Nyala's room (she touched Lolli's cage, to see if that might trigger a helpful vision . . . but nothing), Ephrem's room, the room Mom shared with Grandma Roseline, the hall closets. Nyala had holed herself up in the upstairs bathroom with the two cats; she could hear them howling angrily about being separated from their food bowl or water bowl or litter box or whatever. Major cat drama.

The litter box made her think of . . . *ugh*, the basement. Iris hated it down there; it was dark and damp and smelled like mothballs and cat pee and decay. She would save it for the very end of her search. Or better yet, she would manage to avoid it altogether because Lolli was sure to turn up any second now . . . right?

Just as Iris was finishing up with the last hall closet—it was stuffed to the gills with mismatched sheets, threadbare towels, and about a hundred rolls of discount toilet paper (because, Grandma Roseline)—she remembered the finding-lost-familiars spell from Callixta's book. *Yes!*

Making sure Nyala and Ephrem were out of earshot, Iris clasped her smiley-face moon pendant for extra magical effect and whispered: *"Sortis."*

Nothing.

"Sortis," she repeated.

Still nothing.

She knotted her fists in frustration. *Breathe*, she told herself. She reminded herself that magic was mainly about intention. If the mental intention wasn't there, a spell was pretty much useless.

"Lolli McScuffle Pants, you dumb mouse, where *are* you? *Sortis* right this second or face the full wrath of the High Council!" How was *that* for intention?

Ssssttt.

A strange, barely-there sensation tickled Iris's brain. Like tiny whiskers grazing against her cerebral cortex.

"L-Lolli?"

Another tickle—this time, stronger. Iris continued repeating the spell (quietly) and calling Lolli's name (loudly), and the tickling sensation intensified. It was almost like a weird kind of radar. She moved slowly, carefully in what seemed to be the right direction.

After a moment, she found herself back in her own room. What the hex?

"Lolli?"

On top of her dresser, a fringy black scarf trembled and fluttered, revealing an empty Pasta-in-a-Cup container underneath. A tiny pink nose emerged from the container and sniffed furiously at the air.

"Lolli?"

The white mouse skittered out of the bowl and dashed across the dresser, nimbly navigating a maze of Pokémon figurines and origami dragons.

"Were you in here the whole time? Nyala was super-worried about you! We *all* were!" Iris scolded.

In response, Lolli skittered to the floor, crossed the room, and skittered up Iris's leg. She settled herself in the pocket of Iris's baggy plaid button-up: a small, warm lump.

"W-what are you doing?"

Lolli stared up at Iris with her beady red eyes and sniffed. Iris wasn't sure what to do—she'd never had physical contact with Lolli before—so she stroked the mouse's minuscule head with her index finger.

Happiness radiated up from the tiny creature.

"I *knew* it! You *stole* her!"

Nyala stood in the doorway, her hands on her hips. Her face was hard with fury.

"Oh, hey, Nyala! I *just* found her, like right this second. She was hiding in my dresser . . . well, *on*, technically, except she was inside a . . . never mind, *here*."

Iris reached into her shirt pocket and cradled the soft, warm mouse with her fingertips. She transferred her ever-so-gently to her sister.

Cocooned in Nyala's hands, Lolli McScuffle Pants blinked up at Iris. Iris blinked back. She felt sad all of a sudden . . . why?

Wait. Could *Lolli* be her familiar?

No way.

Or maybe yes way?

Iris coughed. "Yeah. So, hey, Nyala? You should close your door whenever you clean her cage, and make sure the cats aren't in there with you."

"Thank you for stating the obvious, Ms. I'm-the-Boss-of-Everybody!"

"Thank you for finding Lolli McScuffle Pants, Iris. You're welcome, Nyala."

"Ugh! You are such a—*you know what*!" Nyala whirled around and stormed out of the room.

Argh . . . little sisters.

Iris knew she should cut Nyala some slack, though, considering. She and Dad had been extra-super-close. But honestly, Nyala had always shown Iris attitude, and now that she was in middle school, it was probably going to get worse. (Iris had to admit that she *may* have been that way herself, with Kedren.)

Sometimes, a dark mood bubbled up inside Iris and she wished that their parents had never adopted Nyala and Ephrem. Well, Ephrem, maybe, but not Nyala. In any case, whenever she had this bad, terrible thought, she would immediately chase it away with a reversal spell from Callixta's book; Iris was irrationally afraid that her own magical powers, her intention, might make her anger-wish come true. And she obviously didn't want that. She loved her brother and sister. Most days.

Lolli. Iris felt that sad feeling again, being parted from her. *Gah.* So Lolli *must* be her familiar. Which meant that she needed to convince Nyala to give her up and let her live in Iris's room.

Should Iris bribe her? But if she acted like she *wanted* Lolli, Nyala would be doubly determined not to give up her pet. Maybe Iris should cast a spell on Nyala? That seemed like a bad idea, too. She'd have to think about how best to do this.

Sighing, Iris leaned over her desk and refreshed her laptop screen. The two leaders of the High Council were still trash-talking each other. Behind them, their respective coterie of guards had gathered, brandishing various enchanted weapons—everything from wands to swords to spears to thunderwhips.

"But that doesn't mean I wasn't brave . . . oh yeah, ooo-ooo, la la la la la la . . ." Iris sang.

Her phone chimed just then. A message popped up, indicating that she had a Facebook friend request.

Iris logged into her Facebook account, which she hardly ever used because she hardly ever got any "likes," and she had so few FB friends as it was. Someone named Aysha Rodriguez had requested to be her friend. Iris checked out her profile photo. *Oh yeah.* Aysha was in her English class.

Wow! Iris thought as she accepted the friend request. The last time she'd had a friend request was . . . well, she couldn't even remember.

A moment later, a message came through from Aysha:

> Hey, Iris! Thanks for accepting my friend request. I loved
> your comment about teapots in Dalrymple's class! Ha!
> So I was wondering if you wanted to have lunch tomorrow.
> (I have A-lunch.)

Iris smiled in surprise. People at this school were so nice!

> Hey, Aysha! I do have A-lunch, and yes, I'd love to have
> lunch with you!

Aysha replied:

> Fun! I can introduce you to my friends Mira and Div, you'll
> like them. I thought I'd invite this other new girl to join us.
> Her name's Penelope, she's in our English class, too. I
> think the five of us might have a lot in common. K bye!

"Wow!" Iris said out loud. She busted out a spontaneous dance move and accidentally crushed a Pasta-in-a-Cup container with her foot. So much for graceful. Just this morning, she'd wanted to vomit all over the hallway because she was so nervous about being in a new school, a new city, a new *coast*. But since then, she'd made a couple of friends (a real one—a witch!—and a Facebook one) and was well on her way to making even *more* friends.

She was about to return to her game when a text came in from an unfamiliar number:

Hi, it's me, Greta!

Greta! Friend #2! Iris busted out another dance move. She'd given Greta her number at Poe's Market earlier.

The text continued:

I'm really glad we met today! Do you have A-lunch? If so do you want to have lunch together tomorrow?

Iris's eyes grew wide. Now she had *two* lunch invitations for tomorrow! How would she be able to choose? But she had no choice; she'd already said yes to Aysha.

Or maybe she could be creative? The lunch period was approximately forty-five minutes long. That meant she could have two twenty-two-and-a-half-minute-long lunches, right?

Iris wrote:

Lunch is good but I might be a little late if that's okay?

Greta wrote back:

Of course! I usually eat in the courtyard under the purple flower
tree so just meet me when you can. I'll see if my friends Binx
and Ridley are free, too.

"Sure!" Iris said out loud.

She started to type *XOXO*, then deleted it, then retyped it, then
re-deleted it. She didn't want to come across as one of those desperate fan-
girly girls, even though Greta did make her feel kind of fan-girly. After all,
she'd saved Iris from those three Antima bullies. Plus she was a supercool
witch. Plus she smelled like lavender.

There were no further texts. Iris returned to her game.

Life in Sorrow Point was definitely looking up.

Except for the Antima. And for that creepy shadow message that
Greta had shown her. Iris wondered what Jadora would do about *them*?

15

SUNLIGHT AND SHADOWS

If you ignore Discord within a coven,
it will multiply in the shadows.

(FROM *THE GOOD BOOK OF MAGIC AND MENTALISM*
BY CALLIXTA CROWE)

On Thursday at noon, Greta found her way to her favorite bench in the school courtyard, the one under the purple crape myrtle tree. It was a perfect day to be outside—warm but not too warm and with a gentle breeze that carried with it the faint, intoxicating fragrance of abelia blossoms and freshly mown grass. The cedar bench was adorned with a small gold plaque that said: IN MEMORY OF JANE ELIZABETH LEAVENWORTH. She didn't know who Jane Elizabeth Leavenworth was, and she'd resisted the impulse to google her; in Greta's mind, the name had bloomed into a social activist, biologist, and (secret) garden witch who lived in Sorrow Point a century ago with a cat familiar named Orlando and six witchy daughters.

Greta gazed around the courtyard; Binx and Ridley should be here soon. Iris had said she'd be late, but Greta was just happy she could join them at all. Plus, she was glad to have a little time alone with Binx and Ridley first. They had a lot to discuss, and not just about the shadow messages and the Antima.

Ridley had called her last night and told her about Ms. O'Shea. The news had been a (good) surprise—there were now *two* new witches at their school. There was strength in numbers, after all. But with the good came the bad, of course. If Ms. O'Shea and her coven were right, and there really was some rich, powerful Antima organizer in Sorrow Point, then things were bound to get worse . . . not just shadow messages and defaced gravestones, but possibly violence. Like what happened to that witch in Texas. (Also, maybe this Antima bigwig had influence with the local police and would convince them to beef up their witch patrol . . . and witch arrests?)

A sudden chill spidered up Greta's spine. She glanced up abruptly. Nope, no one around. The closest students were all the way by the soccer fields playing Ultimate Frisbee. No sign of Orion or Axel or Brandon, either.

She touched her raw amethyst pendant under her peasant blouse and willed herself to relax. Maybe she should sketch a little until the other girls arrived. She pulled out a slim notebook—not her grimoire, which she only used in private, but a Himalayan rice paper sketchbook—and a green velvet bag containing her drawing pencils. She also opened her recyclable waxed canvas lunch bag and peered inside. She usually packed her own lunches and Teo's, too (she'd been doing this since fifth grade), but this morning her mother had apparently woken up at three— "Middle-aged-lady insomnia," Ysabel had explained with a cheerful yawn—and packed lunches for the whole family. Greta made a mental note to mix a new sleeping elixir for her—perhaps a blend of lavender, valerian root, chamomile, passionflower, and skullcap?

Greta's parents knew she was a witch. They'd known ever since she was eleven, when she'd touched a dead zinnia in the garden, closed her eyes, and willed it to "wake up"—and the withered brown blossom had instantaneously morphed into a profusion of bright red petals. After this discovery moment, Tomas and Ysabel had sat her down and instructed her that even though they'd always taught her not to keep secrets, she *absolutely* had to keep her magical power a secret. *Had* to. They loved her and supported her; they were opposed to 6-129, the law against witchcraft; and they were passionate about equal rights for all. But they also wanted to make sure that the information about her identity never leaked, for her own safety. They'd also told her about her great-grandmother Adelita, on Ysabel's side, who'd been a witch, too. (Adelita had died when Ysabel was a baby, so she had never known her.)

"Hey!"

It was Binx, making her way toward the bench. She was carrying a strawberry yogurt, a bag of potato chips, and a ginger ale. *"Calumnia,"* she said as she sat down next to Greta and shrugged off her Hello Kitty backpack. "So where's the newb recruit?"

"Is that what you're calling her now? Iris will be here soon. Where's Ridley?"

"She had to see Ms. Fein about her paper. She said, like, five minutes."

"Got it." Greta nibbled thoughtfully on a carrot stick. "Did you manage to find the names on those gravestones?"

"No. I tried to blow up the photos, but the quality was too grainy. I guess one of us will just have to go back to the cemetery in person. Fun!" Binx tore open her bag of potato chips and popped one in her mouth. "By the way, I'm curious—why does the newb recruit think 1415 is code for 'no'?" she asked, chewing.

"She touched the shadow message. *My* shadow message; she doesn't know about Div's yet. I didn't even tell her about Div being a . . . Anyway, Iris touched my shadow message and had some sort of vision that indicated that 1415 meant 'no.'"

"Soooo . . . she could be making it up?"

"Why would she make it up?"

"Who knows?" Binx said with a shrug. "You *literally* just met her yesterday. She could be a fake, or a fluffy bunny, or crazy, or whatever. Or she could have sent the shadow message, did you ever think about that? She may not be who she says she is. In fact, I should do more online vetting on her before we let her into the circle, don't you think?"

Greta spread her napkin (actually a dish towel with a map of New Mexico) across her lap and smoothed it carefully. "I guess? But she seemed real to me. Super-sincere. You can see for yourself when you meet her. Besides, we need all the help we can get to figure out who's threatening us. And she seems . . . I don't know, *gifted*. Intuitive."

"Speaking of help . . ." Binx set her food down and leaned toward Greta. "I've been thinking. There's someone else who might be able to help us."

"Who?"

"I have this online friend. We met on one of the *Witchworld* discussion boards. It's a long story, but it turns out he's a cyber-witch, too. *He* might have some thoughts on how to track down whoever wrote those shadow messages."

Greta blinked. "I don't understand. *Who* is this guy?"

Binx lowered her voice, her eyes bright with excitement. "This is totally, hugely confidential, so you can't tell anyone. I haven't even told Ridley yet. I figured I should tell you first because you're our leader or whatever, then the three of us could discuss. Anyway, so . . . ShadowKnight, that's my friend, he belongs to this witch group called Libertas. They started a resistance movement so they can get rid of 6-129 and help protect witches' rights."

Greta took a sip of her kombucha tea and considered this.

"Don't they sound epic? And awesome?" Binx rambled on. "I've actually been thinking about joining them. Things are getting so out of control with the Antima."

"Um . . ." Greta hesitated. "Have you ever met this, uh, Shadowlight person in real life?"

"Shadow*Knight*. No, why?"

"Well, how do you know *he's* not a fake or a fluffy bunny or crazy?"

Binx's expression hardened. "Really? *That's* your reaction to what I just said?"

"We have to be really, really careful about our identities. You *know* that."

"OMG! You are such a hypocrite. So, it's okay that you tell the newb recruit about our coven and share the shadow message with her and everything—without asking Ridley and me, thanks—but it's *not* okay for me to do the same with *my* friend?"

"At least I've met Iris and talked to her in person. I can be sure she's who she says she is," Greta said defensively. "What if ShadowKnight is, like, Antima in disguise? What if there's no such group as Libertas? Or what if there is, and they're *all* Antima, posing as witches?"

Binx stood up abruptly, scattering potato chips everywhere. "You are so paranoid. Libertas doesn't have a website or a social media presence, for safety reasons. *Obviously*. Besides, you don't know him like I do." She shook her head. "Why are you so closed-minded? And selfish? Don't you want to do what's right and what's best for *all* the witches in the world and not just our stupid little coven?"

"*Stupid?* Since when is our coven stupid?"

"Guys!"

Ridley was hurrying across the courtyard toward them. "Why are you arguing?"

Greta touched her pendant and took a deep breath. "We're not arguing. Everything's fine!" she replied with a strained smile.

"Yeah, peachy," Binx said sarcastically.

Greta glared at her.

Ridley cocked her head. "O-kay. I thought you said Iris Gooding was having lunch with us?"

"She is," Greta confirmed.

"Then why is she having lunch with Div and Mira and Aysha? And Penelope?"

"What?" Greta burst out. "And who's Penelope?"

"Penelope is . . . she's a sophomore, too. She's new here. She lives in my neighborhood," Ridley explained, studying her red nails.

"She's a beautuber," Binx added. "She's got over sixty-five thousand subscribers."

Greta tried to wrap her mind around this information. Iris was having lunch with Div and her girls. Which meant that Div must have figured out about Iris being a witch. Which meant that Div might be trying to recruit Iris into *her* coven right this second.

And why was this Penelope girl in the mix? Was *she* a witch, too? (And what on earth was a beautuber?)

"Ugh. Where are they?" Greta asked Ridley.

"At their usual table in the cafeteria."

Greta stuffed her lunch and sketchbook and pencils into her backpack. "Let's go."

16

THE COOL TABLE

If you wish to join another Coven,
do it with care lest you create Enemies where
once you had Friends.

(FROM *THE GOOD BOOK OF MAGIC AND MENTALISM*
BY CALLIXTA CROWE)

D iv found the Iris girl very annoying.

"This is so fun, having lunch with you guys!" Iris was saying in a high, excited voice as she rooted through her Batgirl lunch bag. "Back at my old school, I sometimes ate lunch with the chess club. They met every day at noon . . . five past noon, to be exact. I don't actually know how to play chess. . . . Well, I do, kind of. . . . Like, I know the names of the pieces, pawns and rooks and bishops and knights and queens and kings . . . actually, there's only one queen and one king, so singular queen and king, not plural queens and kings . . . but I'm not great at remembering which pieces are supposed to go where, and when, and how you capture the other person's pieces, and what even is 'castling'? And '*en passant*'? And the 'Sicilian Defense'? It's so complicated!" She paused, unwrapped a corn muffin, and took a big, crumbly bite. "Anyhoo, it's nice to have people to hang out with at lunch. Versus, say, sitting alone in the corner of the cafetorium—isn't that a weird word, *cafetorium*?—and pretend-texting. So, thank you for letting me sit at the cool table!"

Div cocked her head and regarded Iris. She knew she should try to respond with "charming" . . . after all, she was planning to ask Iris (and Penelope, too) to join their coven, pending confirmation that they were both witches, and she needed yeses from both of them. But *still*. She wasn't sure she could stand five more seconds in this girl's presence, let alone see her on a regular basis.

Fortunately, Mira stepped in; even though she could be quite nasty (especially in combination with Aysha, especially when the two of them were hexing Binx or pranking random students), she could also be naturally, genuinely sweet. ("Sweet" was a foreign language for Div.)

"Iris, I am *so* with you about the 'complicated,'" Mira said, punctuating her point in the air with a piece of string cheese. "My dad's been trying to teach me chess, and it seriously hurts my head. But I want to get better, so maybe you and I could play sometime? We can keep it super-caj and also reward ourselves with mani-pedis after. Or before. Or during."

Iris nodded so eagerly that her glasses slid down her nose. She pushed them back up. "Yes! That sounds fun! I've actually never had a mani-pedi, or not a real one, anyway. . . . My sister Kedren, she's my big sister . . . I have a little sister, too, Nyala, she's a total brat . . . Kedren used to try to give me home mani-pedis, but the smell of the nail polish always—"

"*So* interesting," Div interrupted, trying to put the brakes on yet another runaway Iris monologue. She instinctively reached up to pet Prada, then remembered that she'd left her at home to digest her mouse from yesterday. (Snakes didn't like being held during the twenty-four to seventy-two hours after a meal.) "Penelope, what's your position on mani-pedis? Pro or con?"

"Oh, pro, definitely," Penelope said cheerfully. "I did a whole series about them for my YouTube channel last month. I tested different vegan nail polishes, because that's a thing now." She turned to Iris and added, "You might like them. I think they smell nicer than the not-vegan kinds."

"Cool!" Iris exclaimed.

Mira asked Penelope some questions about her YouTube channel. Next to Mira, Aysha fake-smiled through her veggie burger and nod-ded, pretending to listen. (Aysha didn't wear makeup, and the only topics of conversation that held her interest were witchcraft, martial arts, and wolves—she was convinced that her familiar, Nicodemus, was half wolf, half dog.)

Div watched her two witches and her two new maybe-witches. She wasn't a total Crowe disciple—not even close—but she did agree that group spells were more powerful than solo ones, and the bigger the group, the better. Hopefully Iris and Penelope were witches. (And if so, could *they* have enchanted the shadow messages? If yes, why?)

"Hey, guys!"

Speaking of . . . Div recognized the voice, its forced friendliness mask-ing irritation, before she even looked up. Greta was heading toward their table, flanked by Binx and Ridley. *Oh, great.* Div needed to focus on her Iris and Penelope project; she didn't need this distraction right now.

Without waiting for an invitation, Greta pulled up an empty chair from a nearby table. Ridley did the same and sat down next to Penelope. Binx remained standing.

Aysha put down her veggie burger. Her brown eyes flashed at Greta. "We're having a private conversation—" she began.

Div set her iced tea down and held up her hand. "It's fine. Please.

Join us," she said smoothly. She didn't want Iris and Penelope to get the impression that she and Mira and Aysha were mean or unwelcoming.

"Thanks, Div." Greta sat down next to Iris. "Hey, Iris! These are my friends that I told you about. Binx and Ridley. And you must be Penelope," she said. "I'm Greta."

Penelope nodded. "Yup, that's me! Hey, Ridley, when is our history quiz? I forgot to write it down and I'm sort of terrified it's tomorrow."

"It's on Monday, so you have plenty of time. How was that pumpkin spice latte?"

"Yummy, as always. Maybe we could grab one later?"

"Sure!"

Div frowned. Ridley and Penelope already knew each other? And Greta knew Iris, too? This was not good.

Greta didn't suspect that the two new girls might be witches . . . *did* she? She hadn't mentioned a word about it in the car yesterday, and keeping secrets was *so* not Greta. Unless she'd changed. Div eyed Greta with interest, wondering.

Iris stood up and sat down again. She pushed her glasses up the bridge of her nose. "Greta! It's awesome to see you again! I didn't know you guys all knew each other! I'm so, so sorry I'm late for our lunch. I mean, I know that I *told* you I'd be late, but I still feel bad. You and Aysha asked me to lunch at the same time . . . well, not at the *exact* same time, but super, super close . . . so I thought I'd try to hang out with both of you somehow, and your friends, too, but now it's even better because we're all hanging out together!"

"No worries," Greta assured Iris.

Div pretended to pluck a loose thread from her white jeans. So Greta *did* suspect. Maybe she even knew for sure, and she was making her move to recruit them to *her* coven first. She stifled a swear and dug her nails into her palms.

On the other hand, maybe this was a *good* thing—maybe this was the confirmation Div had been looking for. If Greta believed that Iris and Penelope were witches, that backed up Aysha's impressions from yesterday . . . the amulet, the tarot cards . . .

Just then, Div spotted Axel Ngata across the cafeteria; his Antima buddies Orion and Brandon weren't with him. He hovered beside a table where a freshman girl sat by herself. He leaned down and said something to her that made her shake her head agitatedly. The girl tried to pick up her tray and leave, but he wouldn't let her.

Div narrowed her eyes. Did Axel think that girl was a witch? Or was he just harassing her for no good reason? Whatever the case, the guy needed to be put in his place.

Prurio, she thought as she stared directly at him.

Axel stopped what he was doing and began furiously scratching his arms and chest and scalp, as though he'd been attacked by a swarm of fleas. The girl took the opportunity to make her escape. *Good.*

At the same moment, Colter Jessup walked into the cafeteria with the lacrosse coach. Their heads were bent in conversation, and the coach was tracing diamond shapes in the air. Lacrosse plays? Colter and Mira used to date. Div had never liked the guy and was not unhappy when they broke up. There was just something too perfect about him.

Penelope seemed to notice them, too. Her face lit up, and she waved. "Colter! Over here!"

At the mention of Colter's name, Mira's head snapped up, and she swiveled in her chair. She watched intently as Colter said goodbye to the coach and came over to their table.

Penelope wiggled her fingers toward him, and he took her hand and curled his fist over hers. *Oh, that,* Div thought, suddenly bored. Penelope probably didn't know that Colter and Mira used to be boyfriend-girlfriend, and Mira was probably learning about him and Penelope for the first time. Relationship drama. Div herself didn't date unless it served some practical purpose (who had the time?). Like last year, when she'd needed Hakeem Johnson to let her spend time at his family's farm so that she could practice necromancy spells on (dead) animals. Or like in eighth grade, when she'd pretended to return Greta's crush so Greta would stay in Div's coven. (That scheme had worked for a little while, anyway.)

"Colter, these are my new friends. Like, *brand*-new friends," Penelope was telling him. "This is Ridley and Greta and Iris and Binx . . . and this is Div and Aysha and Mira. Did I get all your names right? Or maybe you guys already know each other?"

There was a chorus of *Hi*'s.

"Oh, hey, we met yesterday," Colter said to Iris. "How are you liking your new classes?"

"Hey! They're good, thanks for asking. Well, maybe *good* isn't the right word. They're not *not-good*, if that makes any sense. Which it probably doesn't. Sorry." Iris dropped her gaze and nibbled on her granola bar.

Seriously, this girl, Div thought. She glanced at Mira, who was sipping at her smoothie and not saying anything. That showed great restraint; she normally would have seized the opportunity to make an ex-boyfriend and/or his new girlfriend really uncomfortable. Miserable, even. Like last year at the spring dance when she'd used a nausea spell to make Allison Hofstadt throw up all over Jeremy Cho just as they were being crowned queen and king up on the stage. Div appreciated the fact that Mira was holding back for the sake of their coven.

"Colter and I met at tennis camp this summer," Penelope was explaining.

"She's a *way* better tennis player than I am," Colter said, grinning down at her. "There was a big tournament on the last day of camp, and she and her doubles partner beat me and my partner in straight sets. Pen has a terrifying backhand."

While the tennis conversation continued, Div picked at her lunch—some unrecognizable casserole from the school kitchen (should she use a spell to make it taste better?)—and tried to mentally recalibrate. Her gaze bounced between Greta, Iris, Penelope, and Ridley. So Greta was likely working on Iris . . . and Penelope, too, through Ridley. Did Iris already know that Greta, Ridley, and Binx were witches? Did Penelope? Had Greta *already* extended invitations to join her coven? Div's instincts said no on all counts, although even if the answers were yes, it wasn't too late for Div to try to steal the two girls away.

Binx, who had remained standing, was scrolling through her phone, which had a case featuring a demented-looking purple cartoon creature with huge red eyes. Every once in a while, she slanted a sideways look at Greta, clenched her jaw, and resumed scrolling.

Trouble in paradise? Div wondered, pleasantly surprised. Maybe this *was* a good time to try recruiting Binx again. And if she could get Binx, then Ridley would likely follow. Then finally, Greta—left all alone—would have to come back to her with her tail between her legs. To the coven where she belonged.

Greta was watching her watch the other girls.

That's right, I'm two steps ahead of you, Div thought.

She picked up her phone and composed a quick text to Greta:

Do you play chess?

She hit send. A second later, Greta's phone trilled. She stared in confusion at it, and then up at Div.

No. Why?

Div replied:

No reason. Love your blouse, is it new?

Greta frowned at her. Div picked up her iced tea and lifted it in a toast. She loved loved loved messing with Greta's head.

A moment later, Greta wrote:

You can't have them.

Div raised an eyebrow. So Greta *was* after the new witches. It was good to know for sure. And Greta knew Div was after the witches, too.

She replied:

Whatever you say, Gretabelle.

Greta looked away, her cheeks flaming. Satisfied, Div turned her attention back to Binx and began to formulate a plan. Maybe a pool party at her house this weekend with her girls and Iris and Penelope?

Binx didn't seem like the pool party type, though.

Div would have to think of a different strategy for her.

17

REVOLUTION

Death is the beginning of all transformations.

(FROM *THE GOOD BOOK OF MAGIC AND MENTALISM*
BY CALLIXTA CROWE)

Binx hopscotched up the granite paver driveway, drinking ginger ale and listening to her new Icona Pop album. Icona Pop was Swedish. Swedish people were cool; Sweden seemed cool, too. Sometimes she wished she lived there, like maybe in Stockholm, which had to be way more interesting than the super-small town of Sorrow Point, Washington (population 24,538, home of the Fightin' Buccaneers, the city that invented the sushi doughnut . . . *blurg*).

Still, *okay* . . . she had to admit that her house was in a pretty sweet location. On a cliff overlooking the Pacific Ocean, killer sunsets, lots of privacy (the closest neighbors, whoever they were, lived way down the hill—the closest *living* ones, anyway, since there was the cemetery). Her house also had an infinity pool, two Jacuzzis, a tennis court, and a Japanese Zen garden with a meditation hut. Guess it didn't hurt to have a crazy-rich tech-legend dad, as annoying as he might be. It helped that he now lived full-time in Palo Alto and she rarely saw him; these days, he was even more absentee than usual, with the new trophy wife and new spawn and all. (The wife, Sloane, was a game designer and coder, which sort of redeemed her for having had that affair with Binx's dad. The spawn, Lucas, age eight months, was mostly just loud and wriggly and smelled like applesauce and diaper.)

Of course, Binx wasn't really the outdoorsy type, so the pool and tennis court, as well as the hiking trail that Ridley so loved, were wasted on her. And the only time she'd ever used the meditation hut was to almost make out with LaJon Jamison, although that had been wasted on her, too; LaJon was much more interesting as a Pokémon Go partner, and they'd ended up just talking about Gen 1 versus Gen 2 Legendaries.

There *was* the basketball hoop her dad had installed behind the garage way back when. They used to have free-throw contests, with the loser having to make ice-cream cones for the two of them (which, looking back, wasn't much of a penalty). Maybe she should dust off the old orange ball? She could challenge Ridley to a game of one-on-one.

Her phone buzzed—an incoming call from an unfamiliar number.

Maybe ShadowKnight, finally? She'd left two more encrypted messages for him since yesterday.

"Uxie, who is it?" Binx asked her virtual genie/assistant.

"This number belongs to a wireless caller named Divinity Florescu," Uxie replied.

Div? Did she have new news about the shadow messages? If so, why wasn't she calling Greta?

Binx stopped in the middle of the driveway and pressed talk. "Why are you calling me?"

"Hey, Binx."

Binx, not *Beatrix*. And Div's tone was friendly. Was this an olive branch? Or was it a black locust branch (which was poisonous) in olive branch clothing? At lunch today, Binx had watched the Triad being fake-friendly with the newb recruit (okay, fine, *Iris*) and the beautuber, Penelope. Div must believe that Iris and Penelope were both witches, and she was clearly going for a power grab to turn the Triad into a . . . Pentad? So she could dominate *their* coven into forever?

"Do you have a minute?"

"Yeah, but only a minute. What's up?" Binx strolled over to a stone bench and sat down.

"First of all, can we keep this conversation between us?" Div asked.

"I'll decide on that once I know what it's about."

Now Binx was *really* curious. And nervous. What could Div want to talk about that had to be kept private?

"I'm just going to come out and say it. It seems like Greta wants Iris Gooding and Penelope Hart to join your coven. And you guys have probably guessed that I want them to join *our* coven."

Binx didn't respond.

"I'll be totally honest with you, Binx," Div went on. "Greta's very— how shall I put it?—admirable. Pure and wholesome and old-fashioned in her approach to magic. Flower petals and healing potions and goddesses and all that. And if that's her thing, fine, I respect that. But I'm very worried that her approach isn't going to stop what's coming."

"What's that?"

"The Antima revolution."

"Revolution?" Binx repeated. Was the girl serious? "I mean, the Antima are disgusting and evil, sure, and they absolutely need to be stopped. But this isn't like . . . you know . . . the French Revolution or the American Revolution or whatever. The Antima aren't starting a *war* against witches."

"Actually, I think they are," Div said. "Have you read any of their stuff on social media? They hate us, and they feed off each other's rage. They spread lies about us and act like *we're* the ones who are organizing a revolution to take over. And their power is growing. So is their violence toward witches. You heard what happened to that witch in Texas, right? I heard there are other incidents like that, too, but the witches don't report it because they're afraid to go to the police; they're afraid of getting arrested. And do you know about all the mysterious pet disappearances lately? Dozens of cases in New York and California and Texas. *I* believe those are familiars being taken by Antima. And that it's only a matter of time before pets—familiars—start disappearing here in Washington State."

Binx hadn't heard about the unreported witch beatings or the missing animals. It all made her feel queasy. And scared. And angry. "Continue. I'm listening."

"The Antima haven't killed any witches *yet*. That we know of. But it's going to happen, and we need to stop it—stop *them*—before it gets to that point. That's why I need your help."

"Me? How can *I* help?"

"By joining my coven. And convincing Ridley to join, too, if you think she might be open to it. I'm not sure about Greta," Div said, almost as an afterthought. "But yes, maybe if you and Ridley join, Greta will come to her senses and realize that we need to take extreme measures . . . extreme magical measures, not pretty little flower petal potions . . . to put an end to the Antima. And if I can get Iris and Penelope, too, then we'd have eight witches. Imagine the power we could generate against the Antima, casting group spells with eight witches!"

Binx switched her phone from one ear to the other. "Put an end to the Antima *how*?"

"I'm not talking about *killing* Antima members, if that's what you're worried about. We're better than that. I'm talking about using our craft to change them. Inventing some crazy-powerful group spell, like memory-erase combined with mind-control combined with . . . I'm not sure yet. Something fantastic, something that will force the Antima to stop hating and hurting witches." Div added, "We can start with the Antima at our school, and work our way up from there. And we can inspire other witches across the country to do the same."

Binx didn't respond right away. She realized that she had jumped to her feet, that she had goose bumps, that she was actually *excited* by Div's idea. Which was weird. This was *Div*. Still, the leader of the Triad had managed to come up with an interesting (and possibly effective) plan to defeat the Antima.

"Okay. I'm not going to say I'm not intrigued, but . . ."

"But?"

"I can't do that to Greta. I mean, don't get me wrong. She and I, we don't always get along, and we're really different people." *Understatement.* "But it seems super-disloyal to bail on her and switch to another coven. Especially when it's—" Binx hesitated.

"I know. *My* coven. Greta and I aren't exactly BFFs."

"Yup."

Binx didn't voice her *other* concern, which was that she'd be forced to be coven-mates with Mira and Aysha. She couldn't imagine working side by side with them, even if it *was* for an important goal like taking down the Antima.

Although *something* had to be done about the Antima, obviously. She was thinking more and more that Libertas might be the answer.

"Will you at least think about it?" Div was asking her.

"Yeah, but I'm not going to change my mind. Sorry."

"We'll talk again."

Div ended the call.

Wow. Binx shook her head slowly. She was definitely not going to tell Greta about this. She couldn't. There was already so much tension between them and the Triad, plus now there were the two new witches to fight over, not counting Ms. O'Shea (because that would be weird). Meanwhile, they all needed to focus on smoking out whoever had penned those shadow messages and also figuring out who'd enchanted them with the numbers. They couldn't afford to get distracted by Div's takeover attempt.

Although . . . hadn't Binx herself told Greta that they needed to think about the big picture and not just focus on their little coven? That conversation from lunchtime still irked her. Also, how dare Greta question Binx's judgment re: ShadowKnight and Libertas? Did Greta think she was a total and complete newb?

A breeze rustled the leaves and flowers of a nearby blueblossom bush.

No, not a breeze. There was someone . . . no, something . . . hiding in there.

What the—

Before Binx could react, the thing charged at her. She shrieked and stumbled backward. Her ginger ale splattered everywhere, including on her new pink sweater with the smiling panda bear face and the words HELLO PANDA HAPPINESS on it. Whatever it was, it was four-legged. Was it a coyote or a bobcat or a fox or a . . .

As she regained her balance, she saw what it was.

A dog. A scruffy brown dog. A puppy, actually.

It skidded to a stop in front of her, paws every which way, and dropped something at her feet.

A dead crow.

"Okay, no. That's gross. That is so so so gross. I'm calling your owner . . . who *is* your owner?" Binx dabbed at her ginger-ale-soaked sweater with the back of her hand.

The mutt looked up at her and barked. It didn't appear to be wearing a collar. It dog-smiled at her with its tongue hanging out. Its tail wagged like an out-of-control windshield wiper.

"Yeah, this is not cool. Do you hear me? *Not cool.* Ugh!"

Shaking her head, Binx began scrolling and typing. "Okay, pupster. I'm guessing you belong to the neighbors down the hill. Uxie, please GPS them and cross-check the street address against the phone directory . . . and the Sorrow Point real-estate sale records . . . and the county deeds office and . . . *gotcha!*" Binx nodded as a name and address flashed across the screen. "All right, mini-dog. You must belong to the Noonan family at 1928 Cliffside Drive. A landline—what are they, like, ninety years old? I'm calling them right now, okay? And then you and your, uh, dead poultry friend are out of here."

The puppy panted happily and nudged the crow with its nose. The bird flipped over; its glossy black feathers were flecked with blood. *Ew.*

Binx turned away and dialed the number. A woman's voice answered after three rings. "Hello?"

"Hi . . . I'm calling from the, uh, house up the road. Are you missing your dog? A puppy? Small, brown, kind of annoying?"

There was a silence. "We do not own a dog."

Click.

O-kay. Not very neighborly.

The puppy was barking again.

"Yes, yes, I hear you. So obviously, you belong to someone *else* in this neighborhood. Except, the only other houses around here are way over in *that* direction, and there's a lot of them, and I don't have time to . . .

I know! I'm going to take some photos of you and post them to some sites and— *WAH!*"

Binx's gaze dropped to the single black, bloody feather on the granite paver. What the hex? She spun around in a full three-sixty.

The dead crow was gone. Totally gone.

"Did you *eat* it? That is the grossest thing I've ever—"

Binx was interrupted by a dry flapping of wings. Startled, she glanced up and saw a bird watching her from the crook of a madrona tree. Glossy, black, flecked with blood.

It was the crow. The same crow that had been lying dead on the driveway a second ago.

What. The. Hex.

Binx glanced around—she was alone (except for the haunted crow and the clingy canine, of course). She took a photo of the crow and texted it to Greta and Ridley with an all-caps message:

I THINK I'M BEING STALKED BY A ZOMBIE CROW!!!!!

Then she got her wand, Kricketune, from her backpack and pointed it at the bird.

"*Repellare!*" she said, conjuring a repelling spell.

It didn't budge.

"*Repellare!*" she tried again.

It still didn't budge. Maybe a fire spell would scare it away?

She was just about to try out a new one she'd been practicing when her phone began buzzing. Likely Greta or Binx about the bloody crow photo.

"Just a sec!" she yelled at her phone.

And then she saw that it was a videochat request. From ShadowKnight.

OMG, finally! She quickly hit accept. "Hey! *Hi!*"

The screen was momentarily black as the buffering icon spun and swirled. A second later, ShadowKnight's image appeared—fuzzy at first, then almost intact.

"Hey, Pokedragon2946."

"Hey, ShadowKnight4811! I left you like a gadzillion messages."

"I know. Sorry."

ShadowKnight was cute in an intense, brooding sort of way. His brown hair fell to his chin, and he had the fuzzy beginnings of a beard and mustache.

Now she tried to make out the background behind him. His bedroom? Some other room? Or was he outside? His face was superimposed on a bland, mottled collage of light and dark—and something that could be a window or maybe a glimpse of actual sky—so it was hard to tell.

"Are you okay?" Binx asked him.

"Yeah, not really. I got into a humongous fight with the parental units because my dad found my grimoire under my bed."

"What? No!"

"I told him it was for my art history homework, but I don't think he believed me. They took away my computer and phone for a month."

"Then how are you calling me?"

ShadowKnight shrugged and grinned. "I have my ways. So how are *you* doing?"

"Well, at the moment, I'm engaged in a death-duel with a zombie crow, and I don't mean one of the ones in *Witchworld*."

"Zombie crow?"

"Yeah, kind of. I found this dead crow in my driveway, or I thought it was dead, and then it came back to life."

ShadowKnight laughed. "Maybe it wasn't really dead to begin with? Crows are smart; they can fake you out."

"I didn't know that." Binx glanced up at the madrona tree. The crow was gone. The puppy was still there, though, sniffing at the ground. "Cancel the emergency. The zombie crow has returned to its underworld lair or whatever."

"Whew, close call. Well done, Pokedragon."

"Thanks, ShadowKnight. Anyway, so . . . wow! We have a *lot* to talk about!"

ShadowKnight leaned closer to the videocamera and spoke up. "I know. Listen, before we get to anything else, I wanted to ask you for your help on something. Something Libertas-related. It's kind of urgent."

"Sure, anything! I wanted to talk to you about Libertas, anyway."

"Yeah? Great. And once again, this is top secret. I shouldn't even be discussing it with you, but I totally trust you, and you're already kind of a Libertas member in spirit. So." ShadowKnight glanced over his shoulder. "You've probably heard that President Ingraham is working on a new initiative with Congress. It's a bill to increase enforcement of 6-129 and seek maximum sentences. The rumor is that he's planning on signing it into law during a big ceremony next month, on the anniversary of Callixta Crowe's death. Well, *we're* going to be there, too. We're going to march on Washington, DC, to oppose it, and we're going to present the White House with a *new* law we wrote that repeals 6-129, prevents his other law from happening, and protects the civil rights of witches."

Binx gasped. "Are you serious? That sounds . . . *epic!* And really, really dangerous. Aren't you guys worried about the Antima showing up? And the police, too, and the FBI? What if the president orders all of you to be arrested?"

"Of course there are risks. But we need to take a stand." ShadowKnight nodded to himself, then continued. "So here's what we need from you. You know about Callixta's descendant who posted her book and that letter, right? Well, we've learned that she or he isn't the only Callixta descendant who's still alive. There are others, and we're in the process of trying to find out who they are and where they live—including the letter writer. We think that if we can have some of them with us at the march, it will really help legitimize our cause. Anyway, I kind of designed a magical genealogy app to try to find these descendants. It's super-glitchy, though, and I was wondering if you'd take a look. The group really wants to find some Callixta descendants before the march so they can stand with us in Washington."

Binx felt goose bumps again. "Yeah, of course! I can do that, no problem."

"Awesome. Thanks." ShadowKnight glanced over his shoulder again. "Oh, great . . . there's a car in the driveway. I think it's my dad. I'd better go. I'll send you my app within the hour, through our usual server. Maybe we could chat again this weekend?"

Binx had so many other things she wanted to discuss with him. But it would have to wait. "Definitely. Bye, ShadowKnight."

"Bye, Pokedragon. Stay safe."

"You, too."

She ended the session and peered around. Now the puppy was gone, too. (Maybe it finally went back to its owner?) As she picked up her backpack and headed into the house, her mind churned and raced.

Her back-to-back conversations with Div and ShadowKnight seemed destined to be, somehow. The more she thought about it, the more she realized that Div was right. The Antima movement was growing, and the prospect of more violence against witches (and against their familiars, too?) was really scary. (For the first time ever, Binx was happy she hadn't found her familiar yet.)

Binx *had* to get involved. She needed to help hit the delete button on the Antima . . . and on the anti-witchcraft law (*laws*, plural, if the super-bigoted president had his way).

Binx cast a quick *obex* spell on the front door, then went up the stairs to her room, two at a time. She would treat herself to some *Witchworld* to unwind, then jump into her new C-Squared–related assignment from ShadowKnight (as well as her other assignment, from Greta, researching potential other witches at their school).

Things were happening. Shifting. Changing.

Forget about the Antima revolution . . . Binx felt like she was getting swept up in a *witch* revolution.

And she liked it.

18

PUMPKIN SPICE AND EVERYTHING NICE

Truth spells and potions are sometimes not
as potent as speaking straight from the heart.

(FROM *THE GOOD BOOK OF MAGIC AND MENTALISM*
BY CALLIXTA CROWE)

"Wow. This *is* amazing," Ridley said, taking a sip of her pumpkin spice latte. "Why have I never had one of these?"

She and Penelope were sitting across from each other at a table on the Starbucks patio. Penelope had gone home first to get her dog, Socrates; now the big white poodle lay at her feet, sleeping and snoring quietly. The late afternoon sun barely broke through the clouds, and it was definitely sweater weather; in fact, they were the only customers hanging out outside. *And* Ridley had forgotten to wear a sweater (or jacket or hoodie) to school today.

Still, she was just happy being with Penelope.

"It's how I kick off the season every year," Penelope explained, taking a sip of her latte.

"You mean fall? That's still a few weeks away."

"I mean *the* season. The long celebration season. For me, it starts on the first day these are back on the menu, and goes through Halloween, Thanksgiving, Christmas, and New Year's. After that I take a little break, and then I have a whole bunch of other traditions for Valentine's Day and the first day of spring and Easter."

Ridley laughed. "I guess you're really into holidays."

"Oh yeah. Big-time. You should come to my house at Halloween. I spend, like, *weeks* turning our front yard into a psychedelic graveyard filled with ghosts and zombies."

"Nice!"

Ridley took another sip of her drink and set it down slowly. What should she do now? After the big . . . whatever-that-was with the two covens and Iris and Penelope at lunch, Greta had pulled Ridley aside and given her explicit instructions: to accept Penelope's offer to go out for coffee, find out if she was, in fact a witch, and—if so—invite her to join their coven. Greta was convinced that Div was trying to recruit Iris and Penelope to *her* coven, and she wanted to get there first. Ridley knew that Greta didn't approve of Div's form of magic, and that she wanted all witches to practice *her* way, which was 100 percent Callixta. Natural, creative, nurturing. Love and light.

But sometimes, Ridley wished they'd stop it with their rivalry. Honestly, couldn't they just put their differences aside and help each other—support each other?

Ridley watched Penelope as she bent down and offered a piece of her blueberry scone to Socrates. So Penelope was a witch. Or she was *probably* a witch . . . the only "evidence" they had so far was Div's apparent belief that she was one of them. But she *could* be. Was that why Ridley had been drawn to her yesterday in history? Had Ridley's inner witchness sensed Penelope's inner witchness? Was that even possible?

She and Binx and Greta had *not* found each other via witchness radar. Instead, one evening last September, Ridley had spotted a couple of bullies in the park, beating up on a smaller kid. The park appeared to be deserted, so she'd hidden behind the swing set and brandished Paganini, to stop them. But then she'd spotted Binx behind the slides, doing the same with a video-game console (Kricketune) and Greta behind the monkey bars with a fountain pen (Flora). Afterward, the three witches had carefully, tentatively walked up to each other in the middle of the park, and Greta had introduced herself and invited Binx and Ridley to come to her house for a pot of rose-hip tea and carrot muffins, then burst into (happy) tears and hugged them both.

Thankfully, no one needed magical rescuing on the Starbucks patio at the moment. So how was Ridley going to suss out if Penelope was a witch or not?

"Colter seems nice," Ridley blurted out. *Smooth.* She was supposed to steer the conversation toward witches, not boyfriends.

Penelope nodded and touched something on her right wrist peeking out from under her sleeve; it was a silver charm bracelet with a single heart charm.

"He's *super*-nice. His family's nice, too."

"That's nice." Hadn't Penelope just said that? *Dumb.* "Soooo . . . what are they like?"

"Mr. Jessup's a real-estate developer. Dr. Jessup's a pediatrician. Colter's got an older brother, Hunter, who's at the university, and two little sisters, Cassie and Caitlin. They're twins, fourth grade, and they're *way* into rainbow hair and making music videos of themselves." Penelope grinned and added, "They're kind of obsessed with my YouTube channel, even though their mom said they can't wear makeup until they're in middle school."

"Cute."

"I know. The whole family's super-close. I wish my family was like that. I mean, don't get me wrong! My parents are great. But my dad's always traveling for his work, and my mom has a stressful job, too—she has her own PR firm—so we don't do a lot of stuff together. Plus, I wish I had a sister or brother. Do you have any? Sisters or brothers, I mean?"

"I have a little sister. Harmony. She's four, almost five. And, um . . ."

Ridley hesitated, wondering if she should mention Daniel. *Nope, bad idea.* She'd never even told Binx, or Greta, or anyone else in Sorrow Point. She didn't want to jeopardize her true identity. More than that, it was too hard to talk about, and she'd come to believe that if you didn't bring up certain matters, or think about them even, then you could make them go away.

But. There was something about Penelope. A deep, warm, sunshiny kindness. For the first time in a long time, Ridley found herself wanting to connect, to be vulnerable, to reveal herself to another person.

She dropped her gaze. "I have an older brother. I mean, I *had.*"

"Had?"

"He, um, died. When I was in eighth grade."

"Oh my gosh, I'm so sorry!"

Penelope jumped to her feet, rushed to Ridley's side, and wrapped her arms around her in a fierce hug. Such a tidal wave of emotions hit Ridley—relief, gratitude, grief, sorrow—that she felt as though she might pass out.

And from somewhere within the tidal wave, a small, shimmering voice rose up.

"I'm a witch," she whispered.

Penelope didn't let go. "So am I," she whispered back.

The two of them stayed like that for a long time, holding each other, not saying a word. There would be plenty of time for conversations later. And Ridley hadn't told Penelope *all* her secrets. It was enough to come out as one thing at a time. For right now, the moment was exactly right—not in a happy way or a romantic way, but in a necessary way. A new beginning.

Ridley began to cry. Penelope hugged her harder.

Under the table, Socrates leaned against the girls' legs with a quiet sigh.

It was almost six o'clock by the time Ridley said goodbye to Penelope and Socrates at the intersection of Lilac Street and Coyote Drive, just inside the Seabreeze development. The two girls promised to have lunch together tomorrow, just the two of them, and to meet up over the weekend, too.

Ridley was dizzy with wonder from their talk . . . and also exhausted, spent, weak. She wanted to go home and curl up in bed and sleep for a month. She'd told Penelope about Daniel. They'd revealed their witch identities to each other. They'd told each other about their discovery moments (Ridley's at age ten, when she'd wished for long, beautiful hair and it had spontaneously happened; Penelope's when she was fourteen, when she'd wished for a dog and Socrates had shown up at her doorstep at that same instant). Ridley had told her about Greta and Binx being witches, too, and asked Penelope to think about joining their coven. Penelope had said yes before Ridley even finished her sentence.

They had a lot more to discuss at lunch tomorrow and this weekend and beyond. For now, though, Ridley had to hurry; around 5:15, Daddy had texted that he was leaving work soon and picking up pizza for dinner. By her calculations (he had to finish out his shift, drive from the hospital to Ned's Pizza, pick up the pizza, then drive home), she had about ten more minutes, depending on if he'd remembered to call Ned's with the order first, which was a toss-up with him. She also tried to guess his driving route; he'd likely take Pine, not Laguna, because of traffic.

She couldn't risk running into him. (Yes, there was always a memory-erase spell, but what if it didn't work?) Momma she didn't have to worry about; she rarely left the house anymore. Likely, she was taking a nap in her room while Harmony watched TV.

Ridley eyed one of the still-under-construction McMansions on the street. Half of it was almost finished, at least on the outside, and the other half was just wooden frame. It was also set way back on the lot and out of the neighbors' sight lines. Perfect.

Glancing around, confirming that she was indeed alone, she strolled casually toward the more finished part of the house. She ducked behind what looked to be a future six-car garage.

Reaching into her backpack, she unzipped one of the compartments and pulled out a small black velvet pouch. She loosened the drawstring and shook out a piece of moldavite. The moldavite was a gemstone from the Bohemia region of the Czech Republic, and it was super-rare. Like all other moldavites, it was believed to have fallen from the sky in a meteor shower nearly fifteen million years ago. Which was pretty much the coolest thing ever, in Ridley's humble opinion.

The moldavite had been a gift from her aunt Viola, the other witch in the Stone family (that Ridley knew of, anyway). It was Aunt Viola who'd recognized Ridley's powers when she was ten (she'd accidentally witnessed Ridley's discovery moment with the hair, and helped her reverse it before Daddy and Momma found out), and it was Aunt Viola who'd taught her her first spells. (Back in Cleveland, Aunt Viola had belonged to a small coven that possessed a dozen or so torn, faded pages from Callixta's book.)

Ridley held the translucent green gem against her heart and closed her eyes. Aunt Viola had told her that moldavite was a powerful aid in transformation rituals.

"Muto," she said softly.

Nothing.

Focus on your intention, she reminded herself. Which was not easy, since part of her—a *big* part of her—didn't *want* to transform.

But she had no choice. She hated, *hated,* the twice-daily transformations—each time, the ritual brought up the gut-wrenching pain of the past, of living as someone else—but it was necessary until she perfected a permanent form of the *muto* spell, *vertero,* which would substitute for medicines and surgery. And *dissimulatio,* also an advanced perception spell, way beyond what *calumnia* could do; there was an incomplete entry about it in Callixta Crowe's book, and Ridley had been working in her spare time to fill in the gaps. Once she'd perfected it and *vertero,* too, she would be able to live as her true self twenty-four seven but still appear as Morgan to her family. Some people couldn't see the truth, anyway.

"Muto!" she repeated, more loudly. *"MU-TO!"*

The third incantation did the trick. The muscles in her neck began straining and pulling as her Adam's apple expanded. Her scalp tightened as her long, beautiful curls grew shorter and settled into a neatly trimmed 'fro. Her small breasts sank into her chest, becoming even more invisible under her white button-down shirt. The Crimson Secret polish vanished from her fingertips, leaving them bare.

She touched her upper lip and felt the bristly shadow of a mustache, which made her grimace. Her fingers grazed her cheeks; the skin was rougher, coarser, with tiny bumps. The fat in her body had shifted, too. And . . .

Enough. She didn't want to go through the full checklist in her head; she just wanted to get on with it. Her sad metamorphosis was complete. She could go home.

But just as she was about to leave her hiding spot, her phone lit up with a message.

It was a group text from Greta to her and Binx:

Gofflesby is missing.

19

TRANSCENDING TIME

Your Familiar is not your Familiar forever.
One can lose a beloved spirit companion
to Death or other partings.

(FROM *THE GOOD BOOK OF MAGIC AND MENTALISM*
BY CALLIXTA CROWE)

Greta wandered through her house aimlessly, chewing on her thumbnail and trying to still the wild trembling of her hands. Upstairs, downstairs, and back up again. She cast fleeting glances at every corner of every room, under furniture, on top of furniture, but nothing registered. She felt blind, helpless, powerless; Gofflesby had disappeared, and she had no idea, not a single clue, where he might be. Standing on the second-floor landing, she clasped the raw amethyst pendant. But it, too, seemed lifeless—it offered no vision, no inspiration, not even a sliver of comfort. She *was* useless as a witch.

Tears stung her eyes. She covered her face with her hands.

Don't cry. You're not useless. You have to stay strong. Gofflesby needs you.

The smell of black-bean-and-sweet-potato chili wafted from the kitchen. Her mother, making dinner. Greta swiped at her eyes, took a deep breath, and headed downstairs.

Teo was on the family computer in the living room, playing *Roblox*.

"I didn't let her out," he said without taking his eyes off the screen.

"*Him*. I know you didn't. When was the last time you saw him, though?"

"Dunno. This morning? He was in my room scratching up my closet door again, bad kitty. *Oh no you don't!*" he shouted at a two-headed green zombie moving across the screen.

A lavender candle flickered on the coffee table next to a pile of petitions and voter-registration pamphlets. In the window, the last light of the day caught on the crystal suncatcher and broke into rainbow-colored shards across the old oak floor.

Gofflesby, where are you?

"Greta?"

Ysabel poked her head through the doorway, ladle in hand. "Dinner in five minutes. Don't worry, honey, he'll be back. He probably snuck outside through the bathroom window—I've been meaning to tell the darned landlord to fix that screen."

Greta closed her eyes briefly, trying to discern if the juxtaposition of *Gofflesby* and *bathroom window* resonated. Nothing. Also, *outside* made no sense. He rarely went out. And he was sick.

"I bet he went to one of the neighbors' houses," her mother went on. "That's what happened when I was about your age and our cat, Boots, escaped. He was an indoor cat, too. We found him at Mrs. Zakarian's down the street; he'd gone right into her house and helped himself to a bowl of dog food! He's lucky their shepherd didn't eat *him*."

"Mama! Don't even *say* that!" Greta cried out.

"Sorry, sorry. I'm just trying to . . . I guess I'm not being very helpful."

The front door opened and her father, Tomas, walked in, mopping his brow with a handkerchief. "It got humid all of a sudden. So I walked up and down our street, but no sign of him. I checked the garage and shed, too, in case he was hiding. Listen, Bug, we can make flyers after dinner and pass them around to all the houses." Her father's nickname for her was "Ladybug," which often got shortened to either "Lady" or "Bug."

Her father said something else, but Greta wasn't listening. She was rewinding back to when she'd last seen Gofflesby, in case the memory might trigger clues. This morning, before school. She'd woken up early and filled the upstairs bathroom with eucalyptus steam; it was something her mother had done for her when she had bronchitis. Greta had sat down on the bathroom rug and cradled Gofflesby in her lap, encouraging him to breathe. She'd gently stroked his ears, the way he liked, and told him a Chinese folktale about a woman who'd woven a beautiful tapestry, only to have it stolen by fairies, and about the magical journey her three sons had to undertake to recover the lost tapestry. Gofflesby's emerald eyes had never left her face, and he'd coughed only once the entire time, which seemed like progress. Greta had promised him that they would repeat this ritual every morning and every night, too, until his respiratory infection was totally gone.

She'd also recited a spell of protection to him—a poem—one of her favorites from Callixta's book:

> Goddess of the wild Beasts
> Watch over this familiar
> Favor him with winds from the East
> Take your magic brand of peculiar
> And bless his soul

Keep him safe from harm
Help him feel control
And lots of charm

That was the last time she or anyone else in the family had seen him, except maybe Teo with his story about the closet door.

"Gofflesby, come back to me," Greta prayed out loud.

Only silence greeted her.

For a brief, awful moment, it occurred to Greta that his disappearance might be connected to the shadow message she received yesterday morning. Did the words *you and your kind* mean familiars as well as witches? But she couldn't go to such a dark, dark place in her mind. The Antima couldn't possibly want to hurt an innocent cat.

Could they?

By morning, Gofflesby still hadn't returned. Greta had stayed up most of the night, trying *sortis* and every other finding and scrying spell she could think of. A chaotic assortment of candles, gemstones, herbs, and flower petals covered her floor. She'd fallen asleep just before dawn—fully dressed, her face pressed against her grimoire, her wand, Flora, clasped in her right hand, and Gofflesby's favorite toy clasped in her left.

That day, Greta didn't go to school (her mother called the attendance office to say she had a migraine). Her father drove her over to the SPCA to see if Gofflesby might have shown up there (he hadn't). They also made another sweep through the neighborhood and passed out more flyers.

"He'll be back," Ysabel kept reassuring her. "He's a smart little guy. He'll find his way home."

But Greta wasn't so sure.

Binx and Ridley had been texting her every few hours to check in. They were coming over after school to try some group scrying rituals.

Around lunchtime, Greta received a new text from Ridley:

Is he back?

Greta replied:

No.

I'm sorry. Don't worry, we'll find him. Power of three!

Can you ask Iris to come, too? Power of four would be even better, and she knows about you and Binx. Or five—what about Penelope? You guys talked, right?

Yes. She confirmed that's she's like us. But she's not in school today.

Is she sick?

I don't know. I texted her a couple of times this morning, but she didn't text back.

Just ask Iris, then, okay?

What about Div and Aysha and Mira?

Greta hesitated.

> Maybe later, if we need them. I'm feeling too raw to deal with them right now.

Especially not Div, Greta thought.

> Got it.

A short while later, Ridley texted again:

> Iris said yes. I still haven't heard from Penelope. It's kind of weird.

> She probably turned her phone off.

> I guess so. Anyway the three of us will be over soon. We'll find him!

Later that afternoon, Ridley, Binx, and Iris showed up at Greta's house, holding various packages.

"Any sign of Gofflesby?" Ridley asked immediately as Greta let them in.

"No, not yet."

Iris hugged Greta; her hair smelled like strawberry shampoo. She held up a paper bag. "I brought you some chocolate-chip cookies. Chocolate-chip cookies always make me feel better when I'm stressed, which is basically all the time. They're a thousand percent vegan. Wait, can something be a thousand percent? Is that even a thing?"

"I don't know, but . . . thanks, Iris. This is really sweet of you. Hi, Binx."

"Hey." Binx crossed her arms over her chest and gave a chin-nod. She seemed more subdued than usual. Maybe she was still upset about their argument? But Greta couldn't handle a reprise of that right now—all her energy, mental and otherwise, was taken up by Gofflesby. Maybe the two of them could have a heart-to-heart later, after he'd returned.

"Hey, Greta?" Binx said. "Did you think any more about the . . ."

"The what?" Greta prompted her.

"Never mind. Not important. Come on, let's go find your little furball."

"Yes, let's."

They had to focus on Gofflesby. Greta led the girls upstairs and into her room, where she'd already set up for the magical ritual. Behind them, she closed the door and turned the lock. Her father was at the bookstore, and her mother had taken Teo to his therapy appointment, but she wanted the sense of privacy as well as the sense of security.

"Wow. This is your room!" Iris exclaimed. She swept her arm in a wide arc and accidentally bumped her hand against the dresser. "*Ow!* False alarm, I'm totally fine. Is that a dream catcher above your bed?"

"Yes, although it doesn't get much use."

"What do you mean?"

"I'll tell you later. Okay, so we need to cast a circle. Binx, did you bring your Pokémon cards?" Greta suddenly felt motivated, efficient; her witches were here, and Iris, too, and there was business to be done.

Binx held up her deck. "Need you ask?"

"Do you have more of Gofflesby's hair? We could add that to the ritual," Ridley suggested.

"Of course, I almost forgot."

Greta hurried over to her dresser, picked up Gofflesby's grooming brush, and pulled away a soft, fragile nest of golden fur. The look and feel of it derailed her for a second, made the tears well up again . . . but she took a deep breath and centered herself.

"Have you tried *sortis* yet?" Iris asked Greta, who nodded. "Okay, well . . . whenever Jadora's familiar, Baxxtern, goes missing, she uses this special spell to find him. I could look it up for you; I think it's called Location Lock."

"Yeah, but that one's not as good as Transcend Time," Binx replied.

"True! Wow, so you play *Witchworld*, too?"

"Yeah, a little."

"Nice!"

The four witches sat down in a circle. Greta briefly explained to Iris about the calling of the quarters, since this was her first time. She handed Iris pieces of amber, tiger's eye, white-quartz, and lapis lazuli to use to correspond with the fire, earth, air, and water elements.

Iris handed back the lapis lazuli. "I've got the water element covered. I have this!" She touched her smiley-face moonstone pendant.

"Wonderful!" Greta said.

After calling the quarters, they began the spell. Greta had closed the curtains and dimmed the lights. A dozen candles flickered in the half darkness. Amethyst, rose quartz, and other crystals had been arranged inside the circle along with her scrying bowl. Greta didn't always use the scrying bowl, which was actually one of her mother's black pewter soup bowls; sometimes she preferred to use the vintage mirror she'd picked up at a garage sale instead. Or neither. She often made her choice based on a gut feeling, and today, her gut was telling her to use the bowl.

Now she held Gofflesby's fur a few inches above the bowl. She noticed Iris watching her every move intently, as though memorizing the steps.

In a quiet voice, Greta recited her own version of a time-transcending spell:

Dear Goddess who watches over what is lost
Cast your glance across the universe, let the hours rewind

Land, sea, sky, fire, moon, sun
Return to me my familiar whom I must find.

"Love and light," she added under her breath.

She repeated the spell a second time as the others tried to follow along. By the third time, they were able to join in.

When they'd finished, silence resonated through the air. The water inside the bowl was very still. Greta closed her eyes and drew in the energy of the group to help her see whatever answers the Goddess might offer.

Something told her to open her eyes. When she did, she saw that the water inside the scrying bowl was slowly changing color: from clear to blue to green to red to clear again. It had never done that before. What was happening? She held her breath, afraid and excited at the same time.

Binx and Ridley and Iris were staring intently at the water, too. Iris's jaw had practically dropped to the floor.

This magic was new, different, more intense.

"Gofflesby, is that you?" Greta whispered.

The surface of the water trembled, and a second later, a cloudy image began to form. It dispersed, drew together, dispersed again, drew together again.

It was an image of a house. Actually, a half-built house, part wood frame and part stucco walls, with stacks of lumber and piles of gravel strewn across the bare brown yard. A red pickup truck was parked nearby.

"Do you see Gofflesby? Is he there?" Iris asked eagerly. "I'm sorry, are we allowed to talk during . . . I don't know the rules . . . Okay, I'll shut up now. Sorry, sorry, sorry!"

"It's okay." Greta leaned over and studied the watery image. Worry furrowed her brow. "I don't see him. Do any of you guys recognize this place? I don't."

Ridley leaned closer, too. "I'm not sure, but there's a new development near my house, and a bunch of the houses look like that. They're under construction, I mean. Although I suppose there's lots of houses under construction in Sorrow Point?"

The water began to tremble again, and the unfinished stucco house trembled along with it. Then grew smaller. Then exploded into a rainbow of colors. It was insane, like magic on steroids.

An animal darted in front of the psychedelic house. A cat. A golden cat.

Greta gasped. "Gofflesby?"

The cat stopped and blinked at her with its emerald eyes.

The image vanished, and the water was still again.

"Gofflesby!" Greta cried out.

She jumped to her feet and glanced around wildly, as though her familiar might materialize right then and there. Fresh tears spilled down her cheeks.

She felt a gentle hand on her arm. It was Binx.

"Come on. We're going to go find that house."

20

DEATH AND THE MAIDEN

A spell or other Magical action can be rendered
ineffective in many ways: an inadequacy of
intention; ambivalence or fear; a more
powerful Magical action or presence;
or simple bad luck.

(FROM *THE GOOD BOOK OF MAGIC AND MENTALISM*
BY CALLIXTA CROWE)

The sun had begun to set by the time Iris and the other three girls reached the Seabreeze development. In the distance, down the hill, the lights of downtown Sorrow Point twinkled on as the sky over Puget Sound turned pink, then purple.

Using some magical apps on her phone (before today, Iris had never *heard* of such things), Binx had hacked into the Sorrow Point City Hall records to find current building permits for new houses. She'd turned up forty of them, all in Seabreeze, on eight new streets that extended across a hundred-acre lot. The only other building permits on file had been for an apartment complex near the hospital, a new dorm at the university, and some sort of wellness retreat on the outskirts of the city.

Now, walking down an eerily deserted street (no people, no pets, no cars, just the skeletons of future homes and a single streetlight) with Greta and Ridley and Binx, Iris was nervous. Granted, she was *always* nervous, but this was a different kind of nervous. For one thing, she'd never engaged in a mystery-solving adventure through a strange, eerily empty neighborhood in search of a missing familiar that had communicated to them via scrying bowl. Maybe in *Witchworld*, sure, but not IRL.

And for another thing, her SPD was starting to kick in. Her clothes itched, and her eyes felt hot, and the evening breeze grated painfully against her skin. Greta's voice, calling out for Gofflesby, sounded like a series of mini-explosions.

"Gofflesby? Where are you?" Greta shouted, over and over again.

Iris covered her ears.

"I don't see any houses that look like the one we saw in the scrying bowl," Greta said, chewing on her thumbnail as she glanced this way and that.

"We have a bunch more streets to go." Ridley spoke up. "I walk here on my way home from school sometimes, so I kind of know the area. Kind of."

"What about that red pickup truck? That was part of the vision, too. If we can find it, then we should be able to find the house, right?" Binx pointed out.

Greta nodded. "The red pickup truck . . . right! Ridley, have you ever seen a red pickup truck around here?"

"Umm . . . not that I remember. But this is a pretty big development, so . . ."

Soon, they turned the corner onto another deserted street. There were no streetlights at all, and the block ahead seemed even gloomier than the previous one.

Binx pulled something out of her backpack and pointed it at the ground. Iris was confused; it looked like a gaming console.

"Malorna!" Binx called out. "My wand," she explained to Iris.

"So cool!" Iris replied.

As Binx's gaming-console-slash-wand cast a bright circle of light on the pavement, Iris pulled her own wand out of her backpack. *"Maloona!"*

"Malorna," Binx corrected her.

"Oops. *Malorna!"*

An even larger and brighter circle of light lit up the pavement.

"Wait, why is your light bigger? Did you use a hack?" Binx asked curiously.

"A hack?"

"Yeah, a hack. As in, a shortcut to achieve—"

"We can debate about hacks later. Come on, we need to find Gofflesby!" Greta interrupted.

She and Ridley illuminated their wands, too, and the four girls hurried down the street.

"Gofflesby, where are you? Come back to me."

Still no answer. Greta's lower lip trembled. Iris could sense the distress radiating from her—even the light from her wand dimmed.

A strange whirring noise cut through the stillness. Binx reached into her pocket and held up her phone; today's case was an orange dragon, which Iris recognized as Nyala's favorite Pokémon, Charizard.

"This is weird. My security-alert enchantment is vibrating like crazy."

"Your what?" Greta asked.

"It's an enchantment I put on my phone to warn me if something's up. It's like off the charts. But that doesn't make sense because I disabled it, like, two days ago. Why is it doing that? *Why are you doing that?*" Binx asked her phone. "I wonder if there might be a—you know, like a malevolent magical presence nearby. Something that woke up my enchantment."

Greta stood a little straighter. Her distress had sharpened and became something else. Resolve.

"Formation," she said quietly.

Without a word, Binx and Ridley flanked Greta on either side. The three of them turned so their backs were to each other, their wands directed toward the north, east, and west. They reminded Iris of *The Last Jedi* when Kylo Ren and Rey had positioned themselves that way and fought off a rushing hive of Praetorian Guards, just the two of them. Except Greta and Ridley and Binx were three.

Greta locked eyes with Iris. Iris understood. She quickly joined the formation and directed her wand toward the south. Now they were four.

"I wish Penelope were here," Ridley whispered.

"Lights out," said Greta.

The four witches darkened their wands. They waited, barely breathing. The only sound was the vibration of Binx's security alert.

A cool breeze stirred, carrying with it the scent of pine needles and sawdust and . . . something else. Iris's senses, including her sense of smell, were on overdrive. What *was* that smell? Was it roses?

"Guys, there's the red truck!"

Binx had turned her wandlight back on and was pointing it down the block. A vehicle was parked on the street next to a construction site—the red pickup truck from the scrying bowl.

The girls began sprinting in that direction. As they ran, Binx's security alert grew more frenzied. Iris covered her ears again.

They soon reached the pickup truck. Just beyond it was an unfinished house—the stucco and wood frame one, the one from the vision.

"Gofflesby!" Greta shouted, arcing her wandlight in a wide sweep.

All of a sudden, soft music began to play. Piano music. It seemed to seep out the bones of the house and drift toward them.

Iris uncovered her ears. "Does anyone hear that?" she whispered.

"Yeah. What the hex? Is someone *in* there?" Binx replied.

"Maybe it's coming from somewhere else . . . you know, like a real house with real people in it," Iris said hopefully.

"I know that piece. It's by Schubert. 'Der Tod und das Mädchen,'" Ridley said, looking confused.

"Doesn't the word *tod* mean *death* in German?" Greta asked.

"Um, yeah. The translation is 'Death and the Maiden.'"

"What a *stupid* title for a song," Binx remarked.

"Death and the Maiden." A wave of dizziness swept over Iris. Tiny electric zaps buzzed at her brain.

"Iris?" Greta touched her arm.

A woman's voice joined in with the piano music. She sang in German, her words low and heavy.

"Seriously, where is that creepy caterwauling coming from?" Binx demanded.

From somewhere far away, a dog began howling mournfully. Iris squeezed her eyes shut. The electric zaps were more intense now. She felt sick, delirious. Her feet—had they been hypnotized? Enchanted?—began moving toward the house. The singer's voice and the piano music twined around each other and grew louder. The smell of roses was almost sickly sweet in its intensity.

Something—a force field? a magical barrier?—stopped Iris when she got close to the house. Greta and Ridley and Binx slammed into it, too. It wasn't transparent but manifested as a field of translucent gray, like some sort of mechanical fog.

"What *is* that?" Binx exclaimed. She stepped back and aimed her wand forward. *"Elido!"* she ordered.

Nothing happened.

Greta held out her wand, too. So did Ridley. So did Iris.

"Elido!" they all commanded at the same time.

It worked. Shards of gray light and shadow rained upon them, stinging and hissing. The four witches rushed up to a narrow opening in the Sheetrocked walls and shined their wandlights inside.

A person lay on the ground, eyes staring up blankly at the ceiling beams and the twilight sky. A young woman. A teenager.

A golden cat lay next to her.

"Gofflesby!" Greta shouted.

"Penelope!" Ridley, Binx, and Iris shouted at the same time.

Greta squeezed through the narrow opening and hurried inside. Binx, then Ridley, then Iris hurried in after her. The eerie German music swarmed at them and smothered their ears. The rose fragrance mingled with the smells of sawdust and roof tar.

Greta rushed over to Gofflesby and scooped him up with a cry. His eyelids fluttered, and he meowed weakly at her.

Ridley bent over Penelope and gently touched the side of her neck.

"Guys? She's . . ." Her voice caught in her throat. "Penelope's . . . dead."

Greta leaned forward, still cradling Gofflesby; he was awake now and blinking up at her. *"What?"*

"She's . . . oh my god . . ." Ridley's words dissolved into wild sobs. Binx wrapped her arms around her.

And then they all saw it at the same time.

A shadow message on the ground, near Penelope's body. The words, in glossy black ink, said:

YOU AND YOUR KIND DON'T BELONG HERE.

Then the words began to shimmer and fade away. A few seconds later, a new message emerged in curly script, the ink glittering and purple:

I'm so ashamed of who I am. Please
forgive me. Goodbye.

A suicide note?

The German song was fading to a close. *"Sollst sanft in meinen Armen schlafen!"* the invisible woman sang—except it wasn't a woman anymore, it was a man.

Iris knew a little German, too, from her old school. *Softly shall you sleep in my arms.*

Death was singing to the maiden.

Death had claimed poor Penelope. Death and who else?

Iris swayed, on the brink of fainting. She fell to her knees and grasped her smiley-face moon pendant. But its light was gone. The darkness had extinguished it . . . extinguished everything.

A crow sat above them on a ceiling beam, watching.

PART 2

A MURDER OF CROWS

A murder of crows is a poetic term that
describes a group of crows, like *a flock
of birds* or *a gaggle of geese*. The use
of the word *murder* here has several
interpretations. One interpretation
comes from a folktale that suggests that
crows will sometimes come together to
decide on the fate of a single crow—as
in, should it live or should it die?

(FROM THE GRIMOIRE OF DIVINITY FLORESCU)

21

SYSTEM CRASH

Someone is always watching.

(FROM *THE GOOD BOOK OF MAGIC AND MENTALISM*
BY CALLIXTA CROWE)

"Thank you for coming in to see me."

Mrs. Feathers, the school social worker, waved Iris and Greta and Binx into her office. They took the couch while she sat down on . . . was that a big old yoga ball? Weird.

Binx glanced around the room. The shelves were crammed with books that had titles like *The Power of Positivity* and *Dare to Dream* and *The Self-Esteem Workbook for Teens.* A bright yellow wall clock on the wall indicated that it was eight a.m. Another clock next to it had mood words instead of numbers. HAPPY, SAD, MAD, and so on. (CALM seemed to be in the eight o'clock space. *Yeah, no.*)

Binx wondered how old Mrs. Feathers was; it was hard to tell, with her grayish-blond hair and makeup-less face. Her mom's age, maybe? Or older? Or younger? Her frump-chic outfit screamed L.L.Bean outlet and grandma hand-me-downs. (The school social worker from last year had not been a fashionista, either, preferring cargo pants and T-shirts with sayings like YOU'VE GOT THIS!)

"Will your friend be joining us?" Mrs. Feathers glanced at a clip-boarded form on her lap. "Ridley Stone?"

"She's out sick today," Binx explained. She eyed the new doge back-pack at her feet—her phone was in there—but decided to wait. It probably wasn't cool to be texting in Mrs. Feathers's office. As soon as they were done with this group-therapy crisis-intervention sesh, though, she would send Ridley another text. The girl had been holed up at her house since Friday night, saying she had the flu or something and didn't want to be bothered. Binx had been checking in with her regularly all weekend but gotten no further responses. She was worried; she didn't buy the flu excuse for one second, and her best friend was obviously in bad shape.

Although who could blame her, considering? They were *all* in bad shape.

Except that Ridley and Penelope had grown close.

"Anyway, so . . . how are you girls holding up?" Mrs. Feathers asked kindly.

Iris reached into a brown ceramic bowl on top of Mrs. Feathers's desk and picked up a yellow M&M. She nibbled on the corner of it like a rabid chipmunk. "We're holding up, Mrs. Feathers. Actually, we're *not* holding up. Well, some of us may be holding up, but I'm definitely not holding up. That's kind of a strange expression, isn't it? Holding up? Anyhoo, I haven't slept much since the . . . and yeah, when I do sleep, I have these nightmares about demons attacking the school plus the entire country plus the entire planet. Plus the oceans turn into boiling-hot soup. And we all die and it's basically the Apocalypse. *The. End.* My mom made an emergency appointment with my new therapist—her name is Deanna

Ranger, Dee Ranger, and what kind of name is that for a therapist? Right? Dee Ranger, as in, Dee-Ranged? On Saturday. Her office smells like Dr Pepper and talcum powder." Iris paused and examined the yellow M&M dye on her fingers.

Greta touched Iris's arm gently and whispered something in her ear.

"True," Iris said, nodding.

Mrs. Feathers nodded, too. "Thank you so much for sharing that, Iris. I know it's not easy. There's a lot of trauma and grief happening in our community right now. Everyone here is trying to process Penelope's passing, and they didn't find . . . they didn't have a firsthand experience, like yourselves. Plus, I believe that Penelope was your friend?"

"Kind of. She seemed cool," Binx replied. "Ridley knew her a little better than the rest of us."

"Well, in any case, you're all very brave."

Greta nodded and wept quietly into her handkerchief. Iris took off her glasses and pinched and unpinched the bridge of her nose, then shook her head and began sobbing into a crumpled wad of tissues. Binx, on the other hand, was doing all she could *not* to cry. Crying was a waste of emotion. Crying made it more difficult to defeat the thing that was making you cry to begin with . . . which in this case was solving the mystery of Penelope's death.

They had called 911 that night and, when the police arrived, endured endless questioning. What were they doing in the Seabreeze development wandering through construction sites? How did they happen to find Penelope's body? Greta had told them that they'd been searching for Gofflesby. Ridley had explained that she lived nearby, and added the little white lie that she'd seen a cat resembling Gofflesby running around the neighborhood.

But . . . that suicide note. It had started out as a shadow message, identical to Greta and Div's—the same words, the same handwriting, the same color ink. Then, somehow, it had changed into a goodbye message in Penelope's curly script, and the black had changed to glittery purple.

No, not *somehow*. It was magic. And the freaky German singing and the bizarre energy barrier around the house must have been magic, too.

Which meant that a *witch* must have killed Penelope.

But why would a witch take the life of one of their own?

Also, why had Gofflesby been at Penelope's side? Or the crow with its beady, staring eyes? Binx wondered if it could be the same zombie crow from her driveway. No, it couldn't be. *Could* it?

At least Greta's cat was okay. She was apparently keeping him locked up in her bedroom with his food and toys and other cat stuff. She'd reported that, miraculously, he wasn't sick anymore; his respiratory infection seemed to be gone.

"That's right. Just let it out." Mrs. Feathers was nodding sympathetically at Greta and Iris as they dabbed at their eyes.

When the crying had subsided, Mrs. Feathers shifted and straightened on her yoga ball or whatever. "Are there any other feelings or insights you girls would like to share with me? How about you, Beatrix?"

Binx counted to ten in binary so as not to utter a swear at the mention of her full name. "No, thanks."

Greta sniffled and cleared her throat. "Have the police . . . Did they figure out . . . They asked us a bunch of questions that night, but I don't think we were very . . ."

Mrs. Feathers hesitated. "The school superintendent will be sending out an e-mail to all the parents in the district today. Penelope . . ." Her chin trembled slightly. "Penelope *did* take her own life. With poison. They think it's because . . . well, it turns out that she was a witch. Her parents had no idea."

Greta shook her head. "No. That is *not* what happened."

Everyone stared at Greta. Binx held her breath.

"What do you mean, that's not what happened? Do you have some information that could be helpful to the police?" Mrs. Feathers asked. Greta's face shut down. She sat back in her chair. "Did you girls know? That she practiced witchcraft?" Mrs. Feathers prodded, looking at each of them curiously, probingly.

"Totally not?" Binx said with a pretend-shocked expression.

"No way!" Iris added. "Witchcraft, *blech*, that's awful!"

Enough of this. Binx scooped up her doge backpack and stood up. It was time to end the interrogation; it was also time to strategize with her coven-mates. Plus, she didn't like the idea of having to talk to the police again; she didn't trust them. Just last night, she had seen President Ingraham on TV, talking about his proposed new law to crack down on 6-129 violators. He said that once it was passed, he would be assigning hundreds, maybe thousands, of federal agents to help local police precincts catch witches. ShadowKnight was right; things were heating up fast. "This has been so helpful, thanks, Mrs. Feathers. But would it be okay if we left now? I, uh, think I already have two tardies in homeroom."

"No need to worry. Your teachers know we're meeting. I can give you all passes, though, in case you'd like to take a few minutes to center yourselves, get some fresh air." Mrs. Feathers reached for a pen and pad. "Or do you girls need to go home for the rest of the day? Perhaps that would be best. Self-care is so necessary during a time like this."

"I want to be with my friends," Iris replied, hooking her arm through Greta's.

Greta nodded. Binx nodded, too.

"Of course. But if you change your minds, let me know. And I'm here anytime you need to talk. My door is always open to you . . . and to Ridley, too, when she returns. I'm so sorry about all this."

The girls said goodbye to Mrs. Feathers and walked out of her office. They heard the door closing softly behind them. The hallway was empty except for Becky the cafeteria lady and Seth Zeloski, who was always tardy for who knew what reason.

Iris blew her nose into her wad of tissues. "I think I'm going to need another emergency appointment with Dee Ranger. Do you guys think—"

"Calumnia," Greta said in a low voice. "Okay, we can talk now."

"Sorry," Iris said. "Do you guys think Mrs. Feathers believed us? About Penelope not being a witch, even though she totally was? And was she looking at us funny, like she suspected that *we* might be witches, too, which we totally are, and maybe we should go back in there and cast a memory-erase spell on her? Or maybe a *please-stop-suspecting-us* spell? Does Callixta have one of those?"

"Forget about the yoga-ball lady; we have more important things to deal with," Binx said dismissively. "So I think we can say for sure that a witch killed Penelope and then used magic to make it look like a suicide . . . and used magic to do that other weirdo stuff, too. But why would a witch kill another witch?"

"It doesn't make any sense," Greta agreed. She clutched at something at her throat—her raw amethyst pendant, probably, which she always kept hidden under her clothing. "Do you think . . ." Her knuckles whitened as she curled her hand into a fist. "What about those shadow messages? Do you think Div and I are *next*?"

"No!" Iris blurted out.

"I mean . . ." Binx said at the same time. Greta and Iris both looked at her, horrified, so Binx shifted gears. "Look, whatever this person is planning, we need to find them ASAP. Do we for sure think the Antima are involved?"

"Why would the Antima be teaming up with witches, though? They hate us, right? I mean, not *us* specifically, but our kind," Iris pointed out.

"Yeah, but those shadow messages sure sounded like they came from the Antima, so there's that," Binx mused.

"Did Penelope get a shadow message, too?" Iris asked.

"I don't know," Greta said. "Binx?"

Binx shrugged. "I'll ask Ridley if she knows. Except, wouldn't she have told us? I mean, that's kind of major."

Greta frowned. "Unless Penelope swore her to secrecy."

"Okay, I'll text her. *Again.*" Binx pulled out her phone and began typing.

Greta began typing on her phone, too. "I'm texting Div. Our covens need to meet and figure this stuff out before . . ."

Her voice trailed off as she fought back fresh tears. Binx knew exactly what she meant.

The meeting of the two covens was set up for noon. As Greta and Iris headed off to their respective homerooms, Binx decided to stop in the girls' bathroom to decompress and collect her thoughts. She felt as though she'd undergone a mental system crash, and she wasn't ready to face the day.

Luckily, the bathroom was empty. Leaning against a sink, Binx scrolled through her phone. Still nothing from Ridley.

She typed:

Hey are you getting my texts?

No response.

Are you okay??? I'm worried about you.

Still no response.

Why did Neo cross the road?

That didn't work, either.

Binx sighed and stepped back from the sink. She caught her reflection in the mirror: sleep-deprived, circles under her eyes, a pallor not unlike Baklora the Bloodless, whose witch army was forever storming castles in search of the elusive Chromalian Cure. Which was no surprise, considering that Binx had barely slept in days . . . not after what had happened.

Last night, for example. She'd awoken at two a.m. and tossed and turned for an hour before giving up on sleep altogether. She'd gone to her computer, tried to play *Witchworld*, and stopped after a few minutes (the violent melee at Gasterly Point wasn't amusing). Then, unable to help herself, she'd meandered through the Internet, revisiting Penelope's social media.

Her full name was Penelope Rue Hart, and she would have been sixteen in October. A junior league tennis champion, a competitive gymnast, and a member of the local dressage team (a quick Google search had revealed that "dressage" had to do with horses, not dresses). An only child (just like Binx, unless she was inclined to count the smelly, noisy, infant half brother, which she wasn't).

When Binx had clicked over to Penelope's YouTube channel, she'd been shocked (well, maybe not shocked but disappointed in the human race) that her subscriber base had *tripled* over the weekend. Her other accounts (her Instagram and her Twitter,) had insanely high numbers, too. Nothing like a young girl's untimely death to explode interest in her content.

Binx had noticed, too, that a bunch of randoms had posted disgusting comments. Like: *R.I.P. in Hell, Witch . . . Magic cant save u now . . .* and *One less to deal with LOL.* All with the hashtags *#stopwitchcraft* and *#antima.*

Seriously?

She'd had to use every ounce of restraint in her body to not engage with these haters . . . or send them a powerful cyberspell through the Internet and fry them into oblivion. (She didn't actually have a spell like this in her arsenal, but she was more than motivated to invent one. *Bring. It. On.*)

Penelope's Instagram had included photos of her and Colter—hanging out at the beach, watching a baseball game, sunbathing by a pool. In one of them, Binx noticed a little heart-shaped birthmark just above her bikini top. Her Instagram had *tons* of photos of her dog, Socrates, who was a big poodle with curly white fur and enormous brown eyes. Binx wondered if the poor creature was okay. Did he know that his owner was gone? He must.

For some reason, the Socrates pix made Binx think about the stupid dirt-colored puppy that had shown up at her house last Thursday, along with the undead crow. She hadn't seen it since then; had it gone back to its owner? Was it okay? Over the weekend, she'd gone to Pet Mart on an impulse and spent thirty dollars on different types of dog food—dry, canned, chicken, beef, gravy, no gravy, organic, not organic. (Actually, she'd charged it to the emergency credit card her father had given her, because wasn't that what absentee dads were for?) She'd left the food out for the puppy, rotating the different kinds, but the bowl had remained full.

She checked her phone again. Still nothing from Ridley . . . and nothing from ShadowKnight, either. They'd planned to talk over the weekend, but he hadn't answered her videochat requests; hopefully he hadn't gotten into further trouble with his parents. She'd started analyzing his new genealogy app—the one that was supposed to help him and his Libertas group find C-Squared's living descendants—and made a little progress on Thursday and Friday. But she'd had to take a break because of the Penelope incident. She really wanted to get back to it; killing 6-129 and stopping the president's new bill (and the Antima, too) seemed more urgent than ever.

She also needed to get back to her coven-related assignment, to try to find witches at their school and around town. That, too, seemed more urgent than ever, but for a slightly different reason. At first they'd believed some witch might be *helping* them by enchanting the shadow messages. But now it looked like some witch might be *after* them.

That witch had already gotten Penelope.

In the mirror, Binx saw that her eyes were shiny with tears.

Okay, no crying, you idiot, she chided herself. She hastily dug through her doge backpack for her makeup bag and pulled out a tube of concealer, a bottle of eye drops, and a new lipstick she'd bought at the drugstore after seeing Penelope's dark-lipstick tutorial. It was time for her to perform some anti-Baklora-the-Bloodless magic on her tired features and face the day.

She wished she'd had a chance to thank Penelope for the makeup tips.

The bathroom door burst open, which made Binx drop her lipstick. In the mirror, she saw Ms. O'Shea.

The history sub closed the door behind her and leaned against one of the sinks, catching her breath. "*Calumnia.* I saw you from way down the hall, and I ran, and . . . anyway, I was out of town this weekend, so I just heard about Penelope Hart. That's *awful.*"

Binx picked up the lipstick. "Yeah. It sucks."

"Principal Sparkleman said that you guys found her?"

"Yup. Did you know that she was one of us?"

"She *was*?"

"That's what she told Ridley, the day before she . . ." Binx stopped, uncapped the lipstick, and capped it again. She felt helpless suddenly.

"I wish I'd known. I wish I could have protected her somehow," Ms. O'Shea said quietly.

"Us too."

"Principal Sparkleman said there was a suicide note at the scene?"

"No. I mean, yes, sort of. But she didn't write it; someone used magic to make it *look* like she did."

Ms. O'Shea covered her mouth with a shaking hand. "I can't believe this. Why would anyone do such a thing?"

"I don't know, but we're all pretty freaked out. What if whoever it is comes after Greta or Div next? Or any of us?"

"Tell me everything and spare no detail," Ms. O'Shea said. "Even the tiniest thing might be important."

Binx explained about the handwriting-morphing and the eerie music and the energy barrier.

When she'd finished, Ms. O'Shea was quiet for a long time. "This is bad . . . *very* bad," she said finally. "I need to get this information to my coven ASAP."

"I just don't get it," Binx went on. "What was this killer-witch's motive? And did the same witch enchant Greta's and Div's shadow messages? What's the connection between the shadow messages and Penelope's murder? And are the Antima involved at all, or are they just a bunch of idiots and posers who are doing their own thing?"

"Yes, there's a lot we don't know yet, obviously. But . . ." Ms. O'Shea paused to adjust Theia. Binx gazed at the magical glasses longingly; with her own pair, she could do so much (like search for the dirt-colored puppy across long distances). "I *do* have some new information about the Antima that might be helpful," Ms. O'Shea went on.

"You do?"

"Yes. And now that I know about Penelope's murder . . ." Ms. O'Shea's expression darkened. "Do you remember how I told you and Ridley at the mall that some bigwig in town might be organizing a new local Antima faction?"

"Uh-huh."

"My coven and I have learned that this group definitely exists. They call themselves the New Order. And we came up with a theory about who this bigwig, their leader, might be."

"Who?"

Ms. O'Shea hesitated. "Is Penelope . . . *was* Penelope, I mean . . . dating a guy named Jessup? Colter Jessup?"

Binx nodded slowly. Dread pricked at her insides. Where was Ms. O'Shea going with this?

"We're not absolutely positive—*yet*. But we think that the leader of New Order is someone in the Jessup family."

22

SLEEPYHEAD

Magic cannot manifest something out of nothing.
For example, it cannot find courage
where there is none.

(FROM *THE GOOD BOOK OF MAGIC AND MENTALISM*
BY CALLIXTA CROWE)

"Morgan? You awake, bud?"

Ridley stirred at the sound of her father's voice. Sunlight streamed through the blinds, casting bright white stripes across her room, and the alarm clock on her nightstand blinked 8:40 a.m. Wasn't it Monday? Yes, it was definitely Monday. A school day. Why was she still in bed?

And then she remembered . . . she'd been sick all weekend and asked to stay home. Chills, a marathon headache, fatigue. She'd even canceled her violin lesson with Mr. Jong for later, which was something she never did.

Because, Penelope. Ridley didn't know if the events of last Friday night had made her sick, or if it was a coincidence, or if her illness was all in her mind. What difference did it make, though? Sick was sick. And in any case, Penelope was gone.

But Ridley couldn't bear to think about her another minute; her brain had been on a nonstop Penelope loop. She kept going over their last conversation, wondering *what if, what if, what if* . . .

"Morgan, you all right? I made you some of those cinnamon pancakes you like."

Ridley realized that her father was standing just outside her door.

"Thanks, Dad! I'm not hungry!" Her voice was lower, gruffer. She hated that voice.

"I'll cover them with foil and leave them on the counter for you, then."

Ridley heard his footsteps plodding down the stairs. Come to think of it, Daddy rarely made her breakfast anymore, and certainly not on a weekday morning. He was no doubt trying his best to cheer her up. Of course, he knew only a magically filtered version of the events surrounding Penelope's death. That night, Ridley had been forced to use a series of spells, both on him *and* the police officers, to make sure he wasn't present when they'd questioned her along with Greta, Binx, and Iris . . . *and* to make sure she'd been Ridley the girl with them and Morgan the boy with him. She'd also had to use a calming spell on herself; having to protect her identity so vigilantly in the presence of the police had taken its toll on her. On top of the trauma over Penelope.

The world was spiraling out of control. *She* was spiraling out of control. Maybe she could just stay in bed for the next few weeks. Months. Years. The rest of her life.

The house was quiet now. Momma was no doubt still asleep. Daddy must have driven Harmony to her preschool earlier and come back; Monday was gardening day, which was her favorite because they got to pick peppers and other fresh vegetables for their snack.

Harmony would want to play with Ridley later. There couldn't be two bedridden Stones in the house.

Just get up, she told herself. *Baby steps. You can do this.*

With an effort, she sat up slightly, groaned, and slumped back down again. *A few more minutes.* Out of habit, she held up her hands to inspect her mani for chips . . . and was greeted by the sight of bare, bitten-down nails and thick, slightly hairy knuckles. *Oh yeah.* This happened a lot, especially first thing in the morning, expecting to be her real self and encountering Morgan instead. It was depressing.

Of course, her favorite movie, as always, offered some consoling wisdom on this point: *What is real? How do you define "real"?* In any case, things were going to be so much better, so much more real, once she mastered those two super-advanced spells, *vertero* and *dissimulatio.*

A metallic rattling sound. Across the room, her familiar, Agent Smith, was chewing vigorously on a carrot-shaped toy made of timothy hay (a rabbit favorite) that had been wedged into the wire fence of his exercise pen.

"Hey, guy. I know, you need breakfast. One sec."

Agent Smith watched her with his translucent red eyes as he continued playing tug-of-war with the toy and rattling the fencing.

"I promise, I'll bring you a real carrot, and some kale, too, if we have it. I just—"

With a sudden, swift motion, Agent Smith yanked the toy free with his Dracula-sharp teeth and flung it up in the air. It landed in his litter box, i.e., one of Momma's old aluminum baking pans filled with recycled newspaper bits.

"O-kay. Message received. Be patient with me, I'm having a tough time."

Agent Smith hopped into his litter box, still staring at her. They'd tried a more conventional litter box with him at first, made of plastic, but he'd consumed half of it, so they'd had to resort to something less edible.

Ridley had inherited Agent Smith (formerly Cupcake, which was *so* not the right name for him) from their neighbor back in Cleveland, Mrs. Azar, who was moving to a retirement home and couldn't bring him with her. The moment Ridley had laid eyes on him, she knew. He was her meant-to-be companion. Momma had agreed on their family adopting him on the condition that he got along with Pandy, the dog (technically, *Momma's* dog). It had been touch-and-go at first, but they had eventually developed a grudging cross-species fondness for each other.

Ridley's phone buzzed on her nightstand. *Again.* She really should turn the thing off so she could get some peace.

Another text from Binx; Ridley could barely keep up.

Why couldn't Neo eat his ice cream?

"Because there was no spoon," Ridley said out loud. For someone who claimed not to be a *Matrix* fan, Binx sure knew a lot of *Matrix*-y jokes.

After a moment, Binx wrote:

Dude if you don't text me back soon I'm going to come over to your house and teach your rabbit how to yodel.

Ridley grabbed her phone. She typed:

I'm fine I'm just sick. Are you guys at school? How's everyone doing?

Not good. Did you get my text from before? About Penelope?

I just woke up, sorry. What about her?

When you guys talked last week, did she mention if she got
a shadow message like the one Greta and Div got?

No. Why?

We were wondering if she was threatened, too.

Oh.

Now Ridley felt like a terrible friend. She should have told Penelope
about the shadow messages . . . and also about the defaced gravestones,
about the Antima at school. If Ridley had warned her about all this during their coffee, Penelope might have been more careful; she might still
be alive.

I failed her.

Binx texted:

Also, did she talk about Colter with you?

Colter?

Ridley replied:

She said he was really nice. She seemed pretty happy with him,
I guess.

What about his family?

She said they were nice, too. Why?

> It's complicated. I'm cutting class and coming over
> so I can explain in person. I know your dad doesn't like
> visitors but just this once.

Ridley bolted straight up. *No no no no no.*

> Don't come over I'm super-contagious.

No response.

> Besides I won't be here. My mom's driving me
> to the doctor's. I'll text you later. Swear on a stack
> of spellbooks.

Binx finally replied:

> Okay fine, even though you're totally lying. Call me, okay?

Ridley waited to see if Binx might fire off another text. She didn't. Still, what if she ignored Ridley's orders and came over, anyway? It would be just like her.

Ridley needed a Plan B (besides memory-erase spells, which would be her Plan C). Her mother was not the problem, since she would likely be asleep for a while; she'd been spending a lot of her time in bed since Daniel died.

Her father, though. Would he be out of here in time should Binx defy Ridley's orders and come over? He'd said something last night about his shift starting at nine thirty this morning. Or was it ten thirty?

Ridley swung her feet over the side of her bed and stood up. The sudden motion made her head throb. Pressing her index fingers against her temples, she crossed her room (which she loathed; it was such a boring suburban boy room, with its charcoal-gray walls and blond fake-wood floors and black IKEA furniture) and poked her head out the door. "Dad, did you leave yet?" she called out.

He appeared at the bottom of the stairs. He was dressed in his paramedic uniform: dark green pants, matching polo over a white undershirt, and steel-toed boots. His hair was damp, probably from his shower, and there was a small piece of bloody tissue stuck to his neck. "Just finishing up my coffee. How're you feeling, son?"

She should have been used to the *son* after all these years, but she wasn't. "Kinda crappy. Does Harmony have her raincoat?"

"No, why?"

"I, uh, saw on the weather that there might be rain later," Ridley fibbed. "Do you have time to drop it off? They do outdoor recess even when it's rainy, and you know how she is about getting wet."

Darnell Stone frowned at his watch. "If I leave right now, maybe. Her rain boots, too. Oh, and about later . . . so I'll pick her up at one and drop her off back here, then I've gotta head back to work. I'll try to be home with dinner by six, seven latest. Maybe Chipotle."

"Sounds like a plan."

Ridley stood at the door and waited. After a few minutes, she heard him grab his keys and head out to the garage.

She went over to the window and parted the blinds. The metallic-red Chrysler Pacifica backed out of the driveway and turned west onto Santa Ana Street, in the direction of the Growing Tree Preschool. Afterward, Daddy would have to drive all the way to the hospital via a totally different route. So no chance of running into Binx if she should show up on their doorstep.

Whew. Mission accomplished.

Why was Binx asking questions about Colter Jessup and his family?

And then Ridley remembered about Agent Smith's breakfast. Plucking her daily angel card out of Daniel's old Cleveland Browns mug (today she got *Courage*), she headed downstairs to the kitchen—slowly, because she still felt weak and headachy. Once there, she gathered some carrots and kale from the vegetable bin. On the other side of the dining room, she saw that her mother's bedroom door was closed, and that her father had left a laundry basket of clean, neatly folded sheets and towels next to the doorway.

Back in Cleveland, everything had been different. Her mother, Joyce, had been the multitasker, the organizer of all things domestic, while juggling her high-stress job as a communications manager at City Hall. Daddy had been the deputy chief paramedic at one of the big hospitals and proudly ignorant about how to work the washer and dryer, sew a button, or prepare a simple meal.

Daniel had been a high school senior, straight A's, waiting to hear back from a dozen colleges. His first choice had been Howard University, which was Momma's and Grandpa Henry's alma mater; his second choice had been Case Western Reserve, which was near home and also where his best friend, Victor, was a freshman.

His best friend and secret boyfriend. Daddy had walked in on the two of them kissing one day and practically given himself a rage heart attack. Daddy and Daniel had fought for days, with Daniel insisting that he had the right to date anyone he pleased, boy or girl, neither or both. Daddy had become even more enraged by this; in his bigoted mind, you were either straight or gay, and if you were the latter, you weren't welcome in his home. (Momma had tried to intervene and negotiate a truce, but Daddy had insisted that she stay out of it.)

And so Daniel had packed a bag and taken off one night in his beat-up old Chevy Impala that he'd bought with money saved from his lifeguarding, Domino's delivery, and other part-time jobs.

And then he'd gone to the quarry to blow off steam with his friends. Ignoring the NO SWIMMING/NO DIVING sign, he'd cannonballed off a cliff into the water below and crashed into a boulder, smashing his spine.

After the funeral, Daddy had decided that the family should leave Cleveland forever and move to Sorrow Point, where there was an opening for a chief paramedic at the local hospital. A fresh start. Ridley had decided that it would be a fresh start for her, too. Back in Cleveland, she'd been able to live as Ridley only occasionally, and in the privacy of her room (although she did have an elaborate Pinterest board with pictures of her dream self and dream life). But no one at Sorrow Point High knew that the new girl, Morgan Ridley Stone (who now went by Ridley), had been assigned "male" at birth. All Ridley had to do was use magic to alter her school records and also her appearance (face, hair, body, clothes, etc.) twice a day. *And* to intercept any e-mails or snail mail or phone calls that her parents might receive from the school district, plus keep them from attending school events (which was depressingly easy to do). *And* on the rare occasion when something went awry, use a memory-erase spell.

She just wanted the world to see her for who she really was, twenty-four seven, though.

Once she had those two spells down . . .

Back upstairs, Ridley offered the kale and carrots to Agent Smith. He wrenched them out of her hand and began attacking them methodically. Ridley's familiar held nothing back, ever.

Sitting down on the edge of her bed, she scrolled through her phone and found her playlist. She hit play on one of her favorite songs, "Sleepyhead" by Passion Pit. Listening to the words, she remembered the angel card she had selected from Daniel's Cleveland Browns mug.

Courage.

Hmm. Maybe it was a message from the angels (and Daniel himself?) to deal with what was real. Today.

Or maybe tomorrow. Or later this week.

Ridley lay back down and closed her eyes and let the music wash over her.

A car in the driveway.

Her father must have doubled back. Ridley's eyes flew open as she jumped out of bed and hurried to the window.

But it wasn't the metallic-red Pacifica. It was a silver SUV.

Ridley's entire body tensed. Was it . . . could it be . . . *Brandon Fiske?* Maybe her memory-erase spell from last week had worn off. Maybe he'd remembered about their encounter in the Seabreeze development.

She flattened herself against the wall, breathing hard. Was he here to hurt her? Hurt her family?

"Pleukiokus," she said quickly. *"Pleukiokus, pleukiokus, pleukiokus."*

But a protection spell wasn't enough. She needed to be ready to defend herself. Where was Paganini? Was it still in her backpack, which was in her closet, which was all the way across the room? She needed to use magic that didn't require her wand; should she try *muto* again?

She heard the car shift into reverse and back up out of the driveway. She craned her neck ever so slightly to peer out of the window. The SUV was heading down the street, in the direction of the high school.

Her breathing slowed. *It's okay,* she told herself.

But it wasn't okay.

Maybe she should *really* shore up her courage and just come out to her family, already. That way, she would be free to give up witchcraft; she wouldn't need *vertero* or *dissimulatio*.

Although coming out would present a whole other set of challenges and dangers. Daddy wasn't the only one who was a bigot when it came to the LGBTQIA community. Also, was she really ready to say goodbye to her coven sisters? She needed them more than ever to face what was ahead.

23

(UN)FAMILIARS

Some things, like Life and Death, are sacred
and should be left to higher powers.
Mortality is its own gift. Nature is neither cruel
nor kind; it simply is.

(FROM *THE GOOD BOOK OF MAGIC AND MENTALISM*
BY CALLIXTA CROWE)

At a few minutes past noon, Greta hurried down the East Wing corridor. She had arranged to meet Div, Aysha, and Mira in the parking lot, which was more private than the cafeteria; Binx and Iris would be joining them, too. The hallway swirled with students on their way to lunch, to clubs, and to rehearsals. They were all a blur to Greta, though—a blur of random bodies, fuzzy auras, and clashing conversations. She barely registered the stares and whispers as they walked by.

Everyone knew. Everyone knew that Penelope was dead. That Greta, Iris, Binx, and Ridley were the ones who'd found her body.

And found Gofflesby, too, although no one but Greta and her friends really cared about that.

Gofflesby was at home in Greta's bedroom, hopefully resting. They'd taken him to the Sorrow Point Animal Hospital that night, to get him treated for whatever trauma he'd experienced, but by the time they'd arrived at the reception desk, he was wide-awake and energetic. So they'd turned around and driven home.

Back from the hospital, Gofflesby had promptly devoured five entire cans of cat food—a record for him. Then he'd continued behaving oddly all weekend. He'd been racing around the house as though hopped up on caffeine, climbing curtains, scratching up the wood floors, breaking teacups and other fragile items. Last night, he'd disappeared into the basement for hours and then, at around two a.m., appeared on Greta's pillow with a dead, bloody mouse in his jaws. Totally out of character.

The other strange thing was, his cough was gone. His breathing was normal, like it used to be before his illness.

Was it a coincidence? Or had something—or someone—cured him during his disappearance?

Greta was so thankful to the Goddess that Gofflesby was okay. Still, her heart ached at the thought of Penelope. A sister witch, dead. Murdered. Also, what did that mean for herself and Div and any other witches who might have received a shadow message? Or were the shadow messages not even connected to the murder?

It was all so confusing, and scary, and she felt like it was on her and her fellow witches to figure it out.

Greta reached the double doors leading out to the parking lot. Outside, she spotted Div, Mira, Aysha, Binx, and Iris, all gathered around Div's white car. Binx and Div had their heads bent together and were speaking in low voices while the other three witches were looking at something on Mira's phone.

Binx and Div?

Greta blinked, wondering if her eyes were deceiving her. No, it really was them, talking privately . . . about what?

"Hi, I'm here!" she called out in a voice that sounded too loud, too bright. Binx glanced up abruptly and turned away from Div.

Iris waved. "Hey, Greta! Hi! Hello! Greetings!"

Div regarded Greta coolly. "You're late."

"Sorry, I forgot my English notebook in class and had to go back for it."

"Well, Binx has something important to share with us." Div touched Binx's elbow and said *"Calumnia"* as Binx stepped forward.

Greta crossed her arms over her chest. Annoyance and doubt simmered in her head.

"Um . . . why haven't I heard about whatever this is?" she asked Binx.

"I needed to talk to Div first."

Talk to Div first?

This was getting more and more bewildering. Binx disliked Div intensely. She disliked all three of them; it was *she* who'd invented the nickname Triad of Evil. What was going on?

"So, I ran into Ms. O'Shea this morning." Binx's gaze moved across the semicircle of witches. "She's the history sub for Ms. Hua. Ridley and Greta already know this, but she's one of us, and she belongs to a coven up north," she added.

Mira and Aysha exchanged a look.

"Yay, more witches!" Iris said, clapping. Then she blushed and stopped.

"Ms. O'Shea told me that her coven thinks one of the Jessups might be the head of a major new Antima group in town," Binx announced.

Greta's eyes grew enormous. Penelope's *boyfriend* might be linked to the Antima?

"Wait, what? *Colter's* family?" Mira burst out. "No way. *No way.* They're super-chill and nice. They could never be part of a group like that."

"We should find him and talk to him," Aysha suggested.

"He's not in school today. I checked," said Binx.

Div turned to Mira. "Is Colter aware that you're a witch?"

"Of course not!"

"How well do you know the Jessups?" Binx asked.

"Really well! Colter and I dated for, like, six or seven months. I used to have dinner with the family, like, once or twice a week. His dad always cooked; he makes *the* best homemade pizza. His mom's a doctor, and she is *the* nicest person. His brother, Hunter, is . . . well, he's *hot*, of course, because he's basically just an older version of Colter. He's smart, too; he wants to go to med school someday, like his mom. And the little sisters are just cute little brats, and besides, they're too young to be in some anti-witch hate club." Mira added, "My dad's good friends with Mr. Jessup, too. In fact, Mr. Jessup's helping Dad with his mayoral campaign."

"Your dad's running for mayor? Cool!" Iris piped up.

Really? Greta almost snapped at Iris—but why? Because Iris wasn't in a terrible mood like *she* was? She needed to get hold of herself.

"Beatrix, did this history-sub-slash-witch give you any proof?" Aysha asked skeptically.

Binx glared at Aysha. "It's *Binx. B-I-N-X.* Maybe you've had too many memory-erase spells cast on you; would you like me to fix that for you? And no, she didn't give me any proof, but she seemed pretty sure."

Across the parking lot, a black Jeep backed up and took off noisily. Likely seniors, since they had special privileges and were allowed to leave the school at lunchtime. Greta bit her thumbnail and watched the car driving away into the distance, toward downtown. She felt overwhelmed. Frightened. Angry. *Everything*. Honestly, she just wanted to go home and curl up with Gofflesby, tune out the world. There was just way too much to process.

Including . . . why was Binx acting all friendly with Div? It was bizarre and out of character. Was she getting back at Greta for their argument at lunch last Thursday? Maybe Greta should just ask Binx over for tea and apologize, hash out their issues.

When Greta turned her attention back to the group, she realized that Div was watching her. Greta couldn't read the expression in her snake-like green eyes. Was she studying Greta? Staring her down? Preparing to strike?

Or remembering? For a moment, Greta let her mind travel back to her final coven meeting at Div's house. Div had suggested that the two of them cast a necromancy spell. Greta had refused because Callixta's book was firm on the fact that necromancy was about darkness, not light. Div had, of course, overridden her.

The lucky subject had been a dead gerbil Div had intended to feed Prada for lunch. She had arranged black candles, clear quartz, and thirteen primroses, thirteen blackthorn flowers, and thirteen daffodils inside a circle of salt, and the gerbil had been placed in the center, its body cold and its eyes unseeing.

Div had recited the words of the spell once, twice, then instructed Greta to repeat after her:

> *The dead which I seek*
> *Come to me as I speak*
> *It is not yet your time*

So come back to us fine
Live a life
Free from strife
And return to this earthly plane.

They'd repeated the chant over and over. At first, Greta had moved her lips but not spoken the words, unwilling to participate. But when the gerbil's body twitched, she'd joined in, wanting the small creature to live. Her emotions had been all over the place . . . on the one hand, she hated herself for giving in to the dark side of magic, but on the other hand, she felt exhilarated that the spell had actually worked.

The gerbil slowly and gradually came back to life. It stirred and blinked, stirred and blinked . . . then righted itself on all fours, looking this way and that for an escape route through the maze of candles, quartz, and flowers. For a brief moment, despite her objections about necromancy, Greta had been filled with a sense of wonder. How could it be wrong to help the helpless in this way?

Then Div had spoken into her neck, and Prada had materialized. And swooped in and devoured the gerbil, whole. Right in front of them.

Cruelty against animals was unacceptable to Greta. She'd asked Div tearfully: *"Why bring something back to life, only to put it through an even more horrifying death?"* Div's answer had been blunt: *"You'll never achieve your full potential as a witch if you aren't willing to get your hands dirty."*

That day, she'd walked away from Div's coven—from Div—and never looked back.

Until now. She hadn't *returned*, exactly, but it rattled her nevertheless, joining forces with her ex–coven-mate and ex-friend (and ex-crush, if she was being honest). Even if it was temporary, even if it was an emergency.

Binx's voice cut into her thoughts. "... forgot to mention. Ms. O'Shea's coven said the name of this local group is the New Order."

Iris raised her hand high in the air. *"N-O!"*

"It's okay, Iris, you're not in class," Mira teased her. "Also, why are you spelling the word *no?*"

Iris lowered her hand and jammed it into her jeans pocket. "No, that's not . . . I mean . . . the letters *N* and *O.*"

Greta and Binx exchanged a glance. *1415. N-O. New Order.* Was Iris onto something?

"The first time Greta showed me the shadow message, *her* shadow message, I touched it and then had this vision. . . . I know that sounds crazy, but sometimes I touch stuff and I get these visions, and they might mean something or they might just be my brain making up random gibberish," Iris babbled. "Anyhoo . . . when I touched the shadow message, I had a vision that the number 1415 stood for the letters *N* and *O.* I originally thought it just spelled *no,* but maybe it stands for New Order?"

"Huh. That's interesting." Aysha spoke up. "Some white supremacist groups do that, I think. My cousin Matt, he's technically my stepcousin, was in one of those groups for a while, in Boise, Idaho. His group was called the True Brotherhood; he told us their symbol was the number 202, since *T* and *B* are the twentieth and second letters of the alphabet."

"Do I even want to know what the True Brotherhood is all about?" Div asked.

"No. You really don't," Aysha replied. "Let's just say that side of the family is not welcome in our house. The last time they came for Thanksgiving, my parents made them leave halfway through because Matt couldn't keep his racist mouth shut."

"That's *horrible,*" Mira scoffed. "I would have dumped gravy over his head."

"Yeah, I came *this close*." Aysha pinched her thumb and ring finger until they were nearly closed.

"I think Iris may be right. Good job, Iris," Div said, which made Iris beam, which made Greta even *more* annoyed with Div. "Those numbers on the shadow messages that Greta and I received must stand for the New Order. And if there's a chance the Jessups are connected with the New Order, then we need to check them out. Are we good with that, Mira?"

"I guess so? But I'm like a million percent sure you're not going to find anything."

"We still don't know who enchanted our shadow messages and made those numbers appear, though," Greta reminded Div. "Plus, who did all that magical stuff around Penelope's body? It seems like our killer is a witch, but the New Order, the Antima, wouldn't have witches."

"You're right. It doesn't add up," Div acknowledged. "We need to figure out who enchanted the shadow messages ASAP. Greta, you guys and Iris should get on that while we investigate the Jessups . . . Mira, do you have any ideas on how we could get close to the family?"

"Actually, yes!" Mira scrolled through her phone, then turned it so everyone could see a digital invite. "Tomorrow night is a fund-raising party for my dad's campaign. They happen a lot, and this one's at the Jessups' house."

"Great. Perfect. Can you get Aysha and me on the guest list? In the meantime, we should all continue casting protection spells on ourselves and on our familiars, too. I know they're not perfect, but they're better than nothing." Div regarded Greta. "Speaking of familiars, how is yours? Did you ever figure out why he was with Penelope that night?"

"He's much better, and no, we haven't," Greta replied.

Iris raised her hand again. "Excuse me . . . hey, Greta? Hi! I think I can help with that. Can I come over to your house after school?"

At four o'clock, the Navarro house was quiet; no one was home. Greta led Iris inside and then locked the front door behind them. She wondered why Div had suggested that Iris work on the case with *her* coven and not Div's. Did she no longer want to recruit Iris? Or was she so confident about securing a yes from Iris that she didn't care?

Or had Penelope's death just put everything else on the back burner?

Whatever the reason, Greta was really annoyed with Div, and even more annoyed at herself for letting Div order her and her friends around. She should have said something. She should have stuck up for herself and her coven.

"I thought I could see if my touching-stuff-and-getting-weird-visions thing might work on your cat," Iris explained as they went up the stairs to Greta's room. She paused to study an old black-and-white photograph of a woman with Greta's eyes and smile (Greta explained that it was a picture of her great-grandmother Adelita when she was in high school), then moved on. "No guarantees, though. So far, it's only happened with objects, not animals. Or people." She reached out and tapped Greta's back. "See, I just touched you! No vision! Except maybe my brain just had a vision about popcorn, but that's only because I'm hungry."

"I'll make you some after we see Gofflesby. With brewers' yeast."

"Yeast on popcorn? I was going to say melted butter and nacho-cheese-flavored salt, but sure!"

Upstairs, Greta unlocked her bedroom door with a reverse *obex* spell. Her palms were clammy, and her shoulders were tight with tension. On top of everything else, she'd been worried about Gofflesby all day.

"Gofflesby? I'm home!"

She pushed the door open and gasped.

Her familiar was lapping water and herbs from her scrying bowl.

"Gofflesby, *no!* You can't drink that!" Greta cried out.

Gofflesby arched his back and hissed at her. He dipped one paw in the bowl and scooped the liquid into his mouth. Then he batted at the bowl and tipped it over, spilling its contents onto the wood floor.

"Gofflesby!" Greta grabbed a T-shirt and mopped up the mess.

"I've never seen a cat drink out of a scrying bowl," Iris remarked. "Of course, I don't know a lot of cats. I don't know a lot of people who own scrying bowls, either. Well, just *you* guys, basically."

"He's never drunk from the scrying bowl before," Greta said worriedly. "I don't understand why. . . ."

She stopped as something across the room caught her eye.

"Oh, *no!*"

On top of her art table, empty potion bottles lay cracked and broken. Clumps of herbs collected in wet pools.

Lying in one of the pools was an old notebook with its pages splayed open.

No.

Heart pounding, Greta ran over to her desk and picked it up. Her grimoire! She flipped through it frantically. Some of the pages had been scratched and ripped and streaked with thin spiderwebs of . . . was that blood? Or was it one of her potions that she'd made out of beets and berries?

"Gofflesby!"

He ignored her and lapped at the scrying-bowl water on the floor.

Greta clasped the grimoire to her chest. *"Reparati,"* she murmured.

The pages made a shuffling noise and quickly restored themselves. Greta sighed, relieved. She put the grimoire in a desk drawer, locked it, and hurried back to Gofflesby.

"What's wrong, my love? Why are you doing these things?"

Gofflesby continued lapping at the water.

"Gofflesby! It's *me*!" She scooped him up in her arms and curled herself over him. He hissed and thrashed; she held him tighter, as if her embrace might lull him back to sanity. "Why are you acting like this? Why are you trying to destroy my things? What's *wrong*?"

Iris stood next to Greta. She reached out and laid a tentative hand on Gofflesby's soft orange head . . . and flinched.

"What is it?" Greta demanded.

"You can't feel that?"

"Feel what?"

"He's so hot!"

"No, he's normal. You must be sensing something I can't."

Iris touched him again, more tentatively, and closed her eyes. "What's the matter, Mr. Gofflesby? Is something upsetting you?"

Greta felt Gofflesby's body relax ever so slightly.

Iris stroked Gofflesby's head with her fingertips and nodded to herself.

"It's working! I'm having a vision!" she told Greta excitedly. "All righty, so . . . I'm seeing a man . . . no, a woman. She's standing outside a window— wait, that looks like your house. She's talking to Gofflesby through the window . . . and he goes to her. Now she's taking him somewhere . . ."

"Who is she? What does she look like?" Greta asked.

Iris continued stroking Goffleby's head.

"I don't know. She's wearing a cape, and the hood is covering her face."

"Where is she taking him?"

"She's taking him to a house. A little gray house. But now I'm seeing another house . . . it's that Seabreeze-y house that's still not finished yet, the one where we found . . ." Iris paused and whooshed out a deep breath. "I'm getting dizzy, I think I need to stop."

"Hang on. Did she take him to a little gray house or the Seabreeze house? Or both?"

"Both? Or maybe one is in the past and the other is in the future? I don't know."

"Why is she taking him there? Why is she taking *my* familiar anywhere?"

"I'm not sure. Wait. I think they have some kind of—"

Gofflesby growled suddenly. In the same instant, his body glowed and crackled . . . and a bolt of electricity shot out of him and through the two witches.

The girls screamed and stumbled backward, falling to the floor. Gofflesby landed gracefully on all four paws and circled back toward Greta.

"What . . . was . . . *that*?" Iris panted.

Gofflesby climbed onto Greta's lap and rubbed his head against her arm, purring.

Acting perfectly normal, as though nothing had happened.

24

SECRETS

Secrets cannot be kept securely
where Magic has a presence.
Withhold, or lie, at your own risk.

(FROM *THE GOOD BOOK OF MAGIC AND MENTALISM*
BY CALLIXTA CROWE)

"And . . . *send!*" Binx said as she hit the return button on her encrypted e-mail to Div.

Satisfied, she leaned back in her desk chair and hugged one of her stuffed Pikachus. (She had a small one, a medium one, and a large one. This was the small one, which was her favorite; she'd found her at a garage sale, missing one arm, and repaired her with a *sana* spell—Binx knew it was a *her* because of the heart-shaped tail tip.) After school, Binx had come home to do some research—magically hacking into the server at Mira's dad's campaign headquarters, scoring their guest list for tomorrow night's party at the Jessups', and cross-referencing it against various Antima sites to see if there might be any overlap.

Of course, there was no *obvious* reason to think that there would be Antima members at the event, since it was a political fund-raiser for Mr. Jahani and not a New Order meeting. But Binx had figured it wouldn't hurt to check, especially given what Ms. O'Shea had told her this morning.

And she'd struck gold. Or a few little nuggets of it, anyway. Orion Wong and his parents were on the guest list. So were Brandon Fiske and Axel Ngata and *their* parents. Were the moms and dads Antima sympathizers, too? (So heartwarming . . . families doing Antima activities together!) She'd also found three people on the guest list who'd posted to a new video sharing site, Whatznow, that seemed to be popular with the Antima; their names were Sarabeth Lash, Keemo Malifa, and Essie Tranh. (They didn't go to Sorrow Point High, though.)

Her phone buzzed. Div had texted her.

I didn't realize you were working on this. Thanks, great job!

Binx grinned and typed:

You're welcome!

Div replied:

I've been following the Antima on social media, but I didn't know about Whatznow. Thanks for that, too. No wonder Greta values you so much.

"Yeah, I don't know about that," Binx whispered to her stuffed Pikachu.

She wrote:

The videos on Whatznow will make you barf. Or scream. Or smash your device against the wall. Or all of the above.

Worth it, though, to know everything we can about those losers.

You mean those ignorant, hateful, bottom-feeding, dumpster-fire, if-one-of-them-was-drowning-I'd-throw-the-life-preserver-in-the-other-direction losers.

Exactly! ☺

After saying goodbye, and with a promise to send along cyber-research updates if there were any, Binx set her stuffed Pikachu down, then got up and walked over to the window. She felt lighter than she had all day . . . all weekend. It was nice to be appreciated by someone, even if that someone was Div.

Maybe Div wasn't as bad as she'd thought? Maybe she'd let Greta's negativity about the girl cloud her own impressions and opinions?

At the window, Binx parted her curtains, which were pink with dangly bead trim. The beads made a swishy, plinky waterfall sound that she always found soothing.

Pool. The Jacuzzi twins. Japanese Zen garden. Meditation hut. Tennis court. The beach in the distance.

She leaned farther forward to zero in on the dish of gourmet dog kibble she'd left on the pool deck. Still full. Obviously, the dirt-colored puppy was just gone for good. She'd posted its photo on various pet websites, too, and there had been no hits. *Blurg.*

Her newly lightened mood grew a little heavier again.

Downstairs, the front door opened and shut. Was it the cleaning lady? If so, she was a day early; she usually came on Tuesdays.

Binx stepped into the hallway. "Helloooo?" she called out loudly. "Kathy?"

"Hi, Binxy, it's me!"

Her mother? What was *she* doing home?

Binx went downstairs, her mood deteriorating by the second. Yoko Yamada stood in the foyer dressed in a sleek black pantsuit, riffling through a handful of mail.

"Why aren't you teaching?"

Yoko chuckled. "Hello to you, too. I teach on Tuesdays and Thursdays this semester, remember?"

"Oh. Right. Okay, bye!"

"Bye? Where are you going?"

"Back upstairs. I'm in the middle of a, um, homework thing."

"Binxy."

"What?"

"How are you doing? You must be feeling so awful about that girl from your school. Do you want to talk about it?"

"Nope. I'm coping just fine, thanks," Binx lied.

"Are you sure?"

"Yup."

Yoko reached out and tucked a strand of pink hair behind Binx's ear. Then she stepped back and gave Binx's pink miniskirt and Jigglypuff T-shirt a once-over. "By the way, I hope you don't mind a piece of friendly advice?"

"Actually, I do."

"You're sixteen." Yoko plunged on. "So I don't want to dictate what you should wear—"

"Then don't."

"—or how you should spend your free time—"

"Again, don't."

"—but honestly, and I'm saying this because I'm your mom and I love you. I don't understand why you feel the need to succumb to these superficial Asian American stereotypes. Dressing like that"—she waved at Binx's outfit—"and your obsession with anime and video games. You're better than that."

"Wow, this is *so* none of your business."

"I'm trying to help you. You have a brilliant mind. Your grades are excellent. You could be an academic if you wanted."

"I would rather become a circus clown than do what you do, no offense to circus clowns."

Yoko drew her lips into a tight, thin line. Binx could practically hear her counting to ten in her head, although not in binary because she wasn't cool like that.

"Perhaps it's your father's influence."

"*Please* leave him out of this."

"You've always been obsessed with him, with his work . . . although I'm not sure how churning out a bunch of mindless, violent video games can be called 'work.'"

"O-kay. This conversation is so over. Bye now."

"Binxy—"

"I'll be busy for the next couple of hours, so don't bother me, please."

Before Yoko could reply, Binx ran up the stairs, two at a time, and into her room.

"*Obex,*" she said. The doorknob turned and made a clicking noise. Finally. *Freedom.*

If Binx had been interested in having a *real* conversation with Yoko (which she never would, ever), she would have told her that *one*, she legit liked the K-pop fashion, the anime, and the video games. She wasn't pretending to be someone she wasn't. And, *two*, she used her image as armor, as a disguise. As long as people thought of her as a "shallow Asian girl" with "shallow Asian-girl tastes," they wouldn't suspect what lay beneath the surface—i.e., a powerful cyber-witch.

So whenever someone at school said something idiotic to her (*"Is Binx a popular name in Korea?" "Do they like Pokémon in China?"*), she just shrugged and smiled and made a kawaii hand heart gesture. She didn't throw shade at them or kick them in the shins because they thought all Asian countries were the same, or because they assumed that she wasn't "really American," and that her cultural touchstones were from "over there" instead. She turned their ignorance and bigotry into currency, into a secret weapon. You have no idea, she would think as she passed them by.

(Also, FYI—*For Yoko's Information*—Binx liked *Witchworld* for *Witchworld*, and not because Stephen Kato—her dad and CEO of Skyy Media and Yoko's husband before their bitter, bitter divorce—was its creator.)

Binx listened for a moment at the door. Her mother had not followed her upstairs. *Good.*

A quick glance through the pink beaded curtains . . . still no mutt. *Fine, whatever.* Binx sat down at her desk and put on her noise-canceling headphones. She would spend a little time on her project for ShadowKnight now. She also needed to get back to her other projects, like finding out if there were other witches in Sorrow Point. She wanted to do some digging on the Jessups and New Order, too.

She'd already come up with a few ideas for adjustments to ShadowKnight's genealogy app. As she implemented them now, the program spat out a list of names. Patricia Meeks, Dominick Trovato, Eleanor Guzman, Norman Smythe, and Adelita Suarez. Binx sat up a little straighter. *Nice!* Did that mean the app was working? But after a moment, the names shimmered and disappeared. Did that mean the app *wasn't* working? She opened her note-taking app on her phone and quickly typed in the names before she forgot them.

A faint knocking sound permeated the silence. Binx groaned and whipped off her headphones. Her mother was at her door. "I *told* you I didn't want to be disturbed!" she yelled.

"Binx, it's me."

Ridley?

"Just a sec!"

She reverse-*obexed* the door. Ridley walked in, rainbow-waving.

"Your mom let me in. She told me you were up here."

Binx sized up her friend. She looked tired, and her eyes were bloodshot.

"You look terrible."

"Thanks a lot."

"How's your flu?"

Ridley shrugged. "Better. You said you wanted to talk to me in person, so here I am. I figured I couldn't just lie around in bed forever."

"Actually, you could, but then you'd miss out on so much. Like our excellent trips to the mall."

"Good point. Hey, is that a new lipstick?"

"Shut up."

"No, it's pretty."

"Um, thanks. So are you okay? I was worried."

"Thanks. Yeah, I'm not really okay, but I'm managing. Sort of. Kind of." Ridley sniffled. "I really liked Penelope."

"I know. I'm sorry."

Binx sat down on the pink shag rug, and Ridley did the same. Ridley picked up a stuffed Eevee and hugged it against her chest. "So what did you want to tell me? Is it about her? Did they catch whoever, um . . ." Her voice caught in her throat.

"Not exactly."

Binx reached for her stuffed Pikachu and hugged it to *her* chest. Then she told Ridley about the events of the day, starting with the meeting in Mrs. Feathers's office and ending with the stuff about the Jessup family . . . and about Gofflesby, too. (Greta had texted her about Iris's weird visions and also Gofflesby's un-Gofflesby-like behavior.)

When she'd finished, Ridley was shaking her head in disbelief.

"Penelope's *boyfriend*?"

"We don't know anything for sure. Ms. O'Shea and her coven *think* someone in the Jessup family might be the leader of this new Antima group, but so far there's no proof."

"Aaaaand . . . if they're right, does it mean *that's* the person who killed Penelope? Someone in Colter's family, or maybe even Colter himself? Because she was a witch?"

"Well, except that whoever killed her *was* a witch. Which means they can't be Antima. Or *can* they? No, there's no way."

Ridley's lip trembled. She lowered her head so that her chin was resting on Eevee's fluffy brown ears.

"I know. It's a total mess," Binx acknowledged.

"Did you guys see Colter at school today?"

"He wasn't in school."

"Huh. So what's next, then?"

Binx crossed and uncrossed her legs. "Yeah, so the two covens are going to, like, keep working together. Hurray. Div, Mira, and Aysha are going to this political fund-raising thing at the Jessups' house tomorrow night. It's for Mira's dad, who's running for mayor or whatever. Our coven plus the newb recruit will keep trying to figure out how magic ties into all this and whether there are any other witches in town we don't know about. I'm also going to find out what I can online—about the Antima, about the Jessups, et cetera, et cetera."

Binx didn't mention her genealogy app project for ShadowKnight or even ShadowKnight himself. She'd broken her promise of confidentiality to tell Greta about him, but that had obviously been a huge mistake. She also didn't mention Div's phone call on Thursday, inviting her to join her coven. Binx was so not ready to talk about that, much less think about it.

Although, to be honest, she *had* thought about it a tiny bit. Once or twice, just for a microsecond, when Greta was being annoying.

". . . and let me know what I can do to help," Ridley was saying.

"Are you sure Penelope didn't mention getting a shadow message?"

Ridley bit her lip and nodded.

"Maybe we should ask her parents if she got one."

"She wouldn't have *told* her parents. Her parents didn't know she was a witch, remember?"

"Hmm. True. Maybe we could search her backpack, then?"

"*How* would we get our hands on her backpack?"

"I don't know. Lemme think. Hey, didn't you use *alata* to make Brandon's beer can grow wings and fly back into his car and hit him on the head? Because he super-deserved that? Couldn't you use it to make Penelope's backpack grow wings and fly out of her house?"

"Um, yeah . . . that sounds risky. *Plus* insane."

"Yeah, but it might work. We should try it."

"Let's see what Greta says."

"Oh. Yeah. *Greta*."

Ridley cocked her head. "Is something going on between you two?"

"What? Nah. She bugs me sometimes, that's all. Doesn't she bug you sometimes?"

"Not really. I think she's a great coven leader. Also, you should cut her some slack right now. She almost lost her familiar." Ridley stood up and wandered over to the window, still clutching the stuffed Eevee. She parted the pink beaded curtains and stared out at the view. "Speaking of pets . . . did you guys get a new dog? You didn't tell me."

"What?"

"It's pooping in your fancy Japanese garden. You should teach it not to do that, otherwise it's going to—"

Binx didn't hear the rest of the sentence. She jumped to her feet, ran up to the window, and pressed her face to the glass.

And there was the dirt-colored puppy, squatting next to the Buddha statue with an earnest expression on its little face.

"*Bad* dog!" Binx shouted. And smiled.

Something pinged on her computer. At the same moment, her phone began to vibrate in her pocket.

Ridley wandered over to Binx's desk. "Who's ShadowKnight? Is he your secret boyfriend?"

Binx spun away from the window. Ridley was staring at something on the computer screen.

"Wow, a new boyfriend *and* a new puppy. That's not like you. Did you trade identities with *another* Binx Kato?" Ridley teased her.

Binx ran over to her computer. On the screen was a videochat request from ShadowKnight. She then glanced at her phone; the request had come in through both devices.

"Nope, he's not my secret boyfriend. No way. He's just some gamer. He keeps bugging me for *Witchworld* hacks."

The videochat request continued blinking on the screen, and her phone continued vibrating.

"Aren't you going to answer that?" Ridley asked.

"No! He's annoying. *Just go away!*" Binx yelled at the screen as she hit the ignore icon. "Uxie, end call!"

"The call has been ended," Uxie announced.

Binx tugged on Ridley's arm. "Come on, let's go outside so you can meet the puppy. I think I'm going to adopt it and make it my familiar. How does that work, anyway? Is there a familiar-izing spell in C-Squared's book?"

"It doesn't really work like that. . . ."

As they left the room, Binx glanced back at her computer screen and saw to her relief that ShadowKnight had given up. She would have to call him back later, when she was alone.

ShadowKnight. Div. The invite to Div's coven . . .

Binx's head felt as though it would burst with all the secrets she was keeping.

✳ 25 ✳

VIP

Witches are born that way, although the ability
can skip generations.
Some witches may spend their entire lives
not knowing that they are witches.
Some witches may spend their entire lives
regretting that they are witches.

(FROM *THE GOOD BOOK OF MAGIC AND MENTALISM*
BY CALLIXTA CROWE)

"Your names, please."

Mira poked her head out of the driver-side window of her Miata and smiled charmingly at the security guard. "I'm Mira Jahani. This party is for my dad, Neal Jahani. And these are my friends, Divinity Florescu and Aysha Rodriguez. We're on the guest list."

"Right, I see your names here. Go on through."

Div watched with interest as he spoke quietly into a headset, then pressed a button to open the gates. She wondered why the Jessups had a security guard. Mira proceeded onto a driveway flanked by two lines of glowing paper lanterns.

"You told me the Jessups were rich, but you didn't tell me they were *that* rich," Aysha said.

"Yeah, they kind of are. But they don't *act* super-rich, if you know what I mean."

"How is having a security guard and electronic gates not acting super-rich? Also, that *house*," Aysha added, pointing.

Just ahead of them, past a grove of pine trees and at the end of an enormous front lawn, was a large Victorian mansion. An estate. A line of BMWs and Mercedes and other luxury cars were lined up in a semicircular driveway.

"What kind of party is this?" Aysha asked, leaning forward and resting her chin on the back of the driver-side seat.

"I told you. It's a fund-raiser for my dad's mayoral campaign, so Mr. Jessup probably invited all his super-richest friends. To, you know, raise funds."

"Huh. Must be nice," Aysha remarked.

Gazing out the window, Div wondered why Mr. Jessup hadn't canceled the party in light of his son's girlfriend's death. But maybe political fund-raisers didn't work like that? Div herself had little interest in politics, except maybe national politics because of the new (and Antima sympathizing) president.

As they neared the house, she noticed a large marble fountain inside the semicircular driveway, ringed by neatly trimmed rosebushes. In the center of the fountain was a statue of a winged angel, wearing a crown of stars.

When they reached the front of the line of cars, a valet opened the doors for them and took the keys from Mira. The three witches proceeded inside and found themselves in a huge, beautifully decorated entryway. An ornately carved wooden staircase rose up to the second-floor landing. A crystal chandelier glittered overhead. Gold-framed paintings, mostly portraits, covered the walls. A big vase of dark pink Asiatic lilies sat atop an antique table, giving off their heady scent. A dozen or so guests milled around, sipping champagne and eating canapés. From somewhere in the house, a jazz band played and a woman sang: *"Bewitched, bothered, and bewildered am I . . ."*

Two twentysomething women with iPads greeted Div and her friends. "Hello, welcome! Could I get your names?" one of them said.

Mira gave her the information, and the other woman handed the girls some name tags. As Aysha pinned hers on, she whispered to Mira: "Do we have to pay? It's a fund-raiser, right?"

"We don't have to pay; my dad took care of that," Mira whispered back. "Otherwise, it's a hundred dollars per person, can you believe it? They're expecting about a hundred people, which means like ten thousand dollars total. Mr. Jessup donated the food, drinks, music, decorations, staff . . . all of it. So it's pure profit for my dad's campaign."

Div considered this. Ten thousand dollars . . . that was a lot of money. So probably, the Jessups wouldn't have wanted to cancel the evening and risk losing that amount, even with a recent tragedy like the death of their son's girlfriend.

She reached up to pet Prada, then remembered that she wasn't there. Div felt a brief pang; she missed her familiar's presence. Although she would never admit it to anyone, Prada always gave her an extra jolt of courage, especially in uncertain and potentially high-risk situations (such as walking into the home of a possible Antima leader). But ever since the disappearance of Gofflesby, brief as it was, Div had been too nervous to bring Prada out of the house. Right now, Prada was in her cage under a heat lamp and under a special protective spell that Div had dug up in Crowe's book last night and tweaked to her satisfaction. (She reminded herself to teach it to Mira and Aysha for *their* familiars . . . and maybe Greta, too, although Greta was not likely to take advice from her. She could offer it to Ridley; that might help to win her trust? As far as she knew, Binx didn't have a familiar, and neither did the annoying Iris girl.)

Mira led Div and Aysha to a large living room, which was jam-packed with people. Conversations and laughter rose in the air, mingling with the music from the jazz band, which was playing another Cole Porter song. (Div's father, who lived in Bucharest, was a major Cole Porter fan.) A JAHANI FOR MAYOR banner was draped across one wall, and there were clusters of red, white, and blue balloons everywhere.

Div scanned the crowd. She didn't see Orion or Brandon or Axel. Maybe they hadn't arrived yet. She made a mental note to look for the three who'd posted hate videos on Whatznow: Sarabeth Lash and Keemo Malifa and Essie Tranh.

After a moment, Div spotted Mira's dad holding court with a small group of men. Div had been to Mira's house many times since they first became friends; she'd met Mr. Jahani but didn't know him that well. She also recognized Mrs. Jahani, who was speaking separately with half a dozen women.

Mira's brother, Nick, who was a freshman at the university, stood near the fireplace with two other guys. One of them was Colter . . . and the other one must be his brother, Hunter? They looked alike and had the same broad build. They both had wavy hair, although Colter's was blond and Hunter's was brown.

"Come on, there's Colter," Div said, steering Mira and Aysha toward the fireplace. "Mira, you know what to do."

"Yup. Got it!" Mira plucked a canapé from a passing server and ate it in one quick bite. "Mmm, you guys *have* to try these! They're like little caviar and cucumber sandwiches!"

"We're not here to eat, we're here on business," Div said under her breath.

"Uh-huh, right. Sorry."

They wove their way through the crowd and joined the three guys at the fireplace. They were all drinking champagne.

"Colter!" Mira went up to him and wrapped her arms around his neck. "I am so, so sorry."

Looking startled, Colter hugged her back while carefully balancing his champagne glass in one hand. "Thanks, Mira. Thank you, that's really nice of you."

Div scrutinized Colter. His chiseled face was pale, and his eyes were red, as though he'd been crying . . . or not sleeping . . . or both. Otherwise, he was his usual crazy-hot self. Tonight, he was wearing a navy blazer, white button-down, and khakis; the preppy outfit suited him.

"Hey, ladies," Nick said, waving to the three girls.

Mira turned to Hunter. "Hunter, these are my friends Div and Aysha. Div and Aysha, this is Colter's brother, Hunter."

"Nice to meet you," Hunter said, smiling at Aysha and Div. His smile lingered on Div.

Div knew what that smile meant. She was accustomed to seeing it, and she knew just how to use it.

She swept her hair over her shoulder and moved closer to Hunter. "Great party. It's so generous of your family to do this for Mira's dad."

"Dad and Mr. Jahani go back a long way. So, Div . . . that's a cool name, by the way. Do you go to school with Mira?"

Div wrinkled her nose. "Yes, although I can't *wait* to graduate and start living my life. What about you?"

"I'm a pre-med at the university."

"That is *amazing*," Div said, putting her hand on his arm.

Hunter's eyes flicked to her hand and then back up to her face. "Yeah, I'm pretty passionate about medicine."

"And I've decided to major in political science, thanks for asking," Nick said jokingly. "I'm thinking about law school down the line and then maybe politics, like our future mayor over there." He nodded in the direction of his dad. "You know, saving the world and all that good stuff."

"No one cares, Nicky," Mira teased him.

"No one's listening to you, Meerkat," Nick teased back.

"Your family must be super-upset about Penelope," Aysha said to Colter and Hunter.

Hunter glanced at Colter briefly. "Yeah, of course. It's terrible. But we were also pretty shocked to find out that she was a . . ." He hesitated.

"A witch?" Aysha finished for him.

"Yeah. We had no idea."

Colter's face flushed beet-red. "I told you before, Hunter. I don't believe that," he said emphatically. He gestured with his glass, and champagne spilled out. "She's a . . . she was a really sweet girl. A really good person. There's no way she would have been involved in that kind of criminal activity."

Criminal activity? Div tried to keep her expression neutral, even as fury boiled inside her. Out of the corner of her eye, she saw Aysha curling her hands into fists and then forcing them to relax.

"People *do* keep secrets. Maybe she was too ashamed to tell you?" Mira said to Colter.

"I still don't believe it."

"Well, believe it, bro," Hunter said gently. "I'm sorry she's gone, though. I know you really cared about her."

Mira hooked her arm through Colter's. "You need to let your friends help you move on. We're here for you."

"Boys!"

A middle-aged man strolled up to their group. He wore a red, white, and blue tie with his navy suit. Gray peppered his short blond hair. "There's some folks I want you to meet, from the chamber of commerce; they want us to help organize a charity softball game. Hey there, pretty Mira," he said, kissing her cheek and squeezing her shoulder. *What a lech*, Div thought in disgust. "We've all missed you around here. You need to come around for dinner sometime. And who are these other beauties? Friends of yours? Welcome, welcome. I'm Jared Jessup, but please call me Jared . . . Mr. Jessup is my father's name, you know what I mean?" He chuckled.

Div shook Mr. Jessup's hand quickly, before he had a chance to kiss her on the cheek or squeeze her shoulder. (Aysha busied herself tying her shoelace.)

"We were just talking about Penelope," Div told him with a heavy sigh.

Mr. Jessup sighed, too, and shook his head slowly. "Real shame. She seemed like . . . well, like one of *us*. Who knew that she was involved in all that satanic mumbo jumbo?"

Aysha's hands curled into fists again.

"I don't think—" she began, but Div cut her off.

"Yes, you never know about people. I mean, it's against the *law*. Don't these witches understand that? Sorry, Colter," Div added quickly. "I liked Penelope, too. But I have really strong opinions about this whole witch thing."

She waited a beat and carefully watched Colter's reaction—and Hunter's and Mr. Jessup's, too.

"You're a smart girl, Div. She's a smart girl," Mr. Jessup told his sons.

Colter said nothing and downed his champagne. Hunter was staring at Div with renewed interest. Was he assessing her as a potential Antima member? "Where are my manners? Can I get you something to drink, Div? And you, too, Mira and Aysha?"

"Absolutely!" Mira said cheerfully.

"Love it!" Aysha replied through clenched teeth.

"Thanks, Hunter," Div said silkily. He gave her that smile again . . . the smile that told her that he would be asking her for her number before the party was over.

This little operation was going very well so far.

Except for the fact that Div was really, really tempted to kill the three Jessup men with her bare hands.

Div wandered down the hallway, along an ornate runner that had colorful depictions of exotic birds and flowers woven into it. From the living room, she could hear Mr. Jahani giving his speech, talking about the economy and jobs and taxes while the crowd cheered and clapped and shouted his name.

She was searching for a restroom. Or pretending to, anyway. She was actually on a small side mission—to collect hair samples from each of the Jessup men. The idea had come to her during the conversation with Mr. Jessup (correction, *Jared*, although she felt weird calling him that) and his sons. They had different-color hair, which would make it easier to distinguish any hair samples she might find: Mr. Jessup's was silvery-blond, Colter's was regular blond, and Hunter's was brown.

Her plan was to find their bedrooms and en suite bathrooms (the Jessup mansion looked like it would have a *lot* of en suites) and search through combs, brushes, towels, clothing, pillowcases . . . whatever might have strands of hair clinging to it.

And once she had the hair samples, she could go back to her house with her witches and conduct a series of group scrying spells, to uncover if any of the Jessup men had written the shadow messages.

Div had left Mira and Aysha to keep an eye on the party and make sure no one followed her. Mira was doing a good job fussing and fawning over Colter. Aysha was doing as well as she could, not losing her cool at all the anti-witch talk.

And Hunter. He was going to be an easy one. He was clearly attracted to her, which she would use to her advantage, just as she always did with people who were drawn to her that way.

There was a room to the right; soft classical music drifted from it. Div poked her head through the doorway. Floor-to-ceiling shelves crammed with books, an enormous antique desk . . . it appeared to be a study or a library. The music was coming from an old-fashioned-looking radio, but the room was unoccupied.

No, not a bedroom or bathroom. Move on.

Except . . . an odd sight caught Div's eye. Behind the desk, a piece of red velvet the size of a small tablecloth hung on the wall. It wasn't a curtain, and it looked out of place. Was it covering something? Curious, she walked up to it and pulled up a corner to peer behind it.

Behind the red velvet drape was a large board made of cork. Div lifted the cover higher. Dozens of items were pinned to it with silver pushpins— newspaper clippings, photographs, handwritten notes, sticky flags. Long pieces of red string connected some of the items to others, creating a bizarre sort of constellation.

What the hex?

She'd seen a board like this before. On a detective show on TV. It was called a "murder board," and it was a technique the detectives used to hunt down a murderer.

Were the Jessups hunting down a murderer?

Div leaned forward to study the items on the board. Several of the photographs were faded and sepia-toned, half-torn or crinkled at the edges. Some showed a man with a hawklike nose, bushy beard, mustache, and hair, and small, piercing eyes that radiated coldness even in the mottled, imperfect images.

She then turned her attention to the newspaper clippings. The articles dated all the way back to the 1870s, 1880s. One headline blared: *Famed Witch-Hunter Disappears.*

Witch-hunter?

Had the Jessups put together a murder board so they could hunt down a witch-hunter? But why? Wouldn't witch hunters and the Antima be on the same side, basically? Also, the person would have died long ago.

"Whatcha doing?"

Alarmed, Div let the drape fall to cover the board. She turned around, already preparing to cast a memory-erase spell.

A young girl stood in the doorway. Maybe ten or eleven, she wore black jeans and a black T-shirt with a rhinestone heart on it. Her long blond hair had green and orange streaks. She didn't *seem* to be suspicious of Div; in fact, she was smiling in a friendly way.

Div tried to remember what Mira had told her about Colter's family. She'd mentioned something about twins. . . .

"You must be Colter and Hunter's sister?" Div said pleasantly as she mentally debated—*memory-erase spell or no memory-erase spell?*

"I'm Cassie."

"Hey, Cassie. I'm Div. I was trying to find a quiet place to make a call, but I don't seem to have any bars. Also, where is your bathroom?"

"Which one? We have like three of them down here, for guests, and we have four more upstairs, for the family."

Div registered this. So Colter's, Hunter's, and Mr. Jessup's bathrooms were upstairs. Also, Cassie seemed oblivious to Div's snooping. *No memory-erase spell.*

"Wow, that's a lot of bathrooms!"

"Yeah. I still have to share one with my sister, Caitlin, which is *so* not fair. Do you have your own bathroom?"

"I do. Hey, maybe you could take over one of the downstairs bathrooms and move all your makeup and stuff in there?"

Cassie considered this. "Oh, yeah, that's a good idea!"

"Right?"

"'K, I have to go now because I told my friend Sienna I'd be on *Roblox* like an hour ago. We're in the middle of a zombies-in-the-desert campaign."

"Cool. It was nice meeting you. By the way, I like your hair."

"What? Oh, thanks. I wish it had more colors, though, like pink and blue and purple. Then it would be more rainbow."

Cassie touched the back of her head as she left the room. As she did so, pink and blue and purple strands suddenly appeared, then disappeared just as quickly.

Div clutched at her throat, stifling her shock. *She* hadn't done that, had she? No, she definitely hadn't.

So Cassie Jessup was a witch? And if so, did *she* know that? Did her family know, too? Except that her family—at least, the men in her family—hated witches . . .

She glanced at her phone; the party was halfway over. She needed to get upstairs and get those hair samples. She also needed to find out more about Cassie and about the Jessup family's fascination with witch-hunters (or with one particular witch-hunter, the guy in those long-ago newspaper articles).

Before heading upstairs, she decided to take a quick photo of the murder board (or whatever the hex it was). She turned, lifted the red velvet drape, and held up her phone . . .

. . . and in that same moment, a hand covered her mouth, smothering her. Div tried to scream, but the person's grip was too strong. Panicked, she tried to wrench away . . . except that the hand was holding a silky cloth, and the cloth smelled like chemicals. Suddenly, her muscles felt like jelly. Her brain felt like jelly. She barely registered her phone falling noiselessly onto the soft carpet as her knees buckled, and her legs gave out, and everything went black.

26

ODD WITCH OUT

Keeping a coven together is of the
utmost importance.

(FROM *THE GOOD BOOK OF MAGIC AND MENTALISM*
BY CALLIXTA CROWE)

"This is a *terrible* idea," Ridley whispered.

"Maybe. But it's *my* terrible idea," Binx whispered back.

"Well, I think it's cool! And scary! And cool! It's like we're on a Nancy Drew adventure!" Iris piped up.

"Guys, please . . . let's just get it over with and get out of here before someone sees us," Greta suggested.

The sun was setting, and the four witches were crouched behind an enormous bush in the side yard of 146 Blackberry Lane. Penelope's house. The shrub had peeling brown bark, clusters of small white flowers, and green leaves with jagged edges that reminded Greta of teeth. She recognized it as a ninebark, or *Physocarpus opulifolius*. She tried to recall its magical properties, but right now she was having a hard time concentrating because her nerves were on edge, and all of her focus was on keeping herself and her girls safe.

Earlier that day, Binx had proposed this plan to find Penelope's backpack so they could search for a third shadow message. She'd magically hacked into Penelope's parents' calendar apps to pin down a window of opportunity, learning that they had an appointment across town at six o'clock—something to do with arranging the funeral (which was, although Greta was in denial about it, happening tomorrow).

And so the four of them had driven over in Binx's family's Prius (which was not exactly legal, given Binx's age, but Greta wasn't about to tell her what to do) and parked down the street to wait and watch. Shortly before six, the garage door had opened, and a silver Volvo had emerged and disappeared around the corner. Just to be sure, Binx had hacked into the car's wireless backup camera and manipulated it to show the *inside* of the vehicle. In the front seat were a man and a woman who matched the LinkedIn photos of Penelope's parents.

The four of them had waited a few minutes to make sure the car wasn't turning around, then stealthily made their way to the ninebark bush. Now they were in the process of trying to figure out where Penelope's backpack might be.

Binx scrolled through her phone. "*Calumnia*, even though there are like no human beings around. Besides this house, this whole street is nothing but deserted construction sites . . . yeah, that's not creepy at *all*. Okay, so . . . I'm looking for a magical app that'll tell us which window is Penelope's bedroom. Ooooh, *calcea!* Actually, nah, that's for when you can't find your shoes."

"Maybe we should just do a group scrying spell," Greta suggested.

"Good idea," Ridley agreed.

Greta squeezed Ridley's hand, not just to thank her for the

support but to give *her* support, too. Then all four girls joined hands.

"Close your eyes and take some nice, deep, long breaths," Greta instructed in a soft voice. "Let's all picture Penelope's backpack in our minds. I'm trying to remember . . . was it lavender?"

"Pink," Ridley corrected her. "The material was light pink and soft . . . maybe suede or velvet? There might be a notebook inside with doodles and drawings. Penelope was a really good artist."

Greta squeezed Ridley's hand again. "Good. Thanks. Everyone picture that."

"When you say 'take some nice, deep, long breaths,' what do you mean by 'some'?" Iris asked. "Like, two or three breaths? Or more? Or do you want us to keep doing nice, deep, long breathing while we're picturing the backpack in our minds? Sorry to ask so many questions . . . am I ruining the vibe? I'm ruining the vibe, aren't I? *Argh*, I am so useless!"

"Whatever works for you is fine, and you're not ruining anything," Greta reassured her.

"Oh, *whew!*"

They grew silent again. Greta envisioned the pink backpack in her head. She mentally invited other objects to join the image, objects that might help them identify where the backpack was, like the color of the curtains in the room. But nothing came to her.

Binx broke the silence. "*I* think we should just use a reverse *obex* and go into the house. We could find her room in like thirty seconds."

"Isn't that a little bit illegal?" Iris asked.

"Actually, it's a *lot* illegal," Ridley pointed out.

"Keep breathing and focusing, guys," Greta said, frustrated.

Another minute passed. *Still* nothing came to Greta . . . she tried not to feel discouraged, but instead channel her own powers into the power of her coven . . . her coven plus Iris. She didn't want to be presumptuous. (Iris hadn't said yes yet.)

"Hey, guys? Look!"

Greta opened one eye and saw Ridley pointing to a window on the second floor. Through the flower-print curtains, in the shadows, a person's face was pressed against the glass, watching them. Greta sat up, startled.

But it wasn't a person. It was a *dog*.

"Hi, puppy dog!" Iris called out, waving.

"That's Penelope's familiar, Socrates," Ridley said with a sigh. "A second ago, I saw him in my mind sitting next to her backpack, and now there he is, for real. I bet that's her room, and I bet her backpack is in there."

"Awesome! Now do the beer-can trick. *Muto*, then *alata*, right?" Binx asked Ridley.

"I'll try. But first . . . how do we open the window?"

"I got this." Binx tipped her face up to the window. *"Obex!"*

The window didn't open.

"Really, window? *Obex!*"

Still nothing.

"Let me try," Iris said, raising her hand. *"Open, window, and let in the air. We promise to treat your home with care,"* she chanted.

The window slid open. Socrates stuck his head out, sniffed at the cool evening breeze, and howled mournfully.

Everyone stared at Iris.

"Seriously, *where* did you learn that spell?" Binx demanded.

"Welllll . . . I kind of wrote it in my head. Just now. It's a version of another spell I sorta kinda invented, which has to do with . . . you know when you're walking along a path and there's like a bunch of branches or prickly vines ahead of you, blocking the path, and you want to clear them but you're in a big rush, plus those prickly vines *hurt?*"

"That's amazing, Iris!" Greta exclaimed, and Iris blushed.

"Ridley, you're up," Binx said.

"Right."

Ridley performed the spells, and a moment later, Socrates pulled his head back through the window and was gone. Half a second later he started barking, and then a pink object appeared where he'd been.

Penelope's backpack. It flew out of the window and floated toward Greta and her friends.

"Yessss!" Binx pumped her fist.

Greta glanced around, wondering if they should cast an invisibility spell on the backpack. If the neighborhood wasn't as deserted as it appeared, someone might see it flying through the air and—that would not be good.

But she decided there wasn't time, especially since invisibility spells were complicated. Instead, she stepped forward, reached up, and caught the backpack as it descended toward them.

"Nice catch!" Iris said.

"Thanks!"

Greta unzipped the backpack as the other three gathered around. A faint rose fragrance wafted out, and she could feel a subtle shift in Ridley's aura . . . surprise, remembrance, grief.

"Ridley, you don't have to stay for this if you don't want to," she whispered.

"I'll be okay," Ridley whispered back, although she didn't sound too sure.

Greta rifled through the backpack. Folders. A notebook. A makeup bag. A glittery purple pen. She handed the items to the others, then proceeded to search through the zipped inner compartments.

"No shadow message here," Binx said, flipping through the notebook. "Some cool drawings, though."

Ridley held up the folders. "No shadow message in here, either."

"There's nothing in the makeup bag, except some really pretty lipstick. I didn't know there even *was* a color called *Revenge of the Strawberries*!" Iris piped up.

Greta unzipped the last compartment. "Wait, what's this?"

She plucked out a square cloth and brought it into the light. Embroidered on the fabric was an image of a cage burning over a bonfire.

An Antima shoulder patch.

"What the?" Binx said. "Why would she have an Antima patch?"

"Maybe it was her boyfriend's?" Iris suggested.

"But what's it doing in her backpack?" Greta asked.

"Maybe she found the patch—found out about *him*—just before she . . . before she . . ." Ridley stopped and crossed her arms over her chest. Binx leaned against her and put her head on her shoulder.

Someone's phone buzzed.

Binx straightened. "I think that's me. Uxie, who is it?"

"There is a new text message from Mira Jahani," Uxie reported.

Ridley pulled her phone out of her pocket. "It's a group text. I got one, too."

"Me too," Greta said, glancing at her screen.

Mira had written:

> Guys, Div disappeared and we can't find her anywhere.
> We think she might be in trouble. Can you help?

"*Crap!* This is not good," Binx declared.

"W-what's happening?" Iris asked nervously.

"Div's missing," Ridley explained, then turned to Greta. "What should we do?"

Greta touched her raw amethyst pendant, trying to still her racing thoughts. Div was missing. Was she in danger? What if Penelope's murderer was at the party and they'd done something to her?

Be strong, she told herself. *You need to be a leader.*

"Okay. All right. Ridley, can you and Iris stay here and deal with the backpack and the window, make sure we leave everything exactly as it was? Binx, can you drive us to the Jessups' house and . . . Binx?"

But Binx was already running to her car, smart key in hand.

Fifteen minutes later, Greta and Binx reached the Jessups' house. Mira had texted them again, warning that there was a security guard posted at an electric gate and also a couple of "greeters" inside the house checking off guest names on their iPads.

Binx managed to magically hack into both and add her own and Greta's names, which enabled them to get past the guard and the greeters. Mira and Aysha were waiting inside the house; they stood by a long antique table in the entryway, pretending to check out JAHANI FOR MAYOR buttons and bumper stickers. The sounds of conversations and live music floated in from another room.

Greta and Binx joined Mira and Aysha. The two greeter girls were having a conversation about college applications and seemed oblivious to the witches.

"Calumnia," Greta whispered. "What's going on? Tell us everything!"

"So, we were hanging out with Colter and his brother, Hunter, and their dad," Aysha said quickly. "Div slipped away during the political speeches. She wanted to find hair samples."

"Whose hair samples? What for?" Binx asked, puzzled.

"She wanted to figure out if one of the Jessup guys wrote her shadow message," Aysha replied. "It's this, uh, spell she does." Mira clucked her tongue, but Aysha ignored her. "That was a while ago. She hasn't come back, and she's not answering her texts. Mira and I tried a couple of quick scrying spells to find her, but no go."

"You've been here before, right, Mira?" Greta asked Mira.

"Of course! Lots of times!"

"Can you take us through the house? You could pretend you're giving us a tour."

"Got it! Follow me!"

Mira started down the hallway and began pointing to random paintings and furniture, tour-guide-style, as Greta and Aysha and Binx trailed behind. As they passed the French doors to the living room, Greta could see a big crowd of guests. Colter and—was that Hunter?—were hanging out in a secluded corner, speaking with Brandon and Orion and Axel from school. Their heads were bent close together.

Greta felt a frisson of alarm. Were they discussing Antima business? Did *they* do something to Div? She grabbed Binx's hand and pulled her along so they wouldn't be spotted through the doorway. She considered using a distraction spell on the five guys, but at the moment, she was too distracted to remember how to do it.

Mira waved them into a room on the left.

"And this is the TV-room-slash-den!" she said in a high, cheerful voice. "They used to have family movie night every Friday! I've been to a bunch."

As Mira stood guard in the doorway and jabbered on about movie night, Greta, Binx, and Aysha searched the room for any sign of Div. Greta also tried to sense Div's presence, connect to her aura and her emotions, but came up empty. Her chest tightened; what if they were too late?

What if Div was *dead*? But she couldn't allow that thought to be in her mind or out there in the universe. She shook her head back and forth, back and forth, and envisioned a white light of protection around Div.

Goddess, please watch over my friend.
Keep her safe until we find her.

Part of her couldn't believe she'd automatically used the word "friend," but she went with it. They repeated their search in three more rooms: a home office, a home gym, and a guest bedroom with a private bathroom. Just as they walked into a second guest bedroom, a voice called out to them.

"Are you guys lost?"

It was a young girl, maybe a tween, holding a cardboard box filled with bottles of shampoos, conditioners, and lotions. A tablet was propped on top of the bottles, its screen flashing brightly

"I got this," Mira whispered to the others. "Oh, hey, Caitlin! It's me, Mira!" she called out to the girl.

"I'm Cassie, not Caitlin. Hey, Mira."

"Ohmigosh, I'm sorry! You two look so much alike! Yeah, so, I was just showing my friends around your house. Didn't this room use to be yellow? I like the new color, plus this silk bedspread is to die! Is it Italian?"

"I have noooo idea." Cassie chin-nodded at the box in her arms. "'Scuse me, I just need to get to the bathroom. I'm moving my stuff down here. It was Liv's idea. Caitlin hogs our bathroom all the time, *plus* she uses my stuff without asking!"

"Liv?" Greta repeated.

"She's Colt's friend . . . or maybe Hunter's? She's nice, and she has cool hair. It looks like ice."

Greta's eyes widened. "Is she here at the party?"

"Yeah."

"Could her name be Div, not Liv?"

"Yeah, that."

"Do you know where she is? We've been looking all over for her." Aysha spoke up.

"Dunno. She was in the library before."

"What's the fastest way to get there, Cassie?" Binx asked.

"There's a shortcut through the laundry room. I can show you if you want. I just need to tell Sienna I'm AFK."

Cassie set the cardboard box on the bed, typed a message on her tablet, and gestured for them to follow her down the hallway. Along the way, they ran into some of the catering staff, but no one paid any attention to them. Which was good, because Greta really didn't want to have to resort to memory-erase spells.

A few minutes later, and after a confusing exchange between Binx and Cassie about *Mad City* versus *Jailbreak*, they reached a heavy-looking oak door. Cassie turned the large brass knob and pushed, but the door wouldn't budge.

"I think it's locked. I can get the key from my dad."

Binx coughed. *"Obex."*

The door creaked open.

"Oh, weird, I guess it's *not* locked!"

Cassie ushered the girls into the room. Greta scanned it quickly. Hundreds of books, an Oriental rug, a desk . . . but no sign of Div.

"I guess she left," Cassie said, shrugging. "Oh, well. Maybe she went back to the party?"

"Guys! Over here!" Binx had crossed the room and was crouched on the floor next to the desk. *"Vivifica!"*

No.

"Vivi-what? Is that like a secret code?" Cassie asked Greta.

Greta didn't reply. *Vivifica* was the revival spell for someone who was unconscious or badly hurt. Or dying.

Mira and Aysha rushed to Binx's side. Greta followed, stumbling a little, dreading what she might see.

Div lay on the floor behind the desk, her wrists and ankles bound with rope. Her eyes were closed, and her lips had an odd blue tinge.

"Div!" Greta cried out.

"Vivifica!" Binx repeated.

"Vivifica!" Mira and Aysha said in unison.

Div's eyelids fluttered, then blinked open. Color returned to her lips.

Oh, thank Goddess.

Div coughed and tried to sit up.

"Hold on. *Solvo!*" Binx said quickly.

The ropes around Div's wrists and ankles loosened and slumped to the floor. "Thank you, Binx," she said with a weak smile. "Thanks, Mira; thanks, Aysha."

What about me? Greta wanted to say. But mostly, she was just relieved that Div was okay.

As Binx helped her to her feet, Div turned to look at the wall behind the desk. She ran her hand across the wood paneling.

"It's gone," she murmured.

"What's gone?" Greta asked.

Div twisted around. "What are *you* doing here?"

"Rescuing you," Greta replied, trying to keep the hurt out of her voice.

"I didn't need rescuing."

"Well, you obviously did!"

"I'm quite fine with just my girls here."

"Div, I was scared!" Greta blurted out before she could stop herself.

Div cocked her head. "Yes, that's why you'll never be as powerful a witch as I am. I don't *get* scared."

"You guys are *witches*?"

Cassie was still in the room. Greta had forgotten all about her. . . . They *all* had, in the urgency of the moment.

"Actually—" Div began.

"Praetereo," Aysha interrupted.

Cassie blinked. Her expression went blank.

"Um . . . hey! Are you guys here for Dad's party?"

Mira hooked arms with Cassie and hustled her out of the library. "Yup! Colter invited us. I love your earrings! So, are you dating yet? The last time I saw you, you were crushing on someone named Dylan."

"Dylan? Ew!"

Behind Greta, Div was speaking quietly with Binx and Aysha.

". . . and there's a good chance *she's* a witch, too."

"What?" said Binx.

"How do you even know this?" Aysha asked.

Div whispered a response as she led Aysha and Binx out of the library, but Greta couldn't hear. She trailed behind, suddenly depressed, wondering when she had become the odd witch out.

27

WITCHES DON'T BELONG HERE

Some believe that Witches want
to take over the world with Magic.
They are not entirely wrong.

(FROM *THE GOOD BOOK OF MAGIC AND MENTALISM*
BY CALLIXTA CROWE)

ris was having a strange dream.

In the dream, she was walking through a forest—a forest of syc-amores, pines, and willow trees. Long strands of silvery-green moss dripped down from above. Invisible birds called to her from the shadows, a cacophony of chirps and songs and cries.

She thought it was daytime, but it was hard to be sure; the thick canopy of branches overhead let in only slivers of sunlight. Nervous and unsettled, she wrapped her hand around her smiley-face moonstone pendant. Calm and serenity washed over her.

"Love and light," she whispered. Greta's phrase . . . and Callixta's, too. Just then, a spotlight switched on. Had *she* done that? Would she get into trouble? *Argh*, maybe a detention. A beam like a stage light pierced through the half darkness and landed on a statue, illuminating it.

No, not a statue.

A living thing. A cat.

Gofflesby.

Greta's familiar was sitting under a crape myrtle tree in sphinx position, blinking against the bright, unnatural light. Iris hurried toward him. It was going to be okay, after all.

"Nice kitty. Have you seen Greta?" she asked.

"Elle est avec ma reine," Gofflesby replied. *She is with my queen.*

"Oh, okay. Huh. Where is this queen, then?"

"Elle arrive bientôt." She will arrive soon.

"*How* soon? Who is she, anyway? What country is she from? Does she know Jadora or Amarantha? Or Ilyara and Draska from the Valkyrie Valley High Council? Why are you speaking French?"

Gofflesby meowed, once, twice, three times. The purple blossoms on the crape myrtle tree turned yellow, then silver. A moment later, someone stepped out from behind the tree, shrouded in shadow. A girl. She wore a fancy black dress. A crow sat on her shoulder. Its eyes were milky and opaque, unseeing.

She looked like . . .

"Ridley?" Iris said, confused. "What are you doing here? It's not a school day."

"Did you take the red pill or the blue pill, Iris?"

"I think I took one of each. Is that your familiar?"

"Yes. It's blind. Do you like blind crows?"

Just then, the crow began breaking up into pieces . . . feathers, bones, flesh. A macabre kaleidoscope of crow parts. Slowly, the pieces spun around and gathered together and re-formed into a *thing*, into a violin.

Ridley bent down and picked up a long sycamore branch. She tucked the crow-violin under her chin and positioned the branch on top of the strings.

"*Écoutez.*" Listen.

She began to play, bowing back and forth with the branch. Iris closed her eyes and hummed along.

The tune was eerie, familiar. . . . What *was* it?

It was that piece by Schumann. *Schubert.* "Death and the Maiden."

"Why are you playing that?" Iris asked.

"Because she's dead."

"Yup. Uh-huh. I understand."

Ridley continued to play her violin. Iris watched and listened, mesmerized.

There is so much I need to learn, she thought.

Gofflesby was still sitting in his sphinx position under the crape myrtle tree. A crow, a different crow, flew down and landed on his back. Its glossy black feathers were flecked with red nail polish.

"*Sollst sanft in meinen Armen schlafen!*" the crow sang. *Softly shall you sleep in my arms.*

Gofflesby's head swiveled, birdlike, and his emerald-green eyes fixed on some distant place in the forest. Iris turned to follow his gaze, but all she saw was a labyrinth of trees . . . and beyond the trees, a cave of darkness stretching endlessly into an infinity of sky and space.

"There she is! Ta-da!" Ridley announced.

"Who? Where?"

An ethereal figure was wafting toward them through the cave of darkness. She wore a gold brocade dress with a high neck and long sleeves. An elaborate jeweled crown covered her head. She held a listless body across her outstretched arms. Green velvet cloak, long auburn hair. Was that Greta?

"Greta! *Finally!* I found you!"

Iris began running, running, toward Greta and the woman in gold, the queen. As she got closer, she could see that Greta was asleep in the queen's arms.

No, not asleep. Unconscious?

"Greta?"

Something was very wrong. With Greta. With this place. With everything.

"This isn't fun anymore!" Iris cried out. But no one was listening.

Her chest heaved as she gasped for breath. She was hyperventilating, having a panic attack. She stopped running and reached for her smiley-face moonstone pendant, to calm herself, but it was gone.

Fear coursed through her, and her brain felt scrambled, dizzy. The queen was standing in front of her now. She was beautiful, so beautiful. Greta's face—no, actually, it was *Penelope's* face—was sickly white. Her eyes were open, unblinking, staring vacantly up at the prison of tree branches.

"*No!*"

"It is her time," the queen told Iris.

"Her time for *what*?"

"You know the answer. You've always known the answer. It is the fate of all crows."

The queen lowered Penelope gently, carefully onto the mossy ground. In the same instant, the earth opened up and engulfed Penelope's body.

Iris tried to scream. Instead, she began singing.

"*Sollst sanft in meinen Armen schlafen!*"

The earth closed up over Penelope, the dirt particles glinting red and gold and copper as they avalanched onto her lifeless form, covering it entirely. A hundred, a thousand, a million wildflowers shot up, blossoming frantically into a wild tapestry of colors.

"Let us pray for the crows," said the queen.

She reached up and pulled something out from under her high collar. It was a pendant—Iris's pendant. Except that the edges of the moon shape were changing, bending, curving. Soon, it became a heart.

"I've lost my heart!" Iris cried out.

"That is not your heart. It belonged to Penelope and Greta, but no more."

Gofflesby joined them, the crow still on his back. *"Les sorcières n'appartiennent pas ici,"* he and the crow said in unison.

"Witches do not belong here," the queen repeated.

"Witches do not belong here," Iris repeated, too.

"Witches do not belong here!" Dozens—hundreds?—of angry-looking people holding signs and pitchforks came marching through the forest toward them. Some of the signs said 1415.

It was over.

They had won.

The forest, the dreamscape, began to fade to black. At the last second before it faded, too, the crow whispered something to Iris.

"You must find Margaret."

"Iris! *Iris!* Hey, doofus!"

Iris bolted up. She was drenched in sweat, and her limbs were tangled up in a jumble of sheets, stuffed animals, and dirty laundry.

"Greta!" she cried out.

Nyala was standing over her, her hands on her hips. Her expression was a typical Nyala mash-up of annoyed and skeptical. "Wake up, it's time for school. And why is Lolli with you? Stupid mouse, I am so replacing you with a *new* pet that's loyal. Maybe an iguana!"

Confused, Iris rubbed her eyes. She reached for her glasses, which were on her nightstand. Lolli was curled up on the pillow next to her, her whiskers twitching in sleep. Iris touched her head lightly; she sensed that her familiar was dreaming about her new spinning wheel. Also fruit salad.

"Oh, and by the way, your friend's here," Nyala announced.

"What friend?"

"The one you just mentioned. Gretel."

"Greta?"

"Yeah, her. I have no idea why she's friends with you. She's cool, you drool. You drool more than Mrs. Wendlebaum's Saint Bernard."

"Uh-huh."

"I'm serious!"

Iris got out of bed, jammed her feet into her fuzzy blue slippers, and rushed out of her room. "You're welcome!" she heard Nyala yell behind her.

"Close the door when you leave!" Iris yelled back. *"Pleukiokus,"* she added softly, to make sure that Lolli would stay safe.

Heading down the stairs, Iris tried to shake off her dream fog and return to reality. (*There's my favorite bird on the wallpaper . . . there's a sippy cup on the carpet . . . the house smells like muffins.*) She wondered why Greta was here. Was it Penelope-slash-Antima business or some other kind of business? Or maybe Greta really *did* just want to walk to school together, maybe talk about makeup and boys and whatever else girl friends (not *girlfriends*, one word, but *girl-space-friends*, two words) talked about with each other. Not that Iris would know, since her only real friend back in New York had been Fareeda, and their conversations had been 90 percent about *Witchworld* and 10 percent about their shared hatred of school. Maybe not hatred so much, but a big old casserole of fear, anxiety, and boredom.

Likely, Greta was here on Penelope-slash-Antima business. Iris already knew that Div was safe and sound, because Greta had texted last night about the big rescue mission. So maybe Greta had new news to share? Like, maybe they'd caught Div's attacker and solved the mystery of Penelope's death and invented a super-spell to make all Antima love witches? Case closed?

Or . . . was Greta's surprise visit somehow related to Iris's insane nightmare (or should it be *morningmare*)?

Downstairs, Iris found Greta and Ephrem nestled side by side on the ancient brown corduroy couch; they were poring over Ephrem's rain forest coloring book. Maxina and Oliver P. were both meatloafing on Greta's lap—or Maxina was, anyway, being the petite, prissy creature that she was; Oliver P., who needed to lose at least ten pounds, was spilling over Greta's right thigh like a massive wad of jelly, forcing her to nudge him back up with her elbow as she rooted through a shoe box full of crayons.

"What do you think, Ephrem? Should our macaw be blue or yellow?"

"Blue *and* yellow. *And* red *and* orange *and* green *and* blue." Giggling, Ephrem pulled off one dinosaur-print sock and threw it across the room.

"Perfect. Yellow, red, orange, green, and double blue." Greta glanced up. "Hi, Iris!"

"Are you okay?" Iris demanded.

"Yes, I'm fine. Are *you* okay?"

"How about Gofflesby?"

"His breathing problem seems to be totally gone, and he hasn't . . . he's been acting totally normal."

"Oh, whew." So the morningmare *hadn't* meant Greta was in trouble. Or Gofflesby, either.

"I like your pj's," Greta said.

Iris glanced down. *Argh.* She was still wearing her flannel SpongeBob pajama top and sweatpants. The pajama top had a blobby strawberry jam stain across the front and a ripped sleeve from when she'd accidentally slid down the ladder of Ephrem's bunk bed during action-hero hide-and-seek. The sweatpants had holes in the knees.

"I'm a mess!"

"No, you look cute." Greta leaned over the coloring book. She shaded in the rain forest bird's feathers with a sky-blue crayon, holding it sideways instead of point down, then added on a layer of sunflower yellow. Her long, long hair splayed across the page; she swept it back over her shoulder. Iris's heart skipped a beat. Greta was so pretty, like a figure from a Rembrandt painting.

"I'm sorry to just drop by your house like this. I tried to text you, but you weren't answering," Greta said, still coloring.

Iris blinked. "Oh, I'm sorry! I was asleep . . . well, obviously, right? Since Nyala had to come upstairs and . . . So, what's up? Why did you text me? Although I suppose I could just go back upstairs and read the text for myself?"

"No need. I was wondering if you wanted to walk to school together. I thought we could talk about the . . . the . . ."

"Homecoming Dance! *Got* it!" Iris improvised, remembering the posters in the school halls.

"*Who's* going to the Homecoming Dance?"

Rachelle Gooding pushed at the kitchen door with her hip as she balanced a wooden tray in her hands. On the tray were a platter of blueberry muffins, a teapot, mismatched mugs (the Muppets, D.A.R.E., Monet's waterlilies, a sudoku puzzle), clementines, and honey. She wore her daily uniform (work and non-work) of black leggings and an oversized Café Papillon T-shirt, and her hair was scrunched back in her usual messy *I-can't-be-bothered-with-hairstyles* ponytail.

"Greta, this is my mom. Mom, this is Greta," Iris said.

"Greta and I already met. Before you came down. We had a nice chat about your new school," Rachelle said. "I thought you both might like a little breakfast before you head off. I warmed up the muffins."

"Thanks. Are they vegan?" Iris asked.

"Yes, in fact!" Rachelle set the tray on the coffee table and slanted a look at Ephrem, obviously signaling that she wasn't going to bring up the subject of Penelope in front of him. "Greta told me about some of the clubs and such, and she said she's in the choir. Maybe you'd like that, too, Iris? It sounds low-key."

Low-key was Iris's mom's favorite expression when it came to suggesting activities for her. Stimulating but not too stimulating, no stressors or triggers, nothing that would require a paper bag to breathe into or a special-occasion Xanax or an emergency call to Iris's therapist. Like that time during Mrs. Barber's piano recital, back east. Ten-year-old Iris had performed a solo piano version of Tchaikovsky's "Dance of the Sugar Plum Fairy," from *The Nutcracker*. When some dumb boy in the audience had laughed at her for a slipup, she'd stopped mid-measure, taken off one of her shiny black patent leather shoes from the Shoe Barn, and thrown it at him. (In *The Nutcracker*, Clara had thrown *her* shoe at the Mouse King, so why couldn't Iris do the same?)

"Choir. Huh. Maybe? I'll think about it, okay?"

Two mugs of Earl Grey tea and several blueberry muffins later, Greta and Iris (who'd switched out the SpongeBob and sweats ensemble for jeans and a red-and-gray flannel shirt) headed outside with their backpacks and started up Sycamore Street. The air smelled morning-fresh, and the sky above downtown Sorrow Point was a pale gray-blue. As they passed Poe's Market, they saw the little black cat on the bench; they stopped to sit and say hello, since there was plenty of time before homeroom.

The black cat meowed for attention, and Greta stroked its ears. It climbed onto her lap and settled there. "*Calumnia*. So, I wanted to tell you what Div told us last night. About what happened to her before we got there."

So not *case closed*.

"Div said that before she was attacked, she was checking out this thing on the wall—she called it a 'murder board.' But by the time we found her, the board was gone."

Iris sat up excitedly. "A murder board? Is that like the one in *Witchworld* where Level Twenty-Five and up players can keep track of the enemies they need to catch in order to level-jump?"

Greta looked confused. "I'm not sure. Div thought that maybe the Jessups, or *one* of the Jessups anyway, was collecting information on some witch-hunter so they could hunt him down. It doesn't make sense, though, because witch-hunters don't exist anymore. And even if they did, why would the Antima want to hunt a witch-hunter? They're on the same side."

"Witch-hunter?" Iris didn't like the sound of those two words together.

"Callixta wrote about them in her book," Greta went on. "They hunted and killed witches during the Great Purge. They're really evil."

"*Were* really evil, right?" Iris corrected her.

"Yes. *Were*. Oh, and one more thing. Div thinks that Colter's little sister Cassie is a witch."

"*What?*"

"Div said she has no idea if Cassie *knows* she's a witch. In any case, it's not good news that she lives in a house full of witch haters."

"No, it's *not* good news. It's bad, terrible, scary news. We need to help her!"

"Definitely. We should tell Ms. O'Shea about her, too . . . plus everything else. Hopefully she'll be back in school today."

"Is she sick?"

"I'm not sure. She wasn't there yesterday, though."

Iris plucked at the sleeve of her flannel shirt; it felt itchy suddenly. Should she go home and change? But then she'd probably be late for school. But if she didn't, she would itch all day and be distracted and not be able to pay attention in class. But if she *did* double back, she'd have to explain to Greta why, which would be embarrassing.

Greta seemed easy to talk to, though. And understanding. And wise. Which made Iris wonder . . . should she tell her about her morningmare? But what if it didn't *mean* anything? What if it was just a psychedelic mash-up of recent events, random memories, Iris's personal fears, and the stuff she'd gleaned from Gofflesby during their mind-melding (or whatever) session? She didn't want to freak Greta out with scary fiction about her and her familiar.

Iris *was* really curious about one particular dream detail, though.

"Have you ever heard this saying, 'Witches do not belong here'? It was in this dream I had last night or this morning or whatever."

"It sounds a bit like our shadow messages. Hang on." Greta did a quick search on her phone. "Here. Okay. That's weird. So we were just talking about witch hunters, right?"

"Actually, I was trying to *avoid* talking about them, but technically, yeah."

Greta scrolled down. "This article says that during the Great Purge, there was a witch hunter named Maximus Hobbes. He lived all over the West Coast. He was personally responsible for the deaths of hundreds of witches. It says that he"—she inhaled sharply—"that he put witches in cages and burned them alive."

Iris gulped and scratched furiously at her wrists.

"The article says that Hobbes and his assistants, followers, whatever you want to call them, they used to chant that phrase when they went on their witch-hunting sprees. *Witches do not belong here.*"

"That's really, really super-terrifying."

"I know. I can't even . . ." Greta stopped, shook her head, and began composing a text. "I'm sending this article to Binx. Maybe she could do more research about that phrase."

"But it was just my dream. It's not, you know, like a clue to Penelope's death or anything."

"It *could* be, though. In witchcraft, dreams are very powerful things. They can be messages, prophecies. Plus, you seem to be really intuitive."

"Thanks."

The itching had subsided somewhat. Iris took off her glasses, wiped strawberry jam off the lenses, and put them back on. Was Greta right? Could her dream be a message or a prophecy?

If so, shouldn't she warn Greta that she might be in danger?

"Yeah, so . . . Gofflesby was in my dream, too," Iris said tentatively.

The black cat stirred on Greta's lap.

"You mean he was in the same dream where you heard that phrase about witches?" Greta asked, confused.

"Yes. And Ridley was in it, too. Gofflesby told me a bunch of stuff about a queen, except he was speaking in French. Does Gofflesby understand French? Sorry, dumb question. Anyhoo, then the queen actually showed up—this was the middle of this enchanted forest—and she was carrying you, but then you turned into Penelope, and the queen buried you, I mean Penelope, and all these flowers started to bloom."

Worry flashed in Greta's eyes. "What do you mean she was carrying me? Was I . . . dead? Is that why I turned into Penelope?"

"I don't know. I'm sorry, I didn't mean to freak you out."

"It's okay. I'm not freaked out, I'm just . . ." Greta stroked the black cat. "That's a lie, I *am* a little freaked out. Almost everything about the past week freaks me out."

"Me too." *Except meeting you*, Iris thought. *And Binx and Ridley, too.*

"Hey, are you going to Penelope's funeral later? The real one, not the one in my dream with the flowers and the queen and French Gofflesby. Obviously."

"I'm going, are you going?"

"Yup."

"Binx and Ridley are going, too. I'm not sure about Div and her girls."

"I don't like funerals."

"I don't like them, either. I don't like goodbyes. But we need to honor our witch sister. Maybe we can walk over together?"

"Yes, please!"

The two girls sat in silence, petting the black cat, watching the sun trying to break through the gray morning mist. When a car backfired down the street, Greta jumped and let out a little yelp. "Sorry, sorry," she murmured, and touched her raw amethyst pendant. Iris wished desperately that she could redo their conversation. She shouldn't have told Greta about the dream; for that matter, she wished she could redo the last few hours so she wouldn't have had the dream to begin with. Things were scary and awful enough with Penelope's death, the shadow messages, the Antima, and everything else. They didn't need the dark storm cloud of long-ago witch-hunters—executioners—hovering over them, too.

28

DRESS CODE

Magic cannot cure all Ills.

(FROM *THE GOOD BOOK OF MAGIC AND MENTALISM*
BY CALLIXTA CROWE)

Ridley stood in front of her closet trying to figure out what to wear for Penelope's funeral. She owned two suits—the black one she'd worn for Daniel's funeral and the navy one that was her go-to recital/ audition/competition suit. She also owned two identical white dress shirts and a black-and-blue-and-sort-of-gray paisley tie that matched both paradigms.

Of course, it didn't ultimately matter which suit she chose, since she would be changing outfits (as well as the rest of her appearance) between here and Sorrow Point Cemetery (she'd already picked out a private spot, not in the Seabreeze development, to cast her *muto* spell). So what should *that* outfit be? A black dress? Or maybe a pair of black slacks, a blazer, and a white silk blouse?

Ridley felt a headache coming on. Massaging her temples, she stared at her reflection in the slightly warped closet mirror. After things had calmed down, she would go back to working on the *vertero* and *dissimulatio* spells. She couldn't wait.

A knock on the door. "You in there, son?"

Her father poked his head through the door. He was dressed in his paramedic uniform, and he was carrying a steel thermos and a brown paper bag. "I'm off to the hospital for a few hours. Do you want me to give you a ride to the Hart girl's funeral? It starts at four, right?"

"No, thanks. I thought this was your day off?"

"Rami had a family emergency, so I'm covering the rest of his shift."

"Oh, okay. Is Harmony still over at her friend's?"

"No, she's downstairs. Your mom's playing with her."

Ridley blinked. "Say what?"

"They're having a snack, too. Your mom made her famous grilled cheese. Make sure to say bye before you go."

"*Momma* is with her," Ridley said skeptically.

Her father's face hardened. "I don't want to hear any disrespect from you."

"I'm not disrespecting her. It's just . . ." Ridley took a deep breath. Was her father choosing to ignore the fact that his wife had been MIA for over a year? *Guess we're not going to discuss that particular reality.* "I'm glad she's up, and I'm glad she's hanging out with Harmony. I'll say hi and bye before I take off."

"All right, then. I'll see you at dinner. Thought I'd grill some burgers."

"Sounds good. I might be late, depending on how long the . . . yeah, so I'll let you know."

After her father left, Ridley dressed quickly (she chose the navy suit; she didn't want Momma seeing her in the black suit), ran a pick through her hair (again, for Momma's benefit), grabbed her backpack, and gave

Agent Smith a handful of timothy hay. She also chose her daily angel card from Daniel's Cleveland Browns mug. The card said: *Life.*

Hmm. A life-themed card made zero sense, given that she was on her way to a funeral. But whatever. The angel cards must know something; they were usually smarter than she was.

Still, shouldn't she have selected a card that said *The Return of the Missing Mother* or something like that?

Downstairs, Ridley found Momma and Harmony playing Barbies on the living-room floor. Barbies with a variety of hairstyles and skin colors as well as Barbie clothes, shoes, accessories, furniture, and even a car (pink, one wheel missing) were scattered all over the carpet, mixed up with random other items like Legos and broken crayons and dried-up balls of Play-Doh. Pandy was asleep on the couch, his face twitching and his tail thumping.

Momma was wearing jeans and a Browns sweatshirt. She'd put on lipstick and a little mascara. Not exactly the old Joyce Ibrahim Stone, City Hall communications director, who owned a closetful of power suits and heels . . . but also not the Joyce Ibrahim Stone who'd been living (or not living?) for the past year-plus in pretty much the same powder-blue robe and nightgown.

"Momma?" Ridley said.

Joyce glanced up from the Barbie pile. "Don't you look so handsome. Why're you all dressed up? Do you have a violin recital today?"

"No, it's . . . it's this thing for my friend." Ridley didn't want to say *funeral.* "I won't be gone long. Unless you need me to stay?"

"Harmony and I will be fine. Are you hungry? There's an extra grilled cheese sandwich on the stove. It might be cold, though, so you should put it in the microwave for thirty seconds, on low. Keep an eye on it so the cheese doesn't go melting like lava all over the place."

"Thanks, Momma, but I already ate."

Harmony was squeezing one of the Barbies into a sequined red ball-gown. She rooted through the messy pile and found a pair of gold vinyl boots. She pulled them over Barbie's freakishly high-arched feet.

"Isn't she beautiful? Isn't she the most beautifulest girl you've ever seen?" Harmony said breathlessly.

"Absolutely," Ridley agreed.

Harmony picked up a doll-sized rhinestone tiara, put it back down, picked up a flower-power headband, and put that down, too.

"What about this one, sweetpea?" Momma asked, offering her a beige hat with a peacock feather.

"Yes, that one! Thank you, Momma Goose!"

"You're welcome, Baby Gosling!"

Harmony giggled. Ridley watched, mesmerized, as her little sister draped the peacock-feather hat over Barbie's cornrows and pretend-walked her to the edge of the couch and back. This was how things used to be. Well, not *exactly* how things used to be, because Daniel wasn't here. Also, back then, Ridley had been so jealous of her mother and little sister playing dolls and dress-up and all the other things she wished she could do with them. But right now, she only felt a tiny sliver of that old jealousy. Right now, what she mostly felt was wonder. And hope.

And life, like the angel card had tried to tell her.

She turned to go.

"Morgan!"

"Yup?"

Harmony thrust something at her. It was a tiny gray silk blouse with pearl buttons.

"Isn't it the beautifulest clothes you've ever seen?"

"Sure."

"I want you to wear it. Pretty please?"

"Um . . . okay. Yeah."

Ridley took the Barbie blouse from her sister and tucked it into the pocket of her navy jacket. "What do you think?"

"It's *purr*-fect!" Harmony said, clapping. She'd been angling to get a kitten lately, so her vocabulary was full of cat words.

"Thanks." Ridley hugged her little sister. "See you later, alligator."

"In a while, *cat*-o-dile!" Harmony turned to their mother. "Barbie wants to have a tea party!"

"Well, then, let's have a tea party, Baby Gosling!"

As Ridley walked out the front door, she heard them discussing teacakes versus tea biscuits and whether or not to invite Skipper and Chelsea and Ken.

Huh.

Life.

Ridley arrived at Sorrow Point Cemetery shortly before four o'clock. She was dressed in a gray silk blouse with pearl buttons (she'd managed to transform the Barbie item into a real item), black wool slacks, and ballet flats; she wished Harmony could see her outfit.

It was weird being here for an actual funeral versus taking a shortcut to the mall. Penelope's gravesite was in a far corner of the cemetery next to an enormous weeping willow and a cluster of laurel bushes. (Willow and laurel were both good for headaches, Ridley thought, touching her temples.) It wasn't too far from Daniel's tree.

It wasn't too far from those two gravestones, either, the ones she and Binx had seen last Wednesday with the words DEAD WITCH on them. Ridley could just make them out in the distance. The hideous graffiti was gone. Washed clean. She wondered who'd done that—city workers? Some anonymous Good Samaritan witches? (She and Binx had intended to return to the cemetery to check out who the gravestones belonged to, but then Penelope's murder had happened. . . .)

The funeral service hadn't started yet. A group of mourners formed a somber U shape around Penelope's casket, which was white and covered with some sort of pretty nature design. Ridley noticed a bunch of teachers from the high school and a dozen or so students, too. She didn't see Ms. O'Shea among them, though. Ms. O'Shea hadn't been at school for the last couple of days; Mr. Eggars, the new substitute (was there a word for a substitute's substitute?), said she'd been called out of town for a family emergency. Ridley wished they had her contact info; there was so much going on, and they could really use her advice and assistance. Maybe Binx should hack into wherever and find her phone number? Although maybe Ms. O'Shea was huddling in secret with her coven up north, strategizing about how to deal with the new, witch-killing witch in town?

Ridley found a spot near the back, away from the others, and stood there, not knowing quite what to do. She noticed a well-dressed man and woman behind a nearby tree. The woman was crying quietly into a white linen handkerchief. The man had his arms around her and was whispering in her ear. Ridley recognized them from last night, driving away in the silver Volvo. Penelope's parents. Her heart ached at the sight of them. At Daniel's funeral, Momma had been inconsolable. Daddy, who was usually so tough and stoic, had broken down halfway through his eulogy speech, and Ridley had been forced to finish it for him.

Penelope's mother glanced up at Ridley. She dabbed at her eyes with the handkerchief and walked over to her, followed by her husband.

"Thank you so much for coming. I'm Elena Guzman, Penny's mother. This is my husband, Edwin Hart."

Mr. Hart shook Ridley's hand. "Are you one of her friends from school?"

"Yes. I'm Ridley. Ridley Stone. I'm so, so sorry about Penelope. I . . . she was really nice."

"If only she'd confided in us, we could have helped her. We could have told her we loved her no matter what," Ms. Guzman said in a choked-up voice.

"Did *you* know she was a witch, Ridley? Did any of her friends?" Mr. Hart asked.

Ridley wished she didn't have to lie to Penelope's parents. "Well, she was new to our school, and we didn't know her that well," she managed.

"We should have spent more time with her; we would have noticed the signs. But we were both so busy," Ms. Guzman murmured.

Mr. Hart's eyes—they were the same warm shade of brown as Penelope's—filled with tears. "She had her YouTube and her tennis and all her other interests, though. She seemed so happy, so excited about her future."

She was *happy*, Ridley wanted to say. *She was excited about her future. And she didn't take her own life. Her life was taken from her.* "I'm so sorry," she said instead, meaning it.

Penelope's parents thanked her again for being there, then moved on to greet other newcomers, including Principal Sparkleman and Mrs. Feathers from school.

Ridley had mixed feelings about Mrs. Feathers. She'd come up to Ridley in the hallway yesterday and said that her *"door was always open"* if she wanted to talk. She'd seemed nice enough, although Ridley had picked up a strange vibe from her. An intense watchfulness under the kind, helpful social-worker exterior. Was there a chance that she knew about Ridley's past in Cleveland? That Ridley was trans? She tried to think if she'd been careless at all in altering her school district records, or if she'd missed an e-mail exchange between the school and her parents. She'd have to revisit them as soon as possible, cast more spells if necessary.

Ridley spotted Greta and Iris walking down the path, toward the crowd. She waved to them, and they hurried to her side. She was glad to see her friends; being at Penelope's funeral was making her feel wobbly inside, and not in a good way.

"Hey." Greta gave Ridley a long, fierce hug. "This is so sad," she murmured.

Ridley nodded into Greta's shoulder. "It's crazy-sad. I still can't believe she's gone."

"Group hug," Iris said, wrapping her arms around both of them.

"This group hug's incomplete, though. Where's Binx?" Ridley asked.

"She said she had to stop by the public library first," Greta replied. "She just texted us."

Ridley pulled her phone out of her pocket to check her messages. "Yeah, here it is. The Sorrow Point Public Library? The place with *books*? That doesn't sound like Binx. Does she even know where it *is*?"

"I know. I asked her to research something related to our . . ." Greta paused, then added, "*Calumnia*. Related to our case. I think she might be working on that."

"Huh." This was turning out to be a day of surprises—first Momma acting like her old self, and now Binx looking at physical books.

An elderly-looking minister had moved to the head of Penelope's casket, cradling a black leather-bound Bible in his hands. "I believe we're about ready to begin. Friends and family of Penelope, please gather around," he called out.

Just then, four latecomers came rushing down the path. It was Colter and another guy who looked like him; probably his brother. And with them were Div and Mira—no Aysha.

"What are Div and Mira doing with Colter?" Ridley whispered to Greta.

"*Calumnia*. Div called me like an hour ago and said that she and Mira are doing more undercover work having to do with that family. She said we shouldn't say hi or talk to them or anything. She said she'd explain later."

"Is that his brother?" Ridley asked.

"Yep."

"Why are they even here, if they hate witches so much?" Iris asked.

"Well, Colter was Penelope's boyfriend. I'm not sure about Hunter . . . maybe moral support?" Greta guessed.

The three girls joined the back of the crowd as the minister began the service. As he spoke, Ridley closed her eyes and just breathed. Her head swirled with a ton of emotions. Sadness about Penelope. Regret that she hadn't gotten to know her better. Fear about what she and the other witches didn't know and what might yet happen.

"We are here today to honor the life of Penelope Rue Hart," the minister was saying.

Ridley opened her eyes. In the distance, she saw Binx hurrying down the path. Ridley didn't want to disturb the minister's speech, so she simply nodded at Binx.

Binx stopped in her tracks and gestured for Ridley to come over. Ridley frowned and pointed to the minister, but Binx shook her head emphatically and continued beckoning.

"Be right back," Ridley whispered to Greta.

Greta raised her eyebrows. Ridley mouthed the word *Binx*, and Greta nodded. Then Ridley slipped away as quietly as possible.

She noticed someone noticing her exit, though. Colter.

A chill ran down her spine. Why was he looking at her? Had he figured out that she, too, was a witch? Had Penelope told him about their Starbucks date (*no, not date, just coffee*), about how they'd tearfully confessed their witch identities to each other?

No way.

Ridley soon reached Binx's side.

"Are you okay?" Binx whispered.

"No. What's up that you couldn't wait till after the service?"

In response, Binx grabbed Ridley's arm and pulled her behind a massive stone mausoleum with a bunch of Latin words engraved on it. "Listen up. So I went to the downtown library—"

"Yeah, I know."

"—because I needed to find this old book about the history of witch-hunters by a dude named Dante Basileri. Did you know that the library has a rare book room? It's really cool, and they make you wear gloves to handle the books because the pages are crazy-fragile. Anyway, this morning, Greta asked me to do some research on a witch-hunter from the Great Purge times. Maximus Hobbes. I went online, and long story short, the trail eventually led to Basileri's book."

"Is Maximus Hobbes the one who hunted down and killed like hundreds of witches? I've heard of him."

"Yeah, that's the one. Nice guy, right? So in his book, Basileri explains his theory about Hobbes. And guess what? His theory is related to C-Squared, too."

"Go on."

"Some people believe that she was the greatest, most powerful witch of all time, right? And that *her* book is the reason why most of us who were born witches even know how to practice the craft? Or even know that we're witches? Well, according to Basileri, Hobbes believed that C-Squared had special . . . I don't know, like special genes or special superpowers or something, and that her heart-fire and the heart-fire of her descendants could extend life. Even make you immortal, I suppose, if you had like a never-ending supply."

Ridley crossed her arms over her chest. "O-kay. What's 'heart-fire'?"

"I'm still trying to figure that out. Maybe it's a special potion that only C-Squared and her descendants knew how to make, because of their specialness or whatever? But after I read all this, I thought of something really, really horrifying."

"More horrifying than all the witch murders Hobbes committed during the Purge?"

"Yes. What if Hobbes is still alive?"

29

HEARTLESS

Certain witches may possess a special quality
that makes them more attractive to their Enemies.

(FROM *THE GOOD BOOK OF MAGIC AND MENTALISM*
BY CALLIXTA CROWE)

"The Lord is my shepherd; I shall not want. He maketh me to lie down in green pastures; he leadeth me beside the still waters. He restoreth my soul: he leadeth me in the paths of righteousness for his name's sake."

Iris buttoned up her black cardigan as the elderly minister stood over Penelope's grave and recited from the Bible. The casket, which had not been lowered into the ground yet, was painted white with a fancy design of birds and butterflies. The tag on Iris's sweater was bothering her; she reached back and tried to rip it out, but that didn't work, so she just peeled off the cardigan and bunched it up and held it in her arms. It smelled like mothballs, though, which also bothered her, so she shoved the whole thing into her shoulder bag, next to her wand.

She'd only been to one other funeral in her life—her dad's, which hadn't been a funeral so much as a memorial service with his three friends from college playing the guitar as his ashes were scattered into the waters off Montauk, Long Island, near where he'd grown up. She remembered vividly the honeysuckle and salt in the air, the big waves at high tide. She hoped this funeral, Penelope's funeral, wouldn't make her cry as much as her dad's, although it was entirely possible that she'd cry twice as much because there were now *two* deaths in her life. That was the thing about trauma; it could accumulate like waves and grow bigger, one on top of the other.

She took off her glasses and pinched the bridge of her nose, hard. Mrs. Feathers's trick definitely didn't work for her; tears were already pooling in her eyes. Mrs. Feathers, who was standing just a few feet away, seemed to sense Iris's agitation and gave her a sympathetic nod.

And in addition to her grief, there was her anxiety, which was escalating by the minute. Even with everything going on around her, she couldn't stop thinking about her morningmare. And the more she thought about it, the more it felt like a premonition. What if Greta really *was* in danger? She *had* received a shadow message, after all. Div had received a shadow message, too, and she was attacked at the Jessups' party.

"Yea, though I walk through the valley of the shadow of death, I will fear no evil: for thou art with me; thy rod and thy staff comfort me."

To avoid having a complete emotional meltdown, Iris had performed a calming spell pre-funeral, with a special tea blend. (*As I sip this brew, clear my mind, and help me push through, for inside I can be aligned.*) She crossed her fingers and toes now, hoping that the spell would get her through the next couple of hours.

Iris felt eyes on her. She swiveled her head this way and that, then realized that Colter was staring at her from the other side of Penelope's casket. *O-kay.* Why? She'd only met him twice—on the first day of school, and in the cafeteria when she was having lunch with the two covens and Penelope. Or was he staring at Greta, who was standing right next to her? Nope, his gaze was definitely fixed on *her.* Should she play it cool and smile at him in a casual, *I-don't-know-anything-about-your-Antima-shoulder-patch-or-the-murder-board-in-your-family's-house* kind of way? But people didn't smile at funerals because funerals were sad, so maybe she should just acknowledge him with a slow, melancholy nod?

Wait. But what if he'd figured out that she was a witch? Would he or his 1415, *N-O,* New Order group come after her? Was it even *his* group?

Iris began to scratch furiously at her right arm.

"It's going to be all right."

Greta was whispering in her ear. Her warm hand slipped into Iris's hand and squeezed. Iris squeezed back. At Greta's touch, she could feel the itching subside, the high pitch of unease relax a little.

"It's going to be all right," Greta repeated. "I promise."

Iris nodded, and her glasses slipped down her nose. She pushed them back up again. When this was all over—when they'd solved the mystery of Penelope's death and put the Antima out of commission and eliminated whatever other dangers might lurk over their coven and Div's coven—Iris couldn't wait to really immerse herself and learn more about the craft from Greta and the others. Iris pictured their coven meetings, joining together in their warm candlelit circle and pulling the universe's energy into their hands and hearts so they could make magic together.

Their coven. So she'd definitely decided to join Greta's coven. *Huh. Go, me, making big life decisions and stuff!*

"Surely goodness and mercy shall follow me all the days of my life: and I will dwell in the house of the Lord forever," the elderly minister finished.

"Family and friends, please say your farewells to our dear Penelope before she is laid to her final rest."

People began lining up at the foot of the casket. Iris joined the line right behind Greta. Binx and Ridley were in the distance, still huddled behind a big stone . . . what was it called? A crypt? A tomb? A mausoleum? She wondered what in the hex they were talking about so intently that they would have missed most of the funeral.

Greta reached the front of the line. She picked up a long-stemmed pink rose from a white basket and laid it on top of the casket. She steepled her hands under her chin, in prayer.

"Penelope. May your soul fly to the stars and moons and become one with the universe," she whispered, so softly that only Iris could hear. "May the Goddess watch over you always. May you be joined eternally in heart and spirit with all of your sisters, past, present, and future. Love and light."

Iris was next. Suddenly nervous—more nervous than before—she began scratching at her arm again. *Stop it*, she told herself. *Just do what Greta did.*

She reached into the white basket and hastily extracted one of the pink roses. But a thorn caught the skin on her thumb and drew blood. Stifling a yelp, she shoved her thumb into her mouth.

"Pen-ner-o-*blah*," she began, then pulled her thumb out of her mouth when she realized that she was mumbling incoherently. "*Penelope.* I didn't know you very well. I wish I had. I hope you're happy in heaven. Please say hi to my dad for me. And my grandpa Louis, too. When you meet them, they'll probably be arguing about politics. Or watching NASCAR . . . Is there ESPN up there? There probably is. Anyhoo, please give them lots of hugs for me. I'm sending you hugs, too. Love and light."

Iris lifted the rose to her face to kiss it—she wasn't sure why, but it seemed like a nice gesture—before setting it down on the casket along with the other roses. Its fragrance was sweet—*too* sweet, like those bubblegum-flavored cupcakes that had made her throw up at Ephrem's birthday party last year. Her brain zapped and spun. Nausea rippled and ripped through her insides.

Gasping, she dropped the rose onto the casket. Blood from her thumb dripped onto the white wood; alarmed, she reached down to rub it off with the heel of her palm.

As her hand touched the casket, her brain seemed to short-circuit entirely.

The terrible image hit her like a wave.

She could see Penelope—right here, right now. Lying inside the forever darkness of her casket, alone. Her eyes closed as though in sleep, her flesh cold and hard. Wearing a pale pink dress with gold buttons, her hands folded over her chest . . .

. . . over her heart. Which wasn't there.

Her heart wasn't there.

Iris cried out and stumbled backward. Arms caught her. Greta's.

"Iris, what *is* it?"

Iris could envision the inside of Penelope's chest cavity . . . the bones, the dammed-up veins, the atrophied muscles. And, in the cavity that should be housing her heart, a void. Emptiness.

People were buzzing and whispering. Iris blinked and gazed around wildly. Everyone was staring at her—the minister, Penelope's parents, their friends and relatives, people from school, Div, Mira, Colter . . .

. . . and Hunter, who was moving swiftly in Iris's direction.

"Does your friend need medical help? I'm trained as an EMT," Hunter called out to Greta.

Greta stepped between Hunter and Iris. "Thanks, but—"

"I'm fine!" Iris cut in. "Sorry, everybody! I'm just"—she raised her voice—"I'm just having an anxiety attack! I just need some space and fresh air and . . ."

She took Greta's hand and pulled her away from the crowd.

"Iris? What's wrong?"

Iris led Greta all the way to the tomb, mausoleum, whatever, where Binx and Ridley were still huddling.

"Whoa, girl. You look like you just saw a ghost," Binx said to Iris.

"I . . . I did." Iris sank down on the cool, mossy ground and leaned against the old stone wall. But more visions flashed through her brain—bones, many bones, under the ground beneath her—so she jumped to her feet and scrambled away from the wall. What the hex was happening to her?

"*Guys.* Penelope . . . I saw her and . . . she's missing . . . she's missing her heart."

Binx's jaw dropped. "She's . . . *what?*"

"I don't understand. How could you have seen that?" Ridley demanded.

Greta touched her arm. "Was it another one of your visions?" she asked gently.

"Yup, uh-huh." Iris grasped her smiley-face moonstone necklace, to calm herself, but she was beyond calming (the tea-spell had stopped working, obviously). "I saw all her organs inside her body, except for her heart."

"Soooo . . . maybe they did an autopsy?" Ridley suggested queasily. "Or maybe she was an organ donor, and they gave her heart to a patient who needed one?"

Binx held up both hands. "Guys? *Guys!* What if someone stole it? For her heart-fire?"

"Um . . . what's heart-fire?" Iris asked, although she wasn't sure she wanted to know.

Ridley glanced at Binx, then turned to Greta and Iris. "You guys might want to sit down for this."

After the funeral, everyone gathered at Penelope's house. The dining room table was covered with an array of fancy party foods. People stood around in small groups, eating and drinking and talking; soft classical music played on an invisible sound system.

Iris, Greta, Ridley, and Binx skipped the socializing and sequestered themselves immediately in the family room. Iris sank back in the big, comfy sofa (which bore strands of white dog fur) and hugged a pillow to her chest, hard. The room was a sad place because it was full of Penelope. Dozens of framed photos of her covered the walls—from age zero to the present, from braces to retainer to no braces, from first tennis trophy to junior champion.

Iris was still in a state of shock—not just from the horrific image of Penelope without her heart, which would be burned into her brain forever, but from what Binx and Ridley had told her and Greta at the cemetery. That a witch-hunter—no, not just a witch-hunter, but the most murderous, monstrous witch-hunter in history—may have kept himself alive all this time by killing Callixta Crowe's descendants and stealing some kind of immortality-potion essence from their hearts.

Including, it seemed, Penelope's.

"I've been thinking, too, about that murder board thing that Div saw at the Jessups' house," Binx was saying. "She said it was about some witch-hunter, right? Well, what if that witch-hunter was Maximus Hobbes? Maybe *they* know he's still alive, too. And by *they*, I mean the Jessups, the Antima, the New Order group, whatever."

Iris sat up, still clutching the pillow; the pressure of it made her brain feel a little less spinny. "So really, this murder board isn't about hunting down a murderer to throw him in jail or level-jump in *Witchworld*? But it's about finding a murderer who's actually your hero because of your shared hatred of, plus world-domination supervillain plan to kill, witches?"

"Yeah, basically." Binx turned to Greta. "Is Div here? I should show her a photo of Hobbes and see if it's the same guy she saw on the board. Or I could just text it to her and—"

Greta held up her hand. "No, wait! I'm not sure if she's here yet or if she's even coming . . . but she and Mira might still be with Colter and Hunter, and we don't want to take any chances."

"Are we in *calumnia* mode?" Ridley asked nervously. "*Calumnia* again, just in case. Can we get hold of Ms. O'Shea somehow? I really feel like we could use her help. Like, we were in over our heads before, but now, we're like . . . *drowning*. The new sub said she had some family emergency. Maybe she's with her coven?"

"Maybe, but she never gave us her contact info. Maybe I can get it from the school district database. They must have addresses and phone numbers and stuff of all the subs, right?" Binx began typing on her phone.

"There you are, girls!"

Mrs. Feathers entered the room, a glass of white wine in hand. Binx pocketed her phone. Iris jumped to her feet; had Mrs. Feathers heard them talking? Were they in serious, major trouble? She glanced over her shoulder at Greta, wondering if they should cast a group memory-erase spell or whatever.

Greta stood up, too, and smoothed her skirt. Her face was pale, but she managed to plaster on a smile. "We weren't feeling very social. Sorry. Were you looking for us, Mrs. Feathers?"

"Yes, I was. I know this is such a sad day, so I was trying to find something positive to help us all go forward. I was thinking, wouldn't it be lovely to commission a bench or a sculpture or a fountain for our school, in Penelope's memory? I just spoke with Principal Sparkleman, and he said he could ask the PTA to raise money for it. I've heard you're very artistic, Greta, so I thought I could pick your brain."

"Sure, yes, of course."

"Maybe we could come up with a list of ideas and present them to Mr. Hart and Ms. Guzman in the next week or two? And the PTA, too? Come, I want to show you Penelope's room. Perhaps it will inspire us. Her mother said it was fine for us to go up. Excuse us, girls."

Greta joined Mrs. Feathers, and they disappeared into the hallway. Binx turned to Iris and Ridley. "*Calumnia*. Did she say . . . Ms. Guzman? Who's that?"

"She's Penelope's mom. Didn't you meet her?" Ridley asked.

"Not really. I thought her name was Mrs. or Ms. Hart."

"Nope, it's Guzman. Why?"

Frowning, Binx pulled out her phone and scrolled through it quickly. "Patricia Meeks . . . Dominick Trovato . . . Eleanor Guzman," she read out loud.

"Who are those people? Wait, is Eleanor Guzman Penelope's mom?" Iris asked.

"I thought she told me her name was Elena, though," Ridley said, confused.

"Eleanor Guzman is . . ." Binx hesitated. "So, I found her name through this app. . . . She's part of this, um, project I'm doing. About witches. It's kind of a secret, and . . . *blurg*, I really can't talk about it." She threw up her hands.

"You're keeping a secret from us?" Ridley demanded. "What is it? Spill!"

"I can't. I promised. Maybe soon, though. I'll ask, okay?"

"Ask *who*? Are you saying this Eleanor Guzman is a witch? And that she might be Penelope's relative?"

"Look, I'll explain later. Right now, we need to find Ms. O'Shea."

"Fine."

"Fine!"

As the two girls typed furiously on their phones, Iris's brain began to spin again. She leaned forward and put her head in her hands and squeezed as hard as she could. Sometimes the pressure helped, but at the moment, it made her brain feel even spinnier.

Iris wasn't sure how much time had passed, but at some point, the family room door opened and closed. She glanced up. A poodle with curly white hair lumbered in, its big brown eyes dull with grief.

Penelope's dog. The one in the window.

"Socrates!" Ridley set down her phone and knee-walked across the rug, holding out her hand. "Hey, guy. Remember me? You poor thing, you must miss her so much."

Socrates sniffed at her hand and whimpered. She wrapped her arms around him, kissing his head. Binx joined them, patting Socrates on the side. Iris slipped off the couch and reached out to pet him, too.

The second Iris's hand made contact with his soft, curly fur, her brain seemed to explode. A flurry of strange images ripped through her neurons. She was having a waking nightmare.

A small gray house. A big oak tree. A crow perched on a stone birdbath.

Inside, a prisoner tied up in a red chair.

A teacup full of blood. No, tea. No, poison.

The prisoner was Penelope.

No, it was Greta.

Iris leaped to her feet and began scratching her arms, so hard that she drew blood. "Guys? Okay, I just had one of my crazy visions, and . . . where's Greta? I need to talk to Greta, like, now!"

"She went up to Penelope's room with Mrs. Feathers," Ridley replied.

"I think she might be in trouble. Or she's going to be in trouble. I think she might be a prisoner in a little gray house with a birdbath and an oak tree in the front yard—"

"Are you joking? Is this a joke?" Binx cut in.

"Whatever. Let's just go find Greta, okay?" Ridley said, looking worried.

The three girls left the family room and headed down the hall, Socrates trailing after them. They went up a set of stairs and found Penelope's room on the second floor, way in the back. Iris recognized the flower-print curtains from yesterday's Nancy Drew stakeout mission. The room was large and light-filled, with lemon-yellow walls and a big desk covered with computers, video cameras, and makeup samples.

"Greta?" Iris called out.

Silence.

"Mrs. Feathers? Greta?" Binx said loudly.

More silence.

Ridley's phone was pressed against her ear. "I'm calling Greta now, but she's not picking up."

"I just texted her, too. No answer." Binx's hand shook as she scrolled through her phone. "Guys? This may seem random, but . . . do you know if Greta is related to a Patricia Meeks, Dominick Trovato, Norman Smythe, or Adelita Suarez?"

"Her great-grandma's name was Adelita." Iris spoke up. "I saw her picture at their house. She was pretty, like Greta. I don't know about the Suarez part."

"If her last name *is* Suarez, well . . . I think this might mean that Greta and Penelope are both descended from C-Squared. Callixta Crowe."

"Um . . . what? How do you know this?' Ridley asked skeptically.

"I've been . . . I just do. Please, you have to trust me. I don't have time to explain," Binx insisted.

She continued scrolling through her phone, her fingers flying. Her tense expression grew more frantic by the second.

"What's happening? What are you doing?" Ridley asked.

"A geolocating spell. Iris is right. We need to find that gray house with the birdbath and the oak tree, like, *immediately*. I think Greta might . . . she might be in terrible danger. Or maybe we're too late, and—"

"She might be dead," Iris finished in a choked voice.

✳ 30 ✳

TEA FOR TWO

They began as witch-hunters,
then they discovered that they were
themselves witches.
And oh, how irresistible is Power!

(FROM *THE GOOD BOOK OF MAGIC AND MENTALISM*
BY CALLIXTA CROWE)

Greta was having a dream. Finally. Perhaps the marigolds under her pillow or the wild asparagus root or the peppermint had worked, after all; or perhaps the Goddess had intervened.

Greta hadn't told Iris—she hadn't really even admitted it to herself—but she envied Iris's prophetic abilities. Sure, Iris's dreams and visions could be terribly dark, like the one she'd had about . . . what was that again? Greta lying in a queen's arms, dead? But messages from the magical realm, like poetry and art, often held layers and layers of meaning. And Greta's poetic, artistic temperament was well-suited for receiving and deciphering these layers. And also sitting still with upsetting images, unafraid, letting love and light sift through and illuminate them.

Perhaps it was all part of the Goddess's plan, though . . . the years of dreamlessness followed by this new power. Greta would use it well. This was a beginning.

The dream, her very first dream, was about springtime.

She was in her garden, Bloomsbury, planting new seedlings that she'd cultivated inside the house over the winter. She'd made little labels to go with them, too, recycling dozens of Teo's Popsicle sticks; she'd written the English names on one side and the Latin names on the other, in elegant cursive. Yarrow; *Achillea millefolium*. Dill; *Anethum graveolens*. Cilantro; *Coriandrum sativum*. Eyebright; *Euphrasia officinalis*. Balm of Gilead; *Populus balsamifera*.

"Hi there!"

A woman entered the garden through an ornate black iron gate. She looked familiar. Was it the social worker from school?

"Mrs. Feathers?"

"Yes. How are you, Greta? Are you enjoying the day?"

Greta stood up and brushed her hands against her long wool skirt. She knotted her velvet scarf around her neck. "Yes, thank you! Are you here to see Penelope?"

"Is she here?"

Greta glanced around. "I thought she was, but I haven't seen her in a while."

"No worries. I'm sure she'll be joining us soon. Or perhaps we'll be joining her."

"At her birthday party?"

"Yes, at her birthday party. It should be quite magical!"

Greta's gaze dropped to the ground. The seedlings were already starting to grow. She could see them shooting up, millimeter by millimeter. How miraculous! Bloomsbury must be enchanted, after all. A few feet away, a family of robins splashed around in the stone birdbath. No, not robins. Crows?

And then the dream shifted . . . and suddenly Greta and Mrs. Feathers were inside a room, sitting on either side of a low, old-fashioned-looking table. Dozens of candles cast a warm, glowing light. The room had high, molded tin ceilings, a velvet couch, and a stained-glass window. Also a red chair with a doll on it.

Strange . . . the doll was bound to the chair with thick ropes. Was that part of the birthday festivities?

On the table was a silver tray with a full tea service. The teapot and cups and saucers were bone-white with an unusual flower design.

"Welcome to my home, Greta," said Mrs. Feathers.

"Thank you. Are those lilies?" Greta asked, pointing to the design on the tea set.

"No, they're angel's trumpets. Do you know them?"

"*Brugmansia.* Family name *Solanaceae.* Order *Polemoniales.*"

"Yes! What a clever girl you are! No wonder you're such a talented witch."

Greta frowned. Mrs. Feathers wasn't supposed to know that she practiced the craft. "What do you mean? I'm not a—"

"And these are white baneberry," Mrs. Feathers cut in, pointing to a different flower on the tea set. "Also known as doll's eye."

"*Actaea pachypoda.*"

"Exactly. A-plus. Now, shall I be Mother?"

Greta knew that expression from old English novels, from a time when mothers were expected to pour the tea for everyone.

"Yes. Sure. What you said before, though. I . . . I'm not a witch."

"Of course you are. And as it turns out, you're also a scion of Callixta Crowe. So is Penelope. *Was.*"

"Callixta?" Greta was so confused. She remembered that name from somewhere. And wasn't *scion* the same thing as *descendant*? "Penelope and I are related?"

"Yes, through Callixta's lineage. That's why we had to harvest her heart-fire, and that's why we must harvest yours."

Heart-fire?

Suddenly, Greta saw that the doll was no longer tied up in the red chair. *She* was. The doll was lying on the floor, bleeding. A one-eyed gray cat was licking her wounds. Crying out, Greta strained against the ropes, but they were unyielding.

"You see, Maximus needs the heart-fire of Callixta's scions in order to stay alive," Mrs. Feathers continued.

"I don't understand. Who is Maximus? Are . . . Are you guys Antima?"

Mrs. Feathers laughed. "Antima? No, no, no. We made you and Div and your other witches *think* that the Antima were after you."

"But Ms. O'Shea said—"

"Ms. O'Shea isn't relevant. And she won't be returning to Sorrow Point."

"W-what?"

A slow drumbeat of panic was building inside Greta. She glanced around wildly—what if this *wasn't* a dream? She had to get the hex out of here. This woman seemed off, dangerous.

Her eyes fell on the one-eyed cat. Its whiskers were covered with the doll's blood.

But it wasn't the one-eyed cat anymore. This cat had two eyes, the color of emeralds. And long golden fur.

Gofflesby.

"Gofflesby! What are you doing here?" Greta cried out. She turned to Mrs. Feathers. "Did you hurt him?"

Mrs. Feathers lifted the lid off the flowery teapot. Steam rose in the air, and she smiled, satisfied. "I would never hurt him. He is one of my familiars."

"What? No! He's *my* familiar. And . . . wait, you're a *witch*?"

"I sent him out in the world to help us find Callixta's scions and to confirm their identities. He found you. There are other animals like him out there, my other pets, doing our good work."

"Gofflesby is *my* familiar! He would *never* help someone like you!"

"He gave us the final proof that you are a scion. Your birthmark. Here, above your heart." Mrs. Feathers touched her own sternum. "All of Callixta's scions possess this."

Greta looked down. She'd always had the heart-shaped birthmark above her breastbone. It was tiny and light brown and barely noticeable.

"This is a dream," she whispered to herself. "This is just a dream. I need to wake up."

"It's not a dream, my dear."

Mrs. Feathers tipped the pot over the cup, releasing a thin ribbon of steaming tea. She added a generous dollop of honey and stirred. The silver spoon made a soothing tinkling noise against the porcelain.

The tinkling noise stopped, and she lifted the cup and touched it to Greta's lips.

Greta froze.

Angel's trumpet.

White baneberry.

They were highly toxic plants.

"No!" Greta cried out, wrenching away.

Mrs. Feathers sighed. "I'm afraid you don't have a choice, Greta.

And I must insist you cooperate. There is a specific procedure with the harvesting, and we must follow the steps precisely."

Greta screamed and struggled, twisting her body this way and that. The knots were like cement.

Don't panic. Stay calm. Greta couldn't touch her raw amethyst pendant, but she could imagine it there, connect to its power.

Goddess, please help me.

Solvo. The untying spell. *Yes!* She shuttered her eyes, took a deep, cleansing breath, and began to channel her spiritual energy. *"Solvo,"* she whispered.

"Solvo won't work here, my dear. There's no use fighting it."

"You're a witch. How can you hurt other witches?"

"We're not hurting you, not really. We're allowing you to serve a higher purpose, which is to keep him alive. Maximus Hobbes, the greatest witch and witch-hunter in history. Now, drink up."

A witch and *witch-hunter? How was that possible?*

Mrs. Feathers lifted the teacup to Greta's lips again. The tea trickled into her mouth. It had a warm, green, slightly bittersweet taste that was masked only slightly by the lavender honey.

"Good girl."

"Gofflesby," Greta whispered. She was becoming woozy.

Gofflesby had resumed licking the doll's blood. But it wasn't a doll anymore. It was a bird. A crow.

"Iris . . . Binx . . . Ridley . . ."

"I'm sure they'll all come to your funeral. Now, drink up, my dear."

"Love and light."

"Yes, yes. Love and light. Keep drinking."

Greta felt wetness on her cheeks. Tea? Tears?

Iris. Binx. Ridley. And Div. And Teo and Mama and Papa.

And Gofflesby.

A footstep, light as a feather.

A man was standing in front of her.

No, not a man. A teenager. He had long brown hair that fell to his chin, and the shadow of a mustache and beard.

"Hello, Greta."

"W-who are you?"

"I'm Maximus Hobbes."

"You're . . . Maximus?"

"Yes. And you're Greta Ysabel Navarro. The leader of your own coven. Great-granddaughter of Adelita, whom I had the pleasure of . . . anyway, I know a great deal about you. I'm also a friend of your friend Binx."

"Binx?"

Greta's eyelids felt heavy, so heavy. She was wrong; Maximus wasn't a teenager. He *was* a man. An old man. He had long silver hair and a bushy mustache and beard. He had thick, brooding eyebrows over kind eyes.

No, not kind. Sad.

Maximus turned to Mrs. Feathers. "Get it done."

"As you wish, sir."

Maximus left the room. Greta needed to stay awake, but she couldn't stay awake. Her mind was already returning to a dream state. Or was this a dream within a dream?

Gofflesby had stopped licking the dead crow.

Good boy.

Sitting very still, Gofflesby eyed Mrs. Feathers, who was searching for something. A wand? A knife? When she wasn't looking, he reached out a paw and batted at something, knocking it soundlessly against a silk drape.

The dream was sinking deeper, to a darker place. The end was almost near. Greta could feel it. If only she could hold her familiar one last time, tell him how much she loved him.

But he wasn't Greta's familiar. He was *her* familiar. . . .

Gofflesby continued batting, knocking, moving soundlessly.

The smell of smoke. Greta blinked through the wooziness and tried to see what was burning.

"No!" Mrs. Feathers shouted. She pointed her wand, or her knife, at Gofflesby.

Hissing, he disappeared into the fire.

No! Greta screamed.

Everything was swirling. The dream was collapsing into the other dream.

She closed her eyes.

And then there was no more.

THE FATE OF ALL CROWS

Reality and Dreams can sometimes be
one and the same.
Or in great contradiction to each other. Or both.

(FROM *THE GOOD BOOK OF MAGIC AND MENTALISM*
BY CALLIXTA CROWE)

\\| think I've got it!"

Binx, Iris, and Ridley had slipped out of Penelope's house and were standing next to a row of parked cars. Binx slanted her phone toward the other two girls and jabbed her finger at the screen.

Iris squinted at a tiny blue dot; was that the gray house where Greta was being held prisoner? She reached over and touched the dot and closed her eyes, waiting for confirmation. *Nothing.*

Come on, stupid vision, she thought angrily, because she had no other words, no official spell, to make her brain generate the faraway information she needed. Still nothing. Obviously, they were going to have to rely on Binx's cybermagic to get them to Greta.

"What's the address?" Ridley demanded.

"It's One Hundred Fifty-Eight Spring Street. I'm texting it to Aysha and telling her to communicate with Div and Mira somehow without alerting Colter and Hunter, and for all of them to get their butts over there ASAP. So I had Uxie search through a bunch of real-estate sale records and county deeds looking for gray houses. Once I had those, I hacked into this high-tech global satellite system to zero in on their yards in search of bird fountains and big oak trees. Which was not easy. This is the one, though. I'm a hundred percent. Well, ninety-nine."

"Spring Street . . . that's near my house. Like, a block or two away, on the other side of the Seabreeze development." Ridley pointed. "Come on!"

Ridley and Binx took off running, and Iris ran after them. Her head was throbbing, and she felt like throwing up; her anxiety was off the charts, despite her moonstone pendant, despite her therapy breathing, and despite several attempts at calming spells. She and the others *had* to save Greta. But what if they were too late?

"Did you find out who lives there?" Ridley asked Binx as they took a shortcut through one of the construction sites on Lilac Street.

"I think it's a rental, but I didn't have time to find out who's renting it," Binx replied.

Iris hurried her steps to catch up to the other two girls. "Guys? Isn't this close to that street with the red pickup truck . . . you know, where we found . . ."

Ridley looked around as she ran. "You're right! I think that construction site is, like, half a block over."

"So if Penelope was, um . . . and then they moved her body to . . . it wouldn't have been very far," Iris noted.

"There it is!" Binx yelled.

The sign for Spring Street was just up ahead, half-hidden behind a stand of pine trees. Iris reached into her shoulder bag for her wand; she didn't care who saw it, she wanted to be ready. Binx and Ridley seemed to be on the same wavelength; Binx pulled her wand out of her backpack, and Ridley did the same with hers.

They raced around the corner and onto Spring Street . . .

. . . and stopped in their tracks. At the far end of the street, the windows of a house glowed bright orange. A small gray house. Plumes of smoke seeped out of its sides.

"Is that One Hundred Fifty-Eight?" Ridley cried out.

"It's on fire!" Iris shouted.

"I have a 911 spell," Binx said, pushing a button on her phone.

Iris quickly cast *accelerando* to increase her speed. And then just like that, she was standing in front of 158 Spring Street. Binx and Ridley were still a hundred or so feet behind her.

Fire was blazing inside the gray house, spreading across the walls, licking at the curtains. Iris could make out the outlines of two people inside. One was moving around, the other was sitting in a chair. *Tied* to a chair. Was that Greta?

Stay calm, stay calm, stay calm, Iris told herself.

She squeezed her eyes shut and tried to remember the spell from Callixta's book that extinguished fire.

"Restinguere!" she yelled, raising her wand in the air.

Nothing.

Binx and Ridley came running up to her.

"What about *ceasaro*?" Binx said breathlessly.

"Yes!" Ridley nodded.

The three girls stood in a semicircle, pointed their wands, and yelled: *"Ceasaro!"*

Still nothing.

Just then, a red Miata convertible came tearing down the street. It screeched to a stop in front of 158 Spring Street, and Mira, Div, and Aysha jumped out.

"We got your message. What's going on? Where's Greta?" Div called.

"Inside. Where have you guys *been*?" Ridley demanded.

"No time. Everyone, form a circle, *now*!" Div ordered.

The five witches obeyed. They pointed their wands inward, creating six spokes in a wheel.

"Visualize Greta in the middle. And repeat after me. *Exorior!*"

"Exorior!"

Greta did not appear.

"Exorior!" they repeated, more loudly.

Still no Greta.

The clock was running out. Forget about Div's spells or Callixta Crowe's spells—Iris had to do what Jadora had done when her familiar, Baxxtern, was trapped inside a burning tavern and her magic wasn't working because of the Ongolean Ork king's Weakening Curse.

Run into the fire.

I am strong. I am brave. I can do this. Intention!

Wielding her wand in her right hand and covering her face with her left, Iris spun around, ducked her head, and shouldered her way through the front door. A tsunami wave of heat pounded against her. Smoke burned her eyes like acid. She could hear the girls outside yelling her name.

"Greta, where are you?" Iris shouted.

"I-Iris?" came the faint reply.

Greta!

Hope and resolve cut through Iris's panic and gave her strength. She pointed her wand in front of her. *"Malorna!"*

A beam of light sliced through the dense smoke. Iris could make out Greta slumped in the chair, rope binding her feet and legs.

The smoke was getting thicker by the minute; Iris could feel it scraping and choking her throat, her lungs. Coughing, she aimed her wand at the ropes. What *was* that spell? *Oh yeah.*

"Solvo!"

The ropes splintered and snapped and gave way. Greta started to tumble out of the chair. Gasping for breath, nearly blinded by the smoke, Iris rushed to catch her before she fell.

"We have to get you out of here. Can you walk?"

Greta mumbled an incoherent reply.

"What?"

"S-save. G-Gofflesby."

"Gofflesby's here?"

A crashing sound. A ceiling beam had fallen just inches away from them, kicking up more flames. The fire was accelerating, blooming into an inferno; they had to get out of the house immediately.

Iris reached for Greta's velvet scarf and wrapped it loosely around Greta's nose and mouth. "Breathe through this; it'll be less smoky. Come on . . . this way!"

"G-Gofflesby."

"I know. I'll find him, but we have to get you out of here first."

Iris half led, half dragged Greta to the door. She could hear sirens in the distance; help was on the way.

The girls were waiting just outside the door. Ridley, Binx, and Aysha took Greta from Iris and laid her gently on the grass. Div and Mira immediately launched into a series of healing spells on Greta—first *respiri*, then *medeora*.

Ridley and Binx began casting the same spells on Iris. But Iris didn't have time to be healed. She had to go back in for Gofflesby.

She started to head inside again . . . then stopped when she saw Mrs. Feathers from school, standing behind a column of flames in the burning house.

Was she . . . *smiling*?

"Mrs. Feathers!" Iris shouted. "You have to get out of there! Is there a cat in there with you?"

In response, Mrs. Feathers raised her arms in the air.

She said something, her lips moving furiously, but Iris couldn't hear.

And just like that, the flames vanished.

The smoke cleared.

The siren noises stopped.

Iris turned around, feeling fuzzy and dazed. Greta was rising to her feet and brushing her hair out of her eyes. "What were we talking about?" she asked Iris.

"I—I can't remember," Iris replied.

"Where are we, anyway? How did we end up on this street? *What is our location?"* Binx asked her phone.

The screen flashed an answer.

"Huh. It says we're at One Hundred Fifty-Eight Spring Street. Do we know anyone who lives at One Hundred Fifty-Eight Spring Street?"

Mira strolled over to the mailbox. She reached inside and pulled out a handful of envelopes. "Someone named . . . Margaret Feathers?"

"Who in the hex is that?" said Aysha.

"Not sure. Seriously, how did we get here?" Div asked, brushing dirt off her white dress.

Aysha glared at Binx. "Hey! Did you guys prank us?"

"No! Did *you* guys prank *us*?" Binx shot back.

"You guys used *transfero* on us, didn't you? Maybe that plus *praetero*?" Aysha sneered.

"No, but *you* guys obviously did!" Binx said hotly.

Ridley rainbow-waved. "Excuse me! I'm hungry. Is anyone else hungry?"

Mira studied her French tips. "I know a cool spell that turns rocks into food."

"That's weird. Let's get some *real* food," said Binx.

"Let's go down to my grandma's café. I think she baked scones today!" Iris piped up.

"Yeah, okay, fine. But I have to be home in an hour to walk the puppy," said Binx, glancing at her phone again.

"Mira, you and I don't have time for scones. We're having dinner at the Jessups' house, remember? Colter and Hunter invited us," Div reminded her.

"Oh. Right!"

"How is your undercover work going?" Greta asked.

"The plan is to win Colter's and Hunter's trust so we can find out if one of them is the head of the New Order group. Or whether their father is involved. I guess we should consider their mom, too? Once we know that for sure, I think we'll be a lot closer to finding out who killed Penelope," Div said.

"Whoever did it is going to be so sorry," Ridley murmured angrily.

"Justice *will* be served," Mira said, then took out her smart key. "Who wants a ride? I can drop everyone off, then Div and I can head over to the Jessups'."

"Can that little car fit"—Iris counted on her fingers—"seven people?"

"No worries. I have a spell for that," Mira replied with a wink.

As the two covens drove off down Spring Street, Gofflesby jumped out of the bushes and trotted along behind them.

EPILOGUE

"Hey, Pokedragon."

"Hey, ShadowKnight."

Binx sat cross-legged in the Japanese meditation hut, trying to decipher ShadowKnight's semi-pixelated face on her phone. It was late, almost midnight, and her mother was asleep inside the house. The dirt-colored puppy (which still had no name) was lying next to her with one eye open and one eye closed; it smelled like wet socks and kibble. The air was cool, and a full moon illuminated the velvety blue sky in a way that would have seemed romantic if Binx had been a romantic person (which she wasn't).

"I'm glad I finally reached you," she said to ShadowKnight. "Like, *so* much is going on here."

"Same."

Binx took a deep breath, wondering where she should start.

"Your genealogy app," she said finally. "I think I've finally got it to work. I even got some names from it."

"You did? Callixta Crowe's descendants? That's amazing . . . and maybe we can convince one or more of them to march with us in DC!"

"Yeah, maybe. The thing is . . . are you sitting down? This is pretty dark. Okay, so I went to a funeral the other day. This girl at our school, Penelope, was murdered. And she was a witch. My coven-mates and I are thinking she was killed by a member of this local Antima group called the New Order. Maybe this guy named Colter or his brother, Hunter, or someone else in their family. So we and this other coven are looking into it." Binx paused. "What's weird is, Penelope might be related to one of the names I got from your app."

"*What?* Are you saying your friend Penelope's a *descendant?*"

"*Was.* Yeah, maybe. So, why would the Antima kill Callixta's descendants?"

"Maybe the Antima know about our march and our efforts to find descendants to stand with us? In any case, this may be the first Antima murder of a witch, and there's bound to be more. I'd better share all this with my group ASAP. And we need to warn everyone on that list you got from the app, and tell them to warn *their* descendants, too. Kids, grand-kids, nieces, nephews."

"Good idea."

"We've been brainstorming new strategies to deal with the Antima. Sounds like we need a plan, fast, so they don't hurt any more witches."

Binx nodded mutely.

ShadowKnight gazed at her. His eyes were sad, serious. "Listen. I'm sorry; it's awful that Penelope was killed. Is there anything I can do?"

"Actually, yes." Binx took a deep breath. Was she ready to do this? She was ready to do this. "Let me join your group."

ShadowKnight blinked. "Seriously?"

"Seriously. I want to tackle this full-on. I want to use my magical powers for more than, like, changing my hair color and updating my playlist and pranking other witches. I want to be a superhero, help make our world a better place for people like us. Which means going after 6-129 and all the evil Antima scum, just like you guys are doing."

"Great! That's *fantastic!*" ShadowKnight exclaimed. "What about your coven-mates? Are they okay about this?"

"I'm not sure. I'll figure it out, though." Binx reached down and petted the puppy.

Tomorrow. She would solve that problem tomorrow. For right now, she just wanted to enjoy her conversation with ShadowKnight, her connection with a smart, like-minded gamer-slash-witch who was part of an awesome national community of activist witches. *And* enjoy staring at his cute (in an intense, brooding way) face.

Not that she was crushing on him or anything.

"I'll get back to you about my coven. Hey, new topic . . . have you reached Level Twenty-Three yet?" Binx asked him.

"I'm almost there. I just have to figure out how to defeat the Ethelerean Ghoul and cross the Bridge of Never."

"I can give you a hack."

"Wait, you're already at Level Twenty-Three? *How?*"

A sleek gray cat suddenly appeared in the frame and rubbed up against ShadowKnight's stubbly face.

"Aww, is that your cat?"

"She's my friend's cat. She has like a ton of pets. She named this one Loviatar, after the daughter of the Finnish god of death."

"Nice," Binx said. "I've been trying to think of a name for my new puppy. He's not very 'Finnish god of death,' though. More like 'Can I *Finish* That Breakfast Muffin for You?'"

ShadowKnight laughed. "You're hilarious. Okay, so fork over that hack."

Binx smiled and leaned back and curled her body around the puppy as she continued videochatting with ShadowKnight. This felt right. Her friendship with him, joining Libertas. She was part of a witch revolution now. And after it was over, she, ShadowKnight, Ridley, Greta, Iris, Div, Mira, Aysha, and all the other witches out there were going to be free forever, for real. No hacks necessary.

Binx couldn't wait.

"I wonder where they are?" Greta said, glancing at her watch.

Iris opened her Batgirl lunch bag and poked through its contents. A peanut-butter-and-banana sandwich on whole wheat bread, a bottle of cranberry juice, and a cranberry-walnut muffin from her grandma's café. She picked up the muffin and took a tiny nibble from a corner. *Major yumminess.* "I ran into Ridley after my meeting with Mrs. Feathers. Mrs. Feathers is so nice, she said she refilled her M&M bowl just for me! Anyhoo, she . . . Ridley, not Mrs. Feathers . . . said she might be *un peu en retard*—that means *a little late*—because of a thingama-whatsit having to do with her SAT prep? I'm not sure about Binx."

"Okay. Maybe I'll text them and remind them that we're having lunch out here and not in the cafeteria."

"Okeydokey."

As Greta searched for her phone, Iris leaned back on the cedar bench and gazed up at the branches of the crape myrtle tree. In between the purply clusters of flowers, she could make out puffy clouds drifting lazily across the midday sky.

Her thoughts drifted along with them. Her awesome new familiar,

Lolli. *Happy thought.* Penelope's funeral. *Sad thought.* And just this morning, two more students in her homeroom wearing Antima shoulder patches. *Scary thought.*

At least she was officially a member of Greta's coven now, and they could face the Antima together, catch Penelope's killer together. She'd told Greta the good news the day after the funeral. When she'd told Div later—just because she felt like she should—the girl had just looked at her with those scary green eyes of hers and said that she would be there when Iris changed her mind.

Not *if.* *When.* But Iris had no plans to change her mind; her place was by Greta's side. And Binx's and Ridley's, too.

"Hi, guys!"

Ridley was walking across the courtyard toward them. Today, she wore a gray Columbia University hoodie, pleated skirt, and loafers. Greta and Iris slid over on the bench to make room for her.

Ridley sat down and set her backpack on the grass. "I thought Binx was eating with us."

"She is," Greta confirmed.

"Then why is she having lunch with Div and Mira and Aysha?"

"What?" Greta burst out. "No, she's not. There she is, she's coming over."

Iris swiveled and saw Binx hurrying toward them across the courtyard. Her hair wasn't pink anymore; it was black with platinum highlights. It suited her, and Iris wondered if *she* should get platinum highlights, too.

"Hey!"

Binx stopped in front of them, her face flushed with excitement. Her phone, in her hand, had a cute brown Raichu case.

"Hey! Do you want to sit?" Ridley asked, scooting over.

"In a sec. *Calumnia*. So, I have some news."

"News?" Greta repeated with a tense smile.

"Do you remember that guy I mentioned to you? ShadowKnight?"

"ShadowKnight. Who is he? Sounds like a *Witchworld* username," Iris remarked.

"It's funny you should say that. Don't repeat that name to anyone else, though." Binx turned her attention back to Greta. "Anyway, I've decided to join his group. Libertas."

Greta's smile disappeared. "You mean . . . his secret activist group?"

"*What* secret activist group? Binx, why didn't you mention it to me before? And why did you lie and tell me ShadowKnight was just some random gamer?" Ridley asked in a hurt voice.

"I'm sorry, Ridley. I promised him, like, total secrecy, and . . . listen, guys! Libertas is an *amazing* group; they're trying to get rid of 6-129. And solve the Antima problem. Anyway, I've decided to join them. But I can still do all my coven stuff, too. Like, we have a meeting at my house tonight, right? I'm all set with the snacks, and I even went to Michaels and bought some new—"

"You can't join them," Greta declared flatly.

Binx raised her eyebrows. "*Excuse* me?"

"You can't join them," Greta repeated. "It's too dangerous. For you *and* for us. For one thing, you might accidentally expose our coven."

Ridley twisted her hands in her lap. "Oh. True."

"I am *not* going to expose our coven!" Binx said hotly.

"We can't take that chance," Greta said. "I'm sorry, Binx."

Binx opened her mouth to speak, then closed it. She shook her head. "No. *I'm* sorry. Because if *this* coven isn't going to support my decision, I know a coven that will."

Greta stared at her. She rose to her feet. "You can't be serious—"

"Hells yeah, I am. *They* don't want to stifle me. *They* understand how important it is to fight for witches' rights . . . and safety."

"I understand that, too! I just don't think you joining some sketchy online group who—who knows?—could be just as dangerous is going to help."

"Well, you're wrong. If you'd just listened to me, I don't know, *ever*, maybe you'd get that."

Greta's cheeks flushed. Iris's glance bounced between her three new coven-mates. Actually, her *two* new coven-mates and her about-to-be-ex-coven-mate. *Stressful thought.*

Binx turned to Ridley. "I'm sorry I didn't tell you about Libertas before, and that I lied about ShadowKnight. I'll explain everything soon, and I promise we'll still hang out. But I just can't be a part of . . . a part of *this*." She glanced briefly at Greta. "Thanks for letting me be a coven member. I mean it. But I am *so* ready to grow up and move on."

With that, Binx lifted her Raichu phone in an abrupt goodbye and started back across the courtyard, toward the school building. Ridley jumped to her feet and ran after her. "*Binx!* Can we please talk about this?"

Greta slumped back against the bench. "Oh my gosh. I let this happen. And now we've lost her."

"No, we haven't. We'll get her back!" Iris promised, although she had no idea how.

"She's gone. I know her. Once she makes up her mind about something . . ."

Greta covered her eyes with her hands. Was she going to start crying? She was going to start crying. Iris wasn't sure what to do, so she awkwardly draped an arm around Greta's shoulders and drew her close in a sort-of hug . . .

. . . and accidentally touched Greta's velvet scarf, which was knotted around her neck.

And at that same instance, Iris's brain began to spin and buzz.

A house on fire.

A woman with grayish-blond hair.

A one-eyed cat.

Gofflesby.

Alarmed, Iris jerked back. And just as quickly, her brain stilled.

"I think something big is about to happen. Something bad," she announced to Greta.

ACKNOWLEDGMENTS

We are so grateful to everyone who made this book possible:

Kieran Viola, for believing in us, inspiring us, and challenging us to make *B*witch* what it was meant to be.

Megan Tingley, Alex Hightower, Annie McDonnell, Alex Kelleher-Nagorski, Bill Grace, Savannah Kennelly, Victoria Stapleton, and the rest of our epic team at Little, Brown Books for Young Readers.

Sweeney Boo, for her glorious cover artwork.

Mollie Glick, for always, always having our backs.

Vimbai Ushe, Anaya Truth Rickford, Rebecca Wei Hsieh, Leanna Keyes, Rayne M. J. Richardson, and Lola Bellier, for their invaluable contributions.

★

Paige would also like to thank:

Nick, who knows what he did.

Mum, who taught me to witch.

Scout and Christian, for always being exactly who they are meant to be.

Daddy and Gamma and Papa and Greta, for being my coven.

My familiar, who will always be a part of me.

And Nancy, who believed in me. Love you.

★

Nancy would also like to thank:

Adam, Christa, Cristin, Katie, Michael, Sandy, and Terra, for our incredible community.

Marice Pappo, for her wisdom and kindness.

Baxter, Sweetie, Kimchi, Tiger, and Truffles, for teaching me about all things cat.

Chris and Clara, for introducing me to the world of Pokémon, for the marathon Mario Kart sessions, and for their awesomeness, creativity, and courage. You guys inspire me every day.

Jens, for his endless love and support, and for being so understanding every time I yelled stuff like: "Not NOW, I have to finish the zombie crow scene!"

My amazing coauthor, Paige. Love you back.

★

And last but not least, we would like to thank our dear readers. You are magic.